TWIST

A Mageri Series Novel
Book 2

DANNIKA DARK

Also By Dannika Dark:

THE MAGERI SERIES
Sterling
Twist
Impulse
Gravity
Shine
The Gift (Novella)

MAGERI WORLD
Risk

NOVELLAS
Closer

THE SEVEN SERIES
Seven Years
Six Months
Five Weeks
Four Days
Three Hours
Two Minutes
One Second
Winter Moon (Novella)

SEVEN WORLD
Charming

THE CROSSBREED SERIES
Keystone
Ravenheart
Deathtrap
Gaslight
Blackout
Nevermore

"It is the hard journey that leads to a greater destiny. You can never rise if you never have anything to rise above."

- Sterling

CHAPTER 1

"**C**-8."

"Miss," I said, twisting open a chocolate cookie. I scraped the icing off with my teeth and nibbled at the edge, watching Simon squirm in his chair.

I lifted my chin, feigning confidence. "B-10."

"Hit." Simon leaned on his elbow, planting his cheek against a fist.

"Ready for some humble pie?" I snickered. "B-9."

"Miss!" he sang, wagging his eyebrows. "C-2."

He squinted at me with those brown eyes when I flicked a tiny white peg off the polished table. It skipped across the floor, twirling in a circle near the stove. Simon lacked humility, and I lacked grace.

"You win."

"Say it."

"Come on, Simon, you won. Don't be such a *child*."

"*Say it.*"

He folded his arms. Hell would freeze over before my English friend would let me walk away from that table without saying the words of defeat he longed to hear.

I rolled my eyes dramatically. "You sunk my battleship."

"Atta girl."

He turned my game board around. "You shouldn't be so sensitive, Silver. What you lack is conviction. You're so eager to beat me that you forget all about strategy."

"Perhaps our game sessions should end; clearly I'm not enough of a challenge for you."

"Such a drama queen. Didn't play nice in the schoolyard, did you? If you only see the next move, you'll never win the game. You have to look further ahead. I can give you an example."

"Of course you can."

His lips thinned and I pretended not to notice. Simon loved comparing life with games.

"In chess, you try so hard to protect all your pieces that you wind up spending half your moves running until you've been cornered. You need to be willing to make sacrifices. Perhaps that pawn you so desperately cling to is your pride."

"Don't play that hand, Simon. I'm really not in the mood tonight." I kicked my chair back and stood up. "I know what you're doing, but I don't care to have a life lesson wrapped up in a game analogy. The simple fact is—I'll never beat you."

Simon rested his chin in the palm of his hand, and tapped his cheek playfully. "Self-doubt is a persuasive mistress; careful not to shag her or you'll never get your balls back."

"Why does everything have to be about sex with you?"

A snort escaped. "I thought it was about games?"

"Aren't they one in the same?"

He nodded. "Truer words were never spoken. Learn from your mistakes, love. You can be *so* predictable."

He chomped on a cookie while studying the placement of my ships.

His bad boy looks were deceiving, because Simon was an intelligent and resourceful Mage who was a demon with knives. Teaching new Learners how to protect their light was his bread and butter. I also learned that his reputation preceded him as a strategist. We could contract our services to other Breed, but the Mageri paid well and took care of its own. Simon worked independently. He was an Englishman who recently returned to his way of life in America. Either that, or the country ousted him. He turned down three job offers since the move, insisting he was in retirement. Deep down, Simon hated the politics.

Long ago, there were no governments within the Breed; we were lawless. Humans feared us, wars raged, and there was no order. I read about slavery, and even some who were driven to extinction from conflicts that were ages old. It was necessary for each Breed to establish rules and structure before we destroyed ourselves. For Mage, a higher order called the Mageri was created, with individual Councils for various territories. Rogues who did not comply with the laws were hunted, and there was a sense of comfort among the people.

The Breed has separate laws, places of business, history, and culture. A world brimming with its own magic—a world I rarely saw. My Ghuardian, Justus, kept me under close watch. His responsibility was to protect, educate, and shelter the hell out of me.

He took his job seriously.

Justus schooled me, both mentally and physically. I learned what I was capable of, and he worked to sharpen my abilities. A Mage does not automatically know how to use their gifts; a significant amount of calculation goes into it.

Two nights out of the week were spent with the sexiest game geek this side of the East Coast. That would be Simon Hunt: the man, the myth, the bane of my existence.

Simon's game collection was unparalleled, and it pleased him immensely that I spent countless hours getting my ass kicked. I wasn't bitter, but in my defense—*no one* should have seven hotels on one property.

When I first met Simon, he didn't own a television, but when I started hanging around, it became our late night ritual. He loved the old creature features.

I used to live in what I considered a big city until I moved to Cognito. Nothing compares. It's a metropolis polluted with traffic, cluttered buildings, coffee shops, and nightlife. It's also the capital for the supernatural. Breed live within human society; we are not hideous creatures that lurk in the shadows. We're standing in line behind you at the grocery store checkout, eating burgers at the local diner, sitting two rows ahead in the theater, and coexisting with humans—all without your knowledge. Physically, most of us pass as an ordinary person, but if you look close enough, you'll notice subtle differences. The eyes are often telling, but most humans ignore the strange. Even among Mage, flickers of dim light dance in the irises during an energy burst, often imperceptible to an inattentive eye.

I crossed the living room and sat on the couch, smoothing out the wrinkles on my blouse. Simon plucked the pegs away from the game board, watching me from the corner of his eye.

What he lacked in brawn, he more than made up for in charisma. His eyes were as sweet as candy and flustered many a woman. Simon possessed soft features and a dimple on his left cheek that wouldn't quit. His smile was contagious—lush lips in the center that thinned out to wicked lines. He also knew how to turn the English accent on and off to his advantage. Wavy brown hair dusted his shoulders, and most of the time it never touched a brush. I suspected the real reason he kept his hair long was to cover up the tattoo at the nape of his neck. The one he never mentioned but once.

When I first met the great Mr. Hunt, he came off as the kind of man who would be holding an electric guitar and licking a woman's boot from heel to cuff with his pierced tongue. The usual dress code was jeans and a mangled shirt, but he also owned the most curious collection of leather. Simon's appearance was 50% rebellion, 30% comfort, and 100% attention. He dressed smart when he wanted to. He just never wanted to.

"What is it, love?"

When I didn't respond, he rose from his chair and sat beside me. The cushion sank, and I leaned against him as he curled his fingers through my long black hair.

"Still fretting about that friend of yours?"

He was talking about Adam. The last time we spoke was the night Adam challenged Samil, my Creator. It was a scheme they hatched up to use Adam, because of the rules the Council put in place. They all wanted Samil dead, but the death of a Mage went against the laws of the Mageri. The only way was to remove his power to the weakest challenger—a human.

"Novis is an experienced maker," Simon assured. "He has made many a respectable Mage. If his decision is to separate you two, then it's with good reason. Look here. I do not want to see any long faces tonight. It's *our* night, so don't be a sourpuss."

Simon's wicked fingers wiggled around my rib cage, sending out a flutter of electricity.

"Stop it!" I snapped.

Simon dragged me over his lap and tickled me until I fell on the floor, just shy of hitting the coffee table. A red, lacy article of clothing beneath the sofa caught my eye, and I snagged it. "What's this?"

He snatched the pair of panties dangling from my fingertips. "Last night's dessert; now get up off the floor."

"Why? Afraid I'll find the rest of her clothes down here? I hope she left wearing something decent."

"No woman leaves my apartment decent," he said with a wink.

"If you buy me dinner, I'll be a happy woman."

"That better be a promise," he said. "Now what say we get Twister out for later?" He stepped over me, lifting a black leather coat from the chair.

While he shuffled into the sleeves, I noticed his dimple was on prominent display. It was an adorable feature on his otherwise scandalous face. We played almost every game, except one. Twister was *out of the question* with his flirty behind.

I adored him despite his flaws. Simon was a good friend to me and always kept me in hysterics. He hadn't laid a finger on me in a suggestive way lately, although it wasn't without noticeable restraint. He *was* a man, and I ruffled his needs on occasion. We kindled a fire once, and neither was willing to strike the match again. Mistakes happen.

"Not on your life, but if you pick up a cheesecake, I'll *endure* a game of Risk."

His eyes brightened. "The cheesecake remains in the fridge until I dominate Europe."

"Whatever."

So easy to please.

Risk was his weakness, and I rarely agreed to play. I couldn't stand all that territory and global dominance shit.

He locked the door on his way out and I grabbed my phone. I was breaking the rule about severing human ties. Justus complicated my life with rules, and while I accepted these new expectations, it was a difficult adjustment. My heart ached when I thought about the simple pleasures of my previous life. I missed the feel of southern heat on my skin, the taste of strawberry ice on my tongue from my favorite snow cone stand, and watching life pass me by at a casual pace. I missed going to the movies because Justus never went. I missed the connection I had with girlfriends—the kind you could talk to for hours about nothing. For various reasons, there weren't as many women as men among Breed. I was also new, and it made it that much harder to make friends when I only spent time at the occasional Breed bar.

I missed Sunny. In my human life, we shared an unbreakable friendship. Only now, I feared she would not be receptive to any of this, but my heart was telling me to try.

Sunny had moved out of her downtown apartment, but the girl who sublet it gave me her private number. I decided to make the call at Simon's house where I could have a moment alone. Justus kept a tight watch on me—that man probably had the Mage laws tattooed on his ass.

I tensed when it reached the third ring.

"Hello, who's calling?" she snapped. Her voice was suspicious and reserved, not at all like the affectionate girl I knew.

My throat nearly closed. "Sunshine?"

"*Who* is this? I don't know this number. I'm hanging up."

"You know me." I walked to the window and looked down at the tiny cars zooming down the street. "I'm not sure where to begin." There was a pause as I took a deep breath. "Sunny, it's me, Zoë."

"No, you are not. I know Zoë's voice, this isn't funny."

"It's me, Sunshine. They never found my body, so you had nothing to bury except memories. I've changed, I don't look like the Zoë you remember." My eyes were betraying my stony heart. "I hate crying, *please* don't hang up."

The skeptical voice returned, a little softened. "No one calls me Sunshine." Silence fell between us. "If it is you, then what was the nickname I gave my brother?"

As children, Kane once found Sunny's diary while snooping through her room, so the nickname became a private joke. Sunny's home life was difficult, but she was a tough cookie and more optimistic than I could ever hope to be. Kane left home years before she did. It was hard to keep a lock on him, but he remembered her on birthdays, sent her money, and dropped in to visit on occasion.

"Snoopy."

Sunny wept. "But it doesn't *sound* like you."

"I wanted to hear your voice again. I've been through hell, and I need a little sanity."

"You called the wrong girl, then." She sniffled, attempting to laugh.

I didn't need to glance at a clock to know how much time had elapsed. My internal stopwatch started the second Simon walked out of the door. He never left me alone for long, flashing through empty alleys to get there quicker. Tricks he shouldn't have been doing in public—but Simon was a rule breaker. His mind worked like one of those complicated Swiss watches with all the tiny moving parts, and I couldn't risk him catching me.

"Why didn't you come see me?"

"I live in Cognito. How soon can you get up here?"

"How did you end up there?"

"I can't tell you everything over the phone; we need to talk in person. I don't have much money, but I can wire you some for a plane ticket. Sorry I have to be so secretive, but you can't stay with me. You'll have to find a hotel." My knuckles turned white as I made a nervous fist. "Are you there?"

Her laughter broke the tension. "You live in Cognito? I can't believe I'm agreeing to this." She sniffed a few times, trying to clear her stuffy nose. "I never told anyone about Kane's name except Zoë; I have to believe this is you. Yes, I'll come. How's the weather up there?"

"Warmer than usual, except at night. Bring a raincoat," I said. "By the way, how did everything turn out with Marco?"

"Marco wasn't the man I thought he was." Sadness weighted down her voice. The last time we saw one another, I was shocked to discover she was in a relationship. "What happened to you… was my fault."

"You dropped me off at the train station, Sunshine. That's all." I tucked a strand of hair behind my ear.

"That's not—"

"I have to go," I interrupted. Simon's footsteps sounded in the hall, so I lowered my voice to a baby's breath. "I promise I'll call you back. Text me, but *don't* call. Let me know when you book the flight. I love you, sis." I dove for my purse and slipped the phone inside the zipper just as the door swung open.

Simon set the plastic bags on the kitchen counter and held a container with my favorite cheesecake inside.

"I know how much you like your sweets. For *this*, you're going to give me Australia."

CHAPTER 2

I PEERED OVER THE EDGE OF my book, watching my
Ghuardian enter the main room of our house. Justus smelled
green and fresh, like a sunny morning after a spring rain. It was
his favorite soap, the one with all the little green flecks in it. He lifted
a heavy arm wrapped in tribal ink and leaned against the doorframe.
I set my book down on the expensive leather sofa as he stalled.

Justus was like an ice cream cone: every woman wanted a lick. It
was one of his gifts as a Mage—leaking raw, sexual energy—luring
women, powerless to control it. Women felt an irresistible pull to a
Charmer, but for whatever reason, I was unaffected by his magic. He
was already a handsome man to begin with. An angled jaw outlined
his strength, and cobalt blue eyes reflected his integrity. He shaved
away his dark blond hair to a coarse stubble, and he had the most
powerful legs I'd ever seen on a man. Of course, it was the smug
attitude that preceded his looks when he entered a room that put me
off; there's a difference between confidence and arrogance.

I saw Justus without all that charm—as an ordinary man with
flaws. He snored, lacked table manners, *always* thought he was right,
and was about as lovable as a porcupine, avoiding physical affection.
He had no problem with heavy petting at the bar, but when it came
to personal relationships, he shut down. Buried beneath that tough
exterior was a compassionate man. In rare moments, kind words fell
from his lips. The breakthroughs were brief, and I feared his walls
were too fortified for anyone to crack—even me. Simon insisted it
was good for Justus to have a woman stand up to him, so I considered
my combative nature… *medicinal.*

"Silver, I have something to tell you." A deep crease settled in
his brow.

After Simon dropped me off, we went about our normal routine and I hadn't seen Justus all day. I sat up to make room for him, but he didn't budge a muscle.

His deep, baritone voice filled the room with just a trace of an accent I could never place. "I have business matters to attend to and will be gone for a couple of days. Simon will join me."

"Should I pack now?"

Juicers—who steal energy for a high—are a threat. They frequent Breed bars in hopes of finding young Learners, like me. Flashing, borrowing light, and the ability to tell time are common gifts we all possess. Every Mage receives at least one *rare* gift: I am a Unique. Our light is more potent, but our talents remain an unknown among the Mageri. Rumors circulated for years that a Unique could harness lightning and increase their power over time. I was too young to be anything extraordinary, but I wondered who I might one day become.

I discovered I could move metal objects. It began in Samil's basement when I pulled a flask across the floor by accident. It doesn't work on all metals, and only if a Mage recently handled it. All gifts have limitations. Justus could teach me all he knew about common gifts, but I stumbled learning how to control my new skill. Other than that, the only ability I had was that I could polish off a pint of ice cream in two minutes flat.

"Is this about HALO?"

His blue eyes sharpened.

"I was in your secret room once, with Simon. I saw the red book on your desk with that word etched across the cover. It has the same symbol you put on your business cards," I said, matter-of-factly. "What is HALO? I know it has nothing to do with a holy object hovering over your head."

His shadow played on the wall as he threw his serious eyes to the stone floor. "HALO keeps the peace among the Breed; we share information."

"So that's the big secret?"

"It's no secret I'm a member. If a Vampire pulled information from you—it could undo years of work. It is better that you are not privy to our secrets. We're a select few of different races that represent the Breed. Our alliance is built upon trust, integrity, truth, and secrecy."

"Trust, integrity… wait a minute, your motto's acronym is TITS?"

A deep line etched in his brow. "You always have a comeback," he grumbled, waving a hand.

"You spelled it out." I grinned, deciding I liked the joke. "Halos and tits—it sounds like a strip club."

"I think you need to stop."

"Fine, I know how important tits are to you," I snickered. "Why is Simon going if he's not part of your club?"

"His services for this job were contracted, and… he owes me. We leave tonight," he said, stuffing his hands in his pockets. "I'm not easy about leaving you here alone for that length of time, but you're safe in my home."

"*Our* home," I corrected.

The house was a subterranean fortress with secret passageways, a James Bond garage, and steel doors. It had to be because of HALO. Any position with that much importance meant danger, and the location and structure of his home added a level of comfort.

"I am explicitly ordering you not to step out of that door, do you understand me?"

"What if the house is on fire?"

He lowered his chin, reminding me why he earned the title of lord and master of his house.

"What if I want some ice cream?"

I sensed his anger percolating, so I eased off.

"Do not disobey me, Learner."

I crossed my heart, and hoped not to die.

━━━⊶⬤⬤⬤⊷━━━

In a strange way, I felt naked without Justus in the house. I had grown used to him peering around corners to see what I was doing, feeling a touch of warm air on my skin when I riled him up, and the sound of his deep voice filling the wide spaces in the room. However, regaining my independence was more important than a little loneliness. For the first time as a Mage, I was leaving the house unescorted.

Sunny left a message on my phone:

I'll be there Monday 4ish. Where should we meet?

Breed bars were out of the question; I might as well slap a sign on my head inviting all juicers to form a line. We could maintain a low profile around humans, but the rules state that I must flare in a human establishment. Flaring is an intentional act, releasing energy in small increments. It alerts other Mage that you are on the property, and basically prevents you from getting your ass kicked. The books that filled our shelves dictated these rules, and I decided the risk was low. I chose a human bar.

The problem was that I didn't want to flare and advertise I was alone. If I tried to conceal and my energy leaked by accident, I could be discovered.

I stretched my legs over the red chaise in my bedroom and considered my options. Restless candles flickered on the wall, and the biting chill nipped at my toes.

I needed help.

My finger hovered over a name that Simon gave me a week ago. The scribbled numbers were neatly tucked in the pocket of my favorite blue jeans. I found it when gathering clothes to send to the cleaners and programmed it into my new phone.

Adam Razor. Adam appeared like a guardian angel and carried me through the darkest time in my life. He was my spiritual canteen. I didn't know if Novis was as much of a drill sergeant as Justus when it came to his progeny, but I needed advice.

"Bueno," he replied.

"Hey, Razor."

I could almost feel the breath on my ear as he sighed, but I waited for him to speak first. Pride is a bitch to swallow, and I was choking.

"Why did it take you this long to pick up the phone and call?"

"Me?"

"Yes, *you*."

"You are one stubborn sonofabitch. Here I am thinking that you hate me for what happened that night with Samil. You don't hate me, do you?"

"Woman, I'll bend you over my knee and throttle you for thinking something like that."

I tucked my legs in, picking at the fringe on the cashmere throw. It felt like we were right back where we left off, and a heavy weight lifted from my heart. "That sounds more like something Simon would say," I said with a short laugh.

"Hmm."

"Adam, how is Novis? Is he treating you well?"

"He's the shit, Silver. Truly. Novis has years of experience behind him. There's so much I didn't know."

"I live in a hole, Razor. One stuffed with books that don't make any sense, a fridge that is almost empty, no television, and a Ghuardian who works out six hours a day. I don't know a damn thing."

Adam laughed, and a flood of memories came back. "Has anyone ever told you that you have the mouth of a trucker?"

"I may have a dirty mouth, but it didn't stop you from kissing it." When the line fell silent, I changed the topic. "Have you been presented in front of the Council, officially?"

"Last week. We went through the ceremony with all the robes and speeches. I'm official." He sounded proud.

"Did Novis give you a new name?"

The induction involved each new Mage receiving a new name by their Creator. The tradition was antiquated, but customs were important to the Mageri. I wasn't so fortunate with the one my maker chose for me, but he could rot for all I cared.

"I have a name."

"And? Don't leave me hanging. What is it?" The silence was torture. "Are you kidding me? I'm hanging up if you don't tell me what it is."

"Adam."

I quieted. "I'm still calling you Razor."

"No, you're not," he chuckled. Novis doesn't have a last name and you know the rules."

I preferred to call him by his surname. Adam was too soft and personal. For fuck's sake. Now I was going to *have* to call him Adam and I knew he was eating it up.

"Adam, I need your help."

"What's wrong?" All the soft edges in his voice wore away.

"Nothing's wrong, I just need your advice."

"Shoot."

"And your confidence." I let that sink in; what I really needed was his silence. "I mean it. If you want to help, then what I tell you stays between us."

"On my word, Silver. Tell me what's going on."

"I called Sunny and she's flying in tomorrow. I can't bring her here, so I was thinking about taking one of Justus's cars, but knowing him he probably memorizes the mileage on them and—"

"What time?"

"Her plane comes in around four."

"No, what time do you need me to be there?"

"That's not what I'm asking. I only called because you're the man with the plan; you have ideas, and I need help."

"I can go in public without my Ghuardian."

"Come again?"

I stood up and paced the room. I kicked a dirty sock under the bed and took a cleansing breath.

"Novis is very old, Silver. The light he gave me is strong, and he has no problems with my ability to take care of myself."

"How old is he?"

"*Ancient.* Look, I'll come along and you won't have to worry. It's too dangerous to be out alone and we all know you're a pocketful of trouble."

"Very funny."

"I'm bringing a friend along, remember Knox? He's in town for a little while, so we can all hang out."

"What's Knox doing here? That's not exactly severing human ties," I said through clenched teeth.

"If you don't give me a time, I'm coming over right now and we're having a slumber party."

CHAPTER 3

THE NEXT AFTERNOON, I STARED at the front door for an hour. From my vantage point on the floor, I saw the house in a new light: cobwebs garnished the corners of the wall spattered with mud, shadows moved like dark soldiers, and there was a tiny green candy in the groove of the stone floor. Everything received a thorough inspection because of a deep-seated paranoia that Justus had rigged a trap so he could tell if I left the house. I paced the edges, crawled on my knees searching for string, hair, dental floss, or anything that could serve as a tripwire. I also planned to take a bottle of lemon scented cleaner to that floor later that night.

A knock pounded against the door and I shrieked, springing to my feet.

Someone laughed. "Silver?"

I lifted the latch to the heavy door and pulled it open. "Adam, you scared me to death, why didn't you flare?"

He gave a wolfish smile and I knew it was because I called him by name.

"What happened to your hair?" Someone gave him a bad haircut, and he brushed his fingers through the wavy brown locks. He tried to keep it long on top, but a little too much came off the sides.

"Yeah," he said, scratching at the whiskers on his cheek. "Maybe I better keep my day job."

I looked over his all black attire, as it went against the grain of Adam, who preferred jeans.

I peeked around his shoulder.

"Knox is up top, I don't think he liked the looks of that ladder."

"I don't think the ladder liked the looks of him, either." I smirked and folded my arms.

"Where's my hug, baby doll?"

I gave him one of those awkward hugs where I cradled my arms against my chest. *Since when was I his baby doll?*

Adam grabbed my wrists and hooked them over his shoulders. "Better," he said.

I wrinkled my nose and sniffed his collar. "Are you wearing cologne?" I pulled at the fabric and looked at his neck.

"What are you up to?" he asked. "Because if you're trying to take my clothes off then I should warn you, I'm wearing a thong."

"Oh, *shut up*. I'm just curious where your mark is."

Each Mage carries the mark of their Creator; mine just happened to land on my ass cheek as a promise of future embarrassment.

"Wouldn't you love to know?" he said with a lift of his brow.

"You've seen mine, remember? Doesn't seem fair."

"Maybe someday if you ask me nicely," he said, keeping his arms locked around my waist. My nose drew in his scent, and a flood of memories came back.

"Thanks for coming. I wasn't sure if I could do this alone."

"Are you sure you trust Sunny?"

I fell out of his arms and he backed into the hall.

"As much as you trust Knox."

I looked at the threshold with concern and my gut knotted. Was it worth the risk to ruin the trust I shared with my Ghuardian?

"What's wrong?"

"I promised Justus I wouldn't step outside the front door," I said, shuffling a foot across the floor. "It's not as easy as I thought it would be. My conscience is a pitchfork prodding me in the rear."

Adam bent forward, grabbed me around the hips, and threw me over his shoulder. "What are you doing?" I gasped.

"You can't get in trouble for being kidnapped, can you?"

I hung upside down and stared at his rear. It was a nice view, but it faded in the dark tunnel when the door closed behind us.

"No, but you can," I said, arms swinging like pendulums.

When we reached the ladder, my stomach lurched as he whirled me back on my feet.

I looked up and saw Knox looming over the open hatch like Mount Olympus. He served with Adam in the Special Forces—the kind that no one knew existed and Adam never detailed. It explained a lot about Adam's personality that never clicked for me. Sometimes I saw another side to him that made me wonder about the life he used to live. He worked hard to take care of his sister, and despite dropping out of school, he later obtained a diploma. Adam was loyal and capable, a dangerous mix for someone who lost his twin to murder.

Knox took hold of my arms and lifted me to my feet.

"Hey, dollface."

"It's good to see you, Knox."

Adam shot up out of the tunnel and gave his friend a scornful glance. "Her name is *Silver,* so you can cut the dollface shit."

"I'll call her whatever the fuck I want to, *Razor.* I'm not a Mage. Your rules, not mine, brother."

I looked at Adam. "He knows?"

"He can be trusted. Are you positive you want to tell your friend? Remember, there are consequences if a human breaks our trust."

"If she believes who I am, then she'll have to know *what* I am."

Adam nodded in agreement.

Knox pulled a dark knit cap over his eyes. "Let's roll."

<hr />

The human bar was a smoky, forgettable joint, full of regulars. We stole a table in the back and ordered a few beers. I picked up that Knox and Adam were sharing information based on enigmatic glances and abbreviated remarks. I pressed, but they refused to answer my questions.

"Are you dating anyone, Knox?" Adam kicked my leg and I gave him a "*What the hell was that about?*" glare.

Knox held his beer between two fingers and pointed at Adam. "I have a bone to pick with you, brother."

Lifting his hands defensively, Adam laughed. "It's not my fault she likes to stir it up. I didn't tell her a thing about your situation—or lack of it."

Knox tilted the bottle to his lips like a weapon and cursed with his eyes.

The waitress appeared with fresh beers and a hungry smile.

Knox's eyes slid up her body like a rocket on a launch pad as he admired her long legs. The direction of her stare was obvious as it fell across his thin shirt that hugged him like a long lost lover. His chest was broad and heavy. Knox was an intimidating man who was rough around the edges. He licked his tight lips and flattened his shoulders against the back of his seat.

A flush of color rose in her cheeks, and she played coy—twirling a silver chain around her neck. She wasn't a young demure thing, either. "Sure you don't want something with a little more bite?"

His teeth scraped along his lower lip as they stared at each other. I nudged Adam, but when I turned to look, he was too busy soaking me in with his eyes.

"Stop staring at me," I warned, stripping the label away from the bottle. "You have a television at home, go watch that."

"Where are my manners?"

"Funny, I've been wondering that since we met."

The waitress with small cherry earrings strolled off, passing by the front door where a young woman stepped in, shaking rain from her wet hands.

"That's her," I whispered. "That's Sunny." My stomach twisted into a pretzel as the music switched songs.

Both men leaned around for a look.

Soft light accentuated the curve of her back as she stood on her tiptoes, searching the length of the room. Sunny dressed for the weather in a snug, ashen sweater dress, wide belt, black leggings, and a scarf wrapped over her head. I forgot how much I envied her curves; she could have been a model except she lacked the pissed off, vacant look in her expression. She had a cute button nose and her apple cheeks pushed up those bright blue eyes whenever she smiled. Tonight, she wasn't smiling.

Her blond hair spilled out in short waves when the scarf pulled free, and the bracelets on her wrist clinked together.

My hands were shaking. "She won't recognize me."

"Call her over," Adam suggested, and nudged me with his elbow.

"Sunny!" I stood up to make myself more visible. She looked me over with a blank expression.

"It's me, Zoë."

I put myself in her shoes, and I knew she wanted to bolt. "Please, sit with us for a few minutes. I know it's a lot to take in."

"I don't *know* you." She clutched a small, black purse and raked me over with her eyes. "This was a mistake."

I did the only thing I could think of. "It's me, Sunshine." I reached out and shocked her arm. I always had an unexplainable talent at summoning static electricity. She bounced back and I saw something that wasn't there before—recognition.

"Don't let this be a cruel joke. Please be you."

"I promise it's me. You've come this far and that's more than I expected. Will you sit down and have a beer with us?" I grabbed her hand and we walked to the table.

"I'd like you to meet my best friend—"

Knox stood up so fast the table lifted off the ground. An empty beer bottle sailed into Adam's lap, and he caught the remaining bottles before it turned into a fiasco. Knox pulled off his cap, releasing a mess of black hair that covered the tips of his ears. He wrung the hat between his hands and looked down at her shoes. The man was nothing but muscle and mouth, yet there was something so lovely in the way he looked at Sunny.

I smiled—couldn't help it. "This is Knox."

He started to reach for her hand, but when she only nodded at him, he stuffed his hat in his back pocket and raked his fingers through his hair.

"Hi, Sunny. I'm Adam. It's good to finally put a face to a name." He waved a polite hello from his seat. "Silver speaks of you often."

When I sat beside Adam, Knox moved over and gave Sunny every inch of space the seat would allow. He looked scared of her.

"Who is Silver?" she asked.

"That's me, I'm Silver." I nodded towards the vacant spot. "If you sit down, I'll spill the beans."

Sunny was apprehensive, but set her clutch on the table and folded her hands. Adam dabbed his wet pants with a red cloth napkin, while Knox looked like a molding adhered to the wall.

I detailed the events of the night I disappeared, and everything that transpired since, in thirty minutes. What threw her for a loop was the one detail I had no explanation for—my physical transformation.

It was difficult to accept, and I hoped that someday I would find out the truth. I was a girl who came from a world of explanations, and now I was living in one that lacked them. Sunny knew me as a red-haired girl, a little shorter than her, and pale with pink undertones. Now, my raven colored hair swept past broad shoulders, and green eyes glinted against my warm complexion. I was taller—just by an inch or so—and even my voice was brighter.

The shiny, red cherry swirled in her drink as she digested the information. Sunny always had beautifully manicured nails, and tonight they were a plum color.

I stared in annoyance at Knox who was flipping his silver lighter open and closed.

Click. Click. Click.

Adam's finger traced invisible circles on a glass of ale, and a dribble of water splashed on the wooden table. "Knox, let's go out for a smoke and leave these ladies to talk." Adam didn't smoke, but he was playing *good guy*.

Knox snapped the lighter shut and twirled it on the table. He lifted the pack of cigarettes tucked in his pocket and waited for Sunny to let him out.

They stepped out of the door and moved beneath the awning just outside the window. A shadowy glow illuminated the side of Knox's face from the flame, and he blew out a plume of smoke, tucking the lighter in his back pocket. They turned their backs to us and a cab drove by, splashing water on their feet.

Sunny cleared her throat. "So you're telling me you're a sorcerer?"

If only. "I'm not able to cast spells or brew a love potion, if that's what you're asking. I can't work magic, but there *is* magic in what we can do. I never gave much thought to the idea that some things— beyond explanation—are magic. It's hard to believe the world isn't what we thought it was."

"Prove it."

I leaned forward. "I could be arrested by the Mageri for public display of power. Laws must be followed." *God, I was starting to sound like Justus.*

She looked into my eyes searching for evidence, searching for truth—searching for her old friend. "They never found your body and I… I hoped it wasn't true."

I rubbed my fingertip over a dark stain on the table. "Why did you have the funeral so quickly? I was still missing, and then I turn the page and there I am… in the obituaries."

She rolled her eyes, giving a clear indication she had nothing to do with it. "You know how I feel about your mother so I'm just going to say it: that woman couldn't wait to bury you. She just wanted to move on and not have to deal with it anymore. The photo they took was blurry and didn't even show your face. I guess that's all they needed. I think one of the guys who drove the ambulance got fired."

"How did they find me? I was nowhere near the road."

Sunny shrugged. "If he made you into a Mage, why did he leave you?"

"I don't know. Bringing me close to death, if not killing me, was somehow part of his process. I think he took it too far with me and thought I really died—that he failed. Maybe he planned it so there would be no loose ends to tie up, and he could pick me up at the morgue like a pair of slacks at the dry cleaners. Samil never saw my transition, but somehow he sensed I was alive. He followed me a couple of times, but flashed out of sight before I ever saw him. I don't think he was sure it was me, and I thought I was just getting paranoid. I was in denial, wanting to go on living a normal life. Can you blame me? I was scared," I said, running my finger around a bottle of stout beer. "Everything changed when I met Justus. I can't trust anything Samil said to me. Now he's dead, and I may never know all the facts about why he really did this. It doesn't matter anymore; what's done is done."

"What woke you up?"

"I couldn't breathe," I said, shaking my head. "I'm not sure if I was dead the whole time. I just know what he did to me."

Whatever magic Samil possessed with the gift of creation was dark magic. If he could create a Mage upon their death, or even after, it spoke volumes to that power.

"This isn't how a Mage is created. That part of my life is behind me, and I'm only telling you because I want you to know. It's a sore subject, and I don't like talking about it."

"What have you been doing all these months?"

"Learning who I am, I guess. Do I miss my old life of paper jams at the office? Not really, but I plan to get another job. I'm not sure what I'm qualified to do for the Mageri, but there's got to be something out there for me, and I intend to find out what it is."

"I'm still not sure if I can believe this," she muttered.

"Sunny, I know a million stories about you. It may never be enough. I just want to sit and talk for a little bit." I tore the label off the bottle and let a minute pass by. "How's my mom doing?"

She snorted and swallowed half her drink. "Bat crazy. She won't talk to me anymore. She's found Jesus."

"Really? Where was he hiding?" We laughed together and she ruffled her fingers through her hair. "At least she found somebody. It really tore me up wondering how you two were coping. Did she take Max?"

"You mean that devil cat of yours? Yes, reluctantly your mother took him. I think she felt guilty."

"He isn't the devil, just a little possessed."

"And in need of an exorcism."

I coughed when a trail of smoke stung my eyes from the long fingers of an elderly man lingering by the table. Sunny fanned the air with her hand, giving me a look of disgust for my choice of location. She preferred upscale and fun to mediocre and glum.

"I wanted to believe you were alive because some weird stuff happened."

"What weird stuff?"

"It's my fault." She submersed an ice cube in her glass with the tip of her finger.

A rowdy group of men entered the room and one of them slammed his hands on the bar. "Three beers!" he called out.

"There's no way you could have known that was going to happen to me. Don't even think about blaming yourself."

Her fingers wound through a curl of hair as guilt flooded her eyes. "Marco led me to believe he was the one. What a joke. Marco only wanted to know about *you*."

"*What?*" I asked in disbelief. I met the guy *once*.

"Marco was involved, Zoë—uh, Silver. I can't get used to that name."

"It's fine. You're human, so you can call me whatever you want."

"I went to see him that night after I dropped you off. He discarded me like some floozy. I thought it was because he was messing around, so we argued. When the phone rang, he answered it and went ballistic, yelling in Italian. I couldn't make heads or tails of the conversation. We haven't seen each other since that night."

"Is that why you came up here, because you think this is somehow your doing?"

"Maybe it's why I can believe all of this. Marco scared me, and I moved because of him. I loved that little apartment and hated myself for getting involved with him. None of it mattered. You were gone and my life was a mess."

"What are you not telling me?"

"Well," she began, "we never fought like that before. Most of our quarrels were minor and we always kissed and made up. I never saw that side of him, and I—"

Two fists—one sporting a ring shaped like a knuckle-duster—planted on the table. We raised our attention to a man with a shaved head, dripping from the rain. Deep lines carved across both of his cheeks, and his eyes were small and sunken in. They were also all over Sunny. A foul stench of cheap cologne burned my nose and I angled away from him.

"You ladies want some company?" Drops of rainwater rolled down his head and splashed across my hand.

Sunny didn't even look up because she knew how to handle men. "Scram. You're leaking all over our table."

"Yeah, it's crying like a bitch out there. Me and my boys would like to buy you girls a beer."

His fists remained on the table as if he were claiming his territory. The music switched to an old rock song, and Sunny buffed a nail on her sleeve.

"As you can see," she said, "we already have a drink. Try the next table."

He dropped his ass in the seat next to her as his two companions moved in closer. One covered in tattoos looked like he used a knife to shave his head, while the second guy was bigger, wearing a baseball hat and sweatshirt.

I was a woman with little patience, and these were men with little brains. "These seats are taken."

"Well honey, they look pretty free to me." He lifted his chin. "The more the merrier. I'm Sean, that's John, and Matty's the one with the beer gut. Have a seat, boys."

I moved to get up when Matty muscled his way in the booth, boxing me against the wall.

Sunny reached for her clutch. "I've got pepper spray, so if you don't beat it I'm going to—"

Sean snatched the purse and tossed it to John who held it over his head.

"Let's be friendly. Didn't your mother teach you to be polite?" Sean asked.

"Give me back my purse." She stood up and reached over Sean, trying to grab it. Little did she notice that Sean was getting a private tour of her assets.

"Feisty one. I'd ask you to sit, but you're giving me a lovely view, princess." He curled his octopus hand around her waist and howled, "Always wanted a hellcat!"

I leaned in and grabbed his wrist, prying it away. "Let go of her!"

Matty's fingers hooked in my jeans and yanked me back in my seat. I snapped my arm back, hitting him in the chest with my elbow and he wheezed, grabbing his sternum.

There were pros and cons to being a Mage. The pro was that I could move and heal fast. The con? Well, that meant I couldn't do any of these things around humans. Justus never taught me how to fight someone in a restaurant booth, either.

"Give it to me!" she demanded.

"You hear that, John? She wants you to give it to her," he chuckled.

Sunny may have been saucy with a lot of bite, but she fought like a girl, slapping him with the flat of her hands as he laughed.

"Let go of me or I'm going to call the cops right now. Get your hands... *off* of me!" A few heads in the bar turned, but no one wanted to get involved.

Almost no one.

"You heard the lady," a deep, gravelly voice barked.

Sunny paused from her struggle, looking up with desperate eyes.

Knox had John in a headlock and looked as immovable as a statue. I didn't even see him coming, but he moved in quick and took control. He aimed his eyes at Sean like a firing squad, watching the hands that clutched her hips. Water streamed down his face from the rain outside, and his shoulders were speckled with it.

"Remove your hands and I'll let you keep them."

"This is none of your business," Sean replied.

"Walk out of here," Knox warned, "because I only give one warning and you're two seconds away from getting chin-checked."

Knox wasn't looking for a physical confrontation. Knox *was* the physical confrontation. His skin stretched taut over hard muscle; a chisel couldn't have broken through him.

Adam yanked Matty out of the booth, pinning an arm high on his back as he flung him across the room. I managed to kick him in the rear with my heel, feeling a little embarrassed. It's not that I minded a little chivalry, but I knew I could have handled the situation better, and I failed.

Sean sized up the competition and threw out his hands in surrender. "We're not looking for any trouble. We're just having a little fun with these girls."

"I like fun," Knox agreed, squeezing John's neck between his arms until his face turned a frightening shade of purple. He signaled Adam with his eyes, as if they had their own language. Adam turned his back to watch Matty.

"In fact, why don't you join me outside for some *fun?*" Knox suggested.

Sean weighed his chances with Knox, which were slim to none on a good day. When he stood up, Knox took hold of the back of his neck and shoved him across the room. It wasn't every day I saw a group of guys having a standoff, so it was interesting to see all the chest beating and tail tucking.

Knox directed his focus on John, who was still wedged between his arms. His lips peeled back, and he leaned in close.

"You *should* give the lady back her purse. That would be the right thing to do. Ask me why I hope you don't." John's fingers wrapped around the bicep constricting his air. "Because I want nothing more than to get Medieval on your ass."

He emphasized his threat with a hard squeeze. John cursed and threw Sunny's clutch. It skidded across the table, knocking over an empty beer bottle. Knox shoved the sorry bastard to the floor, waiting for him to fight back.

He didn't.

The music switched to a slow song, and the men angrily left as everyone went back to their drink.

"Some real gentlemen you got in this city," Sunny fussed. She ran her fingers over her dress and blew out a breath. I lifted a napkin crumpled in the corner, wiping the table down when Sunny looked up at Knox.

"I'm sorry, I didn't mean you." She tried to get out of the booth to let him sit down when he touched her shoulder, and pulled away immediately.

"Did he hurt you?"

When she shook her head, a curl sprang out of place and bobbed in front of her nose. She blew out a hard breath and pouted, tucking the hair behind an ear. Sunny was more emotional than I was, and it looked like she was hovering on the edge of tears. Knox snapped his head towards the door, easing around, when Adam pushed a hand against his chest.

"Cool it. This isn't the time."

Knox tightened his jaw and looked at Sunny. "Slide in. I'm taking the end."

Her eyes rose to meet his and the moment they did, his ears turned red. Cherry red. He cleared his throat, pulled the cap from his back pocket, and yanked it over his wet hair. Did she even notice how he looked at her? The man blushed like a furnace. Knox sat on the edge, facing away from us like a loaded shotgun ready to fire.

"Reminds me of that time we went to Shreveport," I said.

Sunny slapped her hand on the table and her voice went up a pitch. "I always said you were a magnet for trouble."

"That was *not* my fault."

"The drink went all over the table." She laughed. *Inside jokes were always the best.* "Maybe if you quit picking at the labels on your bottle, you might not be tipping drinks all over the place."

"He could have been a sport about it."

Her plucked brows arched. "With *that* mouth of yours?"

Sunny got past her doubts and there we were, a couple of girlfriends laughing over drinks. We spent the next several hours talking over cheese pizza. The men occasionally joined in, but it was all about us. We had a lot of catching up to do.

"I need to get this one back," Adam announced, stretching out his legs as he stood up.

He was right. I couldn't risk staying out too late. If Justus came home early, I could expect a tongue-lashing.

"Will I see you tomorrow?" Sunny asked.

Adam frowned, rubbing his chin. "I can only afford a few hours out, but if you ladies want to do this again, we'll come. Knox, you don't mind driving again, do you?" Adam smiled. "I'm afraid I can't fit everyone on my bike."

"Maybe you need to sell that piece of shit," he said.

I hugged Sunny tight and her perfume swirled around me.

"Thank you for believing me, for coming all this way. I'll call you tonight, okay? We'll talk."

She squeezed back hard. "I missed you." I could sense her tears closing in.

Adam and Knox did as men do when women turn on the waterworks—look confused and back away. When we reached the door, I glanced over my shoulder and saw her sit back down.

"Hey, where are you staying?" I yelled out. "We'll drive you."

"It's just a short walk up the road, so don't worry. You always ditch me before I finish my drink," she said, waving a hand. "I'll keep my phone on."

I pulled the strap of my purse over my shoulder.

"What's up?"

I turned my head, but Adam was talking to Knox who fell back a pace.

Knox reached in his pocket and tossed Adam the keys. "Take the Jeep. I'll meet you back at the house. I got some cash I need to spend."

Adam scratched the back of his neck. "With her?"

"Oh, you must have me mixed up with Casa-fucking-nova. Brother, I need a drink, so fucking *deal*."

Knox lifted a heavy hand and tapped beneath my chin with a finger. "See ya, dollface."

I leaned forward, whispering so he could hear. "Watch over my friend."

CHAPTER 4

THE COLD AMBER DRINK SLID down his throat and lit a fire in his belly. Knox scooped a handful of peanuts in his palm and crunched on them, dusting the salt from his fingertips.

He drove a long way to talk to Adam about the Trinity files—a private database owned by the agency he works for—that revealed a world of unexplainable shit. Then, he discovers his buddy is one of them. Talk about kicking a guy in the balls. That was the reason Adam wanted him to come up to Cognito.

Adam and Knox went on a number of dangerous assignments. In their line of work, you just assumed you were the good guy. Most jobs were for information: files, computers, and sometimes the occasional object. They did what they were told, and didn't ask questions. That included hits.

Months ago, Knox's partner hacked the Trinity files and came across a list of names. A background check found nothing out of the ordinary, so when one of the names showed up for his next assignment, Knox took a detour to Texas without his team to find Zoë Merrick. They never went after women, and this order was a hit. That's when he found out Zoë was missing—which would have been fine with him, had he not run into Adam at her apartment. Adam wasn't talking, and while that should have pissed him off, Knox owed him. They both agreed it was in Adam's best interest to skip town while his team ran their investigation. Knox erased prints Adam left behind in Zoë's apartment, and searched his property.

Towards the end of his service, Adam confessed he no longer felt that what they were doing was for a good cause. Knox stayed true and stayed in. Doubt was a plague that ravaged his conscience now that the facts were bubbling to the surface. They saw some weird things in their time, and as it turns out, had been treading in the world of Breed for years. The Trinity files were an inside database for the higher-ups only. It broke down different supernaturals, and a few names listed were ones they had taken out.

Adam fell off the earth, but after an unexpected phone call, Knox drove up and they shared information. Finding out Zoë was Silver took him by surprise, but he needed a good slap in the face to wake the fuck up from his purpose in life.

Knox curled his hand around the chilled glass and peered over his shoulder to check on the girl.

He had no shame admitting he would rather nail a woman than date her. He didn't grow up with a mother, sister, or any woman in his life. His father had a fetish for cheap women that rubbed off on him. Knox wasn't approachable, and at the end of the night, he rarely went home with a woman on his arm.

Her body was like sunshine—warm and intense—something he wanted to soak in with all his senses. Those wide eyes reminded him of azure skies along the southern coastline. Her hips were lush and curvy, leaving everything to the imagination with the layers of clothing she wore. Blond waves of hair spilled across her shoulders like particles of light. He knew she was a woman with class—real class—nothing like the women who came from wealth, pretending they were the very definition of it. Sunny was untouchable.

Knox's chin touched his shoulder as he looked over it. A short waiter with a long goatee pocketed a few bills left beneath Sunny's glass. His heart slammed to a stop when he saw the empty booth.

"Shit," he muttered, throwing his heavy boots on the floor. He twisted around and caught a glimpse of her outside, running by the window. Knox had a choice, and while he could have let her go, that's not how it went down.

He kept a safe distance behind, cursing himself as he stayed in the shadows.

Sunny shielded herself from the onslaught of rain with a small clutch over her head. The water on the dark streets shimmered like glass, collecting a shower of colors from the streetlights and neon signs. When she made it safely to the hotel, Knox took a position by a light pole and lit up a smoke.

Sunny tossed her wet scarf on the dresser. Cognito was miserable with all the rain. She switched on the dim lamp and stood by the window, watching a homeless woman squatting beside a dumpster with a bag over her head.

Marco was eating away at her conscience. In the beginning, he was an attentive lover. He treated her with gifts and expensive dates. She never liked dominant men; it was difficult to break it off with them when it was time. There was never a man in her life that matched his confidence. He was well traveled, educated, and cultured. He was also a liar.

Sunny leaned against the wall as the rain sprayed against the window. The room smelled musty, like a mixture of mold, sweat, and grandpa's shoes. The yellow and brown striped comforter was stained, and it was criminal what they were charging her.

She thought about Knox. He took a stick to those men and she never thanked him. Whether it was the thought of him, or the damp chill in the air, a flurry of goose bumps scattered across her arms.

Her eyes snapped up when a person stepped behind a light post across the street. There was no hiding that frame of solid muscle. That was Knox out in the rain.

Was he watching her?

Without thinking, she ran out of the hotel to confront him. Her leggings soaked up water as she crossed the deep puddles in the road. Sunny stepped up the curb and touched his arm.

"Knox?"

Cold drops of rain pelted her face as Knox spun on his heel and walked in the opposite direction. Fast.

"Wait!" she yelled, knocking into a newspaper stand.

He took off at animal speed, his heavy boots crunching on the coarse concrete.

"Knox wait, don't make me run after you because I will—all the way to Jersey if I have to!" she shouted, "and I don't even know where that is from here, so STOP!"

He slowed down and looked over his shoulder.

"What are you doing out here?" she asked, approaching him

cautiously. His lashes were wet and she couldn't see his eyes, but she felt them on her like heat. A shiver skated across her skin and her teeth chattered.

"You shouldn't be out here," he said. "You'll get sick."

"Where's your car?"

"Adam took it."

She figured as much when she noticed that he stayed at the bar for a drink, but never once did he offer to sit with her. The rain was deafening—but all she could hear was his breath.

"Come inside, let me make you a cup of hot coffee and dry you off. This damsel in distress owes you one."

His shoulders hunched up as he tucked his hands in his pockets, watching her closely but never speaking a word.

"Or, I'll just stay out here with you… in the pouring rain," she said, folding her arms.

Knox wiped a hand over his wet face and moved towards the hotel, escorting her across the street with the palm of his hand between her shoulder blades.

Once inside, Sunny made a beeline to the bathroom and grabbed a fresh stack of white towels. Knox was closing the dingy curtains when she entered the room.

"Those locks on the door are cheap."

Well, wasn't that an odd thing to say?

"It's all I could afford on short notice; most of the hotels were booked," she said. "Here." She flung a towel across the room and he caught it with his left hand. By the looks of him, he needed more than a towel. "Give me your shirt and hat, I'll wring them out and hang them up to dry. I also have a hair dryer."

The shirt he wore didn't leave much to the imagination. While it was the color of iron, the fabric was sheer when wet and she could see every line of muscle.

When she snatched the hat away from his head, the look on his face made her giggle. "Well, at least let me take this before you catch pneumonia."

Sunny marched into the bathroom and wrung out the hat, folding it over the shower rod. She wondered why he wore it all the time because it covered up his beautiful black hair. It was probably the most boyish thing about him.

She tossed her wet clothes in the bathtub and slipped into a pink nightgown that draped past her knees. Zoë used to tease her about her old-fashioned gowns, but she liked them, and Zoë had no room to talk with her sweats and frumpy shirts.

"Are you staying at a hotel nearby?" she yelled through the open door.

"No ma'am."

"Don't call me ma'am unless you're taking my order—and I like extra pickles on my burger," she replied. "Can you put some coffee on?"

Sunny dabbed the ends of her hair with a white cotton towel until the water was no longer dripping. She smiled when she walked into the room and saw Knox holding the coffee pot upside down, staring inside.

"I take it you don't drink much coffee?" Sunny took the pot from his hands. "Sit down and tell me how you know Zoë, I mean… Silver."

"Through Adam."

His eyes darted between her gown and her painted toes. She was a little confused as to why he avoided eye contact with her.

"What exactly is up with that? Are they an item or something?"

Knox laughed; it was throaty and rolled out like a long, suggestive caress that made her toes curl.

"Doesn't he wish? Romeo can't seem to catch that fish."

"You rhymed," she smirked. "That's one fish who doesn't want to be caught. He should cast out his line for another one because he's wasting his time. She doesn't trust men."

"What about you? Do you trust men?" Knox sat down and ruffled his wet hair with the towel.

She slunk in the opposite chair and thought about it.

"I love men with no strings attached. I just want the frosting, not the whole cake." She glimpsed down at his hand, absent of a ring. "No wife?"

A tight smile wound across his face, and he dropped the towel on the floor.

"I'm not hitting on you. I'm just making conversation," she lied. There was something about Knox that reeled her in, and she wanted to kick herself for playing twenty questions. He was the complete opposite of the men she found attractive. He looked as if he lived a rough life, yet even with his brutal features, she couldn't stop looking at him.

"Fuck no. Might as well castrate me, and I like my balls just fine where they are—firmly attached."

She dismissed men like him, and while normally that kind of vulgarity would put her off, Sunny found it refreshing that he was real with her. It had been ages since she knew what real felt like.

What the fuck are you doing here? Knox thought to himself as he scratched the stubble on his jaw. He tried not to stare at Sunny in her satin gown, and almost blushed like a bastard when she walked into the room. She looked like a pink flower, and he breathed in lavender perfume mixed with rainwater.

He would stay, politely drink his coffee, and leave.

"Cream?"

Fuck. "No, black is fine."

"You don't talk much, do you?"

She placed the steaming cup in front of him and his eyes brightened. He never liked the taste of coffee, but he appreciated the smell.

"Do you hate women, or is it just me? I won't be offended."

Knox took a long sip, not giving in to provocation. Some women were always looking for a fight. Through his peripheral, he watched her mashing the tips of her toes against the carpet as she stood beside him. Purple polish. He noticed.

"I don't want to frighten you—just watching what I say."

"You don't scare me, and I don't mind the way you talk. In fact, I kind of like it. I don't know why, but it makes me feel…" She hesitated. "You put me at ease, and that's saying a lot."

"I'm not the kind of man you need to feel comfortable with."

She squeezed a few drops of water from the back of his hair and he shuddered. "I'll be the judge of that." Her voice tickled his spine and he tried to drown out her fresh rain scent with the steam from his cup. "After what I saw tonight, I know there's a decent man in there."

"I don't put up with lowlifes, I was just…" He stopped before he felt the flush in his ears. Damn, how he hated that dead giveaway of his embarrassment. In school, kids taunted him for it, and as a result, Knox learned how to fight.

"Well, you can come to my rescue *anytime*." Sunny drifted over to her seat.

An impulse surged through every muscle in his body. Maybe it was pride talking, but women never spoke that way about him.

"I'm beginning to think I really should carry that pepper spray I'm always threatening to use." She smiled. "I usually don't have to deal with that kind of thing."

Her fingers cupped the mug as she took baby sips. A fluff of steam obscured her face and made the tip of her nose glisten. He took a big mental eraser and tried to work on that emotion swelling inside of him.

"What do you do to earn a respectable dollar?"

Women loved this part. You merely had to suggest you worked in the military and all the visions of uniforms danced in their heads like sugarplums. Of course, the only uniform he wore was all black.

"Military. Top secret shit," he said, with a double arch of the brow.

"Sounds *riveting*," she mocked with a sly smile that had the hairs on the back of his neck standing erect. "Do you work with Adam, is that what he does?"

"No. His kind employs their own and keeps separate from us humans. I don't know what they do precisely."

"So you're human?" she asked warily.

"Born and bred. Your friend—she's been through some rough shit," he said, derailing the subject.

She rested her elbow on the table and it tilted, so Knox planted his boot on one of the legs to steady it. He grimaced at the burnt flavor of the coffee and set his cup down.

Sunny cleared her throat. "I was seeing this guy who kept asking about her, but I didn't think much about it because I thought he was just trying to show an interest in my life. The night Zoë disappeared, I went to his place, and… he said he was finished with me. He deceived me," she said angrily. "Led me to believe there was something more between us. I was an idiot. I can't believe I actually fell for his lies. That's karma coming back to sink its teeth in my rear, and I probably deserve it."

"*He* was the fucking idiot." Knox placed his arms flat on the table.

"I've never led a guy on, Knox, but he did with me. I was so upset by the things he said that we started arguing, and I got even more upset when I couldn't understand half of what he was saying because it was in Italian. When he called me a name—that much I understood. I threw a bookend at him and…"

Her delicate brows pinched together forming a worry line, and he didn't like where this story was going. Knox had zero tolerance for a man who raised a hand to a woman.

"What did he do?"

"He moved so fast. I guess that's something that they can do, right? Well, I was just flabbergasted." Sunny smiled sweetly and it melted him. "Sorry, sometimes I sound a little old fashioned."

He liked the way this woman spoke; it was confident and not muddied up with profanities that came as natural to him as breath. Her voice was clear and bright, like church bells.

"Marco grabbed my arm and threw me out the front door like Monday's trash."

Knox wanted to find the prick and throw him off a cliff.

"I always suspected that Marco had something to do with her disappearance. That's why I moved; I was afraid of him. Now that I know *what* Silver is, everything makes sense. He used me just to get to her; he was probably conspiring with that monster that made her."

She got up and sat on the edge of the bed, dropping her head in her hands. "She's never going to forgive me when I tell her everything."

Knox lowered his eyes to the floor. "You'd be surprised what people can get over."

It was time to make an exit before he started to sound like a greeting card. As he brushed past her, he stopped dead in his tracks as her fingers reached out and curled around his.

"Stay with me tonight." Her voice was quiet, and his heart raced.

"You don't want that." But god, *he* did.

"How do you know what I want?"

"You want to talk about your feelings over a cup of coffee," he said, staring down at her eyes, "but I'm not that guy." Knox bit his tongue. He needed to be crude; it was the only way to smother any idea she held that he was a decent man. Taking a woman whenever she offered was something of a religion to him, but it didn't seem appropriate to do this with her, not just because she was a friend to Silver, but he didn't see her like the other women. "Unless you want to be with someone who will make you feel like a cheap whore, then let go of my hand."

She let go, and hooked her fingers in his jeans. He sucked in a sharp breath, feeling the cold tips against his warm stomach. It triggered a reaction—a need to warm her—and he threaded his fingers through the soft waves of her damp hair. It was silky, just like he imagined.

She rolled up the end of his shirt, spreading slow kisses across the flat of his stomach.

Possession crashed through him like a tsunami. He lifted her by the arms and her body rubbed against his, every curvy inch of it.

"You *don't* make me feel cheap," she said in a breath touching his neck. "I want to know who you are, and I'm asking you to stay with me tonight," she said, rising to her tiptoes to meet his lips.

The kiss, her lips, and the firm way that she gripped his arms were more than he could process. He didn't lean in or offer. She took what she wanted. Knox had always been the aggressor—the pursuer—and he wasn't prepared for a woman to take charge of him this way.

He liked it.

That first feathery brush made his knees lock up. She was insatiable. Her tongue found his and she gripped the back of his neck, pulling him to her even more. Rain and flowers filled his senses, and she deepened the kiss, coaxing him to respond with more passion than he was giving her. She tasted like butterscotch, and their tongues twirled.

"This isn't right," he said, breaking away. She needed someone—anyone—and Knox was nothing more than a convenience of proximity. He refused to be her regret.

"It doesn't have to mean anything," she said.

Those words slammed into him like a brick wall, and it scared the shit out of him. Following her home was a mistake, so Knox moved away and walked out the door.

CHAPTER 5

───◆───

"**W**HAT ARE YOU AND KNOX up to?" I asked.

Adam rapped his fingers on the dining table with confidentiality etched all over his face.

"I can't say."

"The same reason you can't say why he was at my apartment that night?"

Adam rubbed his eyelids with the tips of his fingers and yawned. God, the man was impossible.

A dim candle on the wall sconce flickered out, so I replaced it with a fresh one and lit the wick. I never won the battle for electricity, but I did manage to convince Justus to install it in the bathroom so I could see in the shower.

"Knox isn't trying to become a Mage, is he?"

A sharp laugh flew out of his mouth and his eyes crinkled. "Hell no. Why would you even think that? Knox would never contemplate being anything but human."

"I trust I'll find out soon enough, Captain Confidential."

It was the first time that we had a chance to talk privately, and I struggled with bringing up the topic. "I need to ask you something, and I want you to be honest with me. Do you resent me for the choice you made that night? I knew there was a risk you could die, and that killed me, Adam. But I had no idea that Novis was a Creator and would give you a choice to become something you despised." I paused for a moment as I stood by a chair. "You had every reason to hate us."

His lips formed two thin lines; he didn't appreciate the question.

"It was my choice to become a Mage and I knew what I was bargaining for. I know where you're going with this, woman, and you can rest easy. A Mage murdered the one person who mattered to me, but I feel differently about it now. I can't blame an entire race for the actions of one man. I have no regrets."

I stared at a painting on the wall.

"Are you really upset about this?" he asked.

"It's not the same." I shook my head and wrapped a lock of hair around my finger. "I never wanted you to give up your life, or to make that choice. You had to give up photography, your home, and—"

"And nothing. If you're worried about my career then you need to get your priorities in check. I did that to find meaning in my life when I had none. You're forgetting that it *was* a choice, and not forced on me like…"

Like me, he meant to say. I never had the choice.

He dropped his eyes. "I have peace of mind knowing you never have to see that motherfu—"

"Okay," I said, raising a hand. "Let's not talk about him. I refuse to let that man haunt the rest of my life, and I don't want to make his name part of table conversation, if you don't mind."

It wasn't just how Samil treated me, but I felt robbed of the experience others had with their Creator and first spark. Watching Novis change Adam was a beautiful moment, and part of me would always be envious of that bond.

"If you knew it could have been offered, why were you so willing?"

Adam lowered his eyes without an answer.

I left the table and entered the main room with its majestic warmth and solace. Although we were underground, the ceiling was high, and gave the illusion of a larger house than it was. Justus enjoyed his fire, but I hadn't lit one since he left. The wall on the left contained a deep bookshelf, and a brown rug spread on the floor before the hearth. It was my favorite room. The leather complained as I sank into the chair.

"Your Ghuardian lives in the Stone Age."

"Tell me about it," I chuckled, turning on my side. "Do you know how long I had to beg to have power installed in the bathroom? Justus likes his peace and quiet; you can't imagine how irritated he gets when I start running the hair dryer."

"Is it too late to find another Ghuardian?"

I wondered if he was joking. "I would never do that. Justus won't change overnight, but I trust him with my life. He's more lenient than he used to be. It's not as if I can't go out, but I'd rather not because of all the women licking him up like ambrosia. At least he gives me time alone with Simon."

Adam took a seat on the floor beside my chair and cracked a knuckle.

"Are you and Simon an item?" His throat cleared.

"Can you light a candle? I'm about to fall asleep in this chair."

Adam stretched over on his right arm and lit one of the candles by the fireplace. I lifted the wallet from his back pocket before he could stop me.

The Mageri provided us with new identities to use in human establishments, so I was dying to know what Adam's alias was. Those who monitored law enforcement databases would spread the word to the proper Breed authorities if you were in trouble, and they made sure our names were uncommon. I curled it against my chest when he tried to take it, although I was tempted to snap him with my light. Simon and I often played around, sparking one another with tiny increments of energy—like static, only stronger. I was wary of starting that with Adam. He had never tasted my light as a Mage, and I had to be careful about throwing my power around.

"I want to see your new ID, Adam."

"You didn't answer my question about Simon."

I squinted in the candlelight. "Your name is Lucan Riddle?" Of course, I had no room to talk, because I ended up with Ember Gates. We had no say in what name the Mageri assigned us. I tucked the card back in the sleeve.

"Simon and I are nothing more than friends," I said, fumbling through his wallet.

"Sunny took it all pretty well. You two couldn't be more opposite. I can see why you get along; she's a good girl."

"Are you implying that I'm the bad influence?"

"No comment from the peanut gallery."

"Justus is being unreasonable. He led me to believe it was a law that we had to sever human ties, but they were his laws, not the Mageri's. There's no reason that I can't spend time with Sunny. I finally have someone I can talk to."

"Now I'm hurt by that," Adam said. "You don't want to share your feelings with me, *girlfriend*?"

I flicked my finger on the back of his neck. "Don't be ridiculous. Anyhow, it's not the—hey, what's this?" I pulled a photograph from the inside sleeve of his wallet. It was cut to fit the pocket perfectly. I expected to see a picture of Adam's sister, instead, my fingers held a picture that once hung in a frame in my apartment. It was an old picture of me sitting on a rug in my bedroom when I was a human.

"Where did you get this?"

"The night we went back to your apartment. It's a nice picture and I wanted to keep it."

"Why?"

"It's you."

"It *was* me."

"That's the real you, Silver. That's the girl I found."

Something snapped. I flicked it into his lap. "You see that picture and you think that's me?" His eyes fell on the image.

"Keep it," I said sharply.

He frowned and tucked the picture back in his wallet. "Why are you mad? It's only a photograph."

"You're holding on to a girl who doesn't exist, someone you never even knew. That's not who I am, not anymore." I narrowed my eyes and tapped my chest. "*This* is me, Adam. It's not just about the fact that my brown eyes are now his color, or that I no longer have the same face; I'm different inside. I've changed from the girl I once was in that photograph—the one you never knew. You can't go through the hell I did without changing. You want me to be someone I'm not." My voice softened. I cared about Adam, but I never completely understood him. "You never accepted me as a Mage, and now I know it."

"The hell I haven't." He touched my hand and I jerked it away. "I'm not a human, Silver. You can't hurt me anymore."

"Don't get emotionally attached, I'm not wired like that. It would only end badly for you."

He angrily smiled. "Deny you've been involved with Simon. I dare you."

"What I do is my business."

"Why won't you trust me and tell me the truth?" His voice rose, demanding an answer. I got out of the chair and stood over him, shaking my head.

"What is this conversation even about? I don't know what you want from me, why don't you tell me?"

He fell silent. There it was, neatly folded in my lap. Adam tugged strings of guilt within me, but it was obvious he wasn't even sure of his own feelings.

"My heart is not a piñata. I don't give it away freely, and I don't think you were ever asking for it. I want you as my friend. Why has that never been enough?" I reached down to touch his hair, but he pulled back and stood up, throwing his disapproval at me. He was punishing me for something I couldn't help.

"You have no right to be mad at me, Adam. I can't lead you on if you never asked anything of me. I get more mixed signals from you than a traffic light, and I don't want there to be any tension between us."

"You should never have kissed me, then."

Emotions swirled like one of those whirlpools that suck you to the bottom. It upset me to know that I wouldn't be able to touch him affectionately without him interpreting it the wrong way—that we wouldn't be able to move past this weirdness between us. I became the bad guy, but he had no business feeling a sense of entitlement to me for any reason. I had no clue what role he wanted in my life, because he didn't know himself. My thoughts clouded as anger spilled out in harsh words. I went somewhere I shouldn't have, but that hindsight thing is a real bitch.

"Maybe you just want to fuck me, is that what this is all about? Just tell me the truth, Adam. If I sleep with you, would that be enough to—"

His body shifted so quickly that I flinched.

"Silver," he said reaching out to me, "you know I would never strike you." I backed up and held my arms tightly.

Adam fell silent, staring at the space between us. When he left, his footsteps ruptured through the silent house until he slammed the door behind him. That was our first real fight, and I felt awful about it.

CHAPTER 6

"WHY DID YOU BRING ME here?" I fidgeted in the booth of the same bar we were in the night before, looking into my Ghuardian's eyes, tinted with shades of suspicion and wrath. Fine with me; I always loved a good apocalypse.

Justus returned home early, throwing a wrench in my plans. I called Sunny, but it didn't take the sting away from the fact that I couldn't see her.

Tonight, Justus wasn't dressed in expensive threads, but a muscle shirt and loose pants. In fact, that's what troubled me. I knew something was wrong when he flew out of the training room—dripping in sweat—and told me to get in the car.

He stroked the edgy lines of his tattoo, which was a habit. His eyes fell on me like a jury, and his tongue was the gavel waiting to slam down.

"Tell me, what do you think of this place?"

Like a good defendant, I sipped my vodka and changed the subject. "Did you get that tattoo before you were made?"

"No. In my family, men did not mark themselves."

"If we heal, how can you have a permanent tattoo?"

"Are you reading the books I give you, or staring at the pictures?"

I joked on occasion about there being no pictures to break up the reading, but his condescending attitude rubbed me the wrong way. I spent months learning our history from his books. Granted most of it was boring, but I made every effort to live up to his expectations.

"Liquid fire seals any scar or tattoo; it's an ancient extract and only a few know how it is made."

"Why did you bring me here?" I asked again.

His fingers rapped on the table. "What kind of Ghuardian would

I be if I did not allow my Learner to have some fun? I thought this looked like... your kind of place. What do you think?" He stretched his left arm over the back of his seat and flexed his jaw. "Are the men here to your liking?"

"It's so-so."

His fist slammed against the table. "Why did you defy my orders? I told you not to leave!"

The bartender polished the bar, watching us closely.

"Are these Mageri rules, or *your* rules?" I hissed.

"Don't test me."

"Oh, I'm testing you," I said, pointing a finger. "Adam has the freedom to leave without an escort. You have kept me in a prison with invisible bars."

I cringed at the ugly stare looking my way. I should have been grateful for everything he did for me—and I was—but it wasn't enough.

"How did you know I was here?" I shifted in my seat and the cheap vinyl croaked.

"I don't have to follow you, *Ember Gates*. Every time you pass off your ID or pay for something, it flags our system. I keep a watch on your account, and I know where you go."

I huffed loudly. "Good to know, because next time I'm paying with cash."

He lowered his voice. "I am responsible for you. Your safety is my priority, and I do not approve of your barhopping."

"I wasn't barhopping, I was..."

I pursed my lips when the truth almost slipped out. Justus may not have minded the seclusion of his home, but I came from a life where I had a job and went out with friends, and even by myself. My independence was the hardest thing to let go of, and the thought of how many years this could go on frightened me. I rubbed my cheek and saw the bartender from the corner of my eye. He was pretending to arm-wrestle a man who looked like a bouncer by the way they were keeping an eye on our conversation.

"You were just *what*?"

"Having a drink."

"I do not like secrets," he said, emphasizing every word.

"Of course not, you wear a *halo*. I live with you, Ghuardian. I'm going to find out, so why can't you trust me enough to tell me what you do for HALO? I want to know more about your life."

He leaned forward, lowering his voice. "We work independently from the Mageri, or any other form of government. Two friends organized the group years ago and took an oath to represent and protect all races. There are powerful men consumed with undermining their leaders. We track these unlawful activities and collaborate for the greater good."

"Sounds like a flea circus."

"Don't turn your nose from the fact that we exist to protect your freedoms."

"You implied people know about HALO, so I just don't understand the swarm of secrecy. Why is Simon involved if he's not a member?"

"He has intellect and connections, but Simon is too immature about the politics and refuses to join. We contract his services as needed; the man has skills."

"You got that right," I smirked.

I didn't mean for it to have any hidden innuendos, but to my embarrassment, it spread across the table like a hooker in a brothel. They were old friends, which made it awkward that Simon and I had a careless moment.

"Why did you come here, Learner?"

My lips pressed together like magnets.

"Your nights with Simon are out."

"You can't do that!" I shouted. "You can't—"

Justus scratched his shaved, blond hair. "Punish you? Yes, I can. That is my duty, and if you disobey me again, there will be *no* going out."

"You cannot cage me up like some kind of animal. I may be under your custody, but I have freedoms."

"Not under the Mageri. Once you earn my trust, I'll reconsider the conditions. Until then—"

"Until then, bullshit!" I stood up and threw my finger at his chest. "I am a grown woman, and you should treat me as such." I snatched his wallet from the table.

"You don't behave like much of a woman," he said in a condescending tone. Justus spread his arms across the back of the booth and I was so furious with him I wanted to scream. A plump woman in a red dress slowed down to admire his arms, and bumped into me as she walked past.

"I can't believe how insensitive you are. This is my life, not a social experiment. I've done everything you asked of me; don't treat me differently because I'm a woman."

"A Unique woman," he corrected.

I spun on my heel and marched down the aisle. When he rose from his seat, I shouted to the bartender, "He's trying to leave without paying!"

I got the hell out of there. Fast.

A fine mist coated my face as I stepped on the curb. Through the window, two men confronted Justus, blocking his exit, and an argument heated up. I plucked the phone from my purse and sprinted up the street.

"Dial-a-friend," a cheery voice answered.

"Sunny! I'm in the area, where's your hotel?"

"Where are you?"

"Just passing a bakery on my right."

"Oh, uh…" she paused. "Do you know the Brooks Hotel?"

"No, is that—"

"I'm coming down," she decided. "Keep going straight and you'll see a pizza shop across the street. I'll meet you there."

As I ran northbound, I looked back, but didn't see Justus. I hated my childish behavior around him, but that's exactly what he treated me like.

It was after sunset and when I passed the third bar, I was getting hammered by heavy rain. It was a couple of minutes struggling not to slip in my shoes when I saw the red neon lights of the pizza place. In fact, I smelled the rich spices before I noticed the sign. I darted across the street, splashing through puddles without a thing to cover my head.

I swung the door open and looked around the room, but Sunny wasn't in there. A teenager at the soda fountain wearing an anarchy shirt turned around, half smiling at my drenched appearance.

"Can I help you?" a man offered, in a welcoming voice. He had a handlebar mustache and a red apron that barely wrapped around his potbelly.

My shoes squeaked on the linoleum floor. "I'm looking for my friend—blond hair, real pretty?"

"I'm looking for your friend, too!" He laughed.

I rolled my eyes and pushed out the door, the bell jingling behind me.

Standing beneath the short awning, I scoured the streets. It was a torrential downpour, pelting the cars like bullets. I slicked my hair back and tucked my hands beneath my arms, waiting. Five minutes passed and the rain died down. Sunny never showed.

There was no sense standing around when the hotel was up the road. Knowing that girl, she was still searching for the perfect outfit. It looked desolate straight ahead, so I turned right at the next street. In the distance, I saw there were signs on buildings—possibly hotels. Passing another alley, I heard a noise. I thought a dog followed me so I turned to look, but the dumpster obscured my view. I stepped forward, and peered around the edge.

My heart almost leapt out of my chest. A strong forearm pinned Sunny against a grimy brick wall. Although a scarf covered her head, I recognized those red shoes I used to borrow. Fire filled my veins as I studied my surroundings, searching for a weapon. I learned plenty in the training room, but much of it involved flashing moves. From the weak energy, this was a human, and I was not getting cocky about my hand-to-hand combat skills. I lifted a glass bottle, lying on its side.

Not wanting to give him a chance to see me coming, I rushed in and cracked the bottle over his head. Shards of glass sprayed to the ground as he hunched his shoulders, making a sound between a groan and a yell.

The air squeezed out of my lungs when I was tackled and a large set of arms wrapped around me. Sunny was wide-eyed, and when the man in front of her lifted his chin, I cringed.

Three familiar faces came into focus: Sean, Matty, and John. Except Sean was slightly bloody, thanks to a bottle of carbonated sugar.

He held a chubby hand over Sunny's mouth. John stood to the

side, looking like an ink pen ran over him. His tats covered his neck and arms with the most unattractive and amateur markings. I also noticed how much he looked like Sean. I would have bet they were brothers. They were stocky and close to my height.

Matty tightened his grip, smelling like an ashtray and swinging me like a doll.

Sean snapped the scarf from Sunny's hair as she wrestled against him.

"Remember me, sweets?" he asked. "Your friend sure does, and she's got a mouth on her. I think I like yours much better. Brunettes never did a damn thing for me."

Sunny's eyes went wild with panic when his other arm slid down her side. John was wired with excitement—anticipation.

They looked like a fucking tag team.

My jaw unhinged enough that I could clamp my teeth down on some flesh. Matty pulled his hand away so I twisted his other arm, spun around, and broke his nose with the flat of my hand.

I heard the crack the second my palm struck him, and I didn't pause for his reaction. My knee made a friendly acquaintance with his testicles, and I hit him in the throat with my knuckles. He dropped like a weight, and I kicked him in the crotch. Justus taught me well, but I was also willing to fight dirty.

The time I spent training with Justus—although most of it was basic sparring—was about to be put to the test. I was confident when I could use my Mage abilities, but fighting these men by hand was something else. Justus said it wasn't about strength or speed, but guts and skills.

Skills I knew it would take years to acquire. You can't expect a girl who spent her Sundays at a sandwich shop reading a tabloid to turn into a ninja overnight.

Getting my feet wet in a real fight was the only way to understand my fears, limitations, and weaknesses. Forbidden to use my gifts, it was just me against him.

I faced John, but what rattled me was his confidence.

The smell of garbage was unbearable. Something scurried behind the dumpster, and Sunny scraped her nails against the brick.

"Silver, run!" Sean cut her off with a press of his arm.

John smirked. "Silver? What kind of fucked up sense of humor did your parents have?"

"You tell me? Yours let you live."

Energy buzzed in my fingertips and I felt alive, more than I expected. It was a natural reaction for my light to increase as a defense mechanism. I reined it in, keeping it under control. He bent forward, swinging his arms, waiting for me to strike first.

When he reached for my leg, I planted a solid kick to his shin and threw my hand out, striking him in the face. I wiped the rain from my nose.

"Just so you know, I hit back," he said, spitting out a mouthful of blood.

"Bring it on, Hercules!"

I was asking for it, but smack talk was one skill I perfected. It took years to refine it to an art form. The name I used rubbed him the wrong way, as I guessed him to be a man insecure about his height.

He threw a punch and I ducked, spinning behind him. I was afraid to get too close, so I kicked him behind the knee hoping to knock him off balance. Instead, he bent forward and thrust his leg back. *Moron.* I moved to the side and he stood up, scowling.

Somehow, I was under the impression there was an honor code among street fighters. When Matty suddenly kicked me in the back, I realized how naive I was.

I stumbled forward and John swung his arm, making contact with my face. Pain exploded in my cheek and I hit the ground, falling on my shoulder. The grit from the dirty alley roughed up my chin and I turned my head in time to see him kneeling. I rammed my thumb into his eye and he shouted, squeezing them shut.

"Jesus, John!" Sean yelled out. "You're letting a girl kick your ass?"

Without missing a beat, I punched him in the jaw and kicked him in the gut, which knocked him to the side. I was foolish to think that would be enough to take him down, because when he lifted his eyes, there was excitement flashing in them. I saw an ass-kicking coming in my direction and he was the deliverer.

I scrambled to my feet, but John reached out and balled up the material of my shirt within his iron fist. I saw nothing but thin razors staring back at me.

"When will you bitches ever learn that you don't fuck with—"

I flinched as he swung his arm.

"*Me.*"

The voice that spoke wasn't John, but a baritone that could straighten your spine like an arrow.

Justus held John's fist in the palm of his hand. He caught it mid-swing, and it looked like a ball in a catcher's mitt. I pried John's fingers from my shirt and took a deep, calming breath.

"You like to hit women?" Justus forced him into the shadows until all I could see were his powerful shoulders, illuminated by an overhead light. I shuddered when I heard what sounded like knuckles cracking. John screamed.

"Answer me, you coward!"

My Ghuardian was not only a Charmer, but he was also Thermal. Energy took all forms, including temperature. He was able to control his body heat—except when he was angry. John's eyes watered as if he stuck his head inside an oven.

Justus was karma in a pair of combat boots.

It marked a turning point between us. No matter how often we quarreled, this man would always be at my side when I needed him. Every lesson he taught was invaluable, even if I was too childish to understand it. He had hundreds of years of experience on me, and knew no fear.

While John took a beating, I slicked back my hair and glared at Sean, who twirled around using Sunny as a shield. Her upper lip was swollen, not from him, but something that naturally happened whenever she was upset.

My cheek throbbed where John had hit me, as if my heart found a new place of residence.

"I was thinking about letting you go, but that's not going to happen." I flicked a glance at Matty. "I see you like your friends to do all the dirty work. I bet you fight like a girl. Let her go, and it's just you and me."

"Silver!" Justus bellowed from the shadows.

I ignored him.

"Unless…"

I tried to think of a word that would provoke. Granted, I threw around a cuss word more than a lady should, but I cringed at the vulgarity about to pour from my lips.

"Unless you're a *pussy*."

Fifteen minutes later, I sat in the back of Justus's car with Sunny. He drove to the hotel and put her bags in the trunk. She was coming home with us because I insisted. We made a detour so Justus could buy back his expensive Cartier watch he had traded the bartender. I never understood why he wore those things, but Justus was all about image, even in workout attire.

The heater fogged up the windows, leaving the tips of my fingers sticky from the humidity. Justus breezed out the door, biting down on his wallet as he slipped on the watch.

"He looks really good wet," Sunny remarked in a soft voice. She was feasting on him as he approached the car.

"You are a hot mess; that's my Ghuardian."

"In the flesh," she gushed, with an appraising smile.

The rain polished his arms, and his muscle shirt was so drenched it clung to him. I really didn't need Justus saucing up my friend with his sex voodoo, but we were driving in a small car, so there was no way to put distance between them.

"Sunny, there's something else you should know. We all have special gifts that come with the package."

"Like what?"

Drops of cold water fell to the seat when I squeezed the ends of my hair. "Some move different than the rest of us, others read or send thoughts using energy." I cupped my hands, warming them with a breath. "That man you're fawning all over is a Charmer; he leaks a special kind of energy that's like a love spell. When he's farther away, it's not as strong. Don't get the idea you actually like him, because it's false."

"You mean he can make *any* woman fall for him?"

"Fall isn't the right word, unless you mean in his bed. Trust me when I say that you are better off keeping your distance. He can't turn it off, but he sure can turn you on."

"Oh sweetie, you must be in trouble then," she giggled.

I smiled. "I've been blessed with immunity."

"Wow, I bet that's a blow to his confidence, especially with your good humor."

"I doubt I've put much of a dent in that ego, he's had centuries to perfect it."

"Well, now that I know he's a love magnet, I'll make a conscious effort not to succumb. He's a hottie. Are you sure you don't lust after that body just a teeny-weeny bit?"

"I'm not even going to dignify that with an answer, Sunshine. What did you do last night?"

She made an awful groan, rubbing her face. "I made such a fool out of myself. I invited Knox up to my room and threw myself at him."

"What?" I laughed, turning to face her. "You're kidding, right?"

"No," she said, staring at the roof of the car. "I don't know *what* got into me. I can't explain it because he's nothing like the men I date. He's just… sexy in his own way."

"You're serious? Was it because he came to your rescue, oh princess? Maybe you have that deer in the headlights hero syndrome."

She looked around the Mercedes with detached interest. "Most men play hero, but few men are. There's a chemistry when I'm with him, when I think about him." Sunny sneezed and quickly wiped her nose. "Too bad he wasn't here tonight. I can't believe you found me. When I rounded the corner, I ran right into them, and that guy recognized me immediately. He was talking about Knox like he wanted to kill him."

"Do you think you can keep all of this a secret? Not just about me, but everything you're learning about us."

"I would never break our trust." I caught her eyes looking me over, still skeptical. "I miss the old you," she said wistfully.

"Me too."

CHAPTER 7

MY PUNISHMENT WOULD NOT BE private. Justus hit speed dial as we careened down the road, requesting that Novis come to the house immediately. Each time he referred to me as *Learner,* I squeezed water from my hair onto his leather seat.

"Learner, why did you provoke the human? I had it under control."

Justus had to drag me out of there by the waist. "He let her go, didn't he?" I drew an infinity symbol on the fogged up window. "Ghuardian?"

He flashed his eyes at me in the rearview mirror, and I could see a hint of his light in them. I leaned in close, lowering my voice.

"Pull over and heal me."

The car lurched when his foot slipped on the pedal.

A Mage heals faster than a human does, and sunlight contains healing properties, as does energy from another Mage. Borrowed light is full of moving particles and emotion; it's a personal imprint. Sharing energy with a Mage is like a drug, and I never wanted to get too comfortable with the dependency. It was preferable to allow nature to take its course, or borrow a little sun. That required strict concentration because it is so pure, but the advantage is it doesn't come with the addictive feeling as taking from another. Anyhow, it always zapped my energy later on when I took too much. Anytime you borrow something, you have to give it back.

"You will heal."

"I don't want Adam to see my face."

"Perhaps it serves him right to feel shame for the trouble he has caused."

"Very true," I sighed. "I guess I'll just sit back here with my throbbing cheek so I can be a valuable lesson to someone."

Laying on guilt like thick frosting was something that required a little finesse. I learned that no matter how much he grumbled, Justus had a tender heart.

The car crawled to a stop and I maneuvered into the front seat while he flipped on the interior light.

"You might want to get out your camera, Sunny. He hates touching me, so this one needs to go into the Hall of Fame."

"I think you mean Hall of Lame," she said. "If I have to sit back here and watch you two make out, then you're paying for my plane ticket home. I didn't sign up for this tour."

Justus avoided personal intimacy—the touching kind. There were never any friendly hugs, pats, kisses, or even mussing up my hair. He just wasn't a touchy-feely guy (unless you were a six-foot tall blonde in a pair of pumps). Justus never complained about their affections, but it was curious that he spent most of the time attempting conversations with women when all they heard was *blah, blah, blah.*

"Well come on, let the healing begin!" I exclaimed in my best televangelist voice. I loved needling him.

"Continue to mock me, Learner. Remember who buys your ice cream."

He touched a small mark on my arm, stroking my skin with his rough hand. The light tingled as it stitched the wound, and his fingers lifted to my chin, grazing over the scuff. Finally, he brushed his hand across my swollen cheek, lifting the last of the visible marks. I would have normally healed up in a day or two, but I had enough drama for one night.

Sunny poked her head between the seats. "That's *amazing!* I can't believe you can heal." Her fingers swept my hair back and I smiled. Sometimes I forgot just how amazing it really was. "You really do have magic in you, Silver. Can you do that on me?"

We simultaneously twisted around and Sunny scooted away from Justus. As she pulled her sleeve up, a set of dark prints marked her arm.

"It doesn't work on humans," Justus said. "My apologies."

We arrived at the house nestled deep in the woods. Sunny was impressed when the car lowered into the garage through a mechanical hatch that Justus must have spent millions to install. Money could buy you anything; it's just a shame the man couldn't put a lamp in the living room.

Novis arrived and relaxed in a chair beside the fireplace. As an ancient Mage, he didn't look a day over twenty-five. His features were marked with character and wisdom, but he loved the modern trends. He spiked his hair, and razor cut the sideburns so they were trendy. He dressed in casual clothes, which I liked because it put me at ease. White light sparkled in the depths of his clear blue eyes. Adam inherited the same qualities, but to a lesser degree. His eyes shined, but it was a brief reflection, like a mirror in the distance catching the sun.

"Charmed to see you again, Silver. Adam talks about you… endlessly." He smiled broadly and I wondered if he sensed the tension between us.

Adam was avoiding eye contact, staring at the sleeves of my shirt. The shadows looked like stains, or water, but it was blood. I snatched Sunny by the wrist. "We're going to go change before she catches a cold."

Sunny didn't budge. She was watching Knox who leaned against the far wall by the fireplace. His eyes were preoccupied with the crackling flames—snapping and popping from the fresh log. I pulled her hand and we left the room to dry off and change clothes.

When we emerged in our pajamas, I bumped my knee against a table and grimaced. No one was speaking; they were waiting for us. Candles from the hurricane lamps glowed against the far wall, and Novis twirled a shoelace between his fingers. He looked bored with a cheek resting against his fist.

"Novis, can I get you some wine?" I asked.

"How gracious of you. Yes, please."

Whatever Novis said held weight with Justus. I decided my tactic would be to butter him up with niceties. I handed an empty glass to him and Sunny.

"Gentlemen, I won't delay," Justus began. "I called you here on short notice to clear some air. I do not tolerate deceit and lies in my house." I cringed with the accusatory remark as I poured wine in Novis's glass. "Silver has broken my trust and your progeny was involved."

Novis accepted the statement with a nod of his head.

I took a seat beside Adam on the sofa, and Sunny distanced herself from Justus in a chair across the room. She was heeding the warning I gave her about his charming ability. The lovely pale blue nightgown she wore was stretchable cotton that pulled over her knees as she tucked in her feet. Tiny buttons decorated the front, and pale flowers adorned the bottom. My pajamas, on the other hand, were just a pair of sweats and a black shirt. I preferred boy shorts with a tank top for my sleepwear, but decided that might not go over well.

"Silver was given orders to remain on the premises, and she has defied those orders. She wasn't alone. Who wants to begin?"

"She respects you," Adam spoke up. "You can't divide a friendship. I can promise she didn't do it without hesitation. I simply gave her a push."

"A push to disrespecting her Ghuardian. You put a splinter in our trust. I will not forget this."

"You treat her like a pet."

"Adam, stop it," I said. "Ghuardian, this was my idea. You can't expect me to give up everything from my old life. I agreed to do what you asked of me, but I need my friend. Show me where it's written that we have to cut our ties."

I flicked my eyes to Knox to drive my point home.

"It is easier this way," Novis intervened. "The human will die, and you will not. Leave this temporary world. You no longer have a place in it."

"Nothing is forever," I countered. "Those are your beliefs, but don't impose them on me as if they are the *right* beliefs. Just because a flower will fade, does not mean we should neglect its beauty."

"Poetic." He smiled.

Sunny's voice chimed in. "I didn't mean to get anyone in trouble, but I had to know if my friend was dead, and I needed to apologize to her for what happened. I don't want to drive a wedge in your relationships." She ran her finger over the edge of the crystal glass and it made a bright sound.

Novis paid attention to details, and he caught on to what she was implying. "How was her making any of your doing?" He leaned forward on his elbows, interested in how she would answer.

Sunny bit her lip as everyone stared.

"I met a guy and thought we were moving in the right direction. He asked questions about my life, but mostly about Zoë. Everything he told me, everything I believed about us was a lie. I thought he cared about my life and my friends, so I told him everything I knew about her. I'm so sorry, Silver."

Simon announced his presence with a knock on the door before shoving it open. He looked haggard and a little drunk as he shuffled in the room in his tattered jeans, flip-flops, and a snug red T-shirt.

"Bloody hell, Justus. This better be good."

He slumped in the seat beside me, leaving me sandwiched between two men I went to second base with. Not awkward—not at all.

Simon lifted the wine from the table and wedged it between his legs. In a calculated move, he slid his hand down the neck of the bottle in a suggestive manner and waggled an eyebrow at me.

"Could he be the benefactor of Samil?" Novis wondered aloud.

I shook my head adamantly. "No, I met Marco and he's not the guy in Samil's basement."

Novis set his glass on the table. "It appears there is a fox in the henhouse. The benefactor has informants beguiling humans in order to gain information. The question is—what is he scheming?"

Sunny's voice trembled, "I thought Marco was a good guy. He was so charming and attentive."

"Marco?" Simon murmured. "What was his last name?"

"Fearon," she replied.

"Bloody hell, for a minute there..." He blew out a breath and slouched.

"That's what he told me it was, although it didn't match the name on his credit card." Her fingernail tapped on the glass. "His friends used another name; they called him De Gradi."

Crystal shattered and I flinched.

Shards of glass sprinkled over Justus's shoes, along with drops of blood. His pale expression frightened me, and I sprang into the kitchen to grab a towel.

When I returned, the shift in the room was dramatic.

Simon knelt before Sunny, speaking in soft whispers. Novis stretched out in his chair, crossing his long legs at the ankle with his fingers locked behind his neck.

Wine spoiled the ends of Justus's rug, and blood trickled at his fingertips. I lifted his large hand, wiping the blood away. I stroked a finger over his cut, lending him my light.

The moment he sensed the magic, he jerked his hand free and showed me his back.

"Anything else you remember?" Simon asked. "Anything strange he wanted to know about Silver?"

"He asked more than once about her father."

"What? He wanted to know *what*?" I dropped the towel. I never met my father and knew nothing about him, so I carried resentment for a man who decided to use the "*get out of fatherhood free*" card.

She looked away and Simon consoled her with a gentle pat on the knee.

Knox edged away from the wall, his chest expanding like a silverback gorilla.

Sunny couldn't look me in the eye, and I stepped forward to calm her down. I wasn't mad at her, and she needed to know that.

Suddenly, the breath knocked out of my lungs when Adam lifted me off the ground. He flashed towards me so fast that I couldn't formulate words. "Glass," he muttered, staring at my bare feet as he set me down. One split second was all it took to right what was wrong between us.

"That's what I saw Marco do!" Sunny gasped. "That's how I knew that he wasn't human, he moved just like that."

I lifted my eyes to Justus, but his back was still turned. "Who is he, Ghuardian?"

The room quieted.

"He is my Creator."

CHAPTER 8

COINCIDENCE PARKED ITS ASS IN my driveway every chance it got. It was a fluke that I met Justus in a bar; it could have been anyone, or any Breed. He took me under his wing and in the short span of time we spent together, he became one of the most important mentors in my life. Suddenly, the rug ripped out from beneath us. His Creator was directly involved in the attack that led to my becoming a Mage. The betrayal he felt was palpable.

Justus couldn't look me in the eye. "I cannot *believe* this is true."

"We will summon him," Novis decided. "Tread carefully, Justus. We assigned this case to you, but don't let it become personal. Until we have facts, we have nothing."

I collapsed in my seat. "What case?" Sunny strolled across the room and sat on the arm of my chair.

Novis lingered by the bookshelf, feeling the weathered spines of our collection. "The benefactor is more than just a high paying juicer; we suspect that he's conspiring against the Mageri. We requested HALO take over the investigation."

Without warning, Knox stormed across the room, drawing everyone's attention to his sudden movement. He stopped in front of Sunny and lifted a heavy arm, pointing at her. Every man in that room, including Adam, inched forward.

"*Who* did that?" His lip curled, and something dark flashed in his eyes.

I turned to see what he was looking at. Sunny had lifted her arms to stretch, and the short sleeve fell back, revealing the marks on her arm.

Adam rose from his chair. "That was blood on your sleeve, wasn't it?"

"So what if it was?" I argued.

"Did you fight someone?"

"With my Ghuardian, yes."

Justus faced him directly, lifting his chin. "She bested them." He said it with pride on his tongue and my heart warmed.

"Atta girl," Simon cheered.

"Trouble just seems to follow you, doesn't it?" Adam's lip twitched. "One of these days, no one is going to be there to save you."

"Hey, leave my girl alone," Sunny chimed in. "She doesn't need saving. I always knew she had fight in her, but that was spectacular. Justus had to peel her off that idiot," she said, flipping up my hair in the back. "What were the odds of running into them?"

"I guess they're locals and live in the neighborhood."

"Hold the fuck up. The guys at the bar—*those* are the guys you're talking about?"

If there were such a thing as a testosterone meter, it would have spiked.

Knox lifted her sleeve to get a better look. It was an ugly mark and his jaw tightened like a steel trap.

"I still can't get over how you can heal. That's so amazing." She poked my knee and smiled.

"But *you* can't," Knox said. He turned around and walked across the room, releasing a long sigh as he stared at the fire.

"Take the chair," I said to Sunny. I went to my favorite spot on the sofa.

"Bloody hell," Simon muttered. "You haven't seen Marco in years, Justus. We don't know what he's been up to, but he hasn't kept in touch with you, has he?"

The fire crackled and hissed, sending sparks up the chimney in a twist of light.

Simon's fingers were between the cushions when he pulled out a peanut, studied it, and smiled at me through hooded eyes. He tossed it on the table and sighed. "Marco will never come willingly if the Council calls on him. You can bet he'll go underground."

Novis stretched, and tucked his fingers in his rear pockets.

"Simon, remember that debt you owe to the Council? I think it's time we collect."

"What does that mean?" I asked.

"It means that I'll be taking a trip," he grumbled.

I scoffed at him. "How are you going to get Marco to come with you? Tap him on the shoulder and say 'Excuse me. We think you may have been involved in something illegal. Could you please fly back to Cognito with me so we can put your ass in the slammer?' He'll never talk."

Justus folded his arms and lifted his head to the high ceiling. "If Marco is involved with the benefactor, then he will want to know where you are, because you are a deal that has not been closed. I have his trust, and can use that to bring him in."

Simon snatched my glass and placed it on the table. "No worries, love."

I listened as they questioned Sunny, but it was impossible to fight against the collapse of energy. Justus didn't need to level down because he kept himself under control during the confrontation, while I could barely contain my light within my fingertips.

I nodded off somewhere between plane tickets and hotels. Intense emotions spiked energy levels in a Mage; most of the time we leveled down. It takes concentration to harness your light and shift it appropriately—controlling it, before it controls you. It was my first street fight, and I didn't bother leveling down. I needed the nap.

I woke up stretched across the sofa with my head in Simon's lap. Silence swaddled me. Embers diminished to a curious glow, and the air smelled of bacon and coffee. Simon's fingers had been busy, as tiny little braids skimmed over my face.

"How long was I out?"

"Hours," he said.

"Why didn't you wake me?"

"Wouldn't dream of it—especially after the priceless look on Adam's face."

"I wish you wouldn't try to start trouble." I sat up and rubbed the corner of my eyes, feeling well rested.

"You know, you're more agreeable unconscious. I'd love to sleep with you again sometime."

Braids scattered across my shoulders. "I see you were busy."

"I'm a man who likes to keep my hands occupied."

I noticed a wet spot on his pants and wiped my mouth in embarrassment.

"I think Bam-Bam fancies your friend."

"His name is Knox, and my inside sources tell me otherwise." I yawned.

"Some things are more obvious to other men, I suppose." He tugged a loose thread from his jeans until it snapped off.

"So what's the plan?"

"I talked them out of sending me alone. We don't want him to get nervy. Everyone goes, including Knox."

"Why would he go?"

Simon stretched out like a cat, groaning aloud. "Knox is human, so he can get close and do a little detective work without raising suspicion." He sighed and chewed on a fingernail. "We know a few places he owns, but it's a big city and he could be staying anywhere. We're crashing at Sunny's flat to keep a low profile. No need to worry about our names raising any flags in town."

"How long will we be gone?"

"This time love, you will *not* leave the house." He pinched my nose playfully. "It's safer here. No one has access to get in. He's put his trust in you once more."

My voice softened. "I want to help, Simon. I have more right than anyone to go after him, and I don't want to be excluded."

He groaned, kicking up his feet on the coffee table. "Careful what you choose for your purpose in life; revenge is a swamp you'll get lost in. You're too valuable, which is why we're keeping you safe and sound in the castle."

He dropped his chin and wiped a hand across his lap. "I believe I need a new pair of trousers since these are covered in slobber. I do love it when the ladies drool over me."

"Do me a favor? Don't hit on Sunny. I *know* how much you love to flirt, but you owe me a solid. She's a sensitive girl and I don't want her played by one of my friends. Just keep an eye on her, and… away from Justus."

"No worries," he chuckled. "Something tells me that massive bloke is going to erupt like Mount Vesuvius if Justus so much as charms her. I must confess that I would very much like to see that." His pierced tongue poked at his lower lip. "Novis didn't show it, but he's quite displeased with your Adam. He's the sort that has high expectations of his Learners. I suspect he'll be revoking some of his privileges."

"Great." I slumped back on the sofa and threw my legs over Simon's lap. As if I didn't feel guilty enough. "When are you leaving?"

"Four hours."

"Already?"

"No time to waste, darling."

"Why can't I go?"

"Can't risk it."

"He wouldn't recognize me."

Simon wiggled my toe, the little piggy that had roast beef. "He's a clever Mage, so you stay put."

"What makes you think he still lives there?"

"The pubs Sunny gave us are still in his name. Doesn't even bother to get a different identity from what the Mageri gave him. Marco appears to be quite the entrepreneur. He's taken a fancy to that place."

"It's a hole-in-the-wall town."

Simon laughed. "Your phrases amuse me; they don't mean the same thing where I'm from. Cowardly men prefer to stay out of sight, and out of mind," he concluded. "Why should he leave? Your city is without a Council because of the low population, so that puts him in a powerful position. Marco has years on him, and he's stinking rich."

"Do you think Justus will try to confront him?"

A moment lapsed before Simon answered. "I won't let him."

CHAPTER 9

WITH EVERYONE GONE, I HAD no distractions to pass the time. We didn't own a television, radio, or even a computer. My music player was difficult to charge, and I was tired of listening to the same old songs. I paced the house and discovered a new diversion: cooking. I had a couple of signature dishes, but otherwise, I've always been a catastrophe in the kitchen. Justus filled the kitchen with a few essentials before leaving; little did he know what he was missing out on.

By day two, I managed to cook up a storm. The results included lasagna, noodle casserole (grossly undercooked veggies), a batch of cookies, three cakes, and chicken enchiladas.

On the third night, Simon called to check in on me.

"Are you guys done with your expedition yet?"

"Miss me already?" he purred. "Marco is an elusive bastard. We've sent Knox to his pubs, but the human could not be any *less* conspicuous. We can't afford to have him make too many appearances. Sunny will give him a ring tomorrow—pretend to be the ex who wants to smooth things over."

"Don't do that, Simon. It's better if he forgets all about her."

"I've considered the risk. If this doesn't draw him out, then she's returning to Cognito with us...for good." Simon chuckled like a man with a secret. "Hercules made sure of that."

I swirled my finger in the soft icing of a chocolate cake, decorated with a garnish of strawberries and a dusting of sugar. I liked the idea of Sunny moving to Cognito, so I didn't argue. "I don't see how she agreed to that."

Simon snorted. "She doesn't know."

"Since when does Knox have any—"

My words hit the brakes. In a silent house, any small noise was like a parade. "Hold on."

"What is it?"

A knock sounded at the front door in a friendly rhythm.

"Nothing," I exhaled, sliding off the counter. "Adam's dropping in to check on me. Don't mention this to Justus; I'm already in enough hot water to boil a lobster."

I arrowed through the living room and wiped my fingers on my jeans. The metal door was a security measure that helped Justus sleep at night. I slid the latch and heard whispers on the other end of the phone.

"I'm not kidding, Simon. Don't you dare mention this."

"Silver—"

"Let me call you back."

Simon was my friend, but his friendship with Justus spanned at least a century. I slipped the phone in my rear pocket and pulled open the door.

A man of tremendous height wearing a black raincoat stood before me. Slowly, I lifted my chin to look up at him. Adam always had a few inches on me, but this guy towered at 6'5".

Damn, he was *tall.*

Only the tip of his nose and mouth were visible. An oversized hood cloaked his face, but his pressed lips stretched wide when he smiled. Rain dripped from the ends of his fingers, splashing on the dark concrete. Light from inside glistened off the water-drenched coat, and he smelled like a thunderstorm.

He removed the hood, spilling a stream of water to the floor. Hair the color of sunlight spread across his shoulders, all one length and wet at the ends. The soft ethereal quality of it was a contrast against his pronounced bone structure. Shadowed grooves along his face showcased high cheekbones, and yet there was a softness to his expression. The top of his nose was a little broad, drawing attention to deep-set eyes framed with heavy brows, giving him an animalistic gaze. His light eyes glittered, but I couldn't distinguish the color as they dropped to the floor. His looks were distinct, but not classically handsome. In fact, he was frightening, and... I really needed to stop staring.

"Who are you?" I asked, inching the door closed. We never had visitors.

He wiped droplets of water from his chin and cleared his throat.

"Jiminy, it's coming down like cats and dogs out there! Sorry I'm late; I missed the turn. You must be Silver."

He offered a hand and lifted his brows with a pleasant expression. "I'm Logan Cross."

I stared at his hand wordlessly.

"Justus didn't mention I was coming by to keep an eye on you? I could sit out here if it makes you easier, but I know about the back door and that wouldn't make *me* feel easy. He would have my hide if he didn't think his Learner was protected."

I forced a smile.

Logan had a strong voice that warmed me on the inside like a cup of cocoa. "It was a last minute arrangement, but he said he would prepare you for my visit. Did he not call you?"

I shook my head. "I haven't spoken to him."

"Then showing up at your door unannounced was rude. Forgive me. I didn't mean to startle you. Please, go inside and call Justus," he said, rubbing the corner of his eye. "I'll wait out here." Logan looked battered by the rain, despite his coat.

Throughout our conversation, he never looked me in the eye. Maybe he was introverted, although his strong, confident voice contradicted that. When he shook out of his raincoat, I covered my smile with a hand. His clothing gave everything away. A green shirt hung loosely over a pair of matching pants. The drawstring dangled next to a beeper on his waist, but what set it off were the white sneakers. Logan Cross worked in a hospital to some capacity, although whether he was a surgeon or an intern, I couldn't tell. He was a svelte man of considerable strength—with toned arms, strong hands, and broad shoulders that formed a v-shaped physique. Still, it was that masculine face that caught my attention.

"I came directly from work so I didn't have time to change," he apologized.

"Justus sent you to babysit me?"

Logan scratched his jaw. "Try to think of it more as keeping you company. I owe a favor, and I always pay my debts. Did he mention how long he would be away?" He folded the wet coat and placed it in a neat pile on the floor. "Justus was pretty vague. No offense, but I'm on a tight schedule. I'd rather use up my vacation days on a cruise."

I swung open the door, feeling ridiculous about my lack of manners, and guilty this poor man was put in charge of me.

"Please, come inside, Mr. Cross. I don't mean to be rude. I just wasn't expecting visitors. Are you hungry? I've got mountains of food in there, and I could use some help getting rid of the evidence of my boredom."

His laugh was a deep, throaty rumble. "I'm always a willing victim. My last meal was twelve hours ago, but I should warn you that I have a voracious appetite."

I let him in, locked the door, and reheated the enchiladas. Logan was a polite man who insisted that he serve himself. He prepared his own plate and sat on a stool in front of the kitchen island. I contained my laughter as he shoveled it down like a ravenous wolf, sliding the fork along the plate to catch every morsel. The sound of his lips smacking and the satisfied grunts were a boost to my ego.

"Did you make this yourself?" he asked, pointing at the half-eaten plate with his fork.

"Guilty."

I pulled out a short, chubby glass from the cabinet and poured some cold milk into it.

"Tasty, I've never had it with chicken before," he said, licking the end of his thumb.

"How do you two know each other?"

He tilted his head with an enigmatic smile, looking at his plate. "Justus landed in my ER unconscious and full of holes. There wasn't a reason I can think of he should have made it out of surgery, but when he woke up, he ripped out the IV. I found him crawling down the hallway."

I burst out laughing, dribbling milk on my chin. *Classy.* I wiped it away with the back of my hand. Now I was the proud owner of a mental image of Justus crawling, ass-out, in one of those hospital gowns looking for a slice of healing sunshine.

I set my empty glass in the sink. "I didn't know we could have human jobs. How come you don't work for the Mageri?"

"Oh, I'm not a Mage," he corrected. "I'm just your ordinary, red-blooded male." He was right. When I took a minute to focus on his energy, I sensed it was weaker than a Mage. "I would *very* much like to hear how the two of *you* paired up."

"Coincidence, I guess. Justus found me without a maker and volunteered to be my Ghuardian," I said, tapping my bare foot on the floor.

He scooped up the remaining piece of enchilada, working his jaw slowly, with a satisfied moan. "Tell me more," he said with a mouthful.

"I'm not sure what you want to hear. I live here and he educates me."

When he finished the last bite, his tongue polished the prongs of his fork until it shined. He stared at a spot of sauce on his plate and touched it with the tip of his finger.

"Where's your maker?"

"Six feet under."

"Ah, that's quite unusual for a Mage to die. How tragic for you."

"I think you mean fortunate. Hold on," I said. I could almost feel Simon having a hissy fit as my phone vibrated.

"Hello?"

I sliced a piece of chocolate cake for my guest and set it on a clean, white dish.

"You're a real tart, you know that? Don't hang up on me again; it's very rude," Simon chided. "Are you all right?"

I smiled as I set the plate in front of Logan. His eyes widened.

"Don't call me a tart, Simon."

Logan's brows stitched together as he swirled his finger across the icing. I spun on my heel and went back to the fridge. If I had to watch this man seducing a cake, I was going to have to excuse myself for a cold shower.

"Let me call you back. I'm a little busy at the moment."

"Busy with Adam? Doing *what*, exactly?"

I snorted. "I don't know, but I have two containers of chocolate icing. Got any ideas?"

"When Novis finds out, he will punish Adam severely. Don't underestimate the man; he *will* find out."

"I'm not making out with Adam, you idiot. You're right, Novis probably revoked his privileges—and yes, I feel bad about it."

"Did you bring home a date? Bloody hell—"

"I wish," I said with a short laugh. "It's Justus's friend," I said, pouring milk into an empty glass.

Logan's finger brushed over mine when I handed it to him, and I shivered from the unexpected contact. His Adam's apple rose and fell with every hard swallow, and when he was done, he pushed the glass across the counter with the tip of his finger. A thin milk mustache lined his upper lip, and instead of wiping it off, his tongue crept out and licked it from one end to the other.

His behavior rattled me and I turned around. "Call me later, Simon. I need to do some dishes and there's a slice of cake with my name on it."

"Silver, *do not* hang up. Whoever is in the house with you, I can guarantee that Justus has no idea."

"Have you even talked to him today?"

Logan tilted his chin up and pulled in a long, deep breath. I wondered if he was getting sick from the sweet cake on top of the spicy Mexican food.

"He's sitting right next to me."

Terror crept up my spine, and I knew I had done something I shouldn't have: I let a stranger inside the house.

"Don't say a word," he ordered. "Stay delightful so he doesn't grow suspicious. Hang up the phone, and excuse yourself. Go to Justus's bedroom and lock the door behind you," he said in a rushed voice. "You need time to get out, so don't use the trick door in the hall. Use the one in the bedroom, and you know where he keeps all the car keys. Make up something—anything—just *get the hell out.*"

My heart fired off in my chest like a semiautomatic weapon. I licked my dry lips, clearing my throat as I headed out of the room.

"Mr. Cross, there's more cake on the counter if you would like another slice," I suggested. "I need to find an address book. Simon, give me a minute to get that number and I'll call you back."

I slipped the phone in my pocket and strolled out of the room. What did this man want from me, a free meal?

"I'm not supposed to leave you alone."

Logan brushed by me and pivoted around. I didn't detect suspicion in his tone, and I had no right to throw my power into him without justification.

"Fifty feet of space between us will make little difference." I moved around him. "Make yourself comfortable, I'll just be a minute."

I hurried into Justus's room, but before I could close the door, a white sneaker poked through, stopping it.

"Now, why would you close the door on me?"

He tilted his head to one side, and his shoulder length hair appeared longer on one side. His manner was tranquil, but this man was about as innocuous as a grenade.

Luminous, golden eyes rose to meet mine for the first time. I held my breath and stepped back. His gaze was more than a warning—it was a weapon blinding me from rational thought. Everything tilted, as if reasoning had no place. He didn't blink, and one word came to mind: *predator.*

Logan pushed his face through the open crack where strands of hair floated in, reaching for me. "Would you be so kind as to let me in?"

Thump. Thump. Thump. My heart raced. I couldn't think.

Logan admired the silky texture of my hair between his fingers before he lifted a tendril to his nose and slowly inhaled.

"You don't hide your fear very well, Little Raven."

His words were soft, but his meaning was sharp.

"I'm not afraid," I lied.

The phone vibrated and I reached around to switch it on when Logan's voice snapped at me. "Let me through, I can easily push this door in and we both know it."

To make his point, his sneaker squeaked on the floor, edging inside.

"Are you really a surgeon, Mr. Cross?" I leaned against the door with more effort.

"Of *sorts.* I do have a talent with sharp instruments."

His fingers grazed my cheek, tickling my lashes. I felt for his aura—his energy—but I didn't register anything that remotely felt like a Mage. It didn't feel human, either.

"What are you?"

A smile touched his lips and that's when I got an eyeful. Sharp, animalistic canines ascended from his lower teeth. A light, spotted pattern covered his arms like a thin blanket, as ripples of color flashed across his skin like a mirage. My brow formed a hard line; this wasn't in any of the books I read.

"Your Ghuardian has never spoken of the Chitah?"

"Like the animal?"

Insult played on his features. "No, but you should fear us both." He drew in two quick breaths, like a big cat smelling his prey. "Emotions are a fragrance to our kind. Your scent changed after my second bite of cake."

I refrained from any sudden movement as upper fangs elongated. They were thick, white, and pierced the veil of air that hung between us.

My eyes must have given away my intentions of running. He dropped his chin and a mane of hair fell across his face. I stared into the eyes of a hunter between those strands, and it reminded me of a trip I took to the zoo as a little girl. The big cats were on display behind a glass wall, giving the illusion they were in the room with us. Despite the fact that we were safe, I was too petrified to move—convinced that the wall didn't exist.

"Wouldn't try it, Mage. I can run *much* faster. Open the door."

My skin crawled with each syllable, and the phone slipped from my pocket, clattering to the floor.

"Little bird, little bird, *let me in*." His lips peeled back and I was transfixed on those sharp instruments.

"No," I whispered.

Without warning, the door flew open and slammed against the wall. I staggered backwards, running into the edge of the bed. The tall man loomed in the doorway, cocking his head to the side, collecting me with his eyes like a curiosity.

"What do you want with me?"

"If I had a dollar for every time I heard those words. Don't be coy; you know what I want."

His skin changed again, but it flickered and was gone. The patterns were various sizes, and subtle shades of honey and sand.

"I don't even know who you are; what bone do you have to pick with me?"

"Great choice of words," he mused. "As much as I'd love to pick and chew on your bones, I'm here on orders to collect and deliver."

"Whose orders?"

His tongue slicked around a sharp fang. "If I am here, then you *know* who wants you. He is the man behind the curtain, pulling all the strings."

I couldn't believe it. He was talking about the Mage who stole my light. Novis nicknamed him the benefactor, but I had a few other colorful names for him. Samil lent me over to a man who didn't see me as a person, but a source of power after tasting my light and discovering I was a Unique. Regardless of their business dealings, he was not willing to meet Samil's price, and my Creator put a few obstacles in place by presenting me to the Mageri; it gave him leverage with the bargaining.

Logan's movement was so unexpected that my hair blew back from the rush of air. I didn't think anyone could move faster than a Mage. We stood chin to chest. A rumble filled his throat with every breath against my temple. I hesitated, unsure of how to respond, but I knew one thing: I was afraid of him, so afraid that I couldn't even summon my own energy.

He stepped back and retracted his fangs.

"What's the matter, lose your appetite?" I dared.

Fear was starting to morph into something ugly, and I knew I wouldn't be able to keep my mouth shut.

"My feathers don't ruffle easily, Mage. *Why* does my employer want you?"

"So he can use me." The words hung in the air like dirty laundry, all ripe with humiliation. "Are you his minion for money, or debt?"

"I am no one's lackey. Perhaps I simply enjoy it."

"I call bullshit."

He arched a brow. "You call *what*?"

"No one works for free. You're either a weak man who follows the leader, or the fool that owes a debt. Which is it?"

His cheeks puffed out as he sampled the air. "Your scent is altered. Are you provoking a Chitah?"

"So what if I am?"

He stepped forward. "You would challenge me rather than go to him? I could kill you, lickety-split."

"Death is better than captivity."

"Are you offering to be my prey?" He looked down at me and it became evident that no one challenged a Chitah.

"I'm no one's prey," I said with a sharp tongue. "Do you like to hunt? Well… let's go."

I widened my stance and he widened his eyes. I was ready to take on this man, whoever he was, without hesitation. I swallowed my fear and looked him square in the eye. Then, he blinked.

Twice.

I flashed behind him and threw a punch into his lower back. He snarled and before he could turn, I yanked his long hair, keeping my distance. His back arched and he swung an arm out to grab me. Forced to let go, I leapt back.

Justus helped me identify my weaknesses in our training sessions. Men were physically stronger—that was an undeniable fact. He taught me to fight by keeping my distance. I was stubborn about it, and wanted to make bold moves like he did, but now I understood why he taught me to fight defensively.

When Logan turned around, tangles of hair obscured his face. He surged forward and I threw out my hands, shocking him with a burst of energy. He sailed through the air as if pulled by invisible strings, hitting the corner of the sofa before he slammed against the hard floor.

I tensed when he looked over his shoulder and sliced me apart with his gaze. I'd never thrown my power into another Breed before. My palms were warm, but my core light was cooler from the transference, and I shivered.

"What's the matter? Never been knocked on your ass by a woman?"

Logan didn't stand up, he flew at me so fast that I lost balance and fell flat on my back. The breath knocked out of my lungs and he caged me with his body. His fingers locked around my wrists like shackles. I tried to touch him, but he angled his arms and I couldn't reach them.

I flinched and turned my head to the side, baring my throat to him. Submissive, yes, but maybe he would go straight for the jugular and end this game.

The ends of his hair tickled my forehead as he stared down at me. I braced myself when he lowered his face so close that I could smell mint on his breath. Logan rubbed his cheek against mine, and I stared at him in puzzlement.

He suddenly hopped to his feet, lifting me by the wrists.

"Show me where you lay."

I gave him the middle finger with my over-the-shoulder glare. He took a deep breath and pushed me forward—wrists bound behind my back—until I stumbled across my bedroom.

"I believe I've shown remarkable restraint, despite how you resist. Remove the laces from those shoes and hand them to me," he said, pointing at the red sneakers. "Then you can put them on."

"And what if I say no?"

He stepped in front of the sofa and took a seat, spreading his arms over the wide back and crossing his legs. "Well then, I look forward to meeting your Ghuardian. What time does he arrive?" A threat weaved itself into his words.

There was no choice to consider, as I would never put my Ghuardian's life at risk. I removed the laces from the sneakers, slipped them on, and spun around with a squeak.

A rich, potent aroma filled the air and I pinched my nose. I never smelled anything quite like it. It was dark and heady, filling every pore in my body, and I wanted to yield to it. It was an aromatic aphrodisiac weakening me—relaxing me.

Logan stretched his long back against the red sofa chair I slept on. I couldn't look him in the eye because his gaze was too intimate, but I could feel him watching me. Whatever he was doing felt like a private act, something I shouldn't see. He twisted once more, and the cushion hissed beneath his body.

I had never heard of a Chitah, but I knew one simple, undeniable fact: Logan was marking his territory.

CHAPTER 10

M Y WRISTS WERE BOUND BEHIND my back with slender shoelaces. I had to give him points for hostage creativity. We moved down the outside hall until we reached the metal ladder. A fine mist coated my face as I glanced through the open hatch at the black, abysmal sky. Did he expect me to climb up with my hands tied?

The question was answered when he lifted me off the ground, halfway over his shoulder. His muscles trembled and I thought I was going to slide off, but Logan Cross carried me up that ladder with one arm and never broke stride.

For a tall man, he drove a cheap little car. Someone keyed the silver door on the passenger side, leaving a deep scratch. I don't know why that one little thing stood out, but it did. Justus babied his cars; men like him didn't put up with imperfection.

Once inside, he pulled out a cell phone and slid the key into the ignition.

"I have the female. Where do you want her delivered and… There's no need, she's not going anywhere."

"Tell him he'll never have me," I said.

Logan stared straight ahead, but his eyes shifted just a fraction in my direction.

"I'm a Chitah, are you saying my word is no good?" He gripped the stick shift and squeezed.

Silence.

"No, I did not agree to this and I don't like that you're changing the rules. Tell me why you're backing out of the agreement?" He focused outside the window and lowered his voice. "Let's get one thing clear: I am *not* a delivery service."

I wondered how fast I could whip my foot around and break the key in the ignition.

"Be that as it may…"

His fingers curled around the wheel and he sighed. "I will accept that offer. Where?"

The engine roared to life.

Several minutes crept by. Over the silent hum of the tires spinning along the asphalt, Logan's throaty voice broke the silence. "He said you have something that belongs to him."

"I bet he did. Does he come with a name?"

"We never got to the introductions."

"And you expect me to believe that?"

"I expect nothing, except an answer to my question. What do you possess that's his?"

"I have something he wants, but it doesn't *belong* to him."

Logan squeezed the ends of his wet hair and turned the wheel with a sharp yank. A terrified squirrel dashed through the headlights and scurried into the brush.

"Maybe you should give it to him."

My nature would have been to lash out at him, but I sat quietly in my seat. Power and age should have brought wisdom—but in this world, all it brought was greed.

"What he wants is my light."

"A juicer?" he asked in disbelief.

"Call it whatever you want."

"Maybe I'll call it… bullshit. I can't blame you for trying," he sang.

"To be honest, I don't care what you think, Mr. Cross. You're the least of my concerns." I held my tongue and focused on leveling down the energy that was beginning to surface. The low decibel hum was a symptom, as thirst is to one who is dehydrated. I needed to be alert, and seek an opportunity to lay it on him.

And *boy*, did I want to lay it on him.

"There was a change of plans. I'll be trading you off up ahead."

"Why not take me directly to him?"

"We negotiated over the phone to meet, but he changed his mind at the last minute. I suspect as a Mage, he fears me."

"How do you trust a man you've never met?"

"Who said I trusted him? We will be square after tonight."

"Ah, that explains a lot," I said. "So you are the fool that owes him."

"I pay my debts."

"You should quit getting yourself in a position where you owe people. It makes you look inept."

His eyes flashed at mine. "You sure are a noisy little bird," he snapped.

"Bite me."

He made a frightening sound—deep and low. I knew I was instigating trouble, so I turned my attention on the locking mechanism.

Plan A: I somehow manage to open the door with my hands tied behind my back and roll across the highway, losing skin and breaking bones.

Plan B: I knock him out. What's the worst that could happen? The car flips over, crushing my body between the door and asphalt. Then, a fire sparks from the gas leak, and I slowly burn to death.

Neither was an option. I wiggled in my seat, trying to loosen his impossible knot. I looked out the window and saw we were heading deeper into the woods. A low fog covered the ground like a soft breath.

"We're nearly there," he said.

I was running out of options—and out of time. "Will you take a bribe?" I asked reluctantly. That piqued his interest.

"What do you offer?"

"I have no money on me. What will you take?"

His lower canines rose as if they were hands volunteering.

When the car pulled off the road, we got out. My stomach twisted into a tight knot as he gripped my upper arm. *What Pandora's box did I just open?*

The rain tapered off to a fine mist, leaving a thin film of moisture on my face. An earthy fragrance lifted from the forest like a familiar memory. I stepped on a large twig that rolled, causing me to slip. Logan's other arm swung around and caught me before I fell. We moved down a steep slope until he backed me up against a wide tree.

His eyes memorized every angle of my face before falling to my mouth. Logan's heated gaze was like a pulse against my skin. Frosty wind cooled my cheeks, and the bark of the tree was rough against my back. I felt everything around me: the delicate breeze, a small insect crawling on my wrist, the sound of my heart stammering in my chest, and Logan's rhythmic breathing.

"*Typical.*" I dropped my eyes to the muddy ground.

"You shouldn't jump to conclusions. I am not an animal."

"Then why do you have me cornered against a tree?"

"I despise your kind," he bit out.

Yet, he inched forward and curled his fingers around the ends of my hair. "I might consider letting you go, for a kiss."

"Consider? A bribe means payment guaranteed."

"It's all I can offer. Take it, or leave it."

"Do you normally play with your food before you eat it?"

He soaked me in, top to bottom. His piercing gaze was like a blade running across my delicate skin.

"Then we can go," he said, hooking a hand around my upper arm. I yanked my shoulder back and flattened against the tree. He might be lying—in which case all I would be out was a kiss. But if he spoke the truth and kept to his word, then it meant my freedom. It seemed like such a small pawn to sacrifice.

"I'll agree to this one request, but if you start putting stipulations on it, then I'm telling you up front the answer is no. Go on and take your kiss, Mr. Cross."

I tensed, expecting him to drag me back to the car. The earth crunched beneath his shoes as he parted his legs, leaning forward. My fingers continued working to loosen the knot. Logan lifted my chin with the crook of his finger, and lowered his head to meet mine.

"Give me your lips," he growled. He was insistent, and there was no desire coating his words. This meant nothing to him; I might as well have been a tetanus shot in his ass.

"Why do you want this?"

His lip twitched. "A Mage is my enemy, and I should know everything about my enemy. I've never been close to a female of your kind," he said inching closer, "and I find you... puzzling."

Puzzling wasn't a word a man had ever called me before.

His gaze was detached, as if he were studying the inner workings of a pocket watch.

Logan abruptly planted his warm lips on mine. I stood very still, waiting for those sharp teeth to slice me up, but they remained retracted.

Something changed while his lips explored mine, softening with every stroke.

Bark from the tree snapped above my head, showering small chips of wood in my hair. His fingers clawed against it, and I sensed a shift in his energy.

There was nothing demanding or rough about Logan's kiss. His fleshy lips touched mine with soft pecks on the corners before returning front and center. They diligently tried to coax mine to respond, but I did not reciprocate. Up close, his body carried a masculine smell, one that made it very tempting to capture a breath and hold it in. His lips tasted of peppermint, and his chin was shaved so close it was baby smooth.

Logan didn't kiss me as a man who wanted more—he kissed me adoringly, reverently. I didn't even know this man and he kissed me with more passion than any man I'd ever known. My knees wobbled and I tried to steady myself.

"*Kiss me back,*" he breathed.

When he rubbed his face against my cheek in one long stroke, I grew alarmed. Not because I was afraid of him, but I was afraid of what I was feeling. He was inciting a desire to participate, and I had an urge to nuzzle against his neck.

"I don't like games. I told you—"

My words cut off when a vibration rumbled from his chest.

His brow arched. "What's the matter, cat got your tongue?" he chuckled, brushing those soft lips over mine… again and again.

My lips wanted to obey, and I knew it was wrong. An internal battle was ensuing—instinct vs. common sense—two dominant forces at the root of all decisions.

His breath over my mouth whispered, "*Kiss me, Little Raven.*"

Common sense got its ass kicked.

I kissed back—just a small movement of my trembling lips. Logan groaned, and in a split second, his fangs punched out. I sucked in a sharp breath, and my eyes flew wide open.

He pushed away with a ferocious glare.

"What the fuck do we have here?" a voice shouted from the road.

Two men walked in front of a spray of headlights. The energy flared out and washed over me like an electric current.

"You were supposed to meet us by the tracks, a mile down," one Mage said, pointing as if speaking to a child. "Do you have a problem understanding orders, or do you need a can of tuna as motivation?"

The second Mage hunched over laughing.

Logan turned to confront them.

"I would not advise provoking me, Mage," he warned. "It appears I'm not the only one who has difficulty following orders."

"Oh we're following orders, pussycat. Bring the girl," he said, curling his fingers. When he struck a match and lit the end of his cigarette, I caught a glimpse of a thick mustache. A cloud of smoke swirled around him in the humid air, and he flicked the match on the wet pavement. "You've had your fun with her. Our boss doesn't like to be kept waiting."

"I don't take orders, and the agreement is to deliver her to the appointed location. This is *not* that location. Leave us," Logan demanded. "I will entertain nothing you have to say. When I am ready, she will be all yours."

All yours.

Kiss or not, he wasn't letting me go. I struggled to loosen the knot behind my back when a bold, heavy scent covered me like thick molasses. I became dizzy with it, resting my head against Logan's back. I inhaled, and the fibers of his shirt were rich with the smell. Its effect was like a drug, and when I realized what I was doing, I snapped my head up and stepped away.

The man flicked his cigarette on the asphalt and crushed it beneath his heel.

"We don't have time for this bullshit," he muttered. "Go get her, Nate."

Nate, a very unassuming Mage with scrawny features and a short goatee, made his way down the slope, sliding on the wet grass. Logan stood motionless with his arms passively hung at his side. When Nate was about twenty feet away, he stopped unexpectedly and grimaced.

"Fucking hell, Ethan, he's marked her. Get the gun!"

CHAPTER 11

KNOX PACED ACROSS SUNNY'S KITCHEN floor like a tethered dog. He was a ground zero, balls-to-the-wall kind of guy. Simon and Justus rushed to the airport, and Knox didn't feel right about leaving Sunny alone. Part of him wanted to run into the action, but someone needed to keep an eye on the girl. She was in a panic, and people on the edge do crazy shit.

Knox was restless from lack of sleep, and not because he was stuffed on a tiny couch like a moose in a burrito. No, his sleepless nights were because of Justus. Once Knox discovered his gift of charming the skirts off the ladies, he kept his eyes locked on Sunny's door through the long hours of the night. You can't trust a man with that kind of power. He acted as a buffer by following her around the apartment. She was a conversational creature, always asking Knox questions and offering him food. *So what* if she slept with Justus? Why should he care?

Still, it scratched his back the wrong way.

"You're going to wear a ditch in my floor."

Sunny breezed by him to make a cup of hot chocolate. It was the usual time when she enjoyed her cocoa. Knox noticed.

She reached for a mug on the top shelf of a white cabinet, wearing a short purple robe. Her thigh was wet where it peeked through the slit of fabric.

Yeah, Knox noticed that too.

"Let me get that," he murmured, lifting the cup from the shelf.

"I'm going to make you something special, so have a seat. I know a secret recipe that involves a bottle of Kahlúa, which I just so happen to have," she said, tapping a finger to her chin and looking around. Her eyes lit up and she opened a lower cabinet. "Maybe it'll help those dark circles around your eyes."

It sounded good. Knox couldn't remember the last time someone made him cocoa. Probably never. He dragged his feet to an empty chair, ruffling a hand through tangles of hair as he watched her heat the milk on the stove.

Sunny stirred a long spoon in the blue mugs, setting them down on the table. She tucked her chin in her hand, watching the swirl of foam spin around. The worry on her face shouldn't have bothered him, but it settled at the pit of his stomach like a hot coal.

"She's fine. Just sit tight and wait for them to call."

Her blond locks—colorful with highlights—cascaded over her face. Fingers ran deep into their waves and while he couldn't hear it, he knew she was crying.

"We left her alone. I'm supposed to be her friend and I should have been there." Her voice weakened. "I can't believe this is happening again."

She scooted her chair back and left the room. He listened to the sound of her sticky feet on the wood floor until the bedroom door slammed. Her guilt was ludicrous. What could she have possibly done except put herself in danger?

Knox quietly tasted the cocoa. Damn, she was right; it *was* delicious.

He drank it to the bottom, letting it warm his belly before he cleaned the cup and moved into the living room. Sunny's personality filled the apartment. Lavender was her favorite color; she often wore it, and there were small touches around the place. For every kooky lamp and photograph of her at a party, there was a provocative painting, a romance novel, or small arrangements of handmade flowers. It wasn't the kind of lifestyle Knox was used to, but over the past couple of days, he had never felt more at home. He didn't have a toothbrush on the first night, and she made a trip to the store for food. Before he went to bed, sitting on top of his bag was a purple toothbrush wrapped in plastic.

Knox sat on the pale green sofa and flipped out the light.

He listened to neighbors arguing, a leaky faucet in the bathroom, and the occasional creak as the apartment settled. He closed his eyes for what seemed like a second when they snapped open. His heart pounded, although it wasn't clear what exactly woke him up.

A weak sound came from Sunny's room. Knox vaulted from the sofa and cocked his head, straining his ears. There it was again—a whimper. She had a fire escape outside her window, an easy opportunity for any lowlife.

Motherfucker! Knox saw red. He swung the door open and scanned the room, fists clenched and ready to swing.

The room was empty. The window was closed. A sting of embarrassment touched his ears from the impulsive reaction.

Light filtered through the window, illuminating a figure on the bed. Knox took a moment to admire her. By the fine curve of her hip, she was lying on her side. Sunny took another quick breath and coughed. Something was wrong.

Her face was mashed in the pillow, so he touched her shoulder. "Hey, wake up." She rolled to her back and those puffy eyes flew open.

"You're dreaming. Settle down."

Knox backed up into a shadowy corner. No one needed to wake up to the likes of him.

"You don't have to hide from me," she said, wiping away tears. "I had a dream about Silver and the night she disappeared. Except in the dream, I saw everything that happened to her." Her breath trembled, and voice softened. "Will you sleep in here tonight? I don't want to be alone."

Knox was unable to speak. It wasn't longing in her voice—it was fear. She wanted someone to keep her company, so he eyed the wooden chair by the window.

"I'm sorry about the couch situation. I was saving up for a new one, but my car broke down again. Transmission repairs aren't cheap." She scooted a curvy hip to the far end of the bed. "You can have that side."

That side. The side next to her. Twin beds didn't offer much room, and Knox was the kind of guy who took up a whole lot of mattress. A tiny wave of terror rolled through him.

"I'm sorry about that night at the hotel; I'm obviously not your type."

Well, that remark just peeved him. "What do you think my type is?"

She sniffled and stretched beneath the sheets. "I don't know. I suppose I picture you with a sexy, confident woman."

Jesus, she didn't have a clue. That woman was in the dictionary next to those words.

"It's not a proposition, Knox. I feel bad that I don't have a guest room and you're stuck on that sofa with the loose spring. If it makes you feel any better, we can sleep head to foot."

That mental picture rolled around in his dirty mind with all kinds of wrong attached to it. When he didn't move, she yanked the covers away and threw her feet to the floor.

"Hardheaded are we? Then *you* take the bed and *I'll* sleep on the sofa. You look about as petrified as a fossil, and I didn't even flirt with you."

"Get back in the bed," he ordered.

Without protest, she slipped those long, bashful legs beneath the sheets. When the short gown rose up, he averted his eyes like the gentleman he wasn't.

A nervous creak sounded from beneath the bed when Knox sat down. Sunny chuckled, but kept her back to him. "It's an old bed and sometimes the planks fall out. I got it on sale when I was going through my antique phase."

If that was the case, she was about to be the proud owner of a bed of antique splinters.

The sheets cooled his legs, and he pulled the coverlet over his bare chest. Women like her weren't attracted to him, they were *afraid* of him. That was a hard fact he lived with. Mothers corralling their children, women clutching their purses… People were always making assumptions that he was trouble.

And maybe they were right.

Lavender hung in the air, but it was her apricot conditioner that clouded his thoughts.

"Why don't you like women?" she asked point-blank.

Before he could answer, Sunny continued.

"My dad was a drunk. He spent every night at the bar and when he got home, he used to yell at my mom and put her down." Knox listened to the sound of her feet rubbing together as she took a shallow breath. "He was a miserable man, and I hated the fact my mom put up with it. He threw her clothes on the lawn more than once, but she *always* defended him. She blamed us for making him that way."

"Did he…"

"Hit me? No. He never laid a hand on my mom, either. You don't have to hit someone to abuse them, Knox. But he hit my brother once or twice. The night Kane left home, they were fighting, and my father said that he wasn't his son. How can someone be so cruel?" There was a thoughtful silence. "Sometimes I still wake up with his voice in my head, and the things he said to me, the things he called me. No matter how old you get, you never let go of stuff like that. I don't want to make the same mistakes my mother did, and that's why I don't get serious."

Knox turned his neck and stared at the back of her head. That was a hell of a thing to reveal. He never met a woman with such intimate candor. Quid pro quo, he thought.

"My father hit me. A lot."

Knox never told anyone that story, not even Adam. Abuse was one of those ugly family secrets that revealed far too much about a person. It gained sympathy stares, and most women thought it was a hereditary trait. Knox would cut off his arm before ever striking a woman, or a child. That's what led him to search for Zoë, because in his heart, he knew he couldn't follow through with those orders. He swallowed hard, and decided to finish.

"I never knew my mother; she took off when I was born. The only women in our house were the whores the old man brought home from the bar. To address your question, I like women. They're a good time, that's all."

He expected an argument, waiting for her to throw him out of the room.

"Aren't we a pair?" she sighed.

It was an offhand comment, but he liked the sound of it—the idea of him and Sunny as a pair. A pair of what, he didn't know. They were on opposite ends of the spectrum as far as personality and lifestyle, yet they both sprang from the same, dark past.

"I'm not judging you, Knox. At least you don't lie about it like some men do." She reached over, wrapping her small fingers around his large hand.

With that touch, with those words, something inside of him ignited. Knox was a supernova on the verge of exploding into the dark void.

⸻

Sunny felt an unexplainable connection with Knox from the moment they met. It didn't have to do with him sticking up for her—as impressive as it was—but there was something intangible. Now she understood why. He may have pretended the abuse didn't mean anything, but deep down she knew it mattered. It always mattered.

Knox came across as an insensitive meathead, but deep down, he was a softy. He was the only man at the dinner table who cleaned the dishes and made her sit down. The broken doorknob was suddenly fixed, but no one confessed. Early that morning, Sunny found him kneeling on the bathroom floor trying to repair the leaky faucet. She yelled and shooed him out, but closed the door and smiled, staring at the tools she never used. Sunny spent her life avoiding men like Knox, and he turned out to be an impressive example of a man.

The alarm clock on the nightstand ticked like an impatient fingernail on a table.

She gripped her pillow when the bed shifted, listening as the sheets made a soft hiss. He was moving closer and the bed depressed, causing her to hold on tighter. When a strong arm locked around her waist, she held her breath in surprise.

Knox pulled her flush against him, and his chest warmed her back almost immediately. Once connected, he relaxed.

In those quiet minutes that passed, Sunny thought about how rarely she went to sleep in someone's arms. He nestled his chin against the back of her neck, breathing in the soft smell of her hair. A strong heartbeat pounded between her shoulder blades, drowning out the sound of her own, which was racing.

Knox was thoughtful in ways that didn't attract attention, but made him stand apart from the other men. On the first night, she made okra and meatloaf. It was obvious Knox didn't care for the okra, but he cleaned his plate and complimented her cooking. So on the second night, she cooked meatloaf again, because she watched the way he enjoyed it. Simon grumbled a complaint and Knox stood up at the table, reached over, and scraped Simon's meatloaf onto his plate. That settled that.

God, her mind scrambled in the calmness of that room. Every time his breath skimmed over her shoulder, it filled her up with an insatiable need to be devoured by him.

Bravely, she wrapped her fingers around his wrist and pulled his hand to her mouth, kissing the palm. His reaction was immediate, and Knox tensed. Sunny took it a step further, drawing a circle with her tongue in his hand. He tasted of salt.

"We shouldn't do this." His voice was raspy, filled with the same need.

Denial shouldn't sound so sexy, but it did. Sunny was never put in a position where she was the one making all the moves.

Her fingers worked open the buttons of her gown, and laid his hand over her bare breast. He was putty in her hands and she was putty in his.

When he lightly pinched her tender nipple and caressed the soft skin that surrounded it, she moaned, arching her back. Knox had the physique of a warrior and the hands of a saint.

Desire rolled through her when his tongue slid across her shoulder. Sunny turned over and stared up at him, glossing her lips with her tongue.

"Is that the best you can do?" Over the years, seduction became second nature to her. She discovered little tricks in the bedroom, and men liked to prove themselves.

"Don't say things like that."

Her finger circled around his chest. "Why not?"

Knox captured her mouth and kissed her like he meant to take her; kissed her all the way down to her toes. His warm, wet tongue tangled with hers—deep and slow. She felt like a tiny ball of yarn tumbling down a staircase, unraveling to the very core. When his lips broke free, it left her breathless.

"I don't want you talking like that, you got it? You're not that kind of girl, so don't think you have to be that way with me."

"You said women are nothing but a good—"

"I lied," he cut in, softening his voice. "Not with you, I don't want it to be like that with us. You be Sunny with me, you be yourself."

Knox kissed her reverently, and her nose filled with the musk of male and lust. His lips were soft in contrast to the stubble around his chin. It scraped against hers—but she liked it. Sunny touched his cheek, tracing the line of his jaw. He always covered his hair, so she relished seeing him without the hat. She loved the way it was wavy at the ends. It was unruly—just like him. Sunny scraped her fingers up and down his neck until he involuntarily moaned.

Knox spread her legs, cupping a heated hand over her panties.

"More," she breathed.

"All you want, baby girl," he said, stroking her deep.

He rolled on top, propping himself up on his elbows. Soft, wet kisses showered her. He was far too gentle; Knox came across as a man who just got right down to business. Maybe he was, but not tonight. Not with her.

The kiss grew to an unexpected frenzy. His body was raw power—as if she had her arms wrapped around a hurricane. She curled her fingers behind his neck, sucking on his tongue until Knox spiraled out of control, rocking his hips against her.

She broke the kiss, gasping for air.

"Is this hurting you?" He started to move. "I'm too big, let me—"

She pulled his shoulders until he crashed down on top of her. "Stay where you are," she demanded.

Knox lifted the ends of her gown, peeling it over her head. He balled up the material and flung it across the room.

When his eyes lowered to her breasts, she became self-conscious. Sunny was curvier than she used to be. It was a rough year and those excuses for avoiding the gym were beginning to haunt her. She was always voluptuous in all the right ways, but the last man she slept with was Marco, and the two times they had sex, he never touched her. Only recently did she find out it was because he was a Mage, and their energy spiked during sex, making it impossible for them to touch a human. It seemed kinky, but left her feeling hollow and insecure.

Sunny moved her arm over them in embarrassment; maybe he didn't like what he saw.

"Don't you dare cover yourself," he said, snatching a wrist and stretching out her arm. "You're magnificent."

His mouth came down on the first one and he moaned, like a man tasting food after a long fast. His tongue awakened tiny little nerves she never knew existed, as it swirled in rhythmic circles. Knox was exquisite in how he took his time. He savored her.

She whispered quietly into the waves of his black hair. Not quiet enough as the word reached Knox's ears. Dark eyes rose to meet hers.

"Say it again," he said.

She stroked his cheek with her thumb and blushed at the way he looked at her expectantly. "Lover."

He closed his eyes.

Knox was the opposite of all the pretty boys she dated. His face carried the etchings of worry, his brow wore lines of anger, and secrecy kept those lips pressed thin. Small scars, indentations, and imperfections left her wondering if they were from his line of work… or his father. He was a man weathered, but he was beautiful.

Lips kissed beneath her breast, wandering over the curves of her hip.

She bit her lip when his tongue stroked her inner thigh. Need overwhelmed her. It was more than she could stand, and she scissored her legs against his shoulders.

When the warm heat from his mouth lapped over her panties, Sunny grabbed him by the hair. She didn't mean to be rough, but Knox didn't take any notice. Without hesitation, he pulled them off and went in for the real thing.

Knox didn't tease, torment, or even ask permission. He delivered, and drove his kiss into her, pleasuring with unrelenting strokes.

She clutched his hair, and his large arm snaked around her thigh and held it in place. Did it ever feel this good? A rapid pulse fired off in her chest and her body tensed. He was gentle with her, stroking her hip with his free hand as she let go of his hair and gripped the pillow beneath her head. Just as she closed in on her release… he pulled away and met her face to face.

"Why did you stop?" she panted.

"I don't have anything with me so we're just going to keep doing this because goddammit, I can't stop. I don't do *this* with the other women."

When his eyes skipped to the left and his ears reddened, she knew what he meant.

Her fingers laced around the edges of his sweats, and he sucked in his stomach. "Take them off."

The sweats came off in less than three seconds.

Sunny reached around to the bedside table, pulling a condom from the drawer. He stared at her intimately, in a way no man had ever looked at her before. In the soft glow of the light that shone through the curtain, she watched his lids close as the condom glided over his sex.

Knox cupped the back of her neck and buried himself deep inside of her. There was another connection threading between them on a different level, and a strange familiarity settled over the moment.

She caressed every muscle and groove with delicate fingers. It seemed important that he knew a touch that wasn't just about sex, but about *him*.

There wasn't enough air in the room when he started rocking against her.

His chest was hot and sticky, rising and falling like an empire. She pressed her mouth to his bicep—tasting him—and it was salty, and male. He drove in so deep and fast that it sought for her release.

"So good, feels so good," he muttered. "Want you. God... *want you*."

A poet he was not.

"Harder," she breathed.

He obeyed, and the bed launched itself against the wall and something snapped. Might have been the headboard, or a plank underneath the bed, but it didn't matter.

Wet sounds—delicious sounds—filled her senses. Her manicured nails scored his back and there was no hiding the fact that he liked it. Knox pounded against her—hips crashing, pressure building until the mattress followed his rhythm, tossing her about. Gripping the sheets, she struggled to hold on.

"Grab on to me," he said, planting his fists in the bed. She reached up and locked her fingers around him, finding it easier to stay in control when she held on to Knox.

Desire tightened like a coil and she threw her head back. His demanding thrusts forced the headboard to slam against the wall.

Repeatedly.

Knox stared at her with such intensity that her legs released their hold, falling limp for him to take control.

"I want you," he said demandingly, and fell to his elbows.

The bedside lamp fell over and crashed to the floor along with the alarm clock.

Pleasure crashed through her and she cried out. Knox did, too—a whole string of profanities buried in a pillow that would have to go to church and be sprinkled with holy water before it could be used again.

They melted over one another as Knox dropped to her side. She laughed when she heard her earring roll off the nightstand to the floor.

It took a few minutes to stop seeing tiny flashes of light, and to catch her breath again. Knox rolled onto his back and pulled Sunny over him like a blanket. His chest was warm, and they fit together in all the right places. It was a strange feeling to be exposed to a man— not physically—but in the details of her life that she only told Silver. Most men made it to her bed after a few drinks and meaningless conversation, and maybe that's why there was always a connection lacking. She placed soft kisses on his chin.

"You shouldn't have to hear me curse."

That deserved a laugh. "I'm a big girl, Knox. I think I can handle a swear word or two."

"Or two?" His chin touched his chest and he smirked. She loved the way he smiled with his lips closed. It dropped ten years on his face. Small lines etched the corners of his eyes, and when one side of his mouth curved higher than the other, Sunny curled her toes.

He smothered her with a kiss on the forehead, dipping his nose into her hair. Knox wrapped his massive arms around her back, and she felt safe in them. "Are you ready?"

"For what?"

"My signature full body massage."

"Oh, bring it," she said with a giggle. "I like being pampered."

His lips brushed across the top of her head and they stayed that way for a few more minutes. It was quiet, except for his occasional sigh, and the soft hiss of his hand as it stroked her back.

"I'm just going to say it," he said decidedly. "When I said I wanted you, I didn't just mean sex. I want you to be my girl. You deserve better, but I can't get you out of my head. Shit…Adam is going to give me hell for this, but I'm not a coward. I'm asking you for something I've never asked any woman. Be with me Sunny, and only me."

Sunny held her breath. "You mean, you want to get serious or just—"

Fool around, is what she was thinking. That was the obvious choice, given what just happened between them.

Knox hooked his hands beneath her arms and slid her up a fraction so they were nose to nose.

"Baby girl, if you even *think* about calling this a fling, we're gonna have words. We fit. I'm not the kind of guy you go for, but I'll worship you like the moon. I'm solid in my word, and I'll take good care of you."

Sunny pressed a finger on his lip and thought about it. Marco was the only man she ever let in, and he deceived her in the worst kind of way. He exemplified everything she desired in a man. In the end, he was the worst of them all.

Knox, on the other hand, was the complete opposite. Rough, intimidating, quiet—and yet he never gave her any reason to doubt.

"The last guy strung me along. If you do the same, I'll never forgive you. Hell hath no fury—"

Knox gave a deep chuckle and his chest rocked beneath her. "I wouldn't expect any less. It's the real deal, but this is me, take it or leave it. If it's about looks or money, then you can do better."

"What will everyone say? We just met."

"Does it matter? I feel something in my gut telling me this is right. If you don't feel it too, then tell me to go to hell."

Sunny lowered her cheek to the pillow and rested her head close to his. "It's never been about money, and I think you're handsome, but I'm going to tell you right now that I don't like that you smoke.

It reminds me of… I just don't like it. I'm not asking you to change; I'm just giving you a heads-up when you can't find your cigarettes and the toilet is clogged."

He chuckled, and a deep, wonderful vibration rumbled in his chest. "Is that a yes?"

She paused. "When are you leaving?"

"Who said I was going anywhere? I'm not even asking for a bigger bed to share; I like this," he said, patting the mattress. "It's cozy. How do you feel about a move?"

"To another apartment?"

"Cognito," he mumbled. "The city is growing on me."

She lifted a shoulder, nipping his lower lip with her teeth. "Nothing is holding me here anymore. I don't have roots, if that's what you're asking."

"I don't like the idea of you being in the same city as Marco," he stated as fact. "We'll go back to Cognito and work things out." He placed a kiss on her nose and took pleasure in running his fingers through her short, wavy hair. "It's a fresh start, and I'll help you work things out with a job."

"I don't think you can handle a woman like me," she said with an arch of her brow.

He stroked those large hands up and down her naked body and she relaxed against him. "I think I can handle you just fine, baby girl."

CHAPTER 12

ETHAN DIPPED OUT OF THE stream of headlights and skidded on a patch of wet grass, holding a tranquilizer gun with a long, skinny barrel. It didn't look real, but the deadly intent in his eyes told me otherwise. Nate backed up until they were side by side.

"We can do this the easy way, or we can do this our way," he said to Logan. "Hand over the Mage, or get tranked."

Why didn't they fight him? A Mage could throw power into another Breed, knocking them out. Why resort to weapons when Logan was outnumbered? I turned up my nose at their cowardice.

Ethan and Nate made a slow approach while simultaneously creating distance between each other. Logan's head panned back and forth between them, but Ethan was the imminent threat.

"Here kitty, kitty," Ethan taunted, aiming his gun with a steady hand.

Without Logan's watchful eye, I bent forward, pulling at the laces until I was able to wiggle my arms past my hips and step through the loop. I used my teeth to undo the tight knot.

Nate flicked his eyes in my direction and Logan glanced over his shoulder. I was free, and considered running or fighting. Logan stood up straight and turned his attention to Nate.

A deep sound, like distant thunder, rumbled from his chest. He locked the Mage in like a target, tracking every movement.

Ethan lifted the gun higher and my heart kicked up a beat.

I spoke in a quiet voice. "I'll knock the gun out of his hands while you take the second Mage. If I keep you alive, then you let me go. Deal?"

Logan exploded into action, lunging at Nate with impossible speed. The sound of wet, ripping noises snapped me out of my daze.

I reached out—summoning a gift I rarely used—and pulled the gun from Ethan's hand.

The gun went off. I surged forward and we rolled across the grass. I struggled with him as he held my arms and pressed a knee firmly against my chest until I heard a crack. Logan slammed into him and I gasped, rolling to my side as I watched him bury his face in Ethan's neck.

I turned my head and saw Nate in an awkward position, eyes wide open and glassy.

Ethan sputtered out words I couldn't understand—choking and incoherent as his legs twitched. I rose to my feet, feeling the sudden quiet that enveloped us. Logan turned around and a cold terror chilled me to the marrow. Striking a deal with a man like him was foolish, and I realized how naïve I truly was.

Those weren't fangs; they were weapons of mass destruction. Two dead Mage at my feet punctuated that fact.

I paced backwards with fear on my heels as Logan's penetrating eyes hunted me through the dark. They were black as midnight.

He lifted the bottom of his shirt, exposing his stomach as he wiped the blood from his face.

I had no choice. I ran.

Spinning on my heel, I flashed to the car door and came to a hard stop. Logan was already there, leaning on one arm.

"I won't bite, little bird."

He tilted his head, lulling me with that sweet way of speaking—like poisonous nectar. The eyes were no longer obsidian, but bright amber.

"Isn't that what the cat said to the canary?"

He inhaled deeply and cocked a brow.

"How did you kill them? I don't feel their energy." I was unable to breathe. I knew I needed to level down, but something felt very wrong. "What *are* you?"

"I am a Chitah. Are you afraid?" He reached out and plucked a metal dart from my shoulder. "Your kind keeps their distance for a reason. Why don't you tell me what *you* are?" he said, narrowing his eyes. "That's a nifty trick you have."

He flicked the dart into the grass and pulled in his lower lip, sucking off blood as he bent over and spit it out. "I am your worst nightmare come true; I am more dangerous to you than your own kind." He wiped his mouth with the back of his hand.

"I don't understand how it's possible." My legs wobbled.

I glanced at the two dead men lying in the gulley. Monsters did exist, and I couldn't outrun this one. He crawled right out from beneath my bed and decided to say hello.

"Our bite contains venom we can secrete at will that is poisonous to a Mage."

I was stupid to have gotten that close with a kiss, what was I thinking? All my senses were shutting down as I slipped into a void of darkness. With everything I had left, I reached out to throw my power into him when his eyes widened. He made no motion to stop me, or push my hands away. He took the full force of the energy, even though it was only a minor shock. My knees buckled, and he caught me with a firm hold, shaking his head.

"Foolish Mage. What am I to do with you?"

My eyes rolled back, and my blood ran cold like an arctic wave. I didn't want to go to the benefactor, and I was angry that my body could no longer fight.

His soft voice against my ear was the last thing I heard down a long hallway of nothingness.

"To succumb to death, the bite must be with all four teeth— otherwise it only paralyzes our victim. You are *so* eager to play with fire, but are you ready to get burned?"

Something sharp lightly touched my ear.

CHAPTER 13

I PRETENDED TO BE ASLEEP FOR several minutes, observing my surroundings. My fingers traced along smooth rock overhead. A warm light flickered to my left, throwing shadows on walls made of ancient rocks. I was in a cavern, tucked in a crevice in the wall. The ceiling sloped down at a sharp angle, and tiny sparkles shimmered in the dirt. I threw my legs over the ledge, and dropped to the ground a few feet below, landing hard on my knees.

Someone had dressed me in a brown knit sweater with a wide turtleneck pulled over my nose. I rolled the collar down and the cool, damp air touched my skin. It was *his* sweater. It smelled like him, and the sleeves hung past my hands.

A small fire blocked a narrow passageway, and smoke drifted between the rocks as if the ceiling were breathing it in. To my right was the dark mouth of a cave, ready to swallow any willing victim.

"Come to the fire if you're cold."

"How long was I knocked out?"

"Hmm," his voice rolled out warmly. "However long a Mage sleeps from the energy problem you have. Has anyone solved that energy crisis?" He laughed.

"I was drugged," I said, rubbing my shoulder.

"What they use on a Chitah would have little effect on you."

He was probably right. I hadn't leveled down after the kiss, kills, and adrenaline. The drug triggered a shutdown sooner than I would have liked. I sat back against the wall and dusted off my hands.

Logan was no longer wearing a bloody shirt; in fact, he was wearing none at all. I pressed my back against the uneven wall, and took a seat in the dirt. He leaned against the opposite wall, watching me with detached interest as he wiped a hand over his bare chest.

"Did you bite me?" I asked, remembering the sharp touch on my ear.

He shook his head, staring at the ground.

The fire cracked and I jumped. I debated whether throwing my power into him was a good idea, but I was apprehensive about the risk of getting unnecessarily close. Logan took me off guard because he was fast, deadly, and unpredictable.

"I guess you don't get cable out here?"

"Home away from home," he said. "Material things mean little to me."

Could I reason with him? "You promised to release me, and I've done you two favors. I gave you what you asked, and protected you from getting shot."

"For that, I am in your debt." By the disgusted curl of his lip, he was not pleased about it.

"Consider it paid if you release me."

"To be hunted by the man who hired me to find you?"

"What do you care?"

"I've *never* cared for your kind," he confessed.

"Then it shouldn't be so hard to let me go. I'm not asking you to drop me off at the door, Mr. Cross. Just turn your head and give me back my life." When he didn't answer, I looked at my surroundings. "Why are we here?"

"Gives me time to think."

"About what?"

"I haven't decided what I'm going to do with you," he said, tapping a small stick on the ground.

Logan's eyes glimmered in the firelight, like amber and tiger's eye melted together. The color was striking because the irises were encircled by dark rims. I reached back and twisted my hair, tucking it into the sweater.

"I could throw my light into you," I threatened.

A broad smile exposed his fangs, and I dropped my eyes to the floor.

"I didn't mean to frighten you," he apologized, continuing to tap the stick.

"I think that's exactly what you meant to do."

The man provoked me. His mannerisms were so polished they were impossible to read. I sighed, looking up at the wet walls. Water dribbled down one of the rocks, reminding me of something.

"I need to powder my nose."

Logan stood up and walked to the mouth of the cave. "Follow me and stay close."

The tunnel was narrow, dark, and branched out in several places. He swiped one of the sticks from the fire and used it as a torch. I ducked beneath a low rock and saw a small stream running through an open room.

"Stay here," he said. "Don't make me chase you."

Logan tossed the stick on a rock and left the room.

In captivity, I learned one thing: dark caverns are not awe-inspiring when you're crouched with your pants around your ankles. Humans know that monsters aren't really lurking in the shadows, because things like that don't exist. But I knew better, and those irrational fears weren't so irrational anymore.

Hiking up my pants, I tiptoed down a dark passageway, running my hands along the wall in the blinding dark. I stopped and heard nothing but silence. I envisioned myself getting lost in the tunnels for all eternity, starving to a point where I remained in darkness forever, withering to bones. *This was a monumentally stupid idea.*

I spun around and lost my sense of direction. The wall was no longer in reach, and I searched for something to hold.

A hand captured my wrist and squeezed.

"I told you not to run from me."

"I was just looking around."

He jerked me forward and I winced, stumbling over my feet as I followed at a slow pace. I wondered if he could see in the dark like those nocturnal animals. It made sense by his confident stride.

Logan looked over his shoulder and stopped. I couldn't make out his face, only the outline of his body from the soft firelight in the distance.

"Are you hurt?"

He stepped forward and pointed where I was holding my side.

"Cramps," I offered with a smirk.

A female Mage doesn't have a cycle. If he knew anything about my kind, then he knew it was a lie. That's why it took me several minutes to get myself together when I woke up; I felt a broken rib. Simon taught me never to expose my weaknesses, and it was fine until he jerked my arm.

I pushed past him, but didn't make it three steps when he lifted me off the ground.

"Put me down!" I protested. "I'm perfectly capable of walking."

"Stubborn female," he muttered, walking swiftly back to the room.

Logan set me down beside the fire and squatted on the tips of his shoes to get a better look at me. I scooted as far from him as possible.

"You needn't fear me, Mage."

The light struck his features like a match, setting off his broad shoulders and ferocious stare. His stringy, long hair outlined his face, where shadows played with the grooves of his cheekbones, brightening those eyes to a point where I couldn't look at them.

"I'll remember that the next time you chew up one of my kind."

Logan dropped to his knees, crawling towards me with a curious expression.

"Do you have a broken wing, little bird?"

"I'm fine," I said softly, biting my lip.

"No, you are not. I know the scent of suffering. Let me—" He touched my knee and I slapped his hand.

"*Don't* touch me."

Logan scratched his throat, studying me as if I were a stain on his conscience.

I concentrated on the fire, the way it moved, the sound it made as the wood hissed—scorched by the heat. I could feel him looking at me and I didn't like it.

"Anyone ever tell you it's not polite to stare?" I scolded.

"Tell me where you're hurt and I will stop looking."

"Why? Are you going to take me to a hospital?"

Logan startled me when his rough hand gripped the back of my neck and he searched my eyes. "Perhaps I should toss you where I found you, in the dark. Do you realize that you were only two steps away from a thirty-foot drop? Would you like that?"

I lifted my chin. "Go on and do it, then!"

I cried out when he grabbed my arm. Logan immediately let go, and blew out a long, angered breath.

"Enough of these games; show me your pain."

His face was inches from mine. He was a persistent man; I'd give him that.

"It's only a small fracture."

He snatched my hand and placed it against his bare chest. "Heal yourself."

"Are you kidding?" I laughed, pulling away. When I looked up, his eyes fell to the floor and he arched his brow, anticipating my answer.

"I'd rather endure it," I gritted through my teeth. "I'm tougher than you think I am."

"That I can see, but as you know I'm twice in your debt. I'm offering this as a way to clear that favor owed. Don't ask if I'll release you. The answer is no."

"It doesn't work that way."

His eyes flicked to mine. "Tell me how it works if this is not the way."

"Look, I don't know what you're expecting. We can do this among our own kind, but I don't know if I can take healing light from a Chitah."

"I will be distressed if you cannot. A cut I can mend, but I can't heal bones," he said, rubbing his chin.

"You heal?" I asked in astonishment.

"Superficial wounds."

"How do you do it?"

Logan tilted his head to the side. "With my tongue."

"Is that all you can do?"

"Hmm," he pondered. "As a Chitah, or do you mean *with my tongue?*"

I almost blushed, but Logan was all business as his fangs punched out. "Don't get any ideas," he said, placing his hand over my sweater. "I'm very aware of what you're capable of."

"Skin," I said. "I'm not removing my clothes, and if you so much as touch me in the wrong place, I'm cutting off that hand."

"On my word," he murmured, hand disappearing beneath the

sweater. His warm fingers touched that tender spot and I winced. Logan's eyes flashed to mine, waiting for something to happen.

Justus never said I couldn't take from Breed, only that I *shouldn't*. At least, that's what I remembered during those fuzzy training sessions. I gripped his large hand and focused on the energy. His power was a tightly wound coil that wouldn't give. Pulling healing energy required concentration. Sweat beaded on my forehead, and I began to have second thoughts as I stared at his canines just inches away. What if he attacked when he felt his energy slip?

"Don't pull away, Mage. I won't harm you."

"No offense, but I don't believe you."

"I am a Chitah, and my word is my bond. How is the word of a Mage these days?"

A tingling sensation prickled my skin. Warmth spread between our hands, burning through his fingertips against my skin. I glanced up, and he turned his head away as if catching a scent. The noise he made was a deep purr, so low it was more felt than heard.

"Why do you make those sounds?" I wondered aloud, removing his hand.

"Our body reacts. It can't be controlled. I suppose that I'm calm," he said, flexing his fingers.

Logan made a similar noise while terrorizing me in Justus's bedroom. His version of calm wasn't even in the same ballpark as mine.

"Could you put away your fangs? It makes me feel like a rib eye steak."

He retracted them and stood up, putting distance between us. While it was only a small fraction of his energy given over, he looked weary as he sat down with his arms lazily draped over his knees.

"That was an interesting display back there with the gun," he said. "The gifts your kind conceal are remarkable."

"You don't really work in a hospital, do you?"

Logan shook his head. "I had to gain your trust to get inside. People *do* trust a doctor, don't they?" He laughed richly. "You wouldn't have let me in if I just shown up in a pair of jeans. I scented the change in your comfort level when I removed my coat. A new

Mage is easy to deceive; you still hold on to those human qualities of disbelief that someone could mean you harm."

"You could have pushed your way in and saved me the trouble of making you dinner."

He looked agitated. "I have no need to resort to violence to get what I want. Would you have preferred I be ruthless?"

"No, but I think your tactics were drawn out and unnecessary."

"The enchiladas were worth it." He grinned.

"How many have you killed?"

Logan wasn't shocked by my question; even more disturbing was how quickly he answered.

"I lost count."

"Why aren't we extinct if all of your kind hunts us down?"

"*We* don't. For obvious reasons we aren't allies, but we abide by our laws, just as you do. I hunt alone, and it's personal."

That didn't settle well on my palate. "Are you telling me that you're an assassin? Do you do it for pay, or for sport?"

"I work independently. And before you lay your judgment on me, each and every one of them had it coming."

"Do I have it coming?"

There was no denying the raw power behind his gaze as the fire smoldered in the reflection of his irises. My answer was silence.

CHAPTER 14

MINUTES STRETCHED INTO HOURS. I nodded off against the wall, and when I awoke, I was lying beside the fire. It was quiet, and the embers were dim as if lulling the room asleep.

Logan was sprawled out on his stomach with his face buried in the crook of his arm. He was a very tall man with an athletic build. I was curious about the unusual markings I saw glimpses of, and whether it covered his entire body. His skin glowed with vitality and it made me look at my own arms thinking I could use a bottle of lotion. All of his body hair was baby fine, and light in color.

He was a creature to admire, but only when he was asleep. It wasn't just his sheer size that intimidated me, but the cocksure way in which he carried himself.

I took a step towards the exit when a voice shattered the silence.

"I have no desire to fish you out of a hole. If you break something this time, I will not come get you."

I let out an exasperated sigh and kicked up a cloud of dust. "Why the hell are you keeping me here? Kill me. Eat me. I don't care. Just get it over with!"

He brushed the dirt away from his arms and sat up. "Eat you? What do you think I am?"

I glared at his question. "Walks like a duck, quacks like a duck."

"My, my, my. Isn't that the pot calling the kettle black? Tell me Mage, what happened to your Creator?"

"Don't make assumptions. You don't know anything about me."

A wall of silence descended. I walked around the fire staring into the inky depths of the cavern. My past haunted me at odd moments. I thought about the human life unlived, and the life that almost was, if Adam had never freed me from my maker. I shivered, blowing a warm breath across my white knuckles.

"That was very rude of me, and I apologize."

"I think you enjoy manipulating people. How confident are you that all of your victims deserved what they got? Is that why I'm here? You think that you can uncover some dirty secret that will justify your reason to kill me so you'll have a clean conscience? Good for you for being God's little broom, cleaning up all the evils of the world. If that helps you sleep at night, then the next time you pull the covers up to your chin, I want you to know how *noble* your debt was to the Mage who hired you. I owe him *nothing*. The first time I met him he broke my hands to steal my light."

My heart seized when a shrill sound brightened the room. A scream poured from my lungs and I backed into the wall, electrified with fear. It was involuntary, as if something primal took control of my body.

The cause of that reaction was a deafening roar that filled every space of the cavern, reverberating off the walls. Logan was crouched on one knee, grinding his fists into the dirt. Hair hung wildly over his face, and faded patterns erupted across his torso.

I wound myself tight against the curve of the rock, keeping my eyes low. I moved a fraction when he lunged forward and slammed his hands on the wall, caging me in. Justus always said my mouth would get me in trouble one of these days.

Obsidian eyes stared at me with no familiarity. Rapid breath heated my cheek and I couldn't think straight. If I lifted my hands to throw my power into him, how fast could he sink those teeth into my neck?

He was so close to my neck.

"I'm sorry," I began. "I was only—"

I sucked in a sharp breath when he rubbed his cheek against mine... nuzzling. I forgot how to breathe. I knew it involved pulling in air and pushing it out, but the mechanics of it were lost. Logan's skin was warm, and his lashes tickled my face. The man before me was not Logan, but a feral creature that could not be reasoned with.

What I couldn't explain was why the closer he got to me, the less I feared him.

Logan stormed out of the cave. He suggested that if I went tunnel exploring, to "watch my step". It sounded more like a warning. Through the dark exit, there were too many directions and sharp ledges, and I had a thing about heights.

I scattered a handful of sand on the floor between my legs, wondering how long this temporary infatuation with me would last. Logan Cross was no better than Samil, holding me hostage until his price was met. Maybe his price was nothing more than clearing his debt, but I had no respect for a man without honor.

The sound of footsteps interrupted my thoughts.

Logan ducked beneath the low ceiling entrance, looking refreshed. Those tacky green hospital pants were history, replaced with loose fitting jeans. The top two buttons of his black shirt were undone, and he wore the same white sneakers, which were now green around the rims from the moss on the forest bed. Several plastic sacks were set at my feet, and Logan sat down in front of me Indian style.

Three boxes containing noodles and rice appeared. He tore the top covers off, placing the meals side by side.

"Everyone likes Chinese," he said.

"I'm not hungry."

He wadded up a plastic sack and leaned forward. "You're eating this food, and that is not up for debate."

"You can't make me."

When the corner of his mouth curved into a smile, I decided to choose my battles wisely.

It was a feast of crispy egg rolls, beef and peppers, orange chicken, broccoli, vegetables, and pork. There was no his. There was no mine.

Chinese sugar donuts poured out of a sack when he ripped the bag in half. Logan folded his fingers and waited.

I speared into the pork and he lifted a pair of wooden chopsticks, letting a tangle of noodles slide down his throat. It could have been just an ordinary lunch between two old friends.

"Is Silver your real name?" he asked. "It's unusual."

"My human name was Zoë. Silver is the name I was given by my Creator."

"Silly thing the Mage have with the names—pretentious and unnecessary."

"Were you born a Chitah, or made one?" I asked, changing the topic.

"You can only be born into our kind."

"There must be a lot of you."

He chewed slowly, considering the question. "Not all of our young are Chitah."

"What do you mean?"

Logan shrugged. "We have both human and Chitah DNA. Each child born is either one or the other." He tilted his head back and took another bite.

"So you can have human parents with children that are like you?"

"No, that would create all kinds of havoc in the human gene pool," he said with a mouthful. A noodle slipped from the chopstick and fell on his lap. He didn't think twice about flicking it back in his mouth. "Both parents must be a Chitah in order to produce a Chitah, no exceptions."

"What happens to the human children? What kind of life do they get?"

"They are given up for adoption to the humans."

I dropped my fork, disgusted by the idea. This hit a little close to home because of my father's absence in my life.

"Why would you give your own children away?"

"A parent loves their child enough to protect them, making whatever sacrifices are necessary. Humans are fragile; would you feel easy about raising them among Breed? Not to mention they are prone to disease, and they will wither and die before your eyes. They're better off with their own kind."

He was right. I couldn't imagine protecting a helpless human baby from all of the dangers of our world when I could barely protect myself. The egg roll became suddenly bland and I tossed it back in the box. Logan reached for it and stuffed the entire thing into his mouth, cooties be damned.

"Do you have any brothers or sisters?"

"Four brothers, all Chitah. One human sister," he said proudly.

"Four? Wow, that's a lot. Have you met your sister?"

He paused and looked wistfully at the beef. "I held her when she was an infant, but we have never met. Tell me about your siblings."

"I don't have any brothers or sisters. My best friend is the closest I have to a sister. Simon keeps me company, and Adam—"

"Lover?"

His question felt intrusive and I had no desire to open up my life to a nosy Chitah.

"That would be my personal business, now wouldn't it?"

Logan licked his lips and poured some soy sauce on the rice, unaffected by my response. "Don't be so quick to close a door that you yourself opened. I don't see *you* holding back with getting personal."

"Do you live in this cave, or just come here to explore your Neanderthal ways?"

"I wouldn't mind living here all the time. I'm a man who needs very little in life. But, I do have a condo."

"What do you do for a living? Never mind." My stupid question already had an answer. I forgot myself because Logan had a way of speaking which put me at ease. It was as if he had an internal switch that went between ruthless killer and normal guy. I had to remind myself they were one in the same.

He pointed his chopsticks at me. "Funny you mention that. I am… in-between jobs. If you hear of any openings, be sure to let me know."

I turned my mouth and set the fork down, wiping my fingers on a paper napkin.

"I'm serious. I'm beginning to think it's a dead end job."

"Enough," I said, raising my hand. Under normal circumstances, I might have laughed, but I struggled with appreciating his dark humor about kills when I was still his captive.

His cheeks puffed when he took a breath. "I know you're not mad at me, Little Raven." He licked sauce from his thumb. "I can scent it."

"Maybe you just smell the broccoli."

"Then I'll be sure to order that off the menu next time, as I've never been so aroused by vegetables."

My cheeks heated. His fervent gaze and candid remarks were

only trying to provoke a response out of me. If he kept it up, I might be the first person in history to take out a Chitah with a plastic spoon.

I closed my eyes and thought of Simon—wondering how much he heard over the phone. That's when a giant light bulb flashed over my head. I often forgot myself as a Mage, not remembering that I could go to the Grey Veil to call to Justus and let them know I was safe.

Something gritty touched my lips and my eyes snapped open.

"I've watched you staring at this donut," he said, with an outstretched arm. "Are you going to eat it, or make love to it with those fetching eyes?"

Logan hovered over the food, balancing on the knuckles of his left hand. The muscles in his arms were taut, and even as close as we were, I couldn't look him directly in the eye. I wanted to throw my power at him, but all I could hear in the back of my head was Simon's voice, warning me to choose my opportunities wisely. He would say, "There's a difference between fighting a man who's pointing a gun at you, and fighting with a gun against your head."

He tracked every shift of my body, slide of my foot, and direction of my gaze. Justus watched me in the training room in a similar manner, as did Simon when we played a game. Logan was a man who anticipated moves, and our proximity offered little comfort.

"Eat from my hand, little bird."

When I reached for it, he pulled back. "From my *hand*," he demanded.

I narrowed my eyes and dove for the donuts when he blocked my move and grabbed them. There he stood—holding a donut in one hand and the bag in the other in a game of keep away.

"You are *ridiculous!*" I shouted.

He strolled across the room with a smug expression and sat down, dropping the bag between his legs. The donut disappeared down his throat and he wiped his hand across his chest.

"Sure you don't want one? Mmm, tasty."

"I don't want anything between your legs," I snapped.

I could have sworn color flared in his cheeks. He chewed the donut, watching me with irritated eyes. Lifting a second one, he dramatically waved it beneath his nose.

"While you're busy having foreplay with a pastry, I'm going to crash for a while."

"You just woke up," he said in a flat voice.

"Your broccoli gave me a stomachache."

Logan drew in a deep breath and licked his lips.

I turned my back to him and tucked an arm beneath my head, slipping into the Grey Veil.

CHAPTER 15

I CALLED OUT TO SIMON a second time, leaping from the black rock nestled against a sparkling river. The Grey Veil was a realm that existed between dream and reality. Justus created his own private place because of a gift. When it came to gifts—some magic I would never understand. According to Justus, a Mage could only enter if they shared his light, *and* he showed them the way. Simon and I partially binded, therefore I was able to call to him. The more time that elapsed between light sharing, the harder it was to call to the other. Perhaps that's why he periodically snapped me with his light, sharing small enough increments to keep the connection open. I chose Simon because I was afraid to face Justus.

I always wondered about Simon. He was a private man when it came to his gifts. As a strategist, he was never one to show his cards. Simon either held a royal flush, or a bluff.

He appeared from the trees and approached, touching my face with his hands. "Where are you?"

"I'm being held in a cave, if you can believe that."

"We thought the worst. How are you unharmed?" he asked, looking me over. "We know a Chitah took you, and *bloody hell,* your room reeks of it."

"The Mage, he was taking me to them and, they tried to—"

"Slow down," he said. "Take a breath."

I did as he said. There was no time for details. "He killed a Mage, Simon. Two of them."

"Where would he take you?" Simon asked himself.

"I forgot to bring a map." I met his worried glance, noticing his face was unshaven. Not a very becoming look for Simon; it was patchy and looked like a boyish attempt at a beard. "The next razor's on me."

"I'm delighted to see you can manage a sense of humor at a time like this."

I gave an elegant shrug. "Did you know that we could pull energy from a Chitah to heal? Justus tells me things that I shouldn't do, but he never tells me why."

His jaw unhinged. If it was one thing I loved about Simon, it was his flair for the dramatic.

"You let a Chitah lay a hand on you?"

"Must I have this discussion with a man wearing a ponytail?" I sighed. "I thought the benefactor would have forgotten about me."

"He knows you're a Unique, that's why Justus has kept you so guarded these months, whether you realize it or not. I would have not expected him to send a Chitah."

"I think I can reason with him."

"You cannot reason with a Chitah." Simon took hold of my shoulders. "Unless he has given you his *word* that he will not harm you, do not trust him. Keep your distance; they can kill a Mage. Do you understand me?" Light pulsed in his eyes.

"I understand you perfectly, Mage," a voice interrupted. "Now remove your hands from the female, or I will rip out your throat."

My blood ran cold. Logan stood as an exquisite threat; his predatory eyes glued to Simon like an unwanted inevitability. They judged him from the scuff on his boots to the wave in his hair.

"You are not invited here, dreamwalker. This is the Mage realm."

"Sorry, I seem to have missed the 'no trespassing' sign. Would you mind pointing it out? I do not require an invitation, Mage. My only limitation is that I cannot physically tear you apart in this place. If you want to test that theory, then touch her again. The female is *mine*."

"She is in your custody, but Silver is not *yours*."

"Her Ghuardian does an inadequate job protecting his own." Logan strolled to the edge of the water with a steady eye on us. "It was foolish of him to leave her unattended when a Mage is hunting her. She couldn't be safer than with a Chitah. Do you not agree, Simon the strategist?" His brow winked up on the last word.

"You know me?"

"You've made a lot of enemies. Your reputation precedes you like a red carpet."

Simon's lips disappeared into thin lines. With folded arms, he paced in a circle. "I don't bloody well believe this. Release her and you will be compensated. We will top his price or… be in your debt." Simon wasn't happy about the offer, and frankly neither was I.

"Not enough," Logan said, lifting his chin. "I want full involvement in locating this Mage. Let's just say it's personal."

I could see all kinds of profanities marked above Simon's head in a thought bubble, but he stared at Logan with pressed lips. "Agreed."

"Is this a job offer?" Logan perked up, running his fingers along the collar of his shirt. "I'm in the midst of a career change. You might be surprised at the type of information a man like me has."

"Of that I have no doubt," Simon muttered. "I'm not an unemployment service. Return her to us and we'll come to an arrangement."

Logan dropped his chin and stepped forward. I put my body between them, but Simon kicked up some dirt and cursed at me to move.

A rolling chuckle shook from Logan's chest. "Jiminy. Your kind never ceases to amuse me."

"Let us form an alliance and we will make you a fair trade." Simon held up a hand in good faith.

"I cannot scent if you are truthful here but know this: if you deceive me and fall through on our bargain, I will hunt you down. Cross me, and I will not forget."

Simon nodded once in a silent agreement between men.

"Come," Logan said, cupping his finger at me.

Simon was about to protest, but I touched his arm. "Simon, I'll see you soon."

I took Logan's hand and walked into the light.

Logan shifted to fourth gear—steering with his knee—and folded a stick of gum in his mouth with his free hand. It was late afternoon and the sun battled the brooding dark clouds, which spilled occasional showers of light on the windshield as we drove towards it. This was my favorite time of the day because the world hung in a delicate balance between light and dark.

"What can a dreamwalker do?" I asked.

"Some of us jump into dreams. We can't do it with everyone and I'm not sure why," he said, popping his gum. "If I could control minds or even the subject matter of the dream…"

"Then you would be a pervert."

A loud snap of gum showed his annoyance.

Logan had a unique way of speaking. It was smooth and masculine, but his sentences often trailed off in a deep rumble. He occasionally used old-fashioned phrases, which made me curious of his true age.

"Do me a favor, Mr. Cross, and stay out of my dreams."

The tires crunched over the remaining dead leaves of winter as we rolled up the path leading to the house. Not twenty-four hours ago this man was about to deliver me to my worst nightmare. Now, he was tag teaming with Simon.

"Question?"

He downshifted and looked at me. "Ask me whatever you want."

"Is there any offer that you wouldn't take?"

He lifted the visor and pulled the aviator sunglasses from his face. "Perhaps one day, I'll find out."

The car jerked to a stop, right along with my heart. Justus stood on the edge of the path with his arms folded, pushing out his biceps like a man trying to throw around his macho.

"You are afraid?"

"I don't know if I'm ready for this," I mumbled, rubbing my face. "I just want a shower and a nap, but I can already see he's upset with me."

"Remain in the car," he said, unbuckling his seatbelt.

"What are you going to do?"

Ignoring me, Logan exited the vehicle and approached Justus with a confidence that couldn't be matched. I always thought Justus had swagger, but next to Logan, it was a tough call. Logan towered over him and even their body types were dramatically different. I wondered if the two of them battled it out—who would win.

I waited for Justus to wield his unholy light on Logan, but nothing happened as they spoke. Hiding in the car was a bit childish, so I made my way over to the circle, rolling up the sleeves of my sweater. I was relieved to be home, but ashamed of the error in judgment I made. Live and learn.

Justus took three hard steps until he loomed over me.

"Were you treated well? Don't lie to me."

Logan swept his hair out of his face. "Easy there, hoss. No need to snap your cap."

Justus scraped him from top to bottom with his gaze. "You are the Chitah?"

Logan's fangs descended to answer with absolute certainty. "The one and only."

CHAPTER 16

I T WAS A RELIEF TO walk in and find the room tidy, with no corpses strewn about the floor, spatters of blood, or broken furniture. Instead, all three men behaved like civilized creatures in the main room of Justus's house. I left them alone to take a hot shower, and I used half the bottle of coconut body wash because of Logan's scent, which made Simon scrunch his nose. I could have stayed in there forever, but I was starting to wrinkle.

Lately, my life was either no drama, or an overdose of it. I was a woman living in a new world with old beliefs, concealing a powerful gift, but the kidnapping was beginning to wear thin. *I was no one's object to possess.*

Logan's voice rumbled from the shadows at Simon, who was staring at his cell phone. "The number doesn't come up," he said. "He takes extra measures to hide himself. If you punch the redial it will call, but he doesn't pick up unless he's expecting it."

Tightening the string on my sweats, I looked at Simon. "Did you try my homemade cake?"

I drifted to the brown rug before the fireplace and dropped to my knees. The soft, glowing embers warmed my back.

"None of us had an appetite, love. We tossed them out."

"What a shame," Logan mumbled. "The enchiladas were the bomb."

I smiled at the unexpected compliment.

"Is Sunny coming back?"

"She's already here," Justus said in a tired voice. Their eyes were showing telltale signs of fatigue. "Your friend is staying with Novis for lack of a more suitable place. I *do not* like involving Novis in our personal affairs. Babysitting your human companion is an embarrassing request."

Justus scolded me with every word.

"She could have stayed here."

"To serve as a distraction when you need to remain focused."

"It wasn't my idea to board her with a Council member," I said pointedly.

"Be that as it may…"

"*Mind your tone*, Mage."

Logan emerged from the darkness. His stride was slow and purposeful. All eyes watched as he claimed a position to my right, clasping his hands together. A faint smell cloaked him like a warning, and my hairs stood on end.

"Chitah do not tolerate disrespect to a female."

To which I raised my brow.

Justus spread his arms along the back of the sofa. "Humor me, Chitah; wasn't it you who ripped Silver away from the safety of her home with the intention of trading her off? In my book, kidnapping a woman against her will and terrorizing her qualifies in the genre of disrespect. Not really the Chitah way, is it?"

The temperature in the room kicked up a few degrees, and Justus shredded him apart with those icy blue eyes.

"I did not terrorize the female. I kept her warm and fed her, which is more than I can say you do in this icebox you call a house. Secondly, you are her Ghuardian, which is far more important than a stranger, don't you agree? Each time you disrespect Silver, you're setting the example that this is how a male should treat her. You have an obligation to any female who lives under your roof. We never do that to our own kind; a female will be raised in our house to know that they deserve a male of worth, no less."

Hoping to defuse the Justus bomb, I caught Simon's attention. "Where's Knox? Is he still over at Novis's, or did he go back to… uh—"

"Planet steroid?"

I snorted. I didn't really know where Knox was from. "If you keep calling him names, I'm going to tell him. Where is he staying?"

Simon clattered his fingers on the laptop keys, smacking away at his bubble gum. "With me, for obvious reasons. Spare room in my flat and let me tell you…" He paused to finish typing. "That bloke is a real collector's item. Of course, now that I know he gets his jollies from the daffodil you so thoughtfully brought here—"

"Wait, what… jollies? Simon, revert to American English, please. I hate it when you have one of your spells."

"Your friend and Gigantor are an item."

"Good for her." *I sure didn't see that one coming.*

"Suffice it to say she will be having *no* more sleepovers, not after they broke my favorite plate. I think I'm mentally scarred for life after my kitchen counter was desecrated," he mumbled.

I grimaced. "Remind me not to eat over; we're ordering take out."

"For at least a month, until I properly sterilize—"

"Say no more," I said, waving a hand. We shared a private sniffle of disgust. Poor Simon, he loved preparing food on his counter. His perception of a good seduction involved a foreplay of cuisine.

"Silver, do you remember anything specific you haven't told us about Samil's benefactor during his visits?"

"No, let's change the subject."

"It could help," Simon urged.

I wasn't convinced. "Like what?"

"Clothes, slang, jewelry, scars, or tattoos—maybe there's something in the details we lost. Sometimes it only takes one thing."

"Didn't you find anything when you searched Samil's house?"

"No, the search was unproductive," Justus said, his voice heavy with disappointment.

"He wore glasses, the kind with the gold, round frames. He dressed in suits and they were expensive, like yours," I said, nodding at Justus. "I don't remember any tattoos or scars." I scanned the ceiling, replaying the events in my head.

"His hair was dusty brown, trimmed short to his head and kind of thin. He was always chewing on a toothpick."

I thought of that dirty thing when it rolled over my chest as he slammed my hands into the hard concrete. The memory washed over me like an icy wave. Someone drew in a deep, hollow breath and when I glanced up, Logan was staring down at his shoes as he rocked on his heels. He would only be staying temporarily as part of an agreement he made with Justus, but it was odd getting used to him in our house.

"I don't remember an accent. Cross could tell you more."

"How did he beat you? I'm sorry to ask, Silver, but we need to know." The laptop snapped shut and was set on the table.

I never talked about the details. As much as I adored these men, Sunny was the only person I could really share my feelings with. I hated the benefactor for trying to break me like an animal, and a small part of me wanted to resent Justus and Simon for allowing him to take me. I knew it was out of their hands and the Mageri was to blame, but anger is like a disease that spreads.

"I don't see how that's going to help you, unless it's morbid curiosity."

Justus leaned forward. "Learner, I have seen many things in my lifetime. Specific techniques of torture can be unique to organizations, countries, territories, and cultures. It *may* help."

I curled my legs to the side to get more comfortable. "I was struck in the same spot repeatedly until I either passed out from the pain, or bit into my own arm to welcome a new pain. How's that?"

Someone cursed under their breath.

"You won't learn much from those details," I said. "There wasn't anything that stood out about him, no scars or missing teeth. He carried a silver flask for alcohol, and a necklace—"

"What kind of necklace?"

"A metal chain with a round pendant."

"Do you remember what it looked like?" Simon hopped to his feet and circled the floor.

"This big," I said, sizing my fingers to a specific distance. "Looked dirty, like an old coin."

Justus sat forward. "Can you remember any details or words?"

"Give me a second, I need to think." I remembered how it swung over me like a pendulum. "The edges were uneven, but it was a man's head with leaves."

"Roman," Justus said. "I'd bet on it. He's old, Simon."

"I'm on it." Simon snatched his laptop and walked into the kitchen.

I stole his vacant chair. The seat was still warm, and the scent of bubble gum lingered behind.

"Does this mean he's a coin collector, or just a guy with really bad fashion taste?"

"It narrows our search. Some of the older Mage carry tokens of their former life."

"Has Mr. Cross been of any help?"

"That remains to be seen." Justus rubbed a hand over his shaved head and the bristles scraped against his palm.

The mood was killing my appetite. "Is there anything sweet left to eat in this house, or did you chuck it all in the trash?"

Logan laughed at my sudden change in topic. "I could go pick up some donuts. Just say the word."

I shot him a frosty glare. "Why don't you pick up a rash while you're at it?"

"We're out of sugar." Justus said. "The next time you plan to cook for an army, let me know and I'll stock up."

The man had dry humor that only I appreciated. I grinned at Justus as he walked out of the room. Sunny was in town and I felt like I was beginning to form a circle of friends again. I left Logan and went into the kitchen, only to find Justus and Simon talking in low voices by the fridge. Justus looked upset.

"I don't care, he's still dangerous. She doesn't even realize—"

"What's going on in here?" Their abrupt silence perturbed me. "Tomorrow we're having a dinner party, and I want to invite Sunny. Everyone is going to have a good time. That's mandatory." I put my hands on my hips. "What?"

Justus looked at me with a crooked expression. "I want you to keep your distance from Logan. He is only here because we struck a deal for your return, and he wants involvement."

"There have been several opportunities for him to hurt me, but he hasn't."

"That is the problem, he's grown too…" Justus looked to Simon who finished his thought.

"Attached."

"Grow up—the both of you."

"A dinner party is a wise option. I will send Novis an invitation as I need his consent to access confidential records." Justus leaned on one arm and gave me *the look*. "Dress appropriate?"

He didn't buy *all* my clothes. On a few occasions when I was upset with him, I pulled a shirt from my arsenal. There were three particular T-shirts with vulgar slang written on them that made the vein in his forehead poke out. It was a cute little vein, and I grew fond of seeing its public appearance while I walked behind him like a parade of humiliation.

"I've got a lovely pair of knickers, Mary Janes, and a bustier he might fancy. I think I can swing getting the consent you need," I winked suggestively.

The door swung behind me and I left them to plot—or do whatever men do when they're alone. Laughter pealed out of Simon and he carried on like a hyena until I reached my bedroom. Sometimes the fact that he couldn't shut it off was even funnier than the joke itself.

Logan was reclined on my bed with his fingers laced behind his head. It was a piece of furniture made for someone his size, and he looked like a king in it.

"Comfy?"

"Most definitely," he sighed. "I've been wondering why you chose that shoebox to sleep on. Is this bed not acceptable to your high standards? Perhaps there is a pea tucked between the mattresses," he suggested, patting the blanket.

I looked down at my chaise and back to him. "Some things are too big for their own good."

He snorted. "Indeed. But I rarely receive complaints."

"How do you know I don't sleep on the bed?"

"The night I took you," he said tapping his nose. "I know your scent. I know where you lay."

"I've never slept on Goliath."

Logan scrunched his face, not understanding.

"It's what I call the bed; anything that size deserves a name. We don't have a guest room, so you can take the bed as long as you remain on that side of the room."

"I have no desire to invade your space, Mage."

I ruffled the small blanket and fluffed my pillow.

"Why does it appear that your ulterior motive is to prove something?" he mumbled.

"That a Mage can show more hospitality than a Chitah? I'm not sure what you mean," I said. "I'm only offering you a bed."

"Oh no, this is *not* happening," Justus bellowed. "You," he said, snapping at Logan, "sleep out here on the couch."

"Ghuardian, I invited him to take the bed because we don't have a guest bedroom, and we're better than that. We share a mutual dislike for each other, so you have nothing to be concerned about."

He wrapped his fingers around my wrist. "Come with me."

One blink later, Logan was off the bed and wedged between us. The grip loosened and Logan's voice was low and threatening.

"Why is it so hard for you Mage to keep your hands to yourself? It's a quality I find most unappealing."

When I felt the energy level in the room rise, I separated the two like a referee.

"You are overstepping your bounds, Chitah. This is my home," Justus warned.

"Ghuardian, you make the rules in the house, but I make the rules in my bedroom," I said, hoping to avoid a fight. "I'll keep the door open, and if he so much as looks at me funny, I'll nuke him."

Truthfully, I needed to keep Logan close. I didn't trust him roaming free in the house. Simon had a mouth and Justus had a temper. If an argument fired up while I was sleeping, I wouldn't be there to prevent it from escalating. For reasons I couldn't explain, I felt Logan wouldn't harm me.

"I will not put you at risk," Justus argued.

To prove my point, I reached out with my index finger and poked Logan in the side. I pushed enough power in him that he jolted, snapping his head around in surprise as he grabbed his ribs.

"I can take care of myself," I declared, ignoring Logan's reaction. He strolled to a small table with his back to us, holding his side.

In a low voice I asked, "Don't you trust me enough to make a sensible decision?"

Justus leveled me with his eyes. I felt a million words in that silent stare, but I knew he was glad to have me home because he avoided the fight, turned, and left the room.

"Sometimes father *doesn't* know best," Logan suggested, puffing out a candle on the wall.

He removed his shoes and socks, pulled the belt free from his jeans, and the sheets hissed as he eased inside.

Several minutes ticked by of Logan tossing and turning.

"What's the matter?" I finally asked, punching my pillow and turning to face him.

Silence. I waited for an answer and closed my eyes again.

"I sleep in the nude."

"Not tonight, you don't!"

"Evidently."

"Why don't you put the sweater on? It might be more comfortable."

"I'd rather you wear it."

Those words hung in the air more like a suggestion than a comment.

"You're going to pay for the upholstery cleaning of my sofa."

"Is there something wrong with my scent?"

"It's too strong, and *all over* my bed."

I dipped my nose into the blanket and took a deep breath. The smell was heady and dominating—like an aromatic elixir. I wanted to bury my face in it, and breathe it in all night. Whatever Logan was, he had a power all his own.

"Ah, but you like it," he said softly.

Drifting from the stretch of darkness was a deep, throaty growl that was indescribable. It was as if he had his own internal generator—a soothing sound.

A seductive sound.

CHAPTER 17

I BLINKED THROUGH A TANGLE OF lashes.

"Wakey-wakey," someone spoke.

Logan drifted into focus. He combed his hair nicely this morning, and it looked like Justus lent him a straight razor. Mysterious deep-set eyes looked down expectantly. The candlelight flickered in their lustrous amber and honey depths.

I crossed my eyes and stared down my nose. He pushed a donut against my lips, grinning like the devil.

I groaned, shoving his arm away.

"I made a special trip this morning; Justus already ate nine of them."

"Did he eat them from your hand?" I laughed.

Logan sighed and tilted his head to the side. "You have the most bewitching green eyes."

"My brown ones were prettier," I yawned, rubbing the sleep out of them.

I never liked compliments on my eyes. They were an unusual shade of bright green that attracted attention. They were also the same eyes as my maker, Samil. I accepted my new body, but every time I looked in the mirror, Samil was staring back at me. I carried his mark and his eyes, but I would never carry his black heart.

Logan tucked the donut inside his cheek. "They certainly look attached to you. Do your eyes normally shift colors, or are you pulling my leg?" He sucked his thumb and wiped it on his shirt.

I untangled my foot from the blanket and coughed. "I didn't used to look like this, but something happened after the first spark, and I changed."

"A Shifter? Aren't you full of surprises." He watched me with a pensive stare.

"You know we can't mix species. That much I picked up from my studies. It's more like a metamorphosis, I guess." I frowned at Logan. "Why doesn't that shock you?"

"I'm Breed," he said indifferently. "The longer you live, the more you learn to accept the unexplainable."

I grumbled and sat up to face him.

"Hmm… maybe I should call you butterfly."

I really hoped he didn't. I warmed up a little to the fact that he called me raven, although at times I felt more like a phoenix rising from the ashes of one catastrophe after another.

"Is Justus still here? He needs to escort me to the grocery store."

"Why is that?"

Logan pressed his finger on my clavicle, picking up specks of sugar and sucking on the tips of his fingers. I pushed him away and got off the sofa, dragging the blanket to the floor.

"This Learner must be escorted by her Ghuardian in public. That's the rule."

He sat down in my place and slipped on a sneaker, tying the laces. "I've always enjoyed breaking the rules."

<hr />

The dynamic of Breed relationships was fascinating, and their behavior was nothing like humans. When Logan gave his word to Justus that he would look after me—abduction or not—that was gold. If we were human, Logan would be sitting behind bars. They had a different system and way of life, one I needed to learn more about as it was *my* world now.

It was refreshing to go in public with someone other than Justus. I could push my grocery cart in peace without a cleanup on aisle five because some floozy decided to seduce my Ghuardian by the macaroni. Logan turned a few heads with his stature and penetrating eyes, which he kept low, as they attracted unwanted attention. He carried himself like a man of importance; he also knew his way around the produce aisle. I peered over a mountain of apples and watched him roll a cantaloupe in his hand, lifting it to his nose before he dropped it in the basket.

A dinner party was an informal affair that would allow Justus to strengthen his connections with the Council, but it also served as a needed distraction. Opportunities were arising for a more social climate, and I was looking for any way to incorporate normalcy into my life. I filled five paper sacks and headed home to prepare the meal.

"Who accepted the invitation?" I asked, pulling an avocado out of the bag.

"Everyone," Justus confirmed.

My stomach turned and I stared at the food skeptically.

Logan leaned against the counter on his elbow. "Have you never given a dinner party?"

"Can't be that hard," I said, shrugging my shoulders.

Justus cleared his throat. "We all saw what you did to the turkey."

"I didn't know it had to thaw," I bit out.

I spent hours in the kitchen, chopping and preparing. It was surreal to be passing a knife back and forth to a man who held me captive not twenty-four hours prior. Logan was comfortable in the kitchen. This man knew how to mince and measure where most men barely understood the mechanics of a toaster.

I rarely had an occasion to doll myself up. My black dress was nothing less than sophistication on a hanger, another hand-selected item by Justus. He was nervous about impressing Novis, and wore a dark dress shirt tucked into a pair of expensive slacks. The gold watch was overkill because a Mage didn't need to tell time, but it was his favorite. While Justus usually went to a barber, I heard him in the bathroom shaving his head for what seemed like an hour. Simon was his scandalous self in ass-grabbing jeans. He even applied a smudge of eyeliner for the occasion. Sometimes I adored his spirited personality, but this was not one of those times.

The guests arrived. Knox proudly held Sunny's hand, black hair neatly combed—no hat. I hugged her excitedly and stepped back to look at her date.

"Hey, dollface," Knox greeted, giving me a one-armed hug.

I bowed to Novis and faced Adam, who was memorizing my ensemble. Adam didn't know what had transpired over the past forty-eight hours, and I flicked a glance at Knox. Sunny looked at me with worried eyes, but said nothing. Maybe Justus was embarrassed that it reflected poor judgment on his part by leaving his Learner alone, and asked them for silence.

Adam leaned in for a polite kiss when Logan wedged an arm between us.

"I'm Logan Cross, and you are?"

His eyes snapped open to look up at Logan, who stood taller. "Adam."

"Is that *your* cologne I smell, Mage?" Logan wrinkled his nose. "I never understood the purpose of cologne; the male scent is the most intoxicating thing to a female. Yours must be the exception if you have to bury it beneath layers of—what is that," he asked leaning in, "…buffalo musk?"

Logan stood proudly without a hint of cologne, and I turned my mouth to the side, wondering why he was provoking Adam.

"Could someone crack open the wine?" I asked. "The table is set, so everyone please go in and have a seat while I bring out a few more things."

"Let me help you," Adam volunteered.

Logan raised his hand, "No, this one I got. We spent hours together, *churning*, and mixing. It's the least I can do." He searched Adam's face, nostrils flaring as he pulled in a scent.

"Boys, boys," Sunny chimed in, "I'll help Silver, and you can all duke it out like gentlemen. I'm Sunny, by the way—Silver's best girl. This is Knox." She placed her hands on his bicep.

"Her best guy," Knox cut in.

I almost let out a snort when I saw the jealousy fire up in his eyes, but I didn't. Knox claiming her that way was the most romantic thing I'd seen in a while.

Logan lifted her hand and bowed to it—something he sure never did with me. There was respect on his face, and we could all see it because his long hair was neatly tied back. He inclined his head respectfully to Knox, who slipped an arm around Sunny's waist. Tight.

"Who's the hunk?" Sunny teased, when the kitchen door shut behind us.

"Justus hired him to help catch the Mage I told you about."

"I hope you aren't dating him, he kind of scares me with those eyes. Oh hon, are you okay?" Sunny gave me a tight squeeze and I backed up.

"Everything worked out," I said, not really knowing how to answer. "What did they tell you?"

"We agreed not to talk about it, something about an investigation and if Adam found out, then he would tell Novis," she shrugged. "Simon said the intruder didn't get all the way in. I'm just glad you're not hurt… I was *so* worried."

I squeezed her hand and moved to the stove. "We'll talk about it someday, but I'm fine," I reassured her. "What's up with you and Knox? I wasn't sure if that was a dress you were wearing, or him. Simon mentioned something."

She giggled and gathered up the bowls from the fridge. "Simon's still mad at us."

"I heard *all* about that," I said, dropping the tortillas on a plate in disgust.

"Oh, you know about that?" Her cheeks flushed. "It's not as if we planned it. He was just feeding me some ice cream and the next thing I knew I was polishing the cabinets with my derriere."

"I'm never setting foot in that kitchen again without protection," I sighed.

"Oh, please." Sunny dramatically rolled her eyes. "He's thoughtful and attentive. We spent several days getting to know each other; I feel like he's really looking out for me. Knox has even tried to stop cussing as much; you know how I hate swearing. I didn't ask him to do it, but the other day he actually used the word 'motherfudger'. I laughed so hard I almost peed myself," she snickered. "I want to give it a chance."

"All that from a couple of days?" I arched a brow. *How could anyone feel that sure about something so fast?*

She lifted a shoulder and ran her fingers through those wavy locks. "Stranger things have been known to happen. How do you like my dress?" She twirled, and the fabric spun like a pinwheel.

"You still manage to make me look like a wallflower, Sunshine. Why not Simon? He's sexy, and a really intelligent guy." Not that I wanted her dating Simon, but I thought he had a better chance with her than Knox.

Her eyes sharpened. "*So is Knox*. Besides, Simon isn't my type. Did you see that metal thing on his tongue?"

"I'm beginning to think I don't know what your type is anymore," I replied. "Got to keep getting back on the horse, right?"

She snorted. "Yep, and they just keep bucking me off."

"Is that when you decided to ride the bull instead?"

Sunny shoved me playfully and I returned to the cabinet, peeling the lids from the bowls. "How are you going to manage to get through this evening with Justus throwing off his charm? I didn't really plan for this, but if we end up with War of the Worlds at the table tonight because you start making out with the host—"

"I have it under control," she said. "Now that I know what he can do, it makes it easier to block out. Truthfully, when Knox is near I barely notice. I guess that's why he's stuck to me like glue—not that I mind being stuck to him either," she whispered, taking a handful of plates out the door with a wink.

Candles illuminated the small dining room. We set the table with fine china that came from a box I found in the pantry, and broke out the crystal. Justus took his usual spot at the head of the table, and Novis sat opposite him. I expected Sunny and Knox would sit side by side, which would give me the last seat on that row. Instead, they faced each other.

I stared at the four vacant seats as the remaining three men waited; it was like musical chairs from hell, and Simon mocking me with his dramatic expressions didn't help. I was so thrilled he found this amusing. I touched the chair next to Justus and chickened out, excusing myself to get a bottle of wine.

When I emerged from the kitchen with a bottle of port, Logan won the chair beside mine and stood up as I approached.

"You did all this yourself?" Sunny asked. "Wow, I never in my wildest dreams imagined one day I would see this from a girl who considered tater tots and hot dogs gourmet."

"Thank you, Sunshine," I said, exaggerating my smile. I sat down and lifted my glass, but Logan caught my wrist. A few drops of red wine blotted the white napkin.

"It's bad luck to drink without a toast."

Logan stood up and commanded everyone's attention.

"To a bountiful meal—may we always have friends to share our spoils. To our quests in life—may we always learn from failure and be humbled by success. To those who have found love," he said pointedly to Sunny and Knox, "and to those who seek it—may we deserve what fate puts in our hand. Finally, to our enchanting hostess..."

Logan spun on his heel staring down at me, and I turned five shades of red.

"Your efforts will be rewarded with my appetite. Should the beef be tough and undercooked—then I will lick my plate clean."

Everyone tapped glasses and began conversation.

Logan flipped out the napkin across his lap and whispered in my direction, "You should wear red more often."

I put the back of my hand on my cheek to test if it was still hot. When I heard Justus's stomach growl, I forgot my embarrassment and passed him the guacamole.

Adam lifted his fork. "What line of work are you in, Logan Cross?"

A bell pepper flew down the wrong pipe and I coughed.

Logan lightly patted my back and replied, "I'm between jobs at the moment, but I see an opportunity in my horizon. I'm offering my services to Justus at a reasonable fee."

Logan's hand lingered on my back. I felt the warm stroke of a finger across my skin. I shivered, dabbing the napkin against my lips.

His answer avoided the dreaded question of how *we* met. If Adam knew the truth, he would have pointed out that my forgiving Logan was a character flaw.

Justus leaned over his plate and bit into a fajita, grunting his praise as his eyes floated across the table.

"Novis, we have made progress with our case and hope to bring the truth to light with this Mage." He lifted his crystal glass and removed a quarter of the wine in a swallow. "I have a request to ask of the Council: permission to access the Mageri records on behalf of HALO. What you provide us will remain confidential." Justus cleared his throat nervously.

Novis smoothed a finger across his thin lips. Age seeped through his youthful eyes; you couldn't let the spiky bedhead fool you. He reached for the sour cream with his long slender fingers and spooned it over his beans. I had only met him a couple of times, but I liked him. There was wisdom in every groove of his aura.

"Explore your alternatives, Justus. As the keeper of the records, I'm reluctant to hand over information that will not produce results. While HALO is a separate entity, you continue to involve us in your efforts and that is a conflict of interest. A breach would bring *severe* consequences."

Novis bit into a tortilla chip. "Explore your alternatives first, and be sure you don't neglect your other cases. Last month was a stellar success with the capture of a conspirator, and the Relics are grateful."

Justus offered a respectful nod. "You have our gratitude. The records will be a last resort."

It was evident he respected Novis and sought to gain his trust. The conversation also brought to light the importance of Justus's role with HALO. He spent hours in his room, and I was beginning to see how valued he was.

Knox broke the silence. "Pass me some of that red sh—stuff. My girl needs more for her chips."

Adam's wine went down the wrong way as he laughed into his glass.

We paid attention to every exchange between Sunny and Knox, passing amused glances across the table. Neither of us could have predicted this unexpected pairing.

"You've outdone yourself, love," Simon applauded—literally—at the end of the meal. After I announced I made the enchiladas myself, a competition began between him and Logan to polish off the dish. Simon never backed down from a challenge, even a silent one.

Amid conversation, I flattened my fingers on the table, pulling the energy from Adam's knife. It slid towards me clumsily, and Justus dropped his hand over it.

"Don't use your gifts at the table, Learner."

I watched the interaction between Sunny and Knox—the soft way she smiled at him, how he noticed where her eyes went and quickly brought food within her reach. He was attentive, and I wondered if I wasn't being too harsh with my judgment.

"Novis, I can't thank you enough for taking in Sunny. I know she's anxious to find a place of her own and get out of your hair. Are there any safe areas of the city you would recommend? I'm concerned about Marco."

Knox threw his shoulders back, pressing a finger on the table. "That fucker isn't coming within a ten mile radius of her. She'll have the tightest security in place; that's my specialty."

Well, that settled that.

"Don't worry about me, Silver. I have a feeling I'm going to be inside Fort Knox."

Simon tucked the last of the enchilada in his cheek. "No doubt Fort Knox will be inside of—"

Adam punched his arm, cutting off the thought before it left his mouth. Simon didn't always think before speaking, and I had a feeling Knox wouldn't have seen the humor.

"I want to help find this guy," I announced. "This all began with me, and nothing would make me happier than spoiling his plans."

"No, Learner, you have done *enough*," Justus said.

The tone was accusatory, and my face heated. Novis was an important guest, and confronting my Ghuardian in his presence would have been inappropriate.

When the conversations resumed, I looked at Logan. Something made me turn, and I caught him staring at his empty plate with vacant eyes. He was growling. Maybe I was more attuned to it after spending time alone with him, because no one else noticed.

"Stop that," I whispered, getting out of my chair and leaving the room.

I paced back and forth in the kitchen, blowing out a breath. I couldn't get used to someone dictating my life, making decisions in my interest, and reprimanding me.

I returned with churros, which I had no part in making. It was a cinnamon stick with a rich dipping sauce, and Logan made them.

"You underestimate the female, it's a pity that you can't see how invaluable her abilities are," Logan said, wiping the corner of his mouth with the cloth napkin and tossing it on his plate. "You must always know your enemy. Stupidity is walking into a trap; the advantage comes in setting one. He thinks he's pulling the strings. Well, I for one never cared for puppeteers."

A fork bounced across the table. "You want to use her as bait?" Adam was hot.

"Question my intent once and I will overlook it," Logan bit out, "but question it twice, and the gloves are off."

"Does anyone want to hear what I think?" I stood in my short black dress by the chair and raked them over with my eyes. "There has been too much planning around something that involved me— that is not *involving* me. You have nothing on him right now outside of juicing. He's smart, and if he suspects that we're after him, he'll cover his tracks."

"Learner," Justus warned.

"Let her finish."

I flicked my eyes suspiciously to Logan.

"I also think—and no offense Knox—that sending a human to find Marco was a mistake. Oh, and the plan with Sunny crawling back to him? Anyone who's met Sunny knows how headstrong she is. She would never do anything like that. Why didn't you just send a parade announcing your intention? Have you ever heard of the Trojan horse? Hell, some of you are old enough that you were probably in it."

Simon threw back his head and laughed.

"Marco only met me once in my human form. There's a good chance he has no idea that I'm physically different, so that puts me at an advantage. I can get close to him."

I sat down hard, tempted to drink my glass of wine to the bottom, but I simply ran my finger around the rim. "I know enough about the benefactor to use that knowledge. Marco doesn't know me. *I* am the Trojan horse. Put me in with Marco and I'll get the information we need. If you continue to tiptoe on his turf, he's going to catch on. I'm a female Mage, so that could get me close enough. I can help if you just give me a chance."

I polished off my wine.

A chair slid back and all eyes went to Novis, who rose to his feet. At that point, it was safe to assume I had royally overstepped my bounds as a Learner, insulted a Council member, embarrassed my Ghuardian, made Knox feel like a dipshit, and…

"Fellow Mage," he spoke, resting his fingertips against the table.

"I'm honored to see the beginnings of this Learner. Silver is a worthy addition to the Mageri; wisdom does not always come with age." His eyes locked on Justus. "The weight that holds us down is that of an obese ego. I can offer no advice, nor do I care to listen to these conversations any further this evening, as a member of the Council should have no part. Make your decisions wisely, and I hope that you will see that this Learner has more to offer us than delicious fajitas." Novis flashed a smile at me and winked. "And they are delicious, by the way."

I dreaded what Justus would say. My speaking out was a direct reflection on his ability to teach me properly. Instead, he looked on me with pride. Any compliment to me went indirectly to my Ghuardian.

When I looked back to Novis, I found myself staring at a churro. Logan waved it in a circular motion playfully as he turned it around and shoved it in his mouth.

CHAPTER 18

EARLY THE NEXT MORNING, I joined Justus in the training room downstairs. Simon and Logan were borderline food coma, and I needed to get some practice in. Usually I just worked out, but I felt like buffing up some of my skills. The room had weights and an open mat where we sparred. Down here, we had electricity illuminating the weapons mounted on the wall—mostly knives. I focused on strength building and agility, and occasionally he taught me a new move. Justus had all the moves, and mastered how to concentrate energy to an explosive degree. Some of the older ones learned a trick of balling up energy and using it for a single burst. It looked like a vanishing act, and I saw him do it outside of a bar once.

Four hours in, Justus finally broke the silence.

"I agree to this."

I tossed a dry towel and he caught it, wiping sweat from his neck and face. After a hard workout, his skin took on a sunburned appearance.

"Agree to what?" I sucked down half a bottle of water and bent over.

"I want to know why my maker is involved. He led Samil to you," he said angrily. "This is not the man that taught me about morals and obligations." Justus threw the towel to the floor. "He was a Mage of honor. Regardless of the path he has chosen, I do not believe he would physically harm you. However, you will not meet him unprepared. I will teach you his weaknesses."

"You don't think I can hold my own?"

His steel blue eyes met mine. "I never doubted your courage, only your obedience."

I loved the big guy, despite everything, and a mischievous smile crept over my face. Through my peripheral, I memorized the location and distance of his wrist so I could pull him off balance. My Ghuardian was too clever for my whims of insanity and fell into a fighting stance.

We circled each other.

"I will fight as Marco does. Pay attention and learn from me." His bare feet slid over the mat, and I concentrated on his intent through subtle movements.

Justus moved like a warrior on a battlefield. It was strange to think my Ghuardian had spent years of training under Marco as a Learner. I was so used to seeing him as the man in charge that I forgot he was once himself a student.

His incredible movements made my head spin.

I bent over as he was reaching for my arm, and he clipped me in the mouth by accident. There was no time to think as he pursued me until I was cornered. I couldn't gain any distance between us. These were not Justus's tactics; the style was aggressive.

I kicked off the wall with a flash of energy and threw myself over him, using his shoulder for balance. It took months to learn how to manipulate my flashing abilities, and most of the time I landed on my back. He pivoted around and charged, forcing me against the wall. I did the only thing that came to mind and dropped to one knee, eye level with his crotch.

Marco's moves were not calculated, but like a firestorm. He didn't give his opponent time to think— only react. If Marco taught these moves to Justus, I wondered why *he* never fought this way.

I chomped my teeth and Justus hesitated. I had never threatened his manhood before, but if it meant saving my ass, then I was willing to go the distance.

He swung a heavy arm when a gust of wind cooled my forehead. Bodies slid across the floor in a calamity of sound and tangled limbs.

"No!" I screamed.

Logan pinned Justus to the ground with anger splashed across his complexion. The only thing preventing those canines from piercing my Ghuardian's neck was a strong forearm with a tight fist. Justus grimaced and a vein throbbed in his forehead. Logan held his other arm so he couldn't use his power, and neither man was holding back.

This was no warning.

"Get off of him!"

Simon came up from behind, and swung me by the hip towards the stairs.

"Silver, leave the room."

"They're going to kill each other, Simon. Get out of my way!"

"Listen to me," he said in a calm voice, opening his arms wide. "Leave this room, *now*. You are not equipped to fight a Chitah. He'll kill you in a heartbeat. Do you understand? Let me handle this."

Logan lacked mercy and killed without regret. I knew in that moment that I was willing to fight for my Ghuardian. My loyalty burned so deep it marked me like a river.

"Simon, get out of my way," I said, shoving him.

He shoved back.

Anger culminated in his features, and he firmly gripped my shoulders. Fear struck through me like lightning. *Precious seconds lost squabbling.*

Logan's black, bottomless eyes dragged across the floor and rose to watch us. Something switched gears in his attention, as if Justus no longer existed. My heart skipped a beat from his feral gaze as I struggled with Simon.

Faster than I could track, he lunged at us.

I flew off my feet, tumbling across the floor until I hit the wall. Logan crouched on top of me, knuckles pressed against the hard floor as he looked between Justus and Simon closing in on him. Talk about déjà vu.

Neither man looked Logan directly in the eye—averting their attention to the floor as they talked in low whispers. Logan planted his right foot behind my back and extended his left leg over my body. He was waiting for a challenger.

He pushed my shoulder with his hand when I tried to get up. My hair stuck to my face in sweaty strands. I wrapped my fingers around his arm, pushing at him.

"Ghuardian, stay back. I've seen him kill."

Logan released a deep growl that filled the room like a hunter's call.

Simon eyed one of the daggers on the wall.

Logan noticed.

My fingers burned with energy, but out of nowhere, guilt arrived. What kept me from hurting Logan was the fact he was protecting me. Maybe he had ulterior motives for not handing me over to the Mage that night, but he didn't lack options. I owed him for that.

Seconds away from bloodshed, I squeezed his arm. "You really *are* nothing but an animal."

I meant it, and I knew this would offend him most.

He peered over his shoulder—fangs retracted, skin coloring normal, and eyes ringed in gold.

Logan stood up on his feet and swung a long arm in my direction, pointing towards the small cut on my lip. His eyes never broke contact with Justus.

"Heal the female."

<hr />

I have always hated flying. I came into this world on an airplane, but it always felt more like a coffin than a cradle. Turbulence, barf bags, crying children, the giant engine roaring outside my window—these things were not for me. Nor was riding in coach, because my Ghuardian could afford first class tickets.

"I can't believe Justus agreed to this," I said, crossing my arms over my stomach.

Logan unbuckled his seatbelt and shifted in his seat. "We came to an agreement."

"What kind?"

"That's between us. The word of a Chitah is firm, and I've agreed to guard you in his stead. This was Simon's brainchild, and I can see how he earned his reputation. If you were escorted by a Mage, it would only draw suspicion. I offer better protection to fight against another Mage."

Favors and debts were key elements and overruled personal opinion. As much as Justus didn't trust a Chitah, he trusted they would stay true to their word. After all, it was in their nature.

This trip was giving me an opportunity to do something of value. Having an identity crisis at age twenty-nine was never in my plans, and I was searching for my place in this new life. Justus divulged useful tips on Marco: the type of women he preferred, his drink of choice, and how to speak to him. Simon was confident that if anything would lure him out of his foxhole, it would be a female Mage.

One hour in flight, I burst down the aisle and threw up in the closet they called a bathroom. I returned to my seat with a miserable look on my face. We were hurtling through the air like a missile, and no one batted an eyelash as they continued filing their nails and reading magazines.

Logan's hair was tied at the nape of his neck, and he looked at me with concern.

"Is there something I can do to ease you?"

"Knock me out?"

I shut my eyes and held my stomach. I should have listened to Simon about taking medication, but knowing his sense of humor, he would have slipped me some kind of hallucinogenic drug as a practical joke.

When I opened my eyes, a vomit bag fashioned into a puppet was staring at me. He made it while I was in the bathroom, even took the time to draw large, goofy eyes.

"Why don't you like me, little bird?" he chirped, moving the mouth.

I laughed unexpectedly, and a heavyset man in front of us glared through the seats. He had a pudgy nose, a mole on his cheek, and intolerance in his gaze. Logan looked at him sideways before giving me his attention.

"I can help take your mind off of it."

"Give me *that*." I snatched the bag and held it on my lap, staring at its cartoon eyes. "Don't you have a girlfriend to inflict your humor on?"

A broad smile stretched across his face. "Is that your way of asking me about my *situation*?"

I sighed.

"No, I don't have a female." He stared vacantly at the overhead compartment.

"Maybe if you had a respectable job and didn't kidnap people, a girl might actually take a shine to you."

"I'm not for lack of options."

I rolled my head to the right and stared up at his profile. His lower jaw slightly opened as he periodically tasted the air around him. Logan listened to conversations on two different levels.

"Well good for you."

He smiled with his eyes, still looking ahead. "Jealous?"

"Spare me."

A flight attendant breezed by with a pillow and offered it to an older woman.

"I choose not to mate with them."

I mouthed the word *mate*. Did he mean sex? *Surely not*. It must be their word for wife, or girlfriend, because there was no way in hell Logan was a celibate man.

He chuckled softly. "I use that term loosely. We date around."

"Well you're not dating me."

"Did I miss the part where I hit on you, or is that your way of asking me to?"

Long legs weren't meant for small seats, so he stretched one out in the aisle.

"You nauseate me."

Impatient fingers tapped on the armrest. "I never date females with your dark hair and height."

"What's wrong with my height?"

"Have you ever laid eyes on a female Chitah? They're the stuff legends are made of."

The man was trying to rile me up.

"Are you saying you choose not to mate them or... *mate* them?" I made invisible quotation marks with my fingers.

"Still stuck on that, are we? All Chitah have a kindred spirit, but a few choose to settle with a suitable mate. I have never chased after a woman, for they are too busy chasing after me."

"Player."

"We all play the field, my dear."

"What happens if you settle, and along comes your soul mate?"

"I wouldn't wish that on my worst enemy," he said. "If a Chitah settles, it will be for love. It's not a decision we take lightly, knowing our kindred could appear at any time. We can have young, but most of us wait."

"You didn't answer my question, Mr. Cross."

He gave me an enigmatic stare through the corner of his eyes and rubbed at his jaw.

"Are you really that interested?" He folded his fingers. "We may spend a lifetime searching and never find our Chitah kindred. A male knows her on sight. His desire for her becomes an unquenchable thirst, an undeniable need; he will want her just as sure as he draws breath and will lay down his life for her." Logan sighed. "She does not feel the same pull, so the male must prove himself worthy to her. Nothing comes easy in life. He will always want his kindred, whether she accepts him or not."

This didn't answer my question, and I had a feeling he was avoiding it by giving me details.

Logan absently pulled a lock of hair free from the ponytail. "Every three years, we hold an event called the Gathering. Chitah from all territories come together in search of their other half. The odds are favorable, I've seen it happen."

"All those women, and you haven't found a match? Sounds like you're not getting lucky."

He thinned out his expression. "You choose to see what you want to see, but I *choose* not to take any of the women who throw themselves at me."

"Wow, that's confidence." I laughed. "Be sure to give me a heads up the next time women are throwing themselves at you, I wouldn't want to get knocked unconscious in the melee."

"To admit it is not ego." He shifted closer and spoke in a private voice. "You may not admit it, but you can't deny that men chase you."

"Chase all they want, I'm too fast."

Logan arched a brow.

"I smell their desire. Adam is thick with it. Perhaps you are fast, but you will eventually tire of running."

"You make it sound like they all want me."

"All males lust for the female; it's primal. It doesn't mean they want to marry you; some just want to bed you."

"Justus isn't like that."

"Yes, he's an interesting fellow. He's protective of you and I respect that."

"And it proves that I can have a man in my life without having a relationship with him."

"You share a relationship with everyone in your life, only on different levels."

I felt his heated gaze and pushed my fingers over the puppet's eyes. "I *know* that, I meant the boyfriend kind."

"Why do you play hide-and-seek with your heart? Haven't you ever been loved?"

The paper bag slipped from my fingers and dropped between the seats.

Logan took a deep breath, squinting as if something stung his eyes. Part of me hated him for that. It was no better than someone reading my mind.

"That was not love, Silver. It doesn't count."

I listened to the hum of the engine and pretended I was a million miles away. The real turbulence was going on inside, where my emotions snapped like the contents of a soda bottle that had been shaken, not stirred.

"Don't speak to me about love; you don't know anything about my life. For the record—I don't care about love, because love never cared about me."

I tried to sound like none of it mattered, but it came out angry and hurt. I blinked and felt the sting of tears. Going home was resurfacing old feelings I had buried long ago. I sprang up from my seat, stumbling over his legs as I ran up the aisle with a storm of black hair whipping behind me.

I slammed the bathroom door and stared at the metal sink.

"Don't you even think about crying," I spat.

It felt like the Atlantic fucking Ocean was crashing over me in relentless waves. I glared at myself in the mirror. The wide collar of my green shirt revealed a splotchy red chest, which matched my face. Strands of hair stuck to my tear-stained cheeks. I was a mess, and no one was going to see me have a meltdown, especially not Logan.

I hated him—hated that he knew what buttons to push. I was

too strong to be this weakened by a four-letter word like love. Turning the faucet, I splashed cold water on my face.

Knuckles lightly rapped against the door.

"Occupied."

Drops of water clung to the tip of my nose, and I wondered why it was so hard to let go of my past. My human life clung to me like tiny invisible cobwebs.

"If you don't open this door, I'm going to break it in and get us arrested by the air marshal," he promised. "Try me, because I will."

I reached with one hand and released the latch as I leaned on the sink basin. Logan squeezed inside the tight space and shut the door.

I didn't lift my eyes to meet his gaze as I stared at the drain.

Without a word, he wrapped his strong arms around my stomach and waist, lying flush against my back. Logan held me like it mattered, and I looked at him through the mirror as he eased his head into the crook of my neck.

"What are you doing?" I protested.

Before my ears registered the sound—my body felt it. A soothing vibration deep within his chest rolled through me, calming me on a level I couldn't comprehend. It was as if the problems of the world melted away in his arms and all I felt was safety, compassion, and warmth. A man I barely knew gave me comfort, asking for nothing in return.

I closed my eyes, lowered my head, and accepted his offer.

After a few moments, I collected myself and straightened up. I watched him through the mirror as he reached around, pulling my hair back and detaching the strands that clung to my face. He was gentle and tender, and not at all as I imagined him to be.

"I forget myself—that you were once human. You will toughen with the years."

I turned around. "Like a steak?"

His eyes hooded. "Mmm, and I like mine rare."

"Well I'm rare, that's for sure."

Logan stepped forward, and his fingers grazed my wrist. "Look at me, Silver."

I studied the laces on his sneakers and noticed they were double knotted.

When he moved closer, our legs touched. It was a strange thing to notice when I should have been more concerned about what I was feeling about it.

He lifted my chin with the tip of his finger. "It takes courage to look into the eyes of a Chitah."

I felt the warm insistence of his body and I licked my lips, staring at his mouth. "You make me nervous."

"*Look at me*," he whispered. When I did, something raw flashed in those golden eyes and he stroked my cheek, collecting the last drop of water.

"How did someone like you become a killer?" I asked.

He shrugged with his brows. "I work independently, and I do what it takes to get a job done."

"It was more than a job when you came to me that night; you were *enjoying* it."

"I always enjoy stalking my prey."

"Then why didn't you kill me?"

"Guilt has a scent. Evil deeds have a distinct fragrance—a perfume that you don't wear." His voice lifted an octave. "You also forget that I was not there to kill you, but to retrieve you."

"You could have just given me over to those men."

His face soured as he pushed away. Logan seemed impossibly taller. When I glanced up, the tips of his fangs peeked through. Not all the way, but just enough that I noticed.

"How many Mage do you think have challenged me the way you did? You're fierce-hearted, which is not a common trait I see in your kind. So unlike our females," he said, lowering his eyes to my mouth. "Would you answer the truth to one question?"

I lifted a shoulder.

"When you kissed me back, was it only for your freedom?"

I remembered the moment I gave in, the way his lips warmed against mine. Deep down, I felt guilty. Not just for offering such a thing to Logan, but for wanting it myself.

A powerful heady scent struck with sudden force and filled the room—one that was dark and attractive. It played tricks on my senses as I had a brief flash of our bodies tangling and…

I shoved him back with my hand, pushing just enough power

in him to sting. "Oh, *no*. Do NOT put your scent on this airplane; there's not enough air freshener in Baltimore that could cover that up!"

I squeezed out of the door, shutting him in the bathroom, where he remained the rest of the flight.

CHAPTER 19

"**S**TOP FIDGETING."

"Easy for you to say. You're not the one wearing a Band-Aid masquerading as a skirt," I said.

Logan chuckled and dipped his nose into the glass of brandy. We sat beside each other at the bar, and he stared straight ahead. "If his weakness is legs, then a look at *your* gams should send him to his knees."

When it comes to women, all men have a personal preference. Marco enjoyed long legs and blue eyes. I spent an hour shaving and moisturizing. I couldn't do a damn thing about my eyes because I refused to wear contacts. He also preferred blond hair, but not exclusively. Justus hand-selected my outfit knowing what would lure him—a formfitting white dress with delicate embroidered designs, short enough to show skin, but long enough to show class. Of course, he might have been more impressed by the price tag.

"Could you disappear for a while?"

"He won't see my eyes," Logan said, hunched over. "I'm a man who knows how to keep a low profile. Can you sense what I am? No, because all of the energy these humans are throwing off will dull it out."

True, a Mage could sense a subtle difference in the energy between a human and Breed, but it wasn't sharp enough to detect in such a crowd. That's how Logan managed to get close to all of his victims.

"You're making me nervous, and I can't pretend to be sexy when I'm nervous."

Logan eased out of his seat and reached over me to place a tip on the bar. His body brushed against mine as he spoke in a low voice. "I'll be near."

When Logan cleared out of sight, I held my breath and flared. I released a little more energy than usual. I thought that might grab his attention and I kept a low vibe going, making it easier for him to find me.

I frowned at my posture reflected in a mirror behind the bar. I needed to channel Sunny. She could look sophisticated in a pair of bunny slippers. I swiveled my hips around and leaned against the bar, exposing my legs to the open room.

"You are one fine looking specimen," a man with a southern drawl said.

"Not interested."

I knew he was local by the tattered shirt that read: Bull riders do it in 8 seconds. He was also blocking my view, so I waved a dismissive hand.

"Buy you a drink?"

"No thanks."

"I ain't seen you in here before. Don't worry, I don't bite."

Inside those unfashionably tight jeans was a reason for me to throw a drink in his face. My skirt left a peek-a-boo opening in front, but with the black undies, you couldn't see a thing. It still left the male mind to wander, and his mind didn't just go astray, but fell off a goddamn cliff.

"I'm gay."

"I'll call your bluff."

"I'm not playing hard to get; I'm *impossible* to get. Why don't you go chase the honey over there who's eyeing your ass like gold?"

His tan shirt stretched as he turned to look. He clucked his tongue. "Been there, done *that*."

There was no way to contain my frustrated sigh. "What do you want?"

His finger pressed my knee, "Your legs over my shoulders."

"Good evening," a voice interrupted. "Would you be so kind as to leave the premises immediately? Do so, and I will allow you to return." His accent was as smooth as ice cream—Italian ice cream.

"Yeah? Says who?"

"The owner of this establishment."

The cowboy wasn't as dumb as he looked. He tucked his tail between his legs and turned away.

I remembered Marco from the brief introduction Sunny gave me, but he didn't look this polished. He was wearing jeans at the time, a detail I recall only because I spilled a drink on them. It was easy to see why Sunny fell for Marco; his hair was glossy black and he trimmed his beard close to his face—just a step above a five o'clock shadow. Thick eyebrows were dangerously close to joining in the middle, and his complexion was the most luminous shade of golden brown. The sun didn't just kiss his skin—it made slow, passionate love to it. Everything about the way he dressed and smelled reminded me of Justus.

Marco was definitely not my type.

I didn't make eye contact. Aloof was the way to go. He liked the chase, and I was going to give it to him.

"I overheard your conversation. I cannot tolerate a man who lacks manners. Do tell me—*impossible* to get?" he smirked. "You challenge a man with those words, as you do the lesbian remark. Although, that is more of a cherry on the sundae. If you really want to know how to make a man lose interest, I can teach you the art of rejection."

I had a feeling this man rejected women all the time.

"What would you have suggested?"

"Pretend you're interested, of course. Be sure to bore him with the details of your previous lovers, and your passion for scrapbooking. I am Marco De Gradi, and you are?"

"Silver."

"You are welcome here, Mage. Business or pleasure?"

"Is there a difference?" I mused, twisting around to face the bar again. "Do they serve Pinot here, or is it just another bar?"

I had never tasted Pinot in my life, but I was following Justus's orders. I was also staring at my white dress in the reflection and having second thoughts.

"Allow me." Marco snapped his finger and exchanged a nod with the bartender. He returned with two glasses and a bottle.

"I think you'll prefer this Burgundy."

I held the glass by the stem and let it slide down my throat. I probably should have swirled it, smelled it, or splashed it behind my ears. Damn Justus. I just couldn't pull off sophistication.

"Mmm, very nice," I lied.

He stroked the stem of his glass as if he had other things on his mind. Marco looked me over as if he appreciated what he saw, but the longer we talked, the more disinterested he became. Maybe looks weren't enough. I didn't dwell.

"Is managing a bar your bread and butter?"

One eye drooped. He felt the judgment in my tone. "I am an entrepreneur."

"Ah. Well, nice… *bar.*" I waved a hand.

"You have a very wicked tongue. I collect *many* businesses—including three restaurants, a hotel, and an elite club."

That was his opportunity to boast, because Justus said he was a braggart. I peered at him over my shoulder. "Without the Mageri, funding for such investments becomes challenging, don't you think?"

Marco smoothed his hair with the palm of his hand. I was to raise suspicion without revealing all my cards; Simon called it cat and mouse tactics. In order to discuss the benefactor, we had to be alone. Marco needed time to become paranoid, and I knew I accomplished that goal when he began grinding his teeth.

"Thank you again for the drink, Mr. De Gradi. I want to mingle for a while."

I shot him a cunning smile and eased out of my chair with practiced precision. With a slink of my hips, I immersed into the crowd to strike up a conversation with two women so he could dissect our conversation.

It was strange talking to humans again, and I felt the disconnect Justus once mentioned. There's a hardwired need to be around our own kind. Plus, I couldn't relate to half of the TV shows and songs they mentioned.

I wasted hours talking to strangers, hoping Marco would reappear. A few women complimented my expensive perfume, but not one man approached me. Logan was inconspicuously sitting in a booth, nursing a glass of brandy with his head kept low. He could have passed for a human the way he slumped over the table, face barely visible behind the long strands of hair.

"Did you get lucky?" I sank in the leather seat across from him and grinned. "I didn't hear a stampede."

"The night is still young," he suggested, biting the rim of his glass.

I lowered my voice to a whisper. "Screw Justus and his insider tips; I guess I wasn't Marco's type. He didn't chase me like they said he would, and I played hard to get."

"*That* I believe."

I wadded up a napkin and flicked it across the table.

"Excuse me, Miss?" I turned my neck and looked up at an older man with stormy eyes. "Mr. De Gradi instructed me to deliver this message to you."

He placed a small envelope in my hand and walked away.

"Open it."

I pinched the edges of the fine paper and pulled it out.

You have made quite an impression—but no one is impossible.

Dinner tomorrow at 8pm. Join me.

—De Gradi

I dipped my finger in the envelope and found a small business card with an address.

"Thank God he's not a breast man."

⟢═❈❦❈═⟢

The city was ours for the rest of the evening. I rolled down the windows of our cheap maroon rental car and gave Logan a tour of my old stomping grounds. We drove by my old office, looked inside of my favorite ice cream parlor, and passed by the sandwich shop I used to hide away in. The car rolled to a stop on an old street lined with large oak trees. Jagged cracks ran along the sidewalks, and the mailboxes were in need of repair. I could almost see myself running across the lawn chasing fireflies.

"Why are we here?" Logan asked. "Is there something special about this place?"

I stared at the house across the street with pale green siding and a screen door. The pink crepe myrtles were in need of a trim, and two pots blushing with begonias sat on the front porch.

Logan flipped off the lights and I got out of the car. The night air felt good against my skin and the honeysuckle was in bloom. Spring never felt more profound than it did in the south.

I leaned against the door, tucking my hands under my arms, staring at my childhood home. God, how small it seemed. Logan stood beside me and stretched his arm over the hood.

"What are we looking at?" he asked.

All he saw was a house. All I saw were memories.

"I had my first kiss by that window," I said with a nostalgic smile. "His name was Danny, and he wore braces. Mom locked me outside to teach me a lesson, and I slept on that porch until dawn. When I was seven, I split my lip on a tire swing in the backyard, and I used to run through the sprinklers on hot summer afternoons. After I left home, I visited mom and helped her with the yard a lot. You've always been a Chitah, but I know what I'm missing out on."

"What of *that* life are you truly giving up?" he asked, leaning against the car.

"Not having someone trying to kill me, for one."

"Humans are killed all the time," he replied.

"Having children."

He had no counter for that; Mage could not have children. I never really thought much about having kids, but having that option stolen from me brought an unexpected sadness.

Logan rested his head on top of mine. When something brushed against my leg, I looked down, squinting in the dark.

Meow? It asked.

Two eyes looked up at me—one green and one yellow.

"Max!"

I scooped up the big cat in my arms, forgetting that I wasn't Zoë anymore. Max didn't like strangers; hell, that cat didn't care much for anyone. He let out another demanding groan, and I jerked my neck back, worried he might take a swipe at me. Instead, Max loved me up with an affectionate head-butt.

"Looks like this one knows you."

I nuzzled my face in his fur. "What are you doing outside, panther boy? Doesn't my mom know you're an indoor cat?" I kissed his head and set him down.

Max circled my feet and I smiled sadly. Logan squatted down and made a peculiar chirping sound that had an immediate reaction from Max, who rubbed against his knee as if they were old pals.

Logan stood up with my cat in his arms, scratching his head. "Jiminy. He's a *big* boy."

I brushed away the hairs from my face. "I can't believe he knows me."

"He knows you because he loves you."

Logan flattened the soft ears with a single stroke. Seeing my cat sharpened the pain of the life I left behind—the person I once was. This trip was closure for me, something I needed.

Max purred and I closed my eyes, reminiscing. The wind brushed through the trees and a cricket sang a one-note melody. It was a distant song of my forgotten life, drifting on the winds of my past. It was fading over time, becoming lost to me. One day—maybe hundreds of years from now—all of this would be gone. I lifted Max from Logan's arms.

"I'll always love you." I kissed his nose and placed him on the warm concrete. He looked up with those needy eyes, and before I became upset, I walked around the car and got inside.

When the engine started, Max flashed across the road like a shadow and was gone. My heart sank, and I hoped he would have a good life with lots of tuna. I already knew my Ghuardian's stance on pets, and he would never allow it. Perhaps he was right, and I had to let go.

Logan rubbed the corner of his eye with the heel of his hand. "Tomorrow night when you meet with Marco, I'll be outside on the grounds. I want you to stay near the windows."

"Just don't blow my cover. I hope he still keeps in touch with the benefactor."

"Maybe you should look inside his drawers for Christmas cards." Logan punched the accelerator and we headed back to the hotel.

A television in my room was the equivalent of dying and going to heaven. I stayed up all night watching movies.

In the morning, I ordered pancakes with sausages and slept until noon. Eventually, I shuffled out of bed and dragged my feet across the tight fibers of the carpet when something caught my eye. Sitting in front of the door was a white slip of paper. I reached down and snapped it up with two fingers.

> *Change of plans. Meet with me at your earliest convenience.*
>
> *Do not bring your friend.*
>
> *-De Gradi*

Marco knew Logan was with me, but I couldn't be sure if he had us followed to my mother's house. I didn't like that he peeked at my cards before I was ready to show my hand.

Logan was in the hotel room next door. Because he was more attuned to scent—and I had no idea how sensitive it was—I put Marco out of my head while getting dressed. I didn't want to risk bringing Logan if it meant jeopardizing my only opportunity to get information.

Marco lived in an exclusive neighborhood—the kind with a gated property and long driveways. The train took me far enough that I could walk the rest of the way. My finger pushed the call button and the gate clicked open.

As I walked along the driveway, I noticed that a lot of money went into designing his mansion. The landscaping alone would have cost more than a year's rent at my old apartment. The lawn smelled freshly cut, and the tall trees swayed overhead like watchful giants. I squinted from the bright sunlight and rang the doorbell. The same older man who presented me with the invitation opened the door.

"Come this way. Mr. De Gradi is expecting you," he said flatly. I captured a strong scent of lemon when I stepped inside.

My heels clicked against the glassy floor and I paused when I entered a spacious room. The windows were tremendous, and had not a smudge on them. The focal point was a grand piano where Marco sat. His fingers lightly stroked the keys, and a haunting melody of no particular origin sent chills up my spine.

"I should apologize for the change in plans, but I won't. I am a busy man, and have no—"

"Well if you are too busy to keep your engagements, then I'll leave."

That pompous attitude just rubbed me the wrong way and, Justus be damned, I turned around and walked out. The melody trailed on as I approached the front door. The sudden change in plans and his elusive behavior made me uneasy.

Marco flashed across the room and blocked my exit. "Who are you with and what brings you here?"

"Your invitation brought me here."

He folded his arms and pinched at his beard. "Explain your business in my bar."

"I was ordering a drink. Is that a crime?"

Marco angered at my literal answers. "If you were a man I would have knocked you on the floor. I have no patience for lies, so I am offering you one last chance to speak the truth."

"I was sent."

His expression fell. "Who sent you?"

"Who do you *think*?"

I mirrored his stance, widening my legs and folding my arms.

"Don't play games with me. Why are you here?"

"I don't think he would appreciate me breaking his confidence, do you? These are private business affairs; you're just the detour."

Marco drew a sharp intake of air and I took that as my cue to walk around him and reach for the door.

His voice rang out like the sound of a gunshot in a church, echoing a name I had longed to hear, that when it fell upon my ears, I went deaf.

"Nero has not paid in full, you tell him that."

My fingers loosened from the knob… trembling. *Nero*, my mind whispered. "Not all obligations were filled."

"I did what he asked!" he shouted. "He cannot blame me for Samil's failure. I found her, and that was my job."

"Samil is dead," I said, looking over my shoulder.

Marco blanched and stepped back.

"I don't believe it. How?"

I lightly shrugged, staring at the brass knob on the door. "Sometimes people get what's coming to them."

I grew nervous about staying a minute longer when no one knew where I was. I had the name I needed, and that was enough.

"Samil was the only Creator who could make one so strong. I cannot believe Nero would have done this—no matter how much he despised him, Nero is not a stupid man. Samil was far too valuable a Mage to dispose of. His ability was one we had never seen."

"Marco, I'm not here to threaten you. I was curious what a failure looked like up close. Now that I know, I have other matters to attend to."

CHAPTER 20

"LIKE I SAID BEFORE, I can handle myself. I don't need your permission to do anything, Mr. Cross." Logan hated it when I used his last name, so I made a conscious effort to do it when I was upset with him.

I slid my beer on the smooth surface of the bar, waiting for his reply. With the sudden change in plans, our evening was free. I suggested a trip to a local dive for a few drinks. It would be nice to unwind and have a little fun. I might as well enjoy it; once I returned to Cognito, my social life would be at a crawl.

"You seem to forget that you are just an obstinate young Mage, ill-equipped to handle yourself around one more experienced," Logan said.

"Stop using fancy words, they're unbecoming on your tongue."

Logan was pissed when he shouted his whisper. "I gave my word to your Ghuardian that I would watch over you because he said you have a tendency to skip right into the arms of trouble."

Well, that just disgusted me. "He said that?"

"Now you've put me in a position where my integrity is in question."

"Integrity? Exactly who are you to me? You're not my Ghuardian, brother, best friend, lover—"

Logan spun out of his seat and stalked off, flicking his hand in the air. I took a disgusted sip of my drink and did a little growling of my own.

My phone began to vibrate.

"Hello?"

"Er... ows... eating you?"

"Hold on, Simon, I can't hear you," I shouted, moving into a quiet hallway. "Sorry, the music is loud so speak up. Are you there?"

"Having a good time? Just promise me you'll stay off the dance floor, love. Don't worry, I won't tell Justus as long as you don't end up on the news for sparking half of the city. I know we spoke earlier, but I'm guessing you're alone now?"

"I'm alone. Why?"

"Do you think you can arrange another meeting? I want to ruffle his feathers a little more. It might stir him up enough that he'll come back to Cognito."

"I can try, but he doesn't like me very much."

Simon gave me a quick rundown of a few more questions, so it would not be a wasted opportunity with the remaining time we had. I could sense his frustration, as he would have done a far better job interrogating the man. He wanted to mention Justus, in hopes of luring him back to Cognito.

"Having fun with Knox?"

"Gigantor plays a mean game of poker."

"Well I'm glad you found a playmate. Maybe the two of you can get your freak on with a game of Twister. I'll call you later."

I tucked the phone in my back pocket and made a beeline for the bar. A boisterous laugh slipped out when I thought about Knox and Simon tangled up, reaching for a color, when Knox slips and crushes Simon like a bug. My thoughts cut off when I crashed into someone.

"I'm so sorry!" I clung to his shirt before I lost my balance.

"Watch your step."

Every hair on my arm stood on end when he spoke.

In a past life, I was much shorter and weaker. I changed, but he didn't. The military haircut was still his thing. He always wore sleeveless shirts to show off a vile dragon tattoo that crawled down his arm like a demon in a nightmare. He still wore the same cheap cologne.

With a twist of my arm, I broke the grip he had on me.

"Do I know you?" he asked, narrowing a pair of hazel eyes at me.

The minute they locked on mine, I was Zoë Merrick. Time crawled, as if everyone around us moved at a slower speed.

Brandon was my ex-boyfriend who chiseled me down to a woman who would never trust again. Words tangled in my mouth, and when he reached out with his thick fingers, I slapped his hand.

"Bitch," he muttered, turning on a heel to walk away.

I stood alone in the center of the room with my feet glued to the floor like cement blocks. My heart was a banging drum against my chest, and I could feel my hands shaking. The faces blurred and the music pounded against my shoes like sledgehammers. A current of energy scattered throughout my body like fragmented pieces of a broken past, and I took a slow breath to control it.

One focal point drew my attention above all else. It centered me, and became my northern star before I went adrift.

Golden eyes cut across the room like glass. It was with perfect clarity I saw Logan extract himself from a conversation, stalking across the room until he filled the empty space in front of me.

"Who frightens you?"

"I want to go home."

Logan bent down so that our cheeks touched, and his breath warmed my ear. His voice grew softer, and more dangerous. "Which one is he?"

The growl barely registered, but I heard it.

"I don't know what you mean."

He tilted my chin up with his finger, delicately lifting a scent in the air. Hooded eyes masked the obsidian color that was swelling in the center.

"Emotions are like flavors," he said, stepping in closer. "They blend, and only a skilled Chitah can interpret their meaning. Your scent tells me everything. It's thick like a forest after the rain. This is the same emotion you threw off on the airplane—anger and shame. Only now, it mingles with a sharp scent that burns my eyes. I know that scent... *all* Chitah know the smell of fear." He sniffed lightly.

His thirsty eyes scanned the crowd, darting from one face to the next. When I turned around, he gripped my shoulders and pulled me against him.

Resting his chin on my head, he asked in a soothing voice, "Whose scent is all over you?"

His nose circled through my hair.

"This is not on the agenda."

Showing no expression, he surged into the crowd, dipping his head by each person he passed. A hard swallow seized my throat when he reached Brandon, who was leaning on the bar and cupping a shot of whiskey. Breed rules dictated we could not reveal ourselves in front of humans, nor harm them intentionally as they were a weaker species.

Logan was a man who didn't play by the rules.

He smiled warmly, looking in my direction before he inched forward and lowered his chin. Brandon stood up, but immediately turned his face away as if burned by the heat of Logan's searing gaze. Not even a human could withstand the malice in a Chitah's eyes.

"No need to memorize my face. You'll be seeing it again," Logan promised.

Brandon was the coward I always knew him to be, and chose not to confront the stranger. I expected Logan to do more, but he took my hand and escorted me back to the hotel.

Brandon was the biggest mistake of my life. He liked to dress like a soldier, even though he wasn't one. As it turns out, he was just a control freak.

We briefly dated, but it wasn't until we moved in together that I saw his teeth. It destroyed me, because I *chose* him. After that, I doubted every decision I made. Sunny took me in when my own mother would not, and while she wasn't an emotional rock, she baked delicious pies and made me laugh again.

Nothing spells misery like a large pizza and an action flick. I needed bullets, blood, and mayhem. I replayed the scene at the bar in my head a dozen times, and wished I could have done things differently. In a matter of seconds, that man stripped away all of the tough layers I had worked so hard to build. Logan sensed the obvious shift in my mood and we went to our separate rooms. After greedily stuffing my face, I dozed off on my stomach with my feet on the pillows.

The flickering lights from the television forced me to turn my head towards the air conditioner and an icy breeze cooled my cheek. Then I became aware of a heavy weight and warmth across my lower body. I was stunned when I looked over my shoulder. Logan was unconscious and draped across me like a boa constrictor. Legs entwined around mine, and I was no longer able to tell where he began and I ended. A long arm tucked around my hip, while the other stretched down the length of my arm, clasping my hand. We were like chocolate covered pretzels, and Logan was the chocolate.

"Get *off* of me."

He groaned, flopping onto his back with a fierce stretch. "What time is it?"

"It's time for you to explain what you're doing in my bed uninvited, Mr. Cross." I glared at him.

He languidly rolled to his side, resting his cheek over a bicep. "Why are you so formal with me?"

"Why are you so *informal* with me?"

Logan was not able to conceal a smile, deciding to address my previous question. "The scent of food drew me in. I finished off your leftovers and watched you sleep. Your skin had those little goose pimples," he said, running a finger down my arm. I shivered, and this seemed to please him.

"You could have covered me with a blanket."

"Why would I do that when I can offer the heat you need?"

Silence.

A shadow caught my attention. "What is that stain on your shirt? Is that... *blood*?"

When he didn't answer, I sat up. "Where did you go tonight?"

"Hunting."

"For what?"

"What all men thirst for—justice."

I knew. He didn't have to tell me. Logan went back for Brandon and alarm ran up my spine.

"What did you *do*?"

"Nothing that wasn't deserved."

"Did you kill him?" I almost shrieked.

Logan chuckled. "Would you like me to? Killing him wouldn't be half as fun."

"You're no different than him."

"Not true, Little Raven, because when I hit someone, they *deserve* it."

A knot tightened in my stomach. "There were a hundred men in the bar tonight. Maybe you caught the wrong man."

Logan sat up and leaned forward on his knuckles. He could barely restrain the pride on his tongue.

"I am studious in my efforts. Never doubt my skills, young Mage. I'm a born hunter, and a male who takes his birthright seriously."

"How badly did you hurt him?"

An animalistic sound erupted as he pulled air into his lungs.

"All this for a guy who broke my heart."

"I have it on good authority that he broke more than your heart."

I blinked, and lowered my eyes. "We all make mistakes."

"And some will pay a hefty price," he said, regarding me with strict eyes. "The mistake was not yours; it was his. Men like that should be weeded from the garden before they destroy all the flowers."

I fell back and stared at the ceiling.

"Tell me you're mad, and I'll know if you're lying," he said.

Logan ran his hand across my forehead, smoothing out my hair. "You have every right to push men away as you do. When you know the way a woman has been treated—or mistreated—you understand her in a way that didn't make sense. Lay with me tonight."

Before I could turn my saucer wide eyes towards him, he touched my lips with his finger. "I'm not asking for what you think. Say yes—lay with me and let me have one night to sleep beside my enemy."

In the back of my mind, I heard Justus warning me to keep my distance. His reasons didn't seem good enough, and lately, neither did mine. If Logan meant to bring me harm, he could have done so when he was twist-tied to my body not moments ago. The same curiosity he expressed was one that even I couldn't deny. The more time we spent together, the more he confounded me.

"You have my word that I will never hurt you. Keep your fingertips charged and on standby if you don't trust me," he chuckled.

I nodded.

Logan piqued my curiosity as a Chitah, and as a man. I sharpened my light—just in case.

He sat up and peeled his shirt over his head.

"Wait a minute!"

"Would you rather curl up to his blood? That might actually please me."

"No," I said, watching the fabric fall to the floor. "Just keep your pants on."

When Logan looked at my clothes, I avoided eye contact. I didn't own a collection of adorable gowns and pajamas. I slept in tank tops and boy shorts. They weren't lace or silk, but something told me he liked them when his eyes lingered on the paw print design stitched on the left side.

Logan pulled the sheet away like a child opening gifts on Christmas.

"I have a few rules about sleeping together."

His laughter echoed in the room as he punched a fist into the pillow, softening it. "This should be good."

"Clothes remain on."

"What little we have, yes, that's doable."

"Keep your hands off of body parts, including your own."

This time he smothered his face in the pillow and laughed uncontrollably. I almost wanted to laugh at myself, but men always found sneaky ways around rules.

"Finally, no dirty talk. This isn't an open invitation; I'm not a perk of any deal you made with Simon."

"Cross my heart. You have my word I will not touch you inappropriately." Logan turned to his side, rubbing the short whiskers on his chin. "I never thought I would want to sleep with a Mage."

"What possessed you?" I asked, pulling the cover beneath my arm.

"I like to live dangerously, so please follow your own rules. I think we both know what you can do with your hands."

I smiled. "Why do you despise us so much?"

He let go of a deep sigh and rolled on his back. "A Mage killed my mate."

I turned to face him. "I thought you didn't have a mate."

"I did once… a long time ago." Logan absently stroked his chest and when his eyes drifted upward, I saw him for the first time, not just the outer shell of a hardened man. "Her beauty was unmatched and I courted her for years before she accepted me. I was young and made foolish mistakes. I fell in debt with a Mage, and when I didn't give him what he asked for, he took her life as payment." Anger flickered behind his eyes, but it was distant, buried beneath years of violence all in the name of revenge.

"He knew she carried our young." Logan's lips peeled back in anger.

The room fell so silent that even my heart took pause. Logan not only lost a woman, but an unborn child.

"How long does a Chitah live?"

"I'm not as old as most, but let's just say that I could have played poker with your great-great granddaddy. We have a natural ability to heal, just as you have your own healing magic. But we do age with time, just *very* slowly."

"Do you only have one soul mate?"

"Yes, there is only one Chitah that is our perfect pairing."

I touched the end of his pillow. "I want to apologize for what I said to you on the plane, about not finding a mate at the Gathering. If I knew about your past, I would have never said something so callous."

"Your spirited words did not offend me."

"I mean it."

He turned his head, but couldn't lift his eyes. "I loved her, Silver. Deeply. I would have raised young and lived a good life, but that was not in the fates. She was not my kindred spirit, but it doesn't erase the fact that I adored her."

I learned more about Logan in a single conversation than the entire time we had spent together. He was so direct and willing to share his pain, whereas most people were closed off. He chose a woman who was not his soul mate, eager to start a family with her. I felt selfish for pining over my cat and a tire swing when this man gave up his family to the arms of death. The pieces locked into place, and I knew why he hated my kind.

"Would you have left your family if you had found your soul mate?"

"In the time I was with her I would have said no, never."

"Said, but what would you have done? I'm not doubting you loved her. I guess I'm just curious if—"

"If what?"

"If that whole soul mate crap is true."

Eloquently said, but the thought of predestined lovers was a bunch of bullshit.

"I once had my doubts." He laced his fingers across his stomach and closed his eyes.

"Why should Chitah's have the market cornered on soul mates? If such a thing existed, then we would all have them and the world would be a happier place.

Logan rolled to his side and propped his head in the palm of his hand. "You are a very pessimistic female. Humans have a larger pool of people to fish through and a shorter amount of time. Who's to say that it's exclusive to my kind? Look at your friend; she's a perfect example of how such things are possible. Can they explain their attraction, their connection? No, but it's undeniable." He pinched his lip between his fingers, watching me. "Have you ever binded with another Mage?"

Two words with different meanings exist among Mage: bonding and binding. Bonding is something that couples do to make their relationship more permanent—like marriage—and includes markings of some kind. Binding involves the sharing of sexual energy and emotions by exchanging light through a current in our hands. It can be part of sex, or separate from it. Binding is an exclusive sharing of light like no other.

A warm blush touched my face. Simon and I twirled in the sheets after a night of drinking and shared a little light. Who hasn't?

"You're getting personal."

"You have opened me like a book, and yet you're unwilling to share your own story?"

"Simon wants me to talk to Marco again."

Logan sensually ran his nose along the line of my neck. "Do you always do what Simon says? I never did care for that childish game." He brushed away a loose strand of hair and changed his tone to an inquisitive one. "*He* was the one you binded with. Why would you give yourself to a man who doesn't want you?"

"That's a little insulting," I said, inching away. "That man hits on me all the time."

I refused to let anyone be a killjoy with the only man who spoiled me with compliments. Simon was a luscious flirt, and I loved him for it.

"There's a difference between men who love to eat, and men who hunt for their food."

Logan allowed me to look at him by turning his eyes away. His features were captivating. For the first time, I noticed faint smile lines carved in his cheek. The color of his hair was darker at the root where the sun didn't lighten it, and his brow ridges left him with a serious expression. I shivered, pulling up the sheet.

"I would never have harmed you when I came to you that night," he said. "I want you to know that. You, Silver, enthralled me with those emerald jewels."

"You shouldn't lie just to get in my pants; it's not polite."

"You aren't wearing any pants."

Before I could protest, he ripped the sheet down, exposing my stomach. My heart matched the beat of a hummingbird as Logan spread himself over my body. The moment his warm skin touched mine, I relaxed. He faced the opposite direction, and while I couldn't see his eyes, I felt his breath on my stomach, and the soft tickle of eyelashes with every blink. I was beginning to put aside my human assumptions and understand him from a Breed perspective.

Besides, who was I to insult the man if he wanted to be a human blanket?

"What do you think of me?" he asked.

His soft hair splayed across my stomach, and I lightly touched the ends. I didn't want him to know that I enjoyed his tenderness.

"I think you might be a better man than you allow yourself to be."

"Maybe this is all that I am."

Silence filled the space between us, and several minutes passed.

"Keep running," he finally said.

Puzzled by his statement I tilted my head. "Running from what?"

Logan cleared his throat. "Never settle. Make the men in your life run for it; if they tire of the chase, then they're not worth your affections."

"What if someone keeps chasing?"

"Then you will tire and be caught," he replied. "And that's called settling."

My body flushed from his warmth. He was everywhere.

"So what do you suggest I do?"

"Turn around and face them head on. *Choose.* The female always holds the power, so first make them run for it, then make them wait."

"I make bad choices," I mumbled.

"Give yourself credit," he chuckled. "No one is perfect."

"I'm lying in bed with a man who kidnapped me. You were saying?"

"Fate brought us together for a reason; there are no accidents. Everything that happens in our lives leads us to a greater destiny, even if we don't always understand the purpose."

"Maybe you're deceiving me. I haven't said anything up until now, but I don't completely trust your intentions. I'm stupidly lying in bed with you and I can't explain my actions, but part of me wants to give you the benefit of the doubt. The other part will destroy you if you hurt me, or anyone I love."

"My word was enough for your Ghuardian. Why is it not enough for you?"

"Maybe you have to *earn* my trust."

I sighed, scattering some of his hair around with my breath, and Logan shivered. Tiny flutters tickled my skin where he stretched his throat across my belly.

From out of nowhere, a rush surged through my body. It was raw power in the form of Logan's scent. It was like slipping into a hot bath, skydiving, and a passionate kiss all at once.

"Don't do that with me. You can't mark something that isn't yours."

"You are very correct."

A finger circled around my hip, and he whispered words I couldn't hear.

※∗◎∗☀

The next morning, I woke up in a tangle of limbs. Lines marked Logan's face from the wrinkled sheets, and his hair matted up on one side. He walked to the shower and I checked my phone messages, washing away my thirst with a bottle of water.

Logan was whistling in the bathroom, and I smiled. I often sang in the shower, and the two of us would make quite a duo.

A knock at the door yanked me from my thoughts, and I scraped my feet along the rough carpeting. Maid service was going to have to wait. When the door opened, the hallway was empty. I moved to close the door when it was forced open, knocking me back.

Marco stood brazenly in the doorway.

"I do apologize. Did I catch you at a bad time?" He lowered his head and glared at me.

The shower knob turned with a squeak. A split second later, the door swung open and Logan charged out. Water beaded all over his body and pooled on the carpet. Wet hair clung to his face and neck, and a white towel was the only thing he wore.

Marco didn't break eye contact with me.

"Mage, am I to presume that my visit is unexpected?" He clucked his tongue.

Logan twisted his head and looked down at my panties. I hardly cared.

He did.

In the blink of an eye, he ripped the towel away and tied it around my waist, shedding all modesty, as he stood naked.

Marco chuckled in amusement of the show he was being given.

"I'm Logan Cross. What's your business, Mage?" He folded his arms and took an assertive stance in front of me.

Oh and *boy,* was it assertive. Droplets of water glistened over his backside as they made shiny trails down his thighs. He had a fine curve to his spine that dipped in at the waist. The knotted muscles in his back, arms, and broad shoulders made me appreciate his strength. Logan was as naked as his mama made him, and I couldn't help but notice the subtle shift in his lower body as his legs slightly parted.

My eyes dropped to Logan's bare ass. I bit the inside of my cheek, hiding the lust that slammed through me. When he turned his head to the side, his nostrils flared.

Damn him.

I needed to get my emotions in check before our guest inadvertently got more than an eyeful.

Marco eyeballed Logan. "You are not a Mage. I would guess human, except for that distinctly *telltale* scent."

Logan slicked back a mop of wet hair so Marco could see his eyes. It made a smacking sound as water splattered across my face.

Marco stepped back, unable to meet Logan's gaze.

"Mage, when you have dressed and bathed clean of that offensive odor, I will be waiting in the lobby." He barely stepped out of the room when Logan closed the door and turned on his heel.

My eyes memorized the ceiling. Wasn't it too early in the morning for full frontal?

"You're not shy, are you?"

Retrieving his folded clothes from the dresser, he remarked, "Do you see anything I need to be shy about?"

I didn't have an answer for that.

"Marco didn't flare, did he?" Logan slipped into a pair of jeans with an angry yank of the fabric. The cotton shirt went over his head and soaked up the water, sticking to his skin.

Logan was right; Marco should have announced his presence. In fact, he flashed in the hallway in order to sneak up on me and get into the room. Logan combed his fingers through his wet hair several times until the water shook off the ends.

"That's an open threat, Silver. He's letting you know he could have killed you if he wanted, but that he *chose* not to. This is my language and a game I'm familiar with. He wants the upper hand. It may break his little heart, but you're *not* going to give it to him. You're going to put on that beautiful skirt, brush your teeth, pin your hair up, and join me in the lobby."

Logan approached and spoke in a low voice against my temple. "And under no circumstance will you wash my scent off of you."

I shivered when his finger swiped up a drop of water from my cheek.

CHAPTER 21

LOGAN'S PACE WAS DELIBERATELY SLOW as he walked barefoot across the lobby. The Mage sat in a leather chair on an oversized carpet. Marco's arrogance offended Logan, and he took an inconspicuous draw of breath—picking up his scent through the cloud of aftershave and garlic. He sank into the chair across from him, relaxing his elbows on the armrests, and stretching out his long legs. The mental game of intimidation began. When Marco flinched, Logan inclined his head.

"I once knew a Mage who liked unannounced visits," Logan began, "...until, someone paid one to him."

"I have no business with you, Chitah."

"Business with Silver is business with me."

Logan scrutinized Marco with his eyes. His first impression of the man was that he was an overdressed prick who should have lost his tongue for threatening Silver's life. Logan would never harm a female, and he wasn't pleased at the idea that his assignment was to collect one, but he didn't know a damn thing about Marco's intentions.

"You have an abundance of wealth, Mage, but all the expensive soap in the world will never wash innocent blood from your hands."

Marco's annoyance was an acrid flavor against the roof of Logan's mouth. The easiest ones to bait were those with a conscience. He had a little time before Silver would arrive... time to play.

Marco admired his expensive watch, attempting to ignore him.

"It's not everyday I meet a Mage who has turned his back on the Mageri."

"I find that hard to believe when you are fucking one." Marco laughed with an expressive smile as he buffed the face of his watch.

"You are hardly in a position to place judgment. Since when does a Chitah work for a Mage?"

Logan felt the roar of fury rise within him. He tilted his head, allowing humor to seep across his expression.

"Dear oh dear, what must your *progeny* think of you?"

The remark irritated Marco, who understood Logan knew more about him than just his name. Logan was a master of provocation, something he had cultivated over years of practice. Preying on emotions became the undoing of many—all of it deserved.

"Why does a Chitah have his paws in Mage business?"

"I'm here to clean up your mess; you left things rather untidy, didn't you? I'm fascinated that you seem so aloof about it. I bet the confessional booth burns to cinders when you leave each Sunday."

Logan chuckled when the Mage slammed his fist on the table between them.

"I do *not* respond to threats. If that puttana of yours is not showing up, I will be leaving!"

Marco rose from his chair, but Logan immediately blocked him, staring down his nose. Despite their human surroundings, his lower fangs punched out.

"That *what?*"

———————◦●◦◦◦———————

I had little interest in why Logan and Marco looked prepared to fistfight in the middle of the hotel. Logan was a button pusher, and I was too unnerved by Marco's unexpected appearance to care. My long, brown skirt swished in the air as I silently crossed the lobby. I stopped and stared at them poisonously.

"Marco, my friend doesn't like you very much. State your business, and I suggest you do it quickly before he gets manimal on your ass."

Through the corner of my eye, Logan clasped his hands behind his back and moved to the side.

I walked briskly to a vacant chair and sat down with my legs crossed, collecting my thoughts as the soft sound of classical music drifted from the speakers. The chandeliers were a nice touch, as was the fountain near the front desk that drowned out our conversation. Marco claimed the seat next to mine.

"Tell him I have located another potential."

"What could you hope to gain from this pathetic little offering?"

"Something promised to me. Give him the information, as I have not been able to reach Samil."

What could a man of money possibly want? "All this so you can have a position with Nero?"

Marco laughed and replied in a thick, Italian accent, "Tell me, Mage, why are you here? Surely it is not to amuse me."

"Nero wants Zoë."

Marco sank in his chair as he studied the ceiling. "The first time she came into my bar, I knew she was different. Her energy—it was strong for a human."

Why didn't he just pretend to like me instead of Sunny? Why go through her?

"Maybe you aren't right for this job. It seems you're getting too close and frightening them away."

He pointed his index finger on the arm of his chair, "I do not get near them—ever. I would prefer not to know them."

"Then why get involved? Why are you working for Nero? You have money, you claim to not want a position with him, so exactly what is it?"

"I want something in his possession."

"Yes, isn't that always the case?" To my astonishment, he continued.

"A woman. She was… the first. I want to sever ties with Nero, but he uses her against me. I regret my dealings with him, but he's promised to release her if I give him enough potentials of her value."

"How very noble of you—sacrifice innocent lives to claim a stolen girl as your prize."

Marco scowled. "She is *not* a prize."

He slicked his hair back and regained composure.

"Well, it's been grand," I said, standing up as he rose with me. "Our vacation ends today; I'll be sure to relay the information."

Marco came all this way to confront me, and as it turns out, only to offer himself to Nero once more.

"Did you ever consider that if he did give her up, she might not want you?"

I thought he would say something, but Marco stared vacantly at the sculpture on the table as we turned and walked away.

"That went well," I muttered, tossing the room key on the dresser.

Logan opened the drapes and sat in a chair beside the window. The light caught his hair, giving it an ethereal quality. I carefully removed the pins from my own as I watched him through the mirror. Logan noticed every small gesture.

"Manimal?" The corner of his mouth curved up.

I hopped on the bed and fell on my back.

"I couldn't think straight. Blame Simon and all those cheesy movies he makes me watch." I scratched the soft part of my neck behind my ear. "He's ruined all these lives—all for a girl."

"A man in love would stop time if he could."

"Love? I didn't hear that word come out of his mouth. And what about all the innocent people he handed over like cattle? Are their lives so disposable?"

"To him, yes. I sensed his guilt. He lacks honor, but has a conscience."

"Don't pretend to have honor. Keep in mind how we met."

"You're going to throw that at me every chance you get, aren't you? Well just remember where you are, and it's not with Nero." He pulled off the damp shirt and tossed it on the floor.

"Only because someone made you a better deal."

"I've always preferred the better deal. Your arms will tire of holding that grudge," he said, rising to his feet. "Find something better to hold."

Logan stood in front of the dresser, holding a serene expression as he quenched his thirst with a long swallow of water. He screwed the cap back on the bottle and lifted his eyes. "Why do you look at me that way?"

"I'm not used to someone…"

"Say it."

"I've been told I'm difficult, and not everyone handles it as well as you do."

"Is that all?" He cocked his head to one side. "As it so happens, I like your mouth."

"It doesn't—"

"Challenge me?" He set the bottle down and moved to the end of the bed. "An outspoken woman makes the world a livable place. You have fire in you, and I would never put that out."

"Do you think I did okay out there, Logan?"

The bed rocked as he crawled over the blanket and settled on his stomach. I got a little nervous around him, because I never knew what to expect. The way his eyes fixated on my mouth reminded me of how Justus would eye a plate of prime rib.

Minus the bib.

"What is it now?"

A throaty growl escaped. "I love the way you say my name. Say it again."

"Why?"

"Because I asked you to," he said softly.

"Logan," I whispered, "pick up my dirty laundry."

He wasn't buying it—he stopped listening after his name.

"What shall we do with our morning?" he pondered.

I thought about the water from his shower, dripping down his glorious…

"Be right back," he said, leaping off the bed.

I braided a strand of my hair while he made a phone call. The trip was a success, and that boosted my confidence. Being an immortal with super cool abilities lost its shine months ago. I wanted my life to have meaning, because for so many nights lying awake in bed, I felt adrift. At least now, we knew who we were dealing with, and had information on Marco's motives. Nero was still searching for other potentials. Potential what, exactly?

Logan crawled over the bed like a panther.

Instead of doing anything devious, he pulled my feet into his lap. I frowned as the shoes fell to the floor and he caressed the soles, using deep circles with his thumbs. I was highly ticklish and when I pulled my foot away, it roused a satisfied laugh.

"I've never had anyone give me a foot massage."

"Tell me all the things you've never experienced, and I will give them to you."

"Promise?" I asked jokingly. "I've never been with a man wearing a dress."

That snagged his attention.

"Define, *been with*."

My feet were ancient history when he pushed them off his lap and caged me with his arms. His body heat licked me from neck to hip.

"I would put on a ball gown—the kind with a hundred-thousand sequins. Do you want to *be* with me, Little Raven?"

"Not after that mental snapshot." I smiled.

Logan collapsed in the empty space beside me, throwing an arm over his head.

I spent the next half hour dissecting my feelings for Logan and examining them under a microscope. Staring at his profile made me want to know more about him. The events in our lives mark us, carve away the edges, and determine our shape as a sculpture to an artist. The slaying of his mate outlined the course of his life. Had she lived, we would have never met, and I wondered why that mattered. I knew who he was, but now I was starting to understand *why* he was.

Logan got up and paced across the carpet when a light knock interrupted us.

A young man with pale eyes pushed a food cart across the room. Logan tucked a bill in his hand and escorted him out, securing the locks. I bounced on my knees and lifted a silver lid. Sliced fruit filled the dish, while the others contained bacon, eggs, and sausages with a tomato garnish. He poured orange juice in two glasses and buttered a crescent roll. I reached for the last lid when he flattened his hand on top. "Don't be greedy; one thing at a time."

Unlike Adam (who had a conniption at the idea of eating in bed), Logan encouraged my lack of manners. When I licked the crumbs of bacon from my finger, he nodded just a little bit and smiled.

"Tell me about your brothers. Do you see them?"

His face beamed and a slice of cantaloupe vanished between his lips. "Leo is the eldest and watches over us, keeping the family united. I am the second in line, and Levi is third. He's got it the hardest."

"Why is that?"

"Levi is gay," he said with a shrug.

"And?"

"There's an expectation for us to mate and have young. For that reason, many do not accept homosexuals. I have a feeling most don't care what goes on in the bedroom; it's the fact they're turning up their noses at continuing our line. He's dealt with many harsh words in his life, so we keep an eye out for him. Levi has a hot temper, to say the least. Sometimes I think we've accepted him more than he has."

"Who says he can't have any kids?"

"I don't think the world is ready for little Levi's." Logan laughed. "Right now, we'd settle for him finding a male of worth. He's angry because he fears finding his kindred. Destiny or not, that male will never lay with a female." He licked a crumb off his lip.

"Does he date other Chitah?"

Logan shook his head. "Most Chitah in his position buckle under the influence of family and settle for the opposite sex. Could you hand me the cream cheese?"

I hated the break in conversation because I found myself curious to know more about Logan. I loved the way his eyes lit up as he spoke of his family. With no brothers or sisters of my own, I envied the connection.

"Family bonds are strong, and most aren't willing to sever those ties," he said, smearing the knife across his roll. "Levi doesn't date other Chitah, although I'm not sure why that is. He prefers to interbreed—just a loose term we call for *fooling around with the opposite Breed*."

"Is that a bad thing? Justus never talks about social goodies like this, and his books are…"

"Dull?"

I huffed out a short laugh. "Apparently I have a lot to learn about our riveting history, but half of it doesn't exist in books. So tell me, is dating between different Breeds socially acceptable?" I wiped my fingers with the napkin and reached for a few grapes.

"No. Even with humans, there's little tolerance. If it's nothing serious, then many will turn a blind eye, but those who have offspring are expected to stay with their own kind." Logan rubbed the side of his jaw. "Take a Chitah and Mage, for instance. We're enemies, and that goes way back, so there's little trust among us. I can't think of a single Chitah female who would entertain the idea of hooking up with a Mage; it's not a natural pairing. It's in our nature to have young, and a Mage cannot reproduce."

"Remind me to bring this topic up again," I said.

"Then there's Lucian. He's the little man in the family. Not at all like the rest of us brutes." He stuffed the roll in his cheek trying to wither his smile. "Levi jokes that the stork brought him because he doesn't look like the rest of us."

"Something tells me you boys were hard on him growing up."

Logan shrugged. "Our births were spaced apart. He's smaller and more sensitive. Lucian could shame us in any essay or test; he's as smart as a whip. Our only wish is that he was more capable in protecting himself. Fighting comes naturally, but he fights his own instincts."

"Let me get this straight: you're Leo, Logan, Levi, and Lucian?" I snickered, imagining monogrammed towels and not being able to figure out whose was whose on laundry day.

"Laugh it up," he said. "It's our custom for all male Chitah to retain the father's first name initial."

"What's your sister's name?"

He twisted the stem of a strawberry and a large seed popped off. "Sadie."

"The girls don't take the naming scheme?"

"They do, after the mother. Females are harder to conceive, which is why those who have families have large ones. Women continue having male children until they are able to produce a girl. It's important to ensure the Chitah line goes on. Our mother's name was Susannah."

"Was?"

"She died in childbirth."

"I thought that you could heal and live a long time?" I knew I was treading on sensitive ground by the way he averted his eyes.

"All rules have exceptions and limitations. Once we reach sexual maturity, our aging process slows down. A century puts about five years worth of aging on our bodies. We *can* die, Silver. Childbirth is the greatest gift and biggest threat for our females. Their bodies are vulnerable when they carry our young—no longer able to heal or renew."

Logan drifted off and I knew where his mind went.

"It has to shut down to allow the fetus to grow. Otherwise, the body would instantly absorb it. Our mother's pregnancy was difficult, and she didn't survive the birth of Sadie."

"I'm sorry."

I consoled him with a light touch on the hand. Logan tossed the uneaten strawberry on the plate. His face collected the pain of his past.

"When my father saw that the infant was human, he called the midwife to take it away, but not before I held her."

I looked at him and sensed pride, as an older brother might have for their little sister.

"He left the room after they covered my mother up," Logan said in a distant voice. "My family has opinions about what I do, but my mother insisted that I be there. I think…"

He didn't need to finish, because I knew what his mother was attempting to do. Maybe watching a newborn enter the world would change Logan, make him see the error of his ways, and put his past behind him. He never had the chance to become a father, and if he connected with that little infant, it might be enough for him to walk away from the life he was living. His mother had hopes for him.

Logan cleared his throat. "While my father made arrangements, I held the baby. She cried a little, but I soothed her with my voice and whispered a name in her ear. Sadie."

"How old is she?"

"She turned twenty-four this month. Are you done eating?"

"Yeah, I think that's it for me. Thanks for ordering breakfast; it was a nice change. I usually fend for myself at home and wind up eating toast and jelly."

I pulled up my knees and leaned against the headboard. Why wouldn't a Chitah at least keep in touch with their human siblings? Understandably, it was dangerous for them to live in our world, but to just abandon your own flesh and blood?

Logan propped his chin on my knee and I pulled back when

our faces nearly touched. The sun glinted in his eyes, and a serious expression plagued his features when his heavy brow lowered. A small strand of hair stuck to an eyelash and held my attention.

"I like that you ask about my family."

I reached up and brushed the hair away from his face. A vibration fluttered against my knee from his throat, although I heard nothing.

"Justus doesn't want me around you."

"He's your Ghuardian, and I cannot come between you. I respect a man who keeps the females in his house protected. I will be leaving when we return to Cognito."

Logan held my foot, softly stroking the ankle. "Can I ask a favor?"

I didn't even notice him reaching for the cart.

"Will you eat from my hand?"

Between his fingers was a small, sugar-rolled donut. They were my weakness. I used to call them *heaven on my tongue, and hell on my thighs.*

"Where did you get that?"

Flecks of sugar dusted my chest as he rolled it between his fingers. "Room service will bring anything you pay extra for."

"I really don't understand why this is such a big deal to you."

My reluctance enticed him and he leaned closer.

"I can tell from your reaction that you've never had anyone feed you before." A finger grazed my cheek, which flushed—awakened by his touch.

"I don't like games."

His face soured. "I don't play them."

"Why can't you *hand* me the donut?"

"To you it may seem insignificant, but to the Chitah, it's a sign of trust. There's a lot you don't know about my kind, Silver. We have different customs, and what may seem like a simple gesture to you, holds meaning to us. *I want you* to trust me. *I want you* to see me as something more than I am. *I want you* to eat from my hand."

I knew what he meant, but behind all those words the only thing I heard him say was, "*I want you.*"

Logan's eyes widened when I let him feed me—sugar coating my lips. I became self-conscious as I chewed, embarrassed that this might be a joke. Logan didn't laugh, and when I leaned in for a second bite, he pulled it back so I could only get a small nibble.

He was trying to make this last, so I snatched his wrist and ate the whole thing. When my lips came together, sucking the sugar from his fingertips, Logan moved so close that his breath touched my face. I swallowed my bite with a satisfactory grin.

He examined my lips, sizing them up like prey.

"I'm going to kiss you now," he decided.

Before I even registered what he said, Logan sampled my lips like a man enjoying a decadent dessert. He adored me with his kiss, and lavished me with an affectionate pause.

I was dizzy from the unexpected passion at breakfast. Something kept me from responding, and it was the thought of his poisonous bite.

He opened his eyes, and without fear, hesitation, or regret—I looked right at him. The rims never looked so dark against the pale coloring, and if the eyes were the windows to the soul, I felt as if I were breaking and entering.

"I don't ever want you to be afraid of me," he said, stroking my cheek. "I will never harm you."

"No one can promise that." I looked at the sunlight pouring through the window.

Logan tilted my chin to face him. "I can, and I just did."

"Maybe you lie really well."

He sniffed. "To what gain, getting in your pants? Female, I could have stripped you down and seduced you three strawberries ago. If you want to debate, we can do that later. But right now, I want to kiss you," he said softly. "Kiss me back, not because I asked you to, but because you want to. And I *know*, Little Raven, that you want to. Your words may be sharp, but your scent is soft and tells me that you crave this as much as I do."

I couldn't understand the feelings that surfaced. This wasn't about impulse or lust, nor was it about anything that made sense. An intangible force pulled me towards Logan, and my feet dragged across the ground.

When his cheek nuzzled against mine, we were right back where we started in the woods. I tasted honey on the words that dripped from his tongue. "*Kiss me back.*"

Our cheeks touched and I inhaled, smelling a faint trace of soap on his skin. I moved my head to the side, brushing along his smooth jaw until I found his mouth. He waited, letting me do all the hunting. Fire burned as our lips reacquainted—no introductions necessary—and we fell into a deep, insatiable kiss. Our tongues glided in and out, tasting nothing but explosive desire. His body surged forward, arms trembling where his hands rested on the mattress. Sweet strawberries and velvet strokes stirred a hunger inside of me.

His kiss was not crushing as I expected, but molten. A heat spread across my skin and filled my body, and that heat was the pulse of my light.

Logan encouraged me to take the lead, to make the choice to stop whenever I needed to. But I didn't need to.

I didn't want to.

The sugar melted between us, and when I nibbled his bottom lip—his body went rigid.

"Behave," he growled in a deep voice.

"Make me," I dared.

A challenge rested between us, and I waited for his reaction.

Logan's eyes prowled over my body, and he took in my scent like a flower in bloom. Without warning, he dove for my neck and licked the tender spot just beneath my ear in one seductive stroke.

I shivered.

"Never dare a Chitah," he cautioned, biting my neck gently.

There was no danger in that bite, unless you counted the raw need culminating between us—the one that had my heart in his clutches as it pounded against my chest.

Logan broke away, and when he did, I found myself upset with the abrupt cessation. His hooded eyes hung lazily on me as he wiped a smudge of sugar from my chin with his thumb.

"A kiss is all I asked, and a kiss is all I will take." He placed the tip of his finger in his mouth and slowly pulled it out.

Was every man in my life becoming a kiss and run? I knew it shouldn't have mattered—I wasn't seeking a husband—but I was still a woman with feelings. He must have scented my irritation.

"I know better than to get a Mage overcharged." He laughed. "I don't think that would end very well for me, don't you agree?"

I threw my legs over the edge of the bed, pushing him away. "I should have known better."

In a flash, I was thrown on my back.

Logan dipped his nose down to my chest, slowly taking in my scent in one long inhale until he reached my neck. I felt that breath to the core of my being.

"I want you," he declared. "I want to undress you, and taste you. I want to see the flush in your cheeks, and feel your legs tremble when they can no longer hold against me," he spoke against my neck. "I will not take a female whose lust mingles with doubt. I will *not* take you here in this hotel room out of convenience. Impulse leads to regret, and I *do* like a good seduction," he purred.

My body trembled when his feathery kisses moved along my neck. I wanted to touch him, and feel his skin against my hands. That dark, heady scent he carried was attractive, and it subtly shifted with his moods.

"I can feel your energy," he noticed. "It's tremendous."

"I won't touch you," I assured him, knowing I could release a burst of energy that would undoubtedly drop the curtain on the moment. "I have it under control."

He traced the line of my clavicle with this finger and kissed the corners of my mouth. "Not even if I ask? I want your fingerprints all over me like a crime scene."

I clung to each word that fell from his lips like a spider to a web. "Am I just prey to you?"

"Some things are worth chasing."

"Some things can't be caught."

His finger outlined my jaw as if he were putting me to memory.

"I have spent a lifetime being chased by females, and I know what it means to run. There's something different about you, Silver. You incite the hunter in me."

My saddened eyes wandered up to his, and I made a promise I didn't know if I could keep. "I'll never love again, Logan. If that's what you're asking, then I won't give it to a man that I can't trust with my life and my heart. You kill without regret, and I never know from one minute to the next what your intentions are. I don't want an indecisive man in my life any more than a controlling one."

A torch lit behind those eyes, burning bright as he leaned in and whispered softly beside my ear. "Sweet Little Raven, dusted in sugar—I *will* possess your heart."

CHAPTER 22

A FTER RETURNING TO COGNITO, WE gathered in the living room with a bottle of wine, preparing to discuss the details. You could smell the anticipation in the air like chimney smoke on a winter's night. Logan walked up to the fireplace, commanding everyone's eye—everyone being my Ghuardian, Simon, Adam, and Remi. I didn't know Remi very well, but I guessed that Justus was seeking advice over the Marco situation.

Remi was not a Mage, but a Gemini. They're ancient immortals, and few exist. They have a dangerous streak triggered by negative emotions, so Remi appeared detached. Outside of the dragon tattoo on his neck, he didn't appear menacing. His brown hair was unusually soft in appearance, but his eyes were the most fascinating thing about him; they shifted colors with the light. Justus warned me not to provoke him, and I took his advice. If my Ghuardian was even the slightest bit intimidated by him, then I knew to be respectful.

"Before we get started, there's something I want to say," Logan began.

I took a seat in a chair facing Adam. He was uninterested in what Logan had to say and tucked a bored fist against his jaw. I enjoyed a slow sip of wine, privately admiring the way Logan took command of the room as he rolled up the sleeves of his shirt.

"Silver is a remarkable person; you should commend her for the job she's done. I was impressed by her eagerness to take risks. I will continue to offer my services per our agreement, and would like to extend that beyond this case, if the need arises."

It was then that I noticed something was off with Logan. He wore confidence like an ensemble—straight back, head up, arms hung at his sides—whereas most men with insecurities hid their hands, and found places to scratch. When Logan folded his arms and lowered his chin, a flutter of nerves took over.

"I am announcing my intent to court Silver."

Simon's wine went down the wrong windpipe. While he was choking and gasping for breath in animated movements, Justus sat very still. The room grew warm, and he narrowed his eyes at Logan like missiles.

"Obviously, I don't have your blessing, nor do I seek it. I'm not asking your permission, so there is no need for the drama. It's my right to court whomever I wish. If there are other suitors, they can challenge me for the right of free competition; I will accept that challenge *whenever* it is given."

Logan spoke to the room as a man of worth, a man who knew what he wanted, standing with proud shoulders and a lift of his chin.

Hell, I was flattered.

The odds weren't in his favor, either. He was a man of questionable integrity, but I finally knew where I stood with him. Simon and Adam may have crushed on me, but not once did they declare their intentions for all to witness. Logan had a backbone, and I liked it.

I, on the other hand, sat with my mouth on the edge of the glass not saying yes, no, or hidey-ho. Justus was in a realm of pissed off as I'd never seen. Adam never acknowledged Logan. His dark, brooding eyes bore a hole through my skull, and I poured more wine down my throat.

"Now that we have the cat out of the bag," Logan chuckled, "let's discuss Marco."

Justus rose from his seat. "You are not welcome in my house."

"Be that as it may," Logan countered, "I will still court her. I am aware this is not a preferred match—Mage and Chitah—but I will wait as long as it takes, Justus De Gradi. You don't have to like *me*, but you'll treat her with respect in my presence, despite how you feel."

"You're a Chitah. What could you want with a Mage?"

Logan's tongue flashed across his lower lip and his eyes flicked over to mine. "I like a strong female."

"Go to the gym; there are plenty of strong women there," I blurted out.

I knew he liked me, but I was provoking him to see how much of that ground he was willing to stand.

Logan's brows pinched together. "I find you most agreeable, Silver. Aside from the fact you stuffed me with enchiladas and then tried to kill me."

"I think it was the other way around."

He half smiled.

Logan snapped his fingers at Simon. "Don't think I have forgotten you called her a tart, you arrogant prick."

"What the bloody hell are you talking—" When Simon remembered the offhand remark he made on the phone the night of my abduction, he pressed his lips together and threw his hands up in defeat.

Logan turned his attention to Justus. "If you have an issue with this pairing, you will address it with *me*, not her. Don't put a fracture in your relationship, because she needs a positive influence. As long as Silver lives under your roof, she must not feel bullied by her caregiver for a choice that is hers. You can only have so much control of her life, and you know it."

Adam's eyes were venomous. "Is this what you want?"

"Well I—"

"Do you realize what he is? What he is capable of? That a Chitah can—"

"*Let her finish,* Mage." Logan stepped forward, and his angled features hardened with anger. "When you ask a question, do you want an answer, or are you just puffing out smoke? Allow her to speak. Do you understand me?" Logan flexed a hand at his side and I looked between the two, not sure whose side to take.

"Do *not* get all fucking territorial on me," Adam barked. "You are not one of our kind. You have no right to stand there and stake your claim on her like a piece of property."

"Why?" Logan asked, as a man losing patience. "Because you didn't put your flag down first?"

Simon did a facepalm.

"Does he speak for you now?" Adam was hurt. I saw it in his eyes, but my guilt disintegrated with the tone of his voice. His language was a given, as I couldn't imagine being in the service with Knox all those years and not having that kind of camaraderie, but I was exhausted from being on the defense.

I raised my hand. "Adam, please don't do this. Not here."

He thrust himself back in the chair and scraped his fingers through locks of brown hair, looking like an explosive ready to detonate.

The manner in which Logan watched him was alarming. His nostrils twitched as he pulled in a scent, and he stepped forward.

"Don't turn this into a fight, Mr. Cross. Remember why we're here."

Logan looked at me unapologetically. "I have given my warning and if he interrupts you again, I will knock him to the ground. Please, continue."

"No one speaks for me, Adam. I make my own decisions, and I think it's clear that I haven't made any kind of decision tonight, except maybe to drink this wine to the bottom."

Logan tucked his hands in his pockets and lowered his voice. "Perhaps he would like to challenge me to court you."

Adam lowered his eyes to the floor like heavy weights.

I wasn't sure what a challenge among Chitah entailed, but I had a feeling it didn't involve arm-wrestling. Adam backed down, and I was a little disappointed. He was willing to lay down his life for my freedom, but unwilling to declare his feelings for me. It didn't make sense. Yet, the more I thought about it, the more it did. It left me with a few questions that I decided to keep to myself, because I never did understand why he was so willing to become a Mage.

No challenge was made. Justus spoke privately with Remi, and for the rest of the evening, we discussed everything that happened on our trip.

Well, almost everything.

———◦•◦∞◦•◦———

A few days crept by, and I was getting ready for my first real date in more than two years. I stared in the mirror feeling like a package waiting to be unwrapped. The tall black boots were expensive, and I nervously touched the edges of my short skirt. Even my ponytail revealed more skin than I was used to. I bought a pretty color of eyeliner that looked more like fairy dust, and decided it was my new favorite thing. The woman staring back at me in the mirror was ready for a night out on the town, but it wasn't going to be with Logan.

During the drive, I caught Justus looking at me sideways as we sped through another intersection. He never worried about things like police radar, because an experienced Mage could project the right kind of energy to disable it.

He was apprehensive about letting me go, but trusted the word of a Chitah. Juicers were an epidemic, and I was the equivalent of an energy drink. His concern was justified, but I needed to reclaim my independence and start making choices for myself.

"You look nice," he said, as a headlight splashed across the interior.

"Give yourself a pat on the back; you bought it. I really wish you didn't keep filling my closet. I'm never going to be able to pay you back."

"I would not take payment for something that is my duty."

That's what I liked about Justus; he would never admit that he enjoyed shopping for me. At first, I thought I wasn't up to snuff and he was trying to change me. As it turns out, it was the only way he knew how to express his affection. Wearing one of his dresses was the equivalent of a hug.

Tonight we rode in the Mercedes, his second favorite to the Aston Martin. It was classy, stylish, and in mint condition. We rolled to a stop in front of a fire hydrant outside of Logan's condo. It was nestled in a charming neighborhood with bright yellow lampposts near the sidewalk and small patches of grass.

"Stay out of trouble," he said, as I got out of the car.

Impossible.

Once the car was out of sight, I spun on my heel and hurried up the street.

I discovered Nero's name, but I was not permitted to be involved with the HALO investigation any further. I got the sense that Simon ran into a roadblock with finding reliable information on where he resided. On one visit, Simon got up to use the restroom and left his laptop open. I snooped through his files and found a few notes on

Nero—including rumored hangouts. The one that stood out was a club called Hell; that sounded exactly like the kind of place Nero would frequent. Justus became preoccupied with another case, so I decided to take matters into my own hands. Maybe immortals felt like they had all the time in the world to get things done, but I was still on human time. I wasn't about to let that man become irrelevant.

A few nights earlier, Logan called. He was a great conversationalist, and I enjoyed the playful banter between us. I sensed tension when he said he was going out with his brothers and his father would be meeting up with them. I didn't know much about the relationship they had with their father, but I offered him reassurance. Opportunity presented itself on a platter, and I spun a lie so Justus wouldn't raise a brow.

My heels tapped against the dirty pavement of a narrow sidewalk. When I finally glanced up, a glowing pitchfork marked the building I was looking for. *Cue the mental eye roll.* The club didn't advertise their name. They didn't need to.

I approached Hell with second thoughts; I suppose everyone does. The doorman held up the wall with his back as he scanned the crowd indifferently. His spiked collar made him look like a junkyard dog. The line was nothing but leather, latex, and leashes. Weak energy told me they were all human. They didn't have a chance in hell at getting into a Breed club.

The doorman's eyes lapped me up like a thirsty dog would a bowl of water on a hot summer day. He was a Mage, so I flared and gave him my best sultry smile. He chuckled and rubbed a meaty chin.

"They're going to *love* you, sweets."

When the door swung open, my throat went dry. The heat was the first thing that struck me. The second was a man being whipped as bystanders watched. The rest of the club was as ordinary as they come. I didn't see any disturbing scenes like the one in front that set the tone for what type of place this really was. Black tables scattered across a blood red floor, and a pale blue light bounced off the glasses behind the bar. I ordered a vodka neat and scanned the crowd. It didn't take long before a few persistent men approached me. I didn't look anything like the other women in there, and it was drawing the wrong kind of crowd.

When I was ready to give up, a thick man in wide leather pants and a black jacket approached me. He sized me up and asked, "First timer? I'm Eli. I work here. What are you here for, and how can we pleasure you?"

I anchored my eyebrows. "An old acquaintance recommended this place; he gave it rave reviews, so I decided to check it out for myself."

Eli was a meaty guy who looked like he could bench press a horse. Hell, the man looked like he ate them for breakfast.

"Back to my question: how can we pleasure you? Or is that your pleasure—being punished for disobedience?"

Was this guy serious?

A man walked by and offered a handful of colorful lollipops. I waved him off and he approached a few others who took one and went back to conversations.

"You should be polite and take what's offered," Eli said with a laugh. "It's one of the only things you'll get in this club for free."

"I'm here for a few drinks," I said, lifting my glass. "Just going to hang back and watch."

"Good to know. I'll give you the short tour, then. The stairs on the left lead to the dungeon, the ones on the right go to purgatory. Watch all you want Mage, but you will participate before you leave. Club rules."

"No one told me that!" I was starting to get the full, horrific picture.

He laughed so hard that his eyes were brimming with tears. "I have to know the name of your friend who left out the only rule this club has."

"Nero."

Eli snapped out of his laugh and appraised me. "Yes, that sounds like Nero. Sick little bastard."

"You know him?"

"He's a regular."

"Is he here tonight?" I scanned the crowd as Eli played with the chain hanging from his nipples. I wished I had brought Simon; he would have known how to behave.

"Unh-unh. Should I tell him that you're looking for him?"

"No, don't bother."

Please god, don't bother.

Eli grabbed my arm and yanked me out of the seat. I fought as he towed me down a long hallway, but he was too big. A burst of my energy wouldn't do me any good against a Mage, not to mention that giving out samples of my Unique light would be foolish.

"Let me go!" I struggled, but he didn't slow down. No one helped. I bumped into a Vampire who laughed, and leaned in with mild curiosity.

"Oooh, someone's in trouble!" a tiny voice giggled. I glared at the pixie-sized girl with the short, white hair as Eli tossed me through an open door at the end of the hall and slammed it shut.

"Why are you asking about Nero?"

My eyes roamed across the wall of chains, wrist cuffs, and a wide assortment of whips. It was time for me to grow some balls. "I'm looking for information."

"What position do you have in the Mageri? We don't want trouble here."

"None. This is personal."

He scratched his chin. "Mmm, that makes it interesting, doesn't it?" he murmured. Eli reached behind his back and slid the lock into place. "What kind of information? Perhaps I can help. I'm not partnered with that sonofabitch."

"Do you know if he's keeping any other Mage against their will?"

He tapped a finger against his pants. "You don't look like the sort of girl who's ever visited one of these places before. Ever heard of the bartering system?" Eli pulled a leather whip from the wall and cracked the narrow spray of tails against his pants.

I jumped in my skin but kept my composure.

"Tit for tat. No one leaves this club without participating; that's the rule. I could leave you to some of the twisted men out there," he thumbed, "but I'm willing to trade information for a little fun. I'm curious to know exactly how many questions you can take."

"I'd rather not," I said, moving around him.

He held out his arm, but I didn't get a sense that he was dangerous. Eli was just… persistent.

"This is your last chance; walk out that door and I won't speak to you again about Nero. I can see you want answers. We both know you aren't leaving here without feeling this whip on your back."

"How do I know you have the answers I need?"

He ran a hand down his perspiring chest. "I used to work for him."

I thought about it. It's not as if I was a human—I could heal myself in the morning. "Fine," I said reluctantly.

"Remove your shirt." Eli smirked and held up two fingers. "We'll keep this trade professional. Scouts honor."

Breed clubs were not just a place of recreation, but business. Deals were made and services rendered. Currency was never as valuable as other arrangements. This was the big girl world, and I had to make a decision that could put me in a better position.

All I could think of was Justus telling me to stay out of trouble. Maybe if I knew what kind of club this was, I might have backed out. I doubted Eli was going to hit me that hard—he looked a little sympathetic in the eyes. I removed my shirt and crossed my arms in front of my chest.

"Turn around and put your hands on the desk."

I placed my hands on the wood as the tassels tapped against his leathers. Eli flipped my ponytail over my shoulder. "Ask your question."

"Does Nero work for anyone?"

"No."

I hissed as the leather cracked against my skin and cut through flesh. I thought he would go easy on the first question, but I could tell he was going to make this as shockingly painful as possible. He placed his warm hand flat on my back. *Fuck him and his one word answers.*

"Forget it," I said, grabbing my shirt and putting it back on. "I've changed my mind. I don't care enough about answers to have someone degrade me like this."

He swirled the whip in his hand.

"Hold up, hold up," he said, raising a hand to stop me from leaving. "There's another way we can do this."

I glared at the wall. "Sorry, I'm not into chains either. We made a deal, and I've participated."

He pulled in a deep breath, releasing it with frustration. "I'm a Sensor."

I blanched. "You're a *what*?" Nine million curse words flew through my head. I made a poor assumption that he was a Mage because he knew that's what I was.

Sensor's had the ability to retain emotions and collect them like pet rocks. Any experience could be sold for the right price. According to Simon, most desired sexual exchanges through a Sensor—either one of their own, or someone else's. I didn't know much about their power, except they were also highly sensitive in a room where strong emotions occurred and often worked with investigators. This little evening was going into his collector's box for the highest bidder.

Bastard.

"Buyers love the newbies, and they're not easy to come by," he shrugged. "They don't pay as much when you baby them, so I have to be rough."

I grabbed the whip from his hand and threw it across the room. "You could have at least told me what you were!"

"Would it have made a difference? You're not going to find answers out there," he said, motioning towards the door. "Those men will eat you alive. I'm not a bad guy... just a man who sees an opportunity."

"You should have asked if I wanted to be part of your sales. That makes a difference. I don't like being deceived."

"If you offer me something better, I'll hold to the deal."

"Like what?" I folded my arms.

"Memories. I don't want your first birthday, or skydiving experience. This is a club with specific tastes, so the darker the memory, the higher the bid."

Dark memories were something I owned in abundance. "I had an abusive ex."

Eli laughed. "So does every whore on the street corner. Get more creative."

I swallowed. "I have something. How do I know you'll give me the answers I want?"

"I have to touch you to take the emotion. Go ahead and think about the memory; I'll feel your energy and decide how much information I'm willing to trade," he said, lacking enthusiasm. Clearly, he thought the whipping was more valuable.

I thought about the night that changed my life, when Samil brutally turned me into a Mage. Eli held his hands in front of my chest and tuned out, as if he were under hypnosis. His eyes fluttered and snapped open. "We'll trade," he nodded.

"How much will you tell me?"

"It's an emotion that's hard to sell, but I can find a buyer. I'll give you three more questions." He tucked his hands in his pockets and waited.

"Is he plotting a war?"

There was hesitation, as if uncertain. "Yes, but I don't know the details. No one does."

"How many is he holding against their will?"

"Nine that I know of, but there could be more."

"When will he be in here again?"

"Next Friday."

Eli lowered his chin and stepped forward. "Time to pay up." His fingers spread out across my chest. "All you have to do is think about the memory. Relive it in your mind. It doesn't matter how old it is because I can pull emotions to the surface that have been buried a long time."

I looked at him anxiously, as I didn't know how ready I was to dig up a graveyard of pain. I thought about crossing the field and falling to the ground. I still saw it vividly in my head, and while it was always swirled with shades of hate for Samil, Eli was extracting feelings that burned my senses. I glanced at the soft red glow beneath his hands. When a Mage transferred energy, the light was clean and blue, but for a Sensor, it was just the opposite. It scared me.

The light intensified, and the cruelty of the struggle overcame me. Tears welled at the corners of my eyes, and I turned my head.

"Finish it," he said. "All the way."

When I did, I balled my hands into fists. I felt like hitting something, because a Sensor had a talent for breathing life into emotions that had faded with time. Eli brushed his hands over my shoulders and dropped them to his side. "I can take it away, you know."

"Take what away?"

"The pain. I can't remove the memory, but I can permanently remove the emotions. Do you want that? It'll cost extra, and I'll take a favor."

Meaning I'd be in his debt, at his disposal, to collect in any way he saw fit. Was a clean slate on a terrible memory worth it? My question was answered when I realized that without suffering, I wouldn't be who I am now. Blacksmiths hammer metal in order to change its shape and make it stronger. I would never grow from experience unless I felt the impact of it.

"No, our trade is complete," I said decidedly. "That memory makes me who I am."

"My clients are particular about their requests. You'll bring a fine penny to my pocket. Next Friday?"

I picked up my purse from the floor and left Hell in complete disgust.

CHAPTER 23

WITH TWO HOURS LEFT TO kill before Justus picked me up in his sex-mobile, I sat on the steps of Logan's condo and shook my hair free from the ponytail. Immortality hardened me in ways I least expected. The emotions Eli took still lingered like an unwanted fragrance, but it was worth the trade. I not only had an inside source, but an opportunity to confront Nero. However, Eli still might be able to provide more information. *Jesus, was I really considering this?* A moth landed on my skirt, and I stroked its dusty wings.

"I'd love to say that I'm pleasantly surprised to see you, except that you're unsupervised, and under the impression that I'm out for the night."

Shit.

"I thought you were with your brothers."

"That's exactly my point."

Logan twisted his sneaker on the ground as if he was putting out a cigarette when in reality—he was annoyed. Whatever he did tonight, it was casual by the look of his jeans and pale yellow cotton shirt.

"Why do I smell blood?"

"I went to a bar and there was a fight. You know—Mage drama," I said indifferently.

Logan sat beside me and I looked down at his soft brown sneakers.

"You look pretty in that skirt, Miss Silver."

"Why thank you, Mr. Cross." The little moth fluttered away and I wiped the dust from the dark fabric. "What happened tonight with your dad? You're home early."

"Chitah drama," Logan grumbled, leaning on his elbows. "Levi's date insulted our father and all hell broke loose when Leo jumped him."

"Whose side did Levi take?"

"Ours, of course. Much to the surprise of his boyfriend." Logan smiled and turned a sharp glance my way. "Come inside and we'll talk."

I hissed when he placed his hand across my back.

Logan sprang to his feet and knelt before me, holding my face in his hands. There was no talking, because he was picking up every detail with his nose. He looked me straight in the eye—deep—as if he were collecting thoughts. I remembered why I once feared him as his fangs gleamed from the porch light.

Pulling away from him was an exercise in futility. Logan leaned in, lifted a handful of my hair to his nose, and took a deep breath.

"Tell me what happened, or I will hunt down the male scent that is mingled with *your* blood."

He was serious as he stood up and his lip twitched.

"Logan, wait! Don't. I'll explain everything inside."

<hr />

Logan wasn't kidding when he said he was a minimalist. His condo—with beautiful redwood flooring and sage green walls—was a shell of a life. Two green chairs and a sleeper sofa sat blankly in the living room. He owned no pictures, mirrors, or curtains. As we passed the kitchen, I imagined him eating alone at the island in the center of the room. It had one place setting on the black granite countertop.

He led me by the hand to his bedroom, and I followed behind with cautious steps. The only thing in the room was an oversized mattress lying on the floor, smothered in sheets. Two ceiling to floor windows brought the world inside, as they lacked curtains or blinds. They also lacked privacy. He didn't flip on the switch, but the twinkling lights from the street illuminated the room like fireflies.

"Take off your shirt," he said.

"I don't think so."

He moved closer. "I want it off."

Without waiting for an answer, Logan lifted the delicate straps from my shoulders. I said nothing as he peeled the shirt away and let it slide to my ankles. He rose back up, but kept his eyes centered on mine like an unspoken promise. A finger twirled, instructing me to turn around.

"Lie on the bed."

I dropped to my knees and crawled over the bed, lying on my stomach as Logan ran water in a nearby bathroom. The sheets were cold, and his room smelled of vanilla and earth. The bed moved as he straddled me, wiping the wet towel against the heated wound.

"I need to remove this," he said. I heard the tiny click of latches as Logan unfastened the bra.

"I didn't know what kind of club it was."

"Heal first. Talk later."

"I can't heal until morning," I said, refusing to take light from him. It was a necessity the first time—more about clearing his debt—but a scratch could wait.

"This is going to feel strange, but it won't hurt."

My brows knitted and before I could jerk my head around, a warm tongue glided across my skin.

"What are you doing?" I said, almost knocking him off balance.

"Something I would have rather done under different circumstances. Now be still, little bird, and let me heal your wounds."

The sting I really felt was pride as I let him heal me in a way that was unique to a Chitah. Vulnerability wasn't an emotion I warmed up to, and that's exactly how I felt beneath him. His tongue changed direction, swirling and tracing over the wound as the magic in his saliva numbed the pain. I'm not going to lie; I liked it. I snorted against the covers when I thought of Justus asking me how we spent our evening.

"All done," he said.

I gasped when he fell on top of me and spoke softly against the back of my neck. "Any other places that I need to lick?" he asked, brushing his lips over my skin. "I like to be thorough, so let me know if I missed a spot."

I squirmed.

Logan chuckled and sat up. "Explain why I'm spending my evening licking your wounds?"

Despite the flirtation, everything about his tone showed agitation.

"I went to Hell tonight and met a man who gave me information on Nero."

"Obviously at a price. Why would you do this kind of trading?"

"Simon said people barter all the time. I got the information I wanted, and I don't regret it."

"Was it worth your blood?"

"Pain is incidental. I'm a Mage. I heal."

"You're a Mage. You heal!" he parroted.

I narrowed my eyes at his mocking tone as he tugged at my bra and secured the latches.

"Here," he said. "Put this on."

Something soft hit my hands. While Logan turned to face the wall, I slipped into his yellow T-shirt, scooting to the edge of the bed.

"I only let him do it once."

A minute passed before he said anything. He wrung his hands and paced the floor, making me nervous.

"I feel very… protective of you, Silver. I'm not going to judge your actions because your strength is what attracts me, but do you think I can turn a blind eye to a man who *whipped* a female? Consensual or not, it goes against my very nature, and I would tear him apart."

I decided to leave out the little tidbit that Eli was a Sensor.

"Justus can't find out about this. He would forbid me from seeing you, and might never trust me again. Tonight, we went on a date, and I spilled wine on my blouse. He'll believe that because I'm clumsy with my drinks."

"I'll agree on a single condition."

I sighed. "Name it."

"Include me in whatever you're scheming. Otherwise, it's a deal breaker and I'll spill the beans to your Ghuardian, even if that means you go on lockdown."

I considered if Logan would be a detriment to my plans. I couldn't think of a reason, so I shrugged in agreement.

Logan crouched down and took a seat on the mattress, lifting me onto his lap. It was effortless, as if he had held me a million times before.

"You're going to be a tough one to handle, but learn to trust me. I refuse to tame your independent nature, but know that I would have taken the lashings *for* you. I will prove myself a worthy male to you one day."

"It's a good thing you like to wear sneakers, Mr. Cross."

His lips pressed a tender kiss on my ear, and I sighed against his skin. The sound that poured from him was primal. It rumbled so deep that it reminded me of distant thunder.

"I love the sound your body makes," I spoke softly, looking at his chest. "You don't have any tattoos?"

"Uh… no." He sounded surprised at the question and tilted his head to look at me. "What about you?"

"Just my Creator's mark."

"I don't like that another male has marked you."

I looked up and smiled when I saw his lips were two thin lines. "Every Mage has a mark. I'm sure you know that." I traced the curve of muscle in his arm. "Do you have any scars?"

"We all have scars," he said thoughtfully.

Logan encased me in his arms, and the heat smoldered from him like the fire in the cave where he once held me captive.

"I'm a little offended you lied about being on a date with me, so I'm taking you out next Friday."

"I can't, I'm busy that night."

When he huffed, I smiled, feeling struck by his jealousy. I may have been undecided about where things were going with Logan, but I knew I liked the way he touched me, and the way he spoke of me.

"Busy little bee, aren't we?"

"Nero is going to Hell next Friday."

"Well then, I suppose we'll be going to Hell on Friday and heaven on Saturday. Mark your calendar."

CHAPTER 24

"**H**OW DID YOU COME ACROSS that information?"

"I'd tell you, but I'd have to kill you." I moved the pawn up a space on the wooden board, wondering if Simon would finish the game. Between us, there were nine pieces left, most of them his, but he was merely drawing out the inevitable. I never won. I had information on Nero, and Simon didn't like being one-upped.

"*This* is a game love," he said, tapping the board. Then he reached for my hand. "This is not."

"Nero wants to start a war, Simon. This isn't just about him taking on the Mageri—it's bigger. He's holding others taken by force, like *me*. I don't really care if you tell Justus the facts I found out on Nero, but don't tell him you got it from me. I'm sick of being on the grill. I'm going back in and I need your help. You're the smarty-pants around here, and you'll have better questions. I can't do this without you."

Okay, so I was inflating his ego just a tiny bit, but the great Simon Hunt needed a little inflating now and again.

Simon slumped in his chair, speaking in a heavy accent, which was usually the case when he was nettled about something. "If I find out you were snogging for information, I'll have a real problem with that. Yes, I will."

"I need your total commitment. If not, then you can piss off."

Simon's slang was rubbing off on me, and not in a good way.

"I *suppose* that sodding Chitah of yours put you up to this."

"He knew nothing of it, but he's got my back. Do you?"

Simon's lashes looked like a Venus flytrap around his pale, brown eyes. "Clever girl. I'll help, but you must tell me *everything*."

"If you're with me then it's all the way, and you may not like what you hear. I want your word that you won't tell Justus where you got this information, and especially how I got it." I tapped a finger on my rook and waited for his answer. Simon had to be in the know; it was his nature. But I also had to find out if I could trust him independently.

The chair creaked as he locked his fingers behind his neck and leaned back.

"I give you my word, now spill."

I did, and with no hint of emotion; no need to play out the drama. Simon ghosted when I mentioned the whipping. He said Sensors were valued for their ability to transfer sensory experiences, and most preferred monetary gain to favors. Knowing Simon, he was no stranger to this either. Breed bartered, and everything had a price tag.

He ran a hand over his mouth several times.

"I was ready to walk out of there," I said, "but when he offered to pluck an emotion, it seemed like a harmless trade. I never knew places like that existed. I thought it was just something in the movies."

"Exactly what kind of movies have you been watching?"

"I need help with clothes—appropriate clothes—so I can blend in. Do you catch my drift? I looked too much like Bo Peep having a beer at the bar, and apparently there are a lot of men with a Bo Peep fetish."

"*That* is a definite yes."

I frowned at his enthusiasm.

"You behave like you do in this game, Silver, thinking without planning. You could really get hurt."

I tapped the pawn. "This is what I feel like all the time, Simon. But this," I said, touching the king, "is what I want to be. Important."

Simon smirked. "Life is punctuated by moments, not station or title. Sometimes the little guy has the best move. The king may be important, but he's always on the run and needing protection. Soldiers are strong because they make smart decisions and work as a team. Justus protects you like a King, but his intention is to make you a soldier."

"If you tell me there's no 'I in team', I'm going to shove this rook up your nose."

"Tell the Chitah that I'll be the third wheel. If they cuff his paws to the wall, then you'll be on your own without a backup. Think ahead to avoid traps. Sometimes you have too much moxie for your own good."

"The club rule is that you have to participate. Are you sure you really want to do this?"

"That's my condition, love. Take it or leave it." He moved the pawn up a space. "Checkmate."

"You win."

The next Friday, I went to visit my favorite Englishman for game night. Justus groaned when I bragged about our plans for an all-night Godzilla marathon, but I knew he was glad to be rid of me. He liked to go out and get his freak on, whether he'd admit it or not. Every man has needs, and his were never satisfied when I tagged along. Maybe I *was* a little mean to the women, but it irritated me that he didn't have standards.

Simon became my shopping guru, taking me to the only store in Cognito that would color my cheeks crimson. By the fifth outfit, I caught on to Simon's little game. He dressed me in scandalous outfits—knowing I wouldn't approve—just so he could file the image in his "mental picture drawer" for later recall. *Cheeky bastard.*

We rode down the elevator to meet Logan outside. The leather pants made a sound when I rubbed my sweaty palms over them.

"Stop fussing. You need to look comfortable, like you always wear leather."

"Easy for you to say, this is just another night on the town for you. I feel like I should be saying *trick or treat*."

"I'll take the treat, although I never did turn down a trick."

"Always have a comeback," I said, imitating Justus.

"I learned from the master," he pointed out. "Remember, leather wants to be worn; it craves the feel of your body, so be sure to treat it nice and it will put on a good show."

"Yes, but was the thong necessary? No one is going to see that," I grumbled.

Simon winked. "All or nothing, love."

"I hate you."

"Helen of Troy may have had a face that launched a thousand ships, but you have the body that will launch a thousand—"

I clamped my hand over his mouth.

The pants were tight, low-rise, and paired with a shirt that was an open invitation in the back. I tinted my lips whore red, and the boots had three inches of lift. Simon wagged his tongue when I emerged from the bathroom, and doused me in cheap perfume. If my mother got a glimpse of me, she would have made advanced reservations to roll over in her grave when her time came.

The elevator door popped open and a few heads turned. An old woman holding her Chihuahua clucked her tongue when she saw us.

"Good evening, Miss Behave."

She wrinkled her nose as the little dog bared its teeth. "It's Beatrice Havers, and that's Miss Havers to you, young man."

Simon shot her a sexy wink. She turned up her nose and gave a disgusted sigh, but I could see a twinkle behind her eyes that told me she adored the attention.

"Simon, you are so rude," I whispered.

"She loves it," he assured me. "Every woman should remember that they were once naughty little vixens. I've seen a picture of her back in the day; she was a hot little number."

"I didn't know you went for the cougars." I made small kisses in the air.

"Jealous?"

I laughed. "Absolutely."

Simon pinched my hip as we strutted through the lobby like a couple of punk rock sex kittens. We were a spectacle, and I laughed when I noticed his dimple. He was proud of his little Frankenstein.

"*Geez, Louise!*" Logan said, eating me up with his eyes.

"Not one word."

Between the two of us, I wasn't sure whose outfit was more shocking. Logan wore matching leather pants that fell even lower than mine, showing off the V-cut of his abdomen. He also wasn't wearing a shirt. My eyes returned the gesture, appreciating every line of his svelte body. His normally soft locks were tangled, hanging in small clumps that were thick and unkempt.

Logan towered over me with the confidence of a king. Except tonight, I was a little bit nearer to his face in my heels. A buzz of nervous energy rippled through my fingertips for just a moment.

"Soak it in; take your mental snapshot, but let's go," I said, waving a hand.

He caught my wrist and I looked up at him. "You look lovely in anything, but I don't like the perfume."

"Simon picked it out. What's wrong with it?"

He twisted a lock of my hair between his fingers and held it under his nose. "It's too strong. I can't pick up your scent."

"Oh, so *that's* it," I said, shaking my head. "You can't enjoy my heavenly smell?"

"That's not it." There was a sharp edge to his tone. "I don't like that it will take me longer to track you."

Logan was uneasy, and I stroked his arm reassuringly. "Let's go, Mr. Cross."

I jumped into the backseat and Logan flicked a glance at me. He expected me to claim the seat beside him, which Simon happily took. I needed to mentally prepare myself for the possibility of seeing Nero. After my pitiful confrontation with Brandon, a fear was sprouting inside of me that I might freeze up again.

The car pulled to a stop outside of the club and the engine shut off.

Logan turned around and put a strong hand on my knee. "I won't let anything happen to you, female."

I'm not sure why, but that comforted me. "Eli is our backup plan if Nero doesn't show. I don't want you stalking after him in the bar."

"She's right," Simon agreed. "We don't want to spook our lead. We may end up using him, but let's stick to the plan. Nero won't have his goons around since Hell is his playground. Silver will fish him out, and I'll move in. He should know that we're aware of who he is and what he's doing; I want him on his toes. Men who think they're being watched make mistakes."

We waded through an anxious crowd inside the sticky, hot club. People stood shoulder to shoulder.

I jumped when I heard the crack of a whip. Logan tightened his grip on my hand and led me down the hall. Someone reached out to touch me, and Logan pinned him against the wall in a heartbeat. He turned and nodded at me to go without him.

A girl in a red halter top snatched Simon by the collar and dazzled him with her showy lips. He lingered in the hall, and I moved on to the bar alone.

Breed bars differed from human ones. The magic was a heavy molasses in the air—charged with energy from those who were different—like me. It's dizzying the first time you experience it, but after a while, it feels natural. A man with long brown hair streaked with blond strolled by, holding a handful of colorful lollipops. I recognized him from my last visit and he smiled, handing me a bright red one. I swiveled around in my chair, tore off the wrapper, and popped it in my mouth.

Excitement poured through me. Did everything always have to be about Nero? I needed to cut loose, dance, and let my hair down. What I really wanted was to just follow him home and find out where he lives. Maybe I could break into his house. I leaned forward excitedly, thinking up harebrained schemes.

"Bartender, bring me the whole pitcher!" I shouted, twirling the candy in my mouth.

"You're sure to be the hit tonight," Simon remarked. He leaned in with a low whisper. "Stay visible and don't go wandering off. I'll move in and take over the conversation."

"You just do that." I played with his earlobe and he slapped my hand away. "Simon, you're such a prude. The girl wearing scotch tape for a blouse almost mounted you in the hall, but you would rather babysit me. I'm *so* tired of people watching me like a child." I wrinkled my nose.

"Maybe if you quit acting…"

His eyes narrowed on the white stick poking out of my mouth.

"Bloody hell!" Simon exclaimed, pulling the sucker out. "Didn't anyone ever teach you not to take candy from strangers?"

My lips were numb and tingly. "What's the big deal?"

"The big deal," he said, twirling it between two fingers, "is that it's been spiked by a Sensor."

"Well he can spike me anytime."

Simon grabbed my jaw, squishing my cheeks as he wiped a napkin over my tongue.

"It's called a sampler because they imprint some of their magic on it to heighten your emotions. It's how the Sensors give you a taste of their wares. Stay away from the vodka. I don't need you knackered to boot."

He stuck out his tongue and swirled the sweet candy over it. "Looks like this one got rid of your inhibitions; it's a good thing you didn't suck on that all night."

"I bet you say that to all the girls," I said, laughing so hard I couldn't even make any noise. *God, what was wrong with me?*

"Don't leave the room, and try not to dance on the sodding bar."

Simon bit into the candy, dropped the stick on the bar, and slipped away. The bartender set a frosty glass of beer in front of me and I swallowed a mouthful, leaving a lip stain on the rim of the glass. Bodies moved beneath flickering strobe lights on the dance floor as a techno beat was steadily thumping. Would I be able to sneak Sunny into a Breed bar? Then again, maybe that wasn't such a good idea. She would love the action and strong personalities, but they might eat her alive. I hated the prejudices that existed against humans.

"Well, well, aren't you dressed for the occasion?"

Eli slid a finger down my bare back. "I love the view; such a little tease. Come back for twenty questions?"

"Not on the agenda, Mr. Nipple Chain."

"Shame," he said. "But if you change your mind, holler. I'll come." The way he said the last bit made me squirm. Eli moved away with a nod and disappeared.

An hour stretched by, and the effects of the candy diminished. I heard enough lines that would have made a prostitute blush, but under the influence of candy, I handled them like a pro.

A crowd filtered out from purgatory. Logan towered over them by several inches and was white as a ghost. Whatever he saw down there must have been dark, and I watched him vanish towards the back of the room. Simon was conversing with a woman who had her fingers locked in his belt loop. Although talking didn't seem like an appropriate word—not the way his thumb was stroking her leather top. When I looked back, a figure emerged from the hollow of the doorway—one I knew all too well.

Nero wore a white dress shirt rolled up to his elbows. He always did that right before stealing my light, and it was the first damn thing I noticed. I squeezed the glass with an urge to throw it at him. He looked exactly as I remembered: round glasses, dusty brown hair, crooked mouth, and a narrow nose. Nothing special about him—nothing memorable.

He crossed the room and took a seat at the far end of the bar, lifting a napkin to dab the sweat from his brow.

I catapulted out of the chair, becoming a passenger in my own body. I wasn't supposed to engage in conversation, but the next thing I knew, I was floating over to the stool beside him.

A sultry woman in a short skirt had a man pinned to the wall, pressing a spiked wrist cuff into his neck. Nero glued his eyes to the scene.

"Remember me?" I interrupted.

He turned and that lazy smile dissolved when he got past my outfit and recognition sank in. His cheeks pinkened.

"You're not as bright as you think you are," I scowled.

A little vein protruded from his forehead. "What are you doing here?"

"Having a drink."

"Don't play with me, you stupid little thing."

"I'll do… whatever… I want." I stared with a venomous gaze. "You thought it would be so easy to steal me away, but it backfired in your face. You'll never have me, *Nero*."

I said his name loud, and with purpose.

Nero snatched my hand and splintering shards of pain touched my fingers.

In a flash of movement, his head slammed against the bar. Simon crushed his forearm against the back of his neck, and I yanked my hand free.

"Well look what we have here. Think you're a sly one, do you? Nero, I have heard so—*much*—about you."

The pause between words was a pinch of his arm against Nero's neck. When he finally let go, Nero flung his arm out and grimaced. Simon leaned against the bar creating a wall between us. Even with Simon in the middle, Nero could hardly remove his eyes from me. I guess it was like a turkey walking into your house on Thanksgiving. He had what he wanted right within his reach, but he couldn't take it.

"Did you miss our sessions together?" Nero instigated. "Hell has special rooms for that if you're feeling nostalgic."

Simon slapped him. I'd never really seen a man slap another man, and he wasn't holding back.

"Let's be gentlemen shall we? We know what you're up to, Nero. An open investigation exists with your name on it, and HALO has watch on your little charade. If you're smart, you'll back down, but something tells me you're not."

"You can't prove a thing."

"I wouldn't be so sure of that." Simon grinned.

"Do you think I'm trembling with fear because HALO is watching?" He laughed. "Nothing but a group of misfits who pat themselves on the back for putting important men in jail. All they're doing is divulging secrets that should remain among their own kind, and playing God."

Simon looked over his shoulder. "Silver, I need you to leave us."

"The hell I'm leaving!"

Nero laughed. "That one doesn't know her place."

Simon's eyes narrowed on mine as Nero continued.

"If you want to know how to remedy that, just say the word. It doesn't take much for *that one* to submit."

In a flash, Simon threw his arm out and grabbed Nero by the throat, but he never broke eye contact with me. He jerked his head, motioning for me to leave.

I hopped off the chair and faded into an empty corner. Breed establishments had rules against fighting. If you created disorder, you risked banishment. Simon might end up on that naughty list—not that I cared if he hung out in a place like this—but it wasn't wise to limit your options when they could benefit you in business dealings.

"Nero won't give you what you want."

Eli leaned against the dingy wall in the same unappealing outfit he wore the week before.

"What would that be?"

I stared at the chain hanging across his chest with an urge to yank it off. When he caught the direction of my stare, I saw the faintest hint of a smirk.

"Answers. I can give you those for another even trade." Eli folded his arms and waggled a brow. "Won't hurt a bit. Just a little memory recall."

"I don't think so."

"Just keep in mind that most here don't give a shit what you want. Careful who you tangle with, Mage. You know where to find me if you change your mind. Good luck."

Eli stalked off towards the front of the club and I looked around, wondering where Logan was. We agreed that once Simon had Nero, Logan would drive me home. I walked the length of the club, but didn't see him, so I followed a crowd into the dungeon. When I reached the bottom, I hurried past a woman in pointy heels, walking on a man's bleeding back.

These people had a twisted idea of fun. Was a pint of ice cream and a movie on a Friday night such a bad thing?

Claustrophobia closed in as I shouldered my way through the thick crowd. How hard could it be to find a 6'5" shirtless blond?

The narrow corridor came to a dead end and I stared at the dark wall. Someone grabbed my wrists and held them behind my back.

"Hello, pretty."

"Let go of me," I shouted.

"No one leaves the dungeon once claimed, not until you finish the act."

"I'm not playing, so let me go."

I threw my leg back and kicked him hard, twisting my wrist to break his grip. He was quick, and swung me into an empty room. I fell over the edge of a hard surface. Before I could stand, a man with albino hair strapped a cuff around my wrist, tethering me to the table.

Without thinking, I took his hand and threw my power into him, but quickly realized the man was a Mage. Juiced up with my light, he smiled. Wide. Rule number five in training with Justus was broken—never attack with your power unless you know who your enemy is. I had to be especially careful about throwing my light into another Mage, as the quality was brighter.

"We've got a frisky one tonight, Ryker. Do you want me to tie down her legs?"

"No. That would take the fun out of it."

I pulled at the cuff. "You can't do this without my consent, you sadistic pig!"

"Au contraire. You must participate. There's no rule it has to be consensual," he chuckled. "Play nice; if someone chooses you for their game, you complete the act. Period." He shot a glance towards the albino. "God, I love the newbies."

I could smell Ryker's cologne as he approached. His complexion was pasty which looked even more unattractive against a shaved head. The man needed a bottle of suntan lotion and a trip to Belize. Between his ears, eyes, and mouth—he had more metal than a rock concert. However, what really made my skin crawl was the sinister tattoo inked across his chest. A grim reaper laughed at me with a skeletal smile. The blade of the scythe ran along Ryker's throat.

I launched onto the table—arms bound—ready to kick someone in the skull with my heels.

He tucked his hands beneath his armpits and studied me.

"What do you want to do first?" the albino asked, light pulsing in his eyes. "I say we juice her."

"Later. Let's start with the cane."

I pulled at my restraints. "If you don't take these off, I'm going to scream."

"Go ahead. Do you think they care?" He laughed. "On second thought I'd rather not have a crowd tonight. Hans, get the gag."

When Hans moved closer, I clipped him in the jaw. His head rolled back and his eyes widened like saucers.

"Fucking *hell,* she's really not into this," he said, rubbing his jaw.

Ryker grabbed my heel. "Don't worry, princess. We swing alone; this is just the halftime show."

"We're going to punish you for your disobedience," Hans said. His lashes were as pale as his hair.

You have got to be kidding me. I thrashed my legs out, refusing to submit to this ludicrous game.

"Hold her fucking feet, goddammit."

The albino slapped me, and I shoved him across the room. I was about to leap off the table and do some serious damage with my heels when something caught my attention.

Logan stepped in, just as cool as could be, and closed the door behind him, sliding the lock.

"Get the fuck out of here." Ryker's lip twitched and he cracked a few knuckles. "Private party."

Chills blistered my arms when I looked into Logan's eyes and saw a gathering storm. "Which one of you put that red mark on her face?" His words weren't rushed, and when he opened his mouth and displayed his fangs, their eyes darted back and forth between each other.

Ryker pointed at his friend. "*He* did it."

"Then *he* will die slower," Logan promised.

"Chitah, we have no quarrel with you."

Logan was beyond hearing. When Ryker held up his hand, Logan twisted it until the bone snapped. Cold horror washed over me.

He tossed him to the ground like a rag doll, and I heard the tearing of flesh and groans. The Mage slumped to the floor and shook so violently that his eyes rolled back. Logan struck his victims in the jugular, and there was quite a bit of blood from the struggle, as it tinted the ends of his hair.

"If she's yours, you can have her. This was *his* idea, and if you let me out of here, I'll owe you. I'll owe you fucking big."

Logan took a position by my side, looking at Hans without mercy.

"Logan, *no*," I whispered. Black ringed his eyes and I knew he was only half in control.

He lifted his right hand, rubbing his thumb and index finger together. "Do you know what this is, Mage? It's the world's smallest violin, and it's playing just for you."

One minute Logan was at my side, the next he threw the Mage to the ground. His lips peeled back as his fangs drove into his neck. Only two puncture marks showed when he pulled back, but it was enough to cause paralysis. Logan punched him in the face several times with an iron fist before slicing him with his teeth. I was shocked by the brutality, and just as soon as it began, Logan's venom ended the very short life of a man who merely slapped me.

He freed my wrists from the straps and I struck him in the face with the flat of my hand. "Why did you kill them? Does everything have to end in death with you? We could have called the authorities, or just roughed them up a little."

Ignoring me, he slipped his hands around my waist and nuzzled against my neck. He smelled inexplicably wonderful. The scent was possessive, and I buried myself in its dark sweetness.

"Why did you fly away, little bird?"

"You were gone. I wanted to leave and I couldn't find you."

He gathered me in his arms and pulled me off the table.

My stomach turned, and I stepped back. "You have blood in your hair. Why did you do that? If they open an investigation on the murders, then we're all going to jail."

Breed jail. I read about it, but had no desire to find out firsthand how those living accommodations would be.

"Too many illegal activities are going on; they won't request an investigator."

"How do you know?"

He stroked a hand down his chest, and a muscle ticked in his jaw. "I've been to purgatory."

"Was it worth their life?"

"I've never killed a Mage that didn't have it coming. I can scent guilt much stronger than the slap to your face. Your anxiety flooded through every doorway like a forest fire, but not quick enough. That damn perfume!" he growled. "You have no idea how much I wanted to taste the blood of the one who made you afraid."

I knew. It was obvious in the fire blazing in his eyes, and the way his fingers trembled as they brushed down my arms. Logan knew my scent, and my heightened emotions only amplified it.

"Guilt doesn't make you the judge and executioner."

"What would they have done had I not come in?"

I shook my head. "I don't know, but… you need to learn to control yourself. I don't ever want you to kill in front of me again."

Maybe we differed because I was recently human and retained some of that humanity. Many were older, had less tolerance, and killed in battle. There was no 'my lawyer will call your lawyer'. This was an advanced society living by primitive rules.

"You can't go out like that," I said.

I lifted a folded towel from the floor and ran it over Logan's face, wiping away as much blood as I could. He looked down at me with hardened eyes, lost behind the heavy brow. He still hadn't retracted his fangs, and I carefully wiped his mouth.

Strong hands cupped my cheeks and his eyes glazed over with a passionate stare. Honestly, an intimate moment was the last thing on my mind as I stood there in the torture room with a Chitah and two dead bodies.

"Keep your head down. I couldn't get all of the blood out of your hair."

"Others have blood on them," he argued.

"Did anyone see you come in here?"

"No." Logan's expression looked fuzzy as he tried pulling me close to him. The fact that he killed for me was going straight to his head, giving him a drunken gaze.

"I'll go out first. Wait until I'm out of sight, then follow behind. Keep your distance so nobody makes the connection we're together. If Simon wants to hang out and have a drink with Nero, then I'll signal to him we're leaving. We have to get out of here."

CHAPTER 25

THE ROOM WAS FEVERISH—HEAVY WITH humidity, sweat, and the fragrance of brutality. The music was a deafening roar by the time I reached the top of the stairs. Simon took one look at me and rose to his feet from across the room. I shouldered my way through the crowd towards the front door.

Two men blocked the exit. I was so rattled that I didn't notice they were looking at me in a familiar way. The tall one reached for the handle. "Good luck, Mage. We'll give you a running head start." A malevolent smile flashed across his face and the door swung wide.

I ran against the gusty wind and slid to a stop in front of Logan's gutted car. Tiny pieces of gravel sprayed out from beneath my boots, clicking against the undercarriage. It wasn't a fancy vehicle by any means, but I grimaced when I saw the hood pried open and parts hanging out.

Simon jogged up and threw his hands on the edge, staring at the engine as a curse flew out.

"Simon, we have to run!" I took off down an alley and I don't think my feet ever touched the ground. "I was given a warning!" I yelled out.

"From who?"

"One was a Mage. The other one—I don't know. Tall, sunglasses…" I coughed from the dry wind.

"Chitah," Simon panted, slowing down. "He'll track our scent."

As soon as we turned the corner, Simon skidded to a halt.

"What are you doing?" I reached out, but he stepped back and put his hand on top of his head.

"Let me think, be quiet for a minute."

Empty streets welcomed us like an open hand, trying to lure us into the human bars that lined the edges. Every shadow that moved was an extra tick in my heartbeat. A beer can clattered as it rolled into the gutter, scaring a cat who darted beneath a parked car.

In a blur, Simon flashed across the street from one bar to the next before ending up on a fire escape above me.

"Do what I'm doing!" he yelled.

I flashed in different directions until every square inch of that block carried our scent. Simon had a brilliant idea to throw off our tracker. We covered the area in less than a minute before running northbound.

"Where are we going?"

Simon's hair looked like waves in the wind as he ran ahead of me. "Subway!"

We hurried down stairs surrounded by dirty, red tiles. Simon paid the toll and we jumped on the train, taking the last seat in an empty car.

I collapsed against the window. Air burned my throat with each inhale.

"I didn't think we'd get away," I gasped.

"We haven't," he said, looking out the window. "We're switching trains at the next stop." Red streaks flushed across his cheeks, and he coughed into his shirt.

"Why?"

"If he's a Chitah, he'll track us as long as it takes. Prepare to fight. Bloody hell, prepare to run. I'll hold him off."

"I hope you're kidding."

He stood up and peered through the doorway at the cars ahead.

"What happened with Nero?"

"We had a pleasant conversation that didn't end well. I assumed he would want privacy at a fetish club. I assumed wrong. If he has bodyguards with him at all times, we're going to have a hell of a time getting close again." He combed his hair with the tips of his fingers and murmured, "Well played, Nero."

I groaned and dropped my head in my hands.

"Did you hurt yourself?"

"My head is throbbing."

"It's the adrenaline." He plopped down beside me, rubbing a hand across the back of my neck. "Suck it up, buttercup."

I blew a strand of hair from my eyes. "Where are we going?"

"Back to your place."

"Justus will kill me. You gave me your word that you wouldn't—"

"This has gone too far. We're not putting our lives in jeopardy so that you can salvage your pride. Face the music."

"You mean the firing squad."

When the train squealed to a stop, we jumped off. The floors had random stains with cigarette butts crushed in the corners, and graffiti decorated most of the walls. I grimaced, rubbing at my ankle. My boots were made for walking, not sprinting across half of Cognito.

Simon kicked a soda can, startling a nurse who hurried up the stairs out of sight. We were alone. His gaze drifted towards the open mouth of the dark tunnel.

"Simon?"

His head snapped around. "Run!"

Before I could turn, a sound erupted and it wasn't the train. The figure that stepped out of the shadows was the Chitah. I knew by the distinct roar that decimated any doubt.

He was tall, like Logan, but scrawny and dressed like a bum. The Chitah blew out a hollow breath and stalked forward with large fists.

"You give good chase, female." He threw a leg over the platform and pulled himself up. "Give me more credit; I'm way better than that. I hate to damage the merchandise, but you pissed me off three blocks ago."

His eyes shifted color, and my legs wobbled as I stared into their inky depths.

"Silver, get back," Simon ordered.

"He likes to chase and I'm tired of running. Not a chance. Work with me."

The Chitah's eyes flicked between the two of us.

We looked at each other, and I nodded at Simon. All it took was one tooth to paralyze a Mage. "I'll take his throat," I whispered, "Charge up; you'll only get one shot."

I sprang at the Chitah and he moved to knock my hands away, so I locked my arm around his throat using the force of my body to take him down. We slammed against the hard concrete, knocking my elbow hard enough that I yelled out.

Simon never went for the Chitah, because the Mage emerged from the tunnel wielding a knife. They collided in a blur of movement and engaged in combat. Blood trickled down Simon's arm.

The Chitah moved beneath me and I stupidly held on before realizing I could knock him out with my light. I chanced it—loosening my hold as I cradled his head in my hands. I wasn't charged up enough to do much damage, but I was going to give him what I had. Before I could release, the Chitah rammed the heel of his hands into my chest, throwing me back. I nearly fell off the platform, but caught my balance at the last second.

Gasping for breath, I studied the situation. He obviously didn't see me as competition, as he was dusting off his pants. The only way out of this was to team up with Simon against the Mage, and then take on the Chitah.

I didn't have a chance to finish that thought before the Chitah threw me to the ground, pinning my wrists above my head. Sharp fangs grazed the soft flesh of my cheek and I crumpled away from him.

The knife gleamed against the cement floor to my right, teasing me, as I was unable to use my gift to pull it. Simon wasn't a big guy, but he was a demon with knives.

Logan inadvertently taught me one thing: a Chitah not only scented emotion, but also reacted to it. Anxiety filled his nose, but what would happen if I threw him off with desire? Distraction is a valuable tool. I shut my eyes, searching for a memory—anything that would put me in that frame of mind.

Nothing.

I stared into his murky eyes where rings of gold held on. They reminded me of Logan, and I thought about our smoldering kiss. I could almost taste the strawberry on my tongue.

His nostrils flared. The contours of his face softened, confused as he looked between my green eyes, which I'm sure had points of silver that appear when I'm overcharged. With all the strength I could manage, I curled my fingertips around his wrist and knocked my power into him. The Chitah roared as he flew back like a man electrocuted by a bolt of lightning.

I leapt to my feet. "Simon!"

"Doing fine, honeybunch. How are you holding out?"

I laughed as the Chitah rose to his feet, pissed and ready to tear me apart. "Holding my own."

"Atta girl."

We shared an unspoken look, knowing that this may not end in our favor. The blade made a sharp sound as I lifted it from the concrete. I threw off a scent of confidence. Could a Chitah tell when I was faking it? That roused another intimate question that distracted me. *Need to focus.*

The Chitah knelt down, planted his knuckles on the floor, and showed me his teeth. I trembled, unable to feign confidence any longer. He was eyeing my throat.

His lower canines rose to meet the top.

Out of the darkness, two men emerged from the mouth of the tunnel. Logan leapt onto the platform effortlessly. His chest glimmered from the sweat of a hard run, his hair in tangles, and the leathers looked like they had a good stretch. His face was stone. His body was might, and his low rider pants were *sexy as hell.*

Logan Cross moved in like a predator. Behind him was another Chitah with a thick, brutal set of fangs. A train rushed by like a silver bullet, swirling Logan's hair around like a tornado.

I expected them to circle one another, shouting out threats. There was no warning—they attacked.

"Slide me the knife!" Simon shouted.

My heart raced in the mayhem, and with a flick of the wrist, the knife skated to his feet. He gripped the handle and drove it deep into the chest of the Mage. It sliced through bone and made a sickening sound before the man dropped to the ground. Simon flipped him on his back with his fingers wrapped around the handle. The blade was a stunner—metal forged with magic that could paralyze a Mage.

"Turn away, because you don't want to see this," he said in a raspy voice.

No, I didn't. One of the few ways a Mage could die was decapitation. I threw my hands over my ears and squeezed my eyes shut, rocking on my knees.

Minutes passed, and when I looked up, the station was empty

except for Simon standing in a pool of blood. By the sound of the conversation, he was talking to a cleaner on the phone.

Cleaners have been around for the past couple of centuries. When a body needs disposing, or witnesses require forgetting, cleaners take care of the job. Modern science poses a threat if humans were to perform an autopsy on Breed. Cleaners are also under legal obligation to report their findings to the appropriate leaders. They were referenced in one of Justus's law books, and Simon filled me in on his experiences with them.

Simon networked with people who kept secrets. Dark secrets. Otherwise, we would have faced the Council for killing a Mage. While it was in self-defense, the situation became muddy because it involved an open HALO case.

We jogged up the stairs to the sidewalk. I leaned against a brick wall, legs shaking and exhaustion crashing through me in waves.

"Silver, this is Levi, my brother."

You could see the family resemblance in the eyes and coloring, although Levi was thicker in build and wore his hair closely trimmed to his head. Dark brown stubble ran over his jaw, and his chin punched out a little with a dimple. On the inside of his right forearm was a bold tattoo in thick Old English writing that said: VERITAS.

Levi bowed his head.

"It's *very* nice to meet you, Levi."

That's when I glared at Logan. "I can't believe you dragged your brother into this. He could have been hurt! This is how you want me to meet your family? Where the hell were you? Do you have any idea what we had to go through to get that Chitah off our tail?"

Levi laughed heartily and patted Logan on the shoulder. "I'm *so* beginning to like this one already, Lo." He shuffled out of his lightweight jacket and wrapped it around my shoulders. "She's got bite."

When the cleaners arrived, three men in dark coats stepped out. They were all business as they spoke to Simon, coming to an arrangement. Logan hailed a cab, and we piled in the backseat and waited for him.

Logan brushed a finger over mine. "You two made it pretty

far. Levi lives nearby. When I picked up your trail and scented the trackers, I called him."

"Did you kill the Chitah?"

There was a brief pause. "No, I did not."

He looked past me at Levi. "Did you recognize his scent?"

"No, it was unfamiliar. One of ours is working for a—" Levi cut himself off when the cabbie tilted his mirror. "What are you involved in, Lo?"

"I don't need your judgment brother, only your loyalty. Not here. Let's get this female home first."

I turned my head, admiring Levi's remarkable tattoo. "What does it mean?"

"It means truth." The two brothers shared a private look and fell silent.

My head throbbed, my feet ached, and my energy was going into reverse.

"Can I help it if the ladies like me?"

An unfamiliar smell filled my nostrils. "Did I fall asleep?" I murmured.

It only seemed like a few seconds passed, except that I was snug against Levi's warm chest. The puddle of drool on his shirt was the only evidence needed that I used him as a pillow.

"We're nearly there," Logan said in a low voice. "Go back to sleep. I know how you Mage tire easily after a fight."

I wiped my chin and peered up front. Simon's face was mashed up against the window, fogging it up with each breath he took. I fought to stay conscious, but the lull of tires against pavement knocked me out again.

⫸⬥❈⬥⫷

My nose wrinkled at the sharp sting of frostbitten air. Shoes ate up the forest bed, crunching along its path, summoning my heavy lids to awaken.

I was in the arms of a shirtless god in snug leather pants. My face rubbed against his warm skin, and he purred softly into my hair, "You're awake."

"How long have we been walking?"

"After a mile, I lost track."

"A mile, are you kidding me? Why aren't you running super speed?"

"I'm enjoying this stroll far too much. We should be there in five."

Embarrassment heated my cheeks. One quality I hated about being a Mage was how a surplus of energy weakened the body. I didn't level it out after the adrenaline spike.

My voice was stone cold when I looked him in the eye. "Put me down, Mr. Cross."

With a dark laugh, he set me on the ground.

Coming up behind us was a sight so priceless, it deserved an award. Simon's ass was draped over Levi's shoulder like a sash. Levi looked proud to wear him, too. His hands lovingly gripped those thighs, securing his hold. When Levi's mouth widened like the Cheshire cat, I exploded with laughter.

"I wish Simon were awake to appreciate it as much as I do." I wiped a tear away when Logan reached out and brushed his knuckles across my cheek. I knew it was because he liked seeing me laugh.

"Levi, I may tease a lot, but I want to thank you for helping us."

"Trust me," he said, "the pleasure's *all* mine." He gave Simon a light pat on the inside thigh, looking at me with a lazy grin.

I frowned, remembering the blood. "Set him down for a minute. I think he was hurt."

"Two steps ahead of you honey. I've taken care of it."

A provocative image flashed in my mind. *Damn* Logan for letting me sleep through *that*.

"My Ghuardian is going to chain me to my bedroom," I groaned, staring up at the trees.

Logan's expression was stark, and he lowered his head. "Justus is not a concern."

"Tell me that after he forbids our date tomorrow."

His brows pushed together. "He *better not*."

"Why didn't we go to Simon's place?"

Logan pried apart a clump of hair, glued together by blood. "Nero might send more after you."

"What if they're waiting for us down there?"

Levi stopped to watch as he snuggled his head against Simon's hip.

"We can track their scent better out here than in the city. We're downwind."

"Maybe he sent Vampires," I suggested. Vampires carried no scent, and a Mage couldn't pick up their energy. "I don't want to put Justus in danger."

"He's your Ghuardian. If he thinks he can hide from a Chitah in that bunker, then he's a fool. Remember how easily I found you?"

Simon moaned when Levi shifted his weight. "Can we have this little lovers spat another time? You're waking up my passenger."

"Learner, I want an explanation for this!"

I spun around to see an angry bull named Justus charging from the trees.

Simon unconscious in the arms of a Chitah didn't pique his interest as much as our attire. We looked like a biker gang taking a midnight stroll through the forest to hide a body.

Justus got right in my face and tightened his expression.

Logan inched forward and I threw up my hand. "This isn't your business."

"Explain," Justus demanded, teeth clenched, heat wafting.

"Simon is okay, he's just crashing. This is Levi. He was instrumental in helping us tonight, so I'm asking permission to let them inside. We uncovered something about Nero, and I need your help."

CHAPTER 26

D ATE NIGHT.
    Justus was a man of his word and did not revoke my privileges, even after learning the truth. I stopped Simon when he tried to lie for me. I could never forgive myself if I drove a wedge between two friends. I took full responsibility for my actions, and detailed my first trip to Hell.

That was right before the yelling match began. Justus shouted and Logan stepped between us. Levi was ready to fight anyone with a pulse. I had to commend Simon for smoothing things over. Justus liked to bark a lot, but he rarely held a grudge. Despite how it all went down, I brought valuable information to the table that no one saw coming. Going against the Mageri was one thing, but intent to start a war put Nero in an entirely different league.

I admired myself in the mirror, feeling like a regular girl going on an ordinary date. Sunny would have killed me for wearing black sneakers over pumps, but it was a little slice of sanity in a world of chaos. I reminded Logan that the dress code was jeans, so it might be in his best interest to avoid any five-star restaurants.

Perfume didn't matter with Logan, and neither did makeup. Strands of hair hung loose from my ponytail, and I put on the strawberry flavored lip balm with a nude tint. Logan would have to take me or leave me—just as I was.

We parked outside of a long building and I glanced at the sign and gushed, "I haven't bowled in years! What made you think of this?"

He looked satisfied with my reaction. "You mentioned it once in passing. You'll need to teach me how to play."

I scratched my cheek and looked at him quizzically. "You've never bowled?"

"It's a human thing."

"It's a *fun* thing," I corrected.

Logan opened the door, helped me out of the car, and gave me the full treatment. When he knelt on the dirty floor to tie the laces on my bowling shoes, I didn't recognize the man I first met.

Okay, so he went a little beyond my expectations. Compared to the other men I dated, he stood head and shoulders above the rest—literally.

There was something different about his demeanor. If Chitah women were really God's gift, then I had a lot to measure up to in his mind. Perhaps that's why he looked so weighted by his thoughts.

I learned one fact about Logan: he was an atrocious bowler. My score was bad, but his looked like Morse Code. I thought he was trying to be a gentleman and let me win, but the restrained anger and ruddy cheeks when he threw a gutter ball told me otherwise.

It was hard to poke fun at the man, for I was far too preoccupied watching his magnificent body throw that ball… and so were a few other women. He had no form, but the way his hips swiveled each time he gave it his all was pure magic.

A half-eaten pizza stared at us from the center of the table. We didn't talk about Breed, Nero, or anything supernatural. We spoke about things we enjoyed, things that didn't really matter.

Logan was my date night hero.

One of those slow, sappy love songs hit the speakers and the main lights went out, replaced by a spray of colorful ribbons circling the floor. I fiddled with a pepperoni, feeling nostalgic. He stared intimately at me, and the music became a soundtrack to our date.

"Did you have a job when you were human?" he asked.

I nibbled at the pepperoni and put it back on the plate. "It wasn't the most exciting job, but I worked as an administrative assistant. They had me doing everything from copying files to running reports."

"No male to take care of you?"

I frowned. His uses of words like male and female were one thing, but if he was going to imply a woman should be taken care of,

I was going to have a problem with that. "Does a woman working offend you?"

He tilted his head. "I think it's impressive. Most female Chitah prefer not to work. The ones that do are... well..." He pushed his plate away. "Tell me why your eyes silver in the center."

"You noticed?"

He spoke through clasped hands, with his elbows on the table. "I notice everything about you. There isn't a single hair on your head I haven't put to memory."

"Black hair," I reminded him, because he never dated brunettes.

A single brow arched. He lowered his hands, wet his lips, and spoke very slowly. "Raven hair I want spread all over my satin sheets beneath me."

I turned my head and watched a man throw a strike. Logan knew how to push all kinds of buttons that I didn't know I had.

"You can answer my question or I can color your cheeks. You decide."

"They do that sometimes when I'm charged up," I shrugged.

His reply was dark, and sinful. "Good to know."

"So, you don't have questions about the previous men I've been with? You haven't brought it up."

"Should I? Unless you want me to hunt them down, I have no interest in knowing about any male who took you to bed." His lip twitched and I dropped the subject.

I liked that he wore his hair down. It didn't seem to bother him that part of his face was covered, and it made me want to get a better look at him. But my mind was elsewhere. "Will you promise me something?"

"What can I promise?"

Behind us, a cheer erupted from a group of girls after their ball crashed into the pins.

"That someday you'll look for your sister and talk to her."

He lowered his eyes to the table.

"You owe it to yourself to find her. She could be a remarkable woman and you'll never know. You don't have to explain who you are, but someday she'll be forty, then eighty, and time will have slipped away from you. It might be the biggest regret in your life. I grew up alone, and dreamed of having a sibling. Don't cheat her out of an older brother."

Logan pushed his chair back, and the metal legs shrieked against the floor. He walked around the table and stood over me. Long hair obscured his face, and shadows outlined the cords of muscle in his arms. Unable to see his expression, I became unnerved. It was a sensitive subject, and I should never have brought it up.

I looked down and Logan offered me his hand. Afraid that the date was over, I touched his palm and he pulled me into his arms, holding my hand over his heart.

We swayed.

"Wait, I don't dance like this. Everyone's looking at us." I could feel the eyes crawling over us like a spider.

"Let them look," he said under his breath.

"You didn't answer my question."

"It... pleases me that you think of my family," Logan stuttered. I could feel his heart beating against my fingertips.

He held the back of my neck firmly, pulling me close. A few giggles from the teens in the next lane caught my attention as I stumbled over my feet. Logan towered over me, and I felt like an ugly little weed trying to dance with an oak tree. I closed my eyes, imagining us as a human couple—not Mage or Chitah.

"You are a curious woman, Silver. You'll fearlessly take on a Chitah, but a few humans watching you dance has you rattled. Tell me something else you have never experienced. I want to give you one more thing."

"I don't *know*." I was being difficult.

He slipped an arm around my lower back and dipped me. I squeaked, peering over my shoulder at the wood floor.

"Ah, you've never been dipped, have you? Score one for me." He whirled me back up, and I caught my breath with a startled laugh.

"You are mischief. Anyone ever tell you that? Who ever knew the big bad wolf was just a big ol' pussycat."

Logan pushed me at arms length and laughed unexpectedly. I never saw him so expressive and humored. There was such an agreeable tone in his voice that a few women turned and smiled at him. Why shouldn't they? When he wasn't so serious, his striking features softened and made him appear attractive—in a unique way.

He tired of his sudden outburst and kissed my hand, leading me back to the table. "Have you ever played miniature golf?"

I sipped the grape soda and smiled. "I am the goddess of the volcano."

"Have you ever been on a roller coaster?"

"Unfortunately."

"Have you ever eaten caviar?"

"Uh…"

"Settled."

"I'm not sure I want to eat fish eggs; just because I haven't done it doesn't mean I—"

"Won't try it. That *is* what you were going to say, wasn't it?"

He was impossible. "You win, but you'll have to plug my nose and shovel it in."

Logan lifted my hand to his cheek. It was smooth and freshly shaved, and I imagined it smelled nice. He never wore aftershave or cologne. He didn't need to. A throaty purr rolled over his tongue. "Nothing would please me more than feeding you."

"Your turn." I nodded at the lane, pulling my hand away. "I'll be right back; I need to stretch my legs."

"Silver?"

"Yes?"

Logan cupped my face in his hand and brought everything to a standstill. His thumb traced over my cheekbone and, for the first time, I found myself really looking at him. Deeper than just his irises, deeper than just the way he gazed back at me. Something flickered in there—tender and secretive.

The magic was broken when he let go, looking uncertain about his own behavior. "Hurry back."

"Try not to miss me, Mr. Cross."

I floated like a cloud through the musty smell of sweaty socks, the drunks at the bar, and screaming kids at the arcade. I never felt so disconnected from my old life; I didn't belong in this world anymore.

Can't say it was the most romantic place, but Logan scored points for making me feel human again—even if just for a moment.

I would have skipped to the bathroom if it weren't for the fact that I would look like a bleeding idiot, as Simon would put it.

I made it to the far end of the building by the exit where the bathrooms were tucked away. Two young girls flew out of the open doorway, one splashing the other with water as they ran down the carpeted hall. The bathroom could have used a little cleaning with a mop… or a flamethrower. After I washed my hands and smoothed out my hair, I dug through my purse, searching for a few extra coins when a hand slapped over my mouth.

A sharp needle stung against my neck. The sounds of pins exploding, music, and laughing faded away. I never had a chance to react; an icy wave rushed through my chest, and I blacked out.

<hr>

I lurched forward to vomit, but nothing came up. Rubbing the dust away from my itchy nose, I squinted at the dim light from an outer hall. A bulb flickered as if on the verge of burning out. It reminded me of a horse stall, or Alcatraz.

Scattered patches of straw covered a dirty floor. The walls were made of knotted wood, and corroded bars separated my room from the hall. It was dilapidated, and yet partially remodeled. A small insect scurried through a crevice in the wall behind a wooden bucket.

I put weight on my hand to straighten my legs when a metal sound caught my attention—a shackle, locked around my ankle. The chain snaked across the floor to a heavy bolt plugged into a concrete slab on the wall.

"*What the hell?*" I murmured. The last thing I could remember was staring at the yellow tiles on the bathroom wall.

My temples throbbed as I stood up in my white bowling socks. I could reach all the corners of the room except by the bars; the chain kept me about two feet from it.

"Hello?" I called out.

No answer.

I dropped to my knees and tried to enter the Grey Veil. *Nothing* happened. Stunned, I stood up and tried to flash, but all I did was stumble and fall. There was no sense of time.

Was I human again? No, my core light was bound into a small coil, but it was still there.

The chain scraped across the floor. Could the metal be suppressing my abilities? Stunners were tempered with magic that paralyzed a Mage when driven into their flesh, but merely touching them wouldn't have any effect. I knew because I handled Justus's knives on many occasions. This power was like nothing I'd read about, and it scared the hell out of me.

A door opened in the hall, and I curled up on my side.

"You don't need to pretend. I know you're awake."

It was a man's voice. He squatted on the other side of the door, gripping the bars. Not really a man, but a boy who didn't look a day over twenty-one. His eyes were light—maybe hazel—and shaggy brown hair covered his ears. His physical appearance was boyish, from the slope of his shoulders to his casual posture.

"Hungry? I brought you an apple."

He placed a crimson red apple on the floor. The first thing that flashed in my mind was Snow White, and I glared at him.

"We'll be friends. You'll see. I'm the handler; I bring all the meals and clean up around here, but I can keep you company." He looked down the hall for a few seconds. "It gets lonely at night. Nero doesn't care how long I'm down here as long as I'm out when he comes." He dropped his ass to the floor, claiming a permanent seat.

Nero, that bastard. I stewed on it for a minute, but in a strange way, I was glad he caught me. This was exactly where I needed to be. If Nero was holding others against their will, I had a chance to free them. This wasn't misfortune; it was opportunity.

"My name's Finnegan, but you can call me Finn. What's yours?"

Silence.

"That's cool, you don't have to talk. They usually don't say much at first."

I sat up. Finn was looking at a cheap watch with a blue band.

"Where does he keep the others?"

"They're on the far end of the building. You're in isolation. What did you do to piss him off on your first night?"

"How many are there?"

"Well, four like you, and three transients."

"Transient?"

"That's what we call them when they're still human. Nero's shopping for another Creator. Samil's death threw a wrench in… whatever. I doubt he'll be able to find someone with the same magic he had. That's what Nero is looking for, and he's pretty pissed about it. Samil was a real asshole, anyhow." Finn scratched his shoulder. "Come on, I told you my name. It's only fair you tell me yours."

The kid spoke easy, and nothing about him came across as malevolent. There was loneliness in the way his eyes wandered around the room. Finn avoided eye contact, as if he didn't know how to behave with strangers.

"My name is Silver. Tell me, kid—if that's what you are—why are you involved with Nero?"

"If *that's* what I am?" He laughed. "You're funny. I have no choice because he owns me."

"You can't own someone," I pointed out.

"I'm a Shifter. I was sold to Nero for a price, so that makes me his. Unless he sells me, declares me free, or dies—he owns me."

Finn shrugged matter-of-factly and twirled an apple by the stem. "Do you want this? Mealtime isn't for another four hours. Those in isolation are put on food restriction, but not all the time."

"Are you the one who stuck me with the needle?"

"I never go out," he said, dragging his eyes away. "That was probably Diego. You don't want to mess with him, so if he comes down here, keep your distance. He's not right in the head." Finn tossed the apple in the air and caught it. "Diego is like an apple that looks okay to eat, but there's a tiny hole in the skin. When you cut it open—it's rotten inside."

"Why am I not able to use my gifts?"

Finn set the apple down and lifted a finger. "The metal keeps the power chained up, and not just with your kind, either. I heard he paid a shiny penny for them, too."

"That's what I thought," I said. "I don't understand why you think he owns you. Slavery existed with Shifters, but that was a long time ago." I assumed the books Justus owned were current.

"My father owed a debt and sold me to pay it off. That guy sold me, and three owners later, here I am."

"Jesus."

"Tell me about it."

Finn hopped to his feet and rocked on his heels. "I've got to go, Silver. Strange name. Nero will come, but I don't know when. I hope it's not for a long while; I hate the way they are after he visits them." He glanced down the hall and back. "Stay quiet, and try not to cause trouble."

Little did he know.

Finn smiled and shuffled away. I peeled the label from the skin of the apple and decided to trust him.

CHAPTER 27

HOURS LATER, THE HALL DOOR opened. I curled the chain around my fingers anxiously. I spent the last few hours planning to wrap it around Nero's throat if he attempted to steal my light. When the white tennis shoes came into view, Finn proudly crossed one foot in front of the other while holding a tray.

"Lunch, madam."

"Lunch? I thought it was morning."

"Nope. You were knocked out for a while," he said, unlocking the door. Finn set the tray in the center of the room with a watchful eye.

"My friend will track me down. He's a Chitah."

"Hmm." Finn twisted his mouth. "Nero's guards are good about planning stuff; they wouldn't risk a Chitah tracking them out here." He backed up and swung the door closed.

"He'll come," I insisted.

"I hope he does, but I seriously doubt it. Sometimes they use the spray because it confuses their sense of smell."

Logan was my only hope. Hearing Finn's confident words that I wouldn't be saved was disheartening. All that fairy tale shit I heard growing up was starting to piss me off.

"Where am I supposed to go to the bathroom?"

Two red marks spread across his cheeks. "Sorry, I forgot to... that bucket," he pointed. "Hope you weren't drinking out of it. You're only allowed to leave the room once a week to clean up, but that's the um..." He lifted a shoulder and chewed on his lip.

The food added insult to injury: peas, corn, rice, and sunflower seeds—no utensils. Nero wanted me to behave like an animal, shoveling it in with my hands.

Finn rubbed his nose. "It's what everyone gets in the beginning.

I *know* why. Don't let it get to you. Soon you'll be upgraded to spaghetti and mashed potatoes, so enjoy this while it lasts."

The lock slid into place as Finn sat down Indian style in the hall.

I dropped to my knees and eyed the plate.

"How long have you been a Mage?"

"Less than a year. What can you tell me about the others?"

I wondered if Finn was supposed to be telling me all this, but he perked up whenever I asked him a question.

"Most are girls. Nero doesn't like that for some reason, but that's what Samil brought. Cheri's new, doesn't talk anymore. Ray's pretty coolio. Rena's been here the longest, and she's really nice. She doesn't say mean things to me—not like Lucy." Finn scratched the side of his head and flicked his eyes at me. His ears poked out of his hair just a little bit and I caught the insecurity when he flattened his hair over them. "I feel sorry for her, but I don't talk to her anymore. She's always trying to start a fight."

I studied my plate and folded it like a taco, letting the food slide in through the open end.

Finn laughed contagiously.

I gave him a shit-eating grin. There was no way I was going to be forced into primitive behavior. "Someone may treat you like an animal, Finn, but never act like one. I'm hardheaded. I take after my Ghuardian."

"What's that, a custodian?"

"Not exactly. The meaning is different from the human word, so you won't find it in the dictionary. It's an old word among Mage. After Samil's death, I needed someone to take me in, and the Mageri appointed him."

"Oh. The new ones usually came right after he made them. Except that changed a few months ago when they started bringing in humans. I don't know if that was Nero or Samil's idea; the two of them were always fighting."

"How much do you know about what Nero is planning?"

"Enough to make me dangerous." *Finn looked about as dangerous as a dragonfly caught in a summer breeze.* "None of us know the big picture; we just see our piece of it. The guards know even less than I do, but for what they get paid, I doubt they care." Finn rubbed his nose as if the dust were bothering him. "Are you the one that killed Samil?"

I was surprised by the question. "No, I wasn't the one. He deserved what he got, Finn. Samil was a cruel man."

He twirled a shoelace between his fingers absently. "No doubt."

Finn brought me some water when I finished eating. The stall was hot and stuffy. I wondered what would have happened to me if I'd never met Justus. What were the chances a juicer would have picked me up? Here I sat—once again—in trouble, and yet I would have been worse off living in ignorance.

"Hey Finn?"

"Yeah?"

"Do you mind keeping me company?" My eyelids drooped.

"No problem. Everyone sleeps the first night; the drugs are still in your body. I read about it. They'll wear off in a little while."

Finn spoke softly in a hurried voice, and I listened to his stories about Russia, and old folklore that he found on the internet. My blinks were becoming longer, but that only made him more comfortable with talking to me.

Only a minute or two went by when I snapped my eyes open. Finn was off and running down the hall. Prickles of energy raced across my skin as I felt the flare of a Mage.

Nero stepped into the light with his hands in his pockets. Cool. Collected.

"Look what we have here. What was it you were saying about never being caught?" He stood very still, watching me through the bars. "No leathers today, I see. Tell me, did you really think you could just walk right up to me without consequence?" He clucked his tongue. "Didn't anyone teach you not to leave the house without your Ghuardian? They said you were on a date with a Chitah."

Nero spit, and a puff of dirt rose where it hit the ground. He removed his hands from his pockets and curled them around the bars. "You disgust me with your interbreeding. I'm placing you on food restriction, and I'll return when you are more… cleansed." His nose twitched, and he looked at me like garbage. "Welcome home."

"This is not my home."

"Possession is nine tenths of the law. Your days living under a

Ghuardian are over; enjoy the accommodations." A door slammed in the distance when he walked away.

Time moved forward at a crawl. I could wait patiently for centuries, or I could take charge of my escape. The key to my freedom was in my hands alone.

When the door clicked open, I lifted my eyes. I was anxious to talk to Finn because he was a likable kid, and he might be able to get me out of here. Instead—lifeless eyes watched me from behind the bars.

The dark-haired man stood as silent as a statue. His skin was heavy bronze, as if he spent all his hours in the sun. There was dirt on his rough hands, and mud on his boots.

We engaged in a staring match, a contest I easily won. He lifted an arm to take the key off of the wall.

"Diego, better get your ass out there, man. They're looking for you," Finn yelled from a distance.

Diego squeezed his fingers around the key.

"Did you hear me?"

Finn returned after a long stretch of boredom. The air was thick like summer heat and I rubbed at my sweaty neck. There were no windows or proper ventilation. A pair of sneakers briskly walked along the hall, and Finn took a seat by the door.

"How are you holding out?"

"I think I've lost twenty pounds in sweat."

"It gets cooler in the evening. The sun hitting the roof tends to heat things up."

"That's the infamous Diego? Charming guy."

Finn shifted on his ankle. "If I didn't yell out, that clown would've come in here. I'm not joking around with you. He's hardcore. Diego doesn't react unless someone looks at him; he thinks it means something. Keep your eyes on the floor and play invisible."

I knew he was just trying to help, so I smiled and nodded at him.

"I heard Nero put you on food restriction. Don't worry. I'll bring you a few apples, but I'll have to sneak them in later. Sound cool?"

"Do you think there's a chance he'll move me with the others?"

"Why? Am I too boring for you?" he asked.

"No you don't bore me, Finn," I assured him. "What do you shift into?"

"That's not a very polite thing to ask."

I quickly looked up. "Well la-tee-da! I didn't think it was such a big secret."

Finn looped his finger around his shoelace. "I don't go around showing everyone my animal. That's *personal*."

He was serious, and when his cheeks flushed, I knew I had stumbled upon my first Shifter faux pas. I never attended Breed etiquette classes in the school of Justus.

"Sorry, I've never met a Shifter. I don't mean to be rude with my questions. I was just curious."

"It's like me asking what your gifts are. I may find out eventually. But you're not going to just disclose them to me, now are you?"

He had a point.

"Do you go to school? Do you have a girlfriend?"

"Um, no. I've never been to school," he said, combing his hair down with his fingernails. "I'm not allowed to leave the property so I don't meet girls. They sometimes let me get on the Internet, so I read a lot. I'm not stupid."

"Of course you aren't, I can see you're very bright. How old are you?"

"I think I'm about twenty-two. I forgot the exact day I was born, but I know the month. I'm a Leo."

I wasn't that much older than he was. I stopped aging at twenty-nine when my Creator made me.

"What would happen if you set me free?"

"I can't," he said, shaking his head. "Even if I had the key to those chains and let you go, Nero would beat the snot out of me."

"Scratch that idea."

He lifted his chin and disguised an emotion I couldn't read. "You mean it?"

"No one takes a beating for me."

For the first time, Finn was silent.

His jeans rustled as he stood up to leave. When he was out of sight, I heard him mumble to himself, "I wish I could give you a blanket."

I loved that kid immediately.

CHAPTER 28

A S PROMISED, THE MEALS WERE never delivered to my cell. Late at night, I stared at the ceiling listening to an animal prowling around. Toenails scratched and clawed at the floorboards, and sometimes I heard a snort, or a thunderous run. Whatever lived up there was restless. They shut the main lights down at night, which gave me a sense of time. Finn brought apples, and I hid the cores beneath the straw to bury the evidence. He was good company, dropping in several times a day to talk about movies and facts he read on the Internet. Finn was an inquisitive young man—always wanting to know about the outside world.

When the hall door opened, I brushed a piece of straw off my cheek. No one ever came in this late, including Finn.

At the far end of the hall, a light switched on, throwing shadows across the floor. A silhouette of a man drifted in front of the cell. The door unlocked.

"Finn?"

It wasn't Finn. It was Diego.

He came inside and I swept my leg out, knocking him off his feet. I didn't have time to think—only react. I lifted my leg to stomp on his throat when he grabbed my ankle and pulled me off balance. I hit the floor and knocked my head hard enough that I saw flashing lights.

A growl rolled through the open door like a starting motor. It was vicious, causing all the little hairs on my arms to stand up as it moved in closer. Diego stood up and I scurried across the dirt until I met with the wall, pulling the chain in my hands to use as a weapon. Diego I could handle, but something that wild made my heart beat out of control.

Diego moved slowly, and the growl became more ferocious than before. He slipped through the door and jogged out of sight.

My nerves seized up when the hall light went out, throwing me into darkness. That was the first time I ever fell asleep with my eyes open.

⚜

In my dream, the cavern floor was hard, but that's exactly how I remembered it. Glowing embers from the fire crackled, and a familiar face leaned against the wall, kicking up a spray of shimmering dust.

"Do you know who I am?"

"Yes, you're Mr. Doublecross."

Logan furrowed his brow. "What is that supposed to mean?"

I pointed an accusing finger at him. "Did you sell me out? What was this date really about, Logan? How much did Nero pay you to get me out of the house?"

The temperature dropped twenty degrees. "I would never do that!" he shouted, his upper lip trembling in anger.

"Can you promise me that? I will *never* forgive you if you were part of this."

"On my word," he said softly. "On my very word I would never consider it." Logan looked down, hair falling in front of his face like a veil. "I couldn't track you; they blocked the scent. How did they take you without a fight?"

"*Drugs, drugs, drugs,*" I sang.

He looked at me sideways and a sly grin spread across his face. "You seem in good spirits. I hope you realize that I'm not a dream."

I felt more lucid than usual, so I knew he was right. "I have a new friend. Isn't it interesting where I'm meeting all my new friends lately?"

We sat down against the uneven wall and Logan held onto my knee.

"Where are you?" he asked.

"Nero is keeping me locked up in some kind of barn. There are others here, but I haven't seen them because he's kept us separated.

I think Nero is trying to replace Samil, but good luck on that," I muttered.

"Nero," he whispered. Something dark flashed across his face. "Is your friend a Mage or human?"

"Neither. He's a Shifter."

Logan squeezed my knee. "A Shifter is half animal, and their animal cannot be trusted."

"Finn is just a kid. He couldn't hurt anybody."

Logan threw his head back and stared ahead. "I should have never let you go alone. I had a feeling before you left the table that something wasn't right. It could have been their adrenaline, or smell…"

"Then why did you let me go?"

"Because I'm not Justus. I don't require you to wear a leash. You should be able to go to the bathroom without a shadow, and I wanted…" He slammed his head against the wall angrily.

"I've never kissed you in my dream."

He didn't move, so I stretched until my lips pressed to his. They were soft, but unresponsive.

Logan turned up his chin. "Not like this."

"I know you want to kiss me," I said, stroking my mouth softly over his cheek. That's when he pushed me off and stood up.

"It's not real, Silver. I don't want anything with you if it's not real."

<hr/>

The next morning, the guards allowed me to bathe in a narrow stream just a short walk from the building. Finn was my handler, so they linked us together with neck shackles and a long chain.

"Make it easy or make it hard. I could give a fuck," one of the guards huffed.

I decided to make it easy and let them switch out the chains.

The guards didn't follow us, and there was no need to. I wouldn't get far trying to drag Finn through the woods against his will. The neck shackles contained the same magic suppressant. I guess it just made things easier for Nero if we couldn't put up much of a fight.

The water was chilly and clear. Finn sat on the shore and never spoke a word. He looked a little embarrassed, but went through the motions as if he'd done it a million times. I wondered why Finn never escaped. Perhaps he did and learned a hard lesson, but most likely, he didn't know how to live outside of captivity. When you belong to someone for that many years, you forget how to belong to yourself. While *my* chains were physical, Finn's were psychological, and this was something I knew a little about.

When we returned to my cell, the guards locked me inside.

"Diego visited last night," I said.

Finn's knuckles whitened, squeezing the bars.

"I couldn't see much," I continued, "but I had a protector watching over me."

You would have thought I presented him with a medal. Finn puffed out his chest proudly. How much did a Shifter remember in their animal form? I guessed very little, but not wanting to ask another inappropriate question, I left it alone.

"Why does Diego obey you the way he does?"

"He's a human. I've already established that I'm the alpha and he's the beta."

Shifters were interesting creatures, indeed.

I spent the rest of the day alone and hungry. I had visions of Justus sitting at a table brushing barbeque sauce over a rack of ribs. While the hunger was uncomfortable, I had a few laughs remembering the quirky things about how he liked to eat his food.

By evening, the temperature dropped. It was unusual that Finn hadn't stopped in. I wanted to know more about the others Nero was keeping.

When the hall door clicked open, I was relieved. "Finn," I sighed. "I was beginning to worry. Where have you been all day?"

"Misbehaving," a voice replied. "Sorry to disappoint. Were you expecting someone else?"

Nero walked by the bars without making eye contact. He pulled the corners away from a white napkin, holding the dirty remains of apple cores. I felt sickened at the sight of them. Finn brought them to me, and they must have searched the room while I bathed.

"Where's Finn?"

"I'm making sure that he stays an obedient dog."

"Don't you hurt him!"

"I'll send him your regards. My, don't we look all fresh and clean today?"

A smile polluted his face as he slid the key into the lock. The door opened and my pulse quickened. I picked up the chain, rehearsing a scene I'd imagined in my head a hundred times. I ran the slack through my hands expectantly. He wanted to taste my light, and I would die before I gave it to him willingly.

"What you're doing with these humans is reprehensible. They're people, not possessions. Without Samil, you can't even make whatever it is you were making."

"What I already have will suffice. In time, you will see that what I'm doing is for the greater good."

I laughed. "The greater good of what?"

"Someone as young as you will never understand the thumb that has been pressed over our lives for so long by the higher order of law. Not just the Mageri, but *all* law," he emphasized. "It goes against nature to live in peace with our enemies. It weakens us. Through the centuries, the Mageri has recorded the gifts of every Mage."

"So?"

"Did you ever consider how valuable that information might be to our enemies? Give them a list of the few Creator's we have, and we offer up our extinction."

"Your logic is to kill everyone else in order to preserve our race?"

He shrugged. "Better them than me."

"You're delusional," I said. "Building an army this way would take forever. Not all of us are going to see things your way, no matter how long you keep us here. I'll never fight for your cause, Nero."

He rubbed the side of his nose with a long, skinny finger. "I never thought Samil had it in him to create a Unique; it's a shame it has to be wasted on someone as repugnant as you."

"The others aren't Uniques?"

"They're special, but they're not like you. Samil had a gift at multiplying the power of his progeny, and some have extraordinary gifts. A stronger Mage makes a stronger army."

"Or a dangerous enemy. I'll never go your way."

He grinned with small teeth and thin lips. Nero slipped out of his jacket and neatly folded it on the floor before rolling his sleeves up. "I have more houses than this. You're just a drop in the bucket. The beautiful thing about immortality… is that I have all the time in the world to change your mind."

My grip tightened around the metal, but it was in vain.

CHAPTER 29

LYING IN THE DARK SHADOWS, I thought about home. I wanted Justus to comfort me in a way that I couldn't articulate. I wanted someone to tell me it would be okay, that someday I would be a woman who could stand on her own two feet and protect her light.

For the last several minutes, I secretly watched Finn washing my feet. While touched by his compassion, I was different now—hardened. Once you get over the fact that you won't die from your injuries, your mind learns how to absorb the pain. For Nero, his objective wasn't physically beating me down, because that would diminish the quality of my light. His methods were about subordination. Once he juiced my light, I fell to the ground like gravity's child.

Nero carried a simple wooden stick. I could have done it the easy way and let him take my light, but I never believed in the easy way. I would never let someone take from me what I wasn't willing to give.

He struck the soles of my feet repeatedly until they blistered. I gave him a pretty good fight—all things considered.

"I can't believe he did this," Finn murmured with his back to me. "This is worse than the first Mage he brought in."

"Finn, did he hurt you at all? Turn around and look at me."

He tilted his neck, but looked all right.

"What happened last night?"

Finn squeezed the wet rag and pressed it on the bottom of my swollen foot. I winced.

"Nothing I can't handle."

"I don't want you in here. Get out."

Ignoring me, he let water spill through his cupped fingers over my feet. I shuddered as my nerve endings were like a raw string on a guitar, strumming a horrible melody. It was then that something else occurred to me. I flipped the tail end of his green shirt up, staring at red marks all over his back.

"Finn!"

I pulled it a little higher, revealing how much punishment this kid took. There were several lashes across the skin. When he stood up, I cursed myself. I cursed Nero. He ruined too many lives and now it felt personal. "Oh Finn, I'm so sorry he hurt you. If I had known Nero would do this because you brought me apples, I would have stayed hungry. It wasn't worth it."

"It's no big deal," he said, straightening the shirt. "It'll heal up when I shift a couple more times, and the magic works its way through. I closed the wounds with the last shift so it didn't scar. I'm used to it."

"Yeah, no big deal," I muttered, repeating the same sentiment Logan did with me. Now I understood how he felt. Finn could heal, but it still marked my conscience knowing he took a beating because of me.

"Don't ever think that we're all like this, because we're not. I'm not that kind of a Mage, and I don't know how many you have been around, but Nero is the exception, not the rule. I don't want you helping me anymore, just tell me where we are."

Finn shook his head. "I don't know where we are. Been living here since I was a teen. There's no street sign, no address, and we don't get mail. I can roam the area a little, but I can't leave the property line. He fixed up one of the rooms down the hall for me, and that's where I live."

"Are you the one scratching around at night in the attic?"

"Yeah, sometimes my animal likes to sit on the roof. Sorry," he said, tugging at his hair. "There's something else going on. Two of the women weren't in their rooms this morning."

I eased up, alarmed. "Which ones? The humans?"

"All of Lucy's things were cleared out. She could have pissed someone off, but then Rena's room was also empty. That's when I got rattled."

"What's so special about her?"

"He spends time with her. She actually looked forward to his visits. What's that called... Munchausen's syndrome?"

"I think you mean Stockholm; maybe she was faking. He didn't take the other two?"

"He left Cheri behind. She's been here less than a year and doesn't talk much anymore. I'm not sure why, but I think it's because of Diego. Some of the humans say that he takes her from the room during his shift. I don't have access to that part of the building at night. Ray is still here, too."

"Why would he leave them?"

He lifted his shoulders in a light shrug and winced, remembering his back.

"What about the humans? Has he done anything with them?"

"Not yet, but one of them had a visitor last night that I'd never seen."

"What's he up to?" I muttered. "You said their things were gone. What things?"

"He let them have personal belongings such as books and a bed; I guess he made it like a reward or some shit. Rena kept animal carvings I made for her." His voice filled with pain as if he were speaking of a friend. If we were just possessions to Nero, why would he care to pack their stuff? It's as if they had a choice. Perhaps they were the strongest, and he was moving them to another area to make room for newcomers. The thought was chilling.

"Finn, where do they keep the keys to my shackles?"

"Only the guard on duty is allowed to carry the key. The chains all have the same lock, so it makes it easy not to lose track of keys."

"You mean the guys who came in my cell?"

"Yeah, one of *them*. There's another who does the morning shift, and of course, you know Diego. I don't let him in here since I run this end of the building," he said, scrunching his nose.

"He's a guard?"

"If you want to call it that. He's not really guard material, so they gave him the evening shift. He does all the manual stuff around the property."

The wheels in my head started to—like the bus—go round and round. "Finn, if you're not in the building, then that would eliminate any suspicion that you were involved. Is there a way you can leave for the night, maybe go to the main house?"

Finn tossed the rag in the pail he brought in. "Why the hell would I leave?"

I covered my face. "I care about you Finn, and I don't want you to get in trouble. If Diego has the key—"

"You can't fight off Diego! My wolf had to come in here to save your butt... Do you hear what I'm saying?"

"No," I argued.

"I'm not going to let you do this."

"*Let* me? You just said that to the wrong person. Do you think I'm just going to lie down like a—" I bit my tongue before I said something insulting. "Scratch that. He's going to do this to me every night until I have no more fight left. Do you want me to end up like your friend, Cheri? Where does Diego keep the key?"

Finn spun away. "You're the only friend I've got. I don't *want* you to leave—I'll be stuck alone here with no one to talk to."

His voice broke, and I felt for him. I really did.

"Then come with me."

He dropped his head. "I can't."

I sighed thoughtfully. "Then I'll come back for you. We'll force him to release you, Finn. That's my promise. Do you hear me?"

He sniffed and wiped his nose with a quick swipe. "He keeps it in his back pocket. Left side."

Finn stood up and gripped the bars, looking away. "If it helps any, deep down he wants you to like him. He's insecure. Don't hit him because that'll just piss him off and you don't have enough strength to fight. You're not going to get far, not with your feet like that."

"Finn?"

"Yeah?" He peered over his shoulder, but a mop of hair covered his expressive eyes.

"I need to do this while I have the energy. The more he takes, the harder it will become. I can't sit around waiting for opportunity; I have to make it myself. Can you be gone tonight?"

"I guess. Once or twice I've played cards in the main house with the guards." Finn sighed reluctantly. "You sure you want to do this?

If something goes wrong, I won't be here." He scraped his tennis shoe across the floor.

Which is exactly what I wanted. It mattered to me that Nero might punish him for something he had no part in planning. Finn didn't deserve to be Nero's pet, and as much as I wanted to drag him along, Finn would never come of his own free will.

"My plan is to chain Diego and release the others. Do you think they'll hear him shouting from the house?"

Finn sniffed. "He won't call out. Diego is mute; Nero cut out his tongue a long time ago. Someone slammed his fingers in a truck door once and he didn't make a peep. Even if he can, he probably won't."

"Why not?"

"Pride."

"Make sure Diego knows you won't be here. I promise I'll come back for you. You're a good friend, and you deserve a better life than this."

Before he turned away, a tear spilled down his cheek and he wiped it with the heel of his hand. If fate brought me here—I knew that above all, it was to free Finn.

CHAPTER 30

LOGAN APPEARED IN A CLOUD of dust. Only, he wasn't an apparition, he was dreamwalking.

"I'm escaping tonight."

"Tell me how," he said, eyes brimming with concern.

"Nero's unpredictability is scaring me. Two of the women are missing, but he left the others behind. I want you to make me a promise."

"A promise to do what? That's a serious thing to ask a Chitah, Silver."

"The Shifter I told you about—Finn—swear to me that if I don't make it out, you'll free him. I'm in his debt, and if I can't keep good on my word, I want you to do it for me."

The muscles in his face tensed. "What are you planning that would make me keep such a promise? One that I could only make if you were cut from this earth?"

"These people deserve their freedom, and this has gone on long enough. My plan is to release them all, including the humans. Once I'm out of these shackles, I'll be in touch."

A deep growl rose in the back of his throat. "Shackles? He put you in shackles?"

"Promise me, Logan."

I didn't think he would agree, but his shoulders relaxed and he bowed his head. "You have my word."

"Tell Simon and Justus that once I have an idea where I am, I'll reach out to them."

He smoothed a hand over my cheek and looked at me gravely. "You're as crafty as you are stubborn. Be careful, and keep your wits about you."

"Wish me luck. I have to go."

My primary focus that evening was pushing back the pain. I had no intention to stay close to Diego for long, and his healing light was not sufficient as a human. Plus, I could inadvertently kill him. Killing someone in self-defense was one thing, but just to heal a few cuts on my feet? A murderer I was not.

Diego appeared in the doorway, sliding the key into the metal lock. I lay motionless in the center of the room, erasing my fears.

I never talked about it later. What happened with Diego was a necessity, and while I didn't do anything beyond kissing that troll, it violated my conscience. I lifted the key from his pocket and reclaimed my freedom.

Diego wasn't just submissive to Finn. I ordered him to turn around and strip off his clothes near the door. He was surprisingly obedient and willing to play. It bought me time to unlock my chains in the darkness and prepare to fight. When I looked up, he was waiting for instructions.

"Walk this way, and turn around."

I shuddered when he bumped into me. As he stood there with his ass in my face, I put weight on my feet, leaned forward, and locked the shackle around his ankle.

I flashed to the door and slammed it shut, blowing out a heavy breath. He tested the chain with his strength and anger seeped across his expression—betrayal.

"Sorry Diego, no nookie for you tonight."

Two parts of the building connected through a central room by the front door. I stared at an empty desk, and smelled the heavy, wet stench of cigars. It was Diego, because the taste still lingered on my lips. Soda cans and empty potato chip bags filled a small wastebasket. Guard duty seemed like a boring job. I opened the far door.

"Is anyone in here?" I whispered loudly.

"Down here!"

I cautiously looked through the bars into the shadows. "Who's in there? I can't turn on the lights."

"My name is Ray."

"Ray, I'm going to come in, so stay where you are and don't try anything. I've got the key to your shackle."

"Yes, come in!" he said in a hurried voice.

I moved slowly until my foot tapped against someone. "Take the keys, they're in my hand."

"Hey, we're in here!" a voice shouted from the other side of the hall.

Irritated, I turned around and glared. "I'm here to save you, so could you please shut the hell up?" With my chains removed, my abilities were returning, and I sensed human energy. It was weak, like a dying battery.

A scrawny man emerged from the room. By the looks of his dirty hair and long beard, he had been in captivity for a long time. Ray ignored me and unlocked the door to the adjacent cell. A moment later, a young blonde stepped out with an expression as blank as a chalkboard.

He saw me staring at the room where people were rustling around. It didn't sound like Nero chained them up, but why should he? "Leave them here. They're human and won't get far."

"I'm not leaving them. He may not have a Creator, but if he finds a replacement, then their lives will be at his disposal. Look, just give me the key."

"Give her the key, asshole!" one of the humans spat.

"Shut the hell up!" I hissed. "If you want the guards to tie you to a tree and sprinkle blood all over you to attract wild animals, just keep on yelling."

My sympathy card was played.

"I'll yell at the top of my lungs if you don't open the goddamn door," he challenged.

Ray tossed me the key and the second the door unlocked, three humans knocked me over and took off.

"Do you need my light?" Ray asked, looking down at my feet and the way I leaned to the side.

He was a seasoned Mage, but when I looked at his gaunt features, I decided not to take from his already depleted light.

"No, we don't have time to waste."

Ray dropped to one knee and held my foot. A feathery blue light skimmed the surface of my skin, numbing the pain. It didn't heal all the way, but it was enough.

We scattered across the property like leaves.

"Have you ever flashed before?" I yelled at Ray.

"Of course! I was Samil's Learner before he gave me over to Nero."

That chilling revelation stopped me dead in my tracks. The man who beat me in a basement had a progeny he tried to teach?

"You were his Learner?"

Ray pulled Cheri by the hand, glancing back. "Of course. Unlike the others, I'm a man."

I blinked, and tilted my head. "What's that supposed to mean?"

"Men are more valuable than women as progeny. Creators expect loyalty, so the older ones consider it strength building to have men below them—like having their own small army. They see women as more trouble than they're worth."

"Well if that isn't the most sexist—"

"We don't have time to debate," he said, cutting the air with his hand.

I shook off a chill and looked back. "What about her? Can she flash?"

"Give me a minute and I'll work with her."

I looked for landmarks while Ray gave Cheri a crash course in flashing. The forest was a thick maze of distorted trees and biting vines. Within a minute or two, I was impressed to see the girl could move like a Mage.

I ripped a hole through my shirt with a broken stick, tying strips around branches as we flashed through the dark woods. It was the only idea that sprang to mind in case we needed to retrace our steps.

The hill was a terrible experience. Each time I lost traction and my foot slipped, a terrible pain gripped me. I staggered and fell to my knees when we reached the top, tempted to kiss the dirty asphalt. A road was a symbol of hope, even if I didn't know where it would take me.

"I need to contact a Mage. Can you keep a lookout?"

Ray nodded.

I spent less than a minute at the Grey Veil. Ray knew the name of the road, so I relayed the information to Justus, along with the mile marker. The temptation to go back and confront Nero was strong, but he didn't live on the property. According to Finn, Nero owned a multitude of homes.

We flew up the road like a flame racing over kerosene.

Ray's pace slowed to a crawl. "We need to stop. None of us are in a condition to keep this up."

"We can't," I panted. "We've got to keep moving. If he has trackers on us, then it won't be long before they catch up."

"It'll take time for the guards to find us."

"Nero has a history of hiring Chitah. Do you want to take that chance?"

Ray blanched and tugged at Cheri. "Come on."

The pavement was unforgiving—each step becoming a test in faith.

"What's your name?" Ray coughed.

"Silver."

He slowed down, tugging at his beard. "So *you're* the one."

I frowned. "The one?"

"Nero talks about you. We heard you were responsible for Samil's death."

He extended his arm and I stepped back. "I want to shake the hand of the person who killed him."

I shook my head. Ray was his Learner, and maybe he felt the same way I did about Samil, but I didn't know him well enough to trust if he was baiting me or not. "That's not our custom, Ray. And I didn't kill Samil. Come on. Let's keep moving."

Headlights sprang up from behind, illuminating us like a guilty party. We sensed the energy moving in our direction. They were flaring on purpose.

"You two get out of here. My friends will be coming soon. Just go!"

Ray grabbed Cheri by the arm and ran. I faced the oncoming car giving the appearance of a panicked woman when the high beams flipped on. I darted off the road into the woods, hearing several doors open behind me.

It was futile to outrun them. In the dim light of the moon, I searched for a tree with low branches, as hiding out seemed a better option.

When I found one, I hoisted myself up. I scaled that tree in one minute flat, thanks to my formative years as a seven-year-old wannabe Olympian. Strength training with Justus also provided me with the endurance to push myself when I thought I couldn't go on.

The bark scraped my arms and feet, but I didn't stop. I couldn't stop.

Perched high on a branch, I pressed my body against the aging tree. I saw blackness below, and guessed I had climbed at least two or three stories. My stomach knotted as figures moved through the brush, so I silenced my heavy breaths.

"That way," someone shouted.

Energy radiated from all directions. My breath caught when voices drifted up from below.

"I don't know. I mean... I can *feel* her."

"Circle that way," the other said. "She's holed up somewhere."

I panicked because my energy was leaking.

A gunshot shattered the silence, and I clawed the tree to keep from falling.

"What the hell are you doing?" someone shouted.

"She's up there. *Look.* You see her now? Just above the branch... to the right."

"*Fuck me,*" a voice exclaimed. "How did she get up that high?"

"I don't know, but I'm not going after her if you catch my meaning."

I heard the safety release. Another gunshot fired. This time, the branch above me cracked as the bullet flew by.

"I haven't had a good target practice in a while. How many bullets you got on you?"

When the third shot exploded, I involuntarily screamed. That one grazed my leg. They laughed as if they were at a carnival, and I was the target.

"It's my turn. Let me try."

"I think I got her that time."

Another shot fired off, followed by a high pitch laugh.

The air charged with energy, and the hairs on my arms stood up.

In the distance, something was tearing through the forest, growing louder and louder like an oncoming locomotive until it collided with one of the men.

A blood-curdling scream cut off, followed by a terrible silence. Then more struggling as the gun went off again.

Twigs cracked in the silence as something circled the tree below me.

A chilly breeze rustled through the branches, and a few strands of hair licked around my neck. I suppressed a shiver, remaining as lifeless as a statue. The tree became my best friend as I hugged against the rough grooves of the bark.

Whatever found us was deadly, and I wasn't about to take any chances. I lived in a new world now, where monsters were real.

My muscles were shaking when I heard the crack of wood below. It was climbing up.

It was coming to get me.

My heart hammered against my chest so insistently that I became dizzy. It moved closer, and the branches creaked until it was directly below me. I had nowhere to go, and my energy was not restored enough to give me any form of self-defense after the flashing.

I thought it would be Justus who would come to get me, but Logan was every bit the tracker he professed to be. With unbelievable agility, Logan swiftly pulled himself up to my branch.

"Don't ever say I didn't go out on a limb for you."

My teary eyes were wide with fear, and his humored expression quickly faded.

"Put your arms around my neck," he said, turning himself about and gripping a branch overhead. He angled his body so I could piggyback off him. "Do as I say, and hold on tight."

I spread over his back and he reached around, pulling my legs one at a time until Logan was the only thing holding me up. I looked down nervously, and nestled my face in his hair. He sensed my fear and turned his head so that our cheeks touched. "Do not be afraid, female. You're safe with me," he said.

"I can't hold on, Logan. I'm going to fall." Heights terrified me.

"You have my word that I will never let you fall."

Logan pushed himself away from the tree and we sailed through the air to a lower branch of another tree. The impact loosened my grip, but his arm swiftly locked around me.

He leapt to a lower branch and I let go. Logan caught me by one arm as I swung in midair. His hand was an iron grip that would not let go—as promised. With impossible determination, he lifted me into his arms. My entire body shook, like one of those leaves trying desperately to hold on to the tree. All the worry melted away when his soft lips kissed my neck just seconds before he jumped. We hit the ground, and a rush of air punched out of my lungs.

Logan buried his face in my neck, rolling me on my side. A strong vibration rose within his chest and the full force of his scent embraced me. This time, I did not push away, but pulled myself in tighter.

"Logan, are you alone?"

His voice was just a whisper, but it unleashed a chaos in my soul. "*Not anymore.*"

He carried me in his arms, running through the woods at an uncalculated speed. I was uncertain of our direction, but I knew one thing with perfect clarity: I was in the arms of a man who loved me.

CHAPTER 31

"WHAT IS IT?" I WHISPERED.

He fell to one knee and scanned the woods. I slipped off his back and sat down.

"How many are out there?"

"At least eight. Subtract the three I put in a coma." He flicked a glance at me and read my mind. "Yes, they still live. The one that tangled with Justus wasn't so lucky, but he was a pain in the drain."

"Who else is with you?"

Logan lifted his chin, opened his mouth, and captured a breath. "Where are you hurt?"

He smelled the blood. The earth crunched beneath me when I shifted my body.

"As much as I'd love you to lick me, I'm not coming out of these jeans."

"Maybe not now, but you will later on."

"One of the bullets scraped my leg and my feet hurt; I'll just slow us down."

He slung me over his back as if I weighed nothing. We hit Chitah run in a few strides, but it didn't last long. I flew off, flipping over several times until I slammed into a tree.

I spit a leaf out of my mouth and looked up to see what happened. Two men were closing in on us. Logan faced off with one of them, while the other Mage moved to the side, walking in my direction.

In the pale moonlight, Logan's eyes were wide and animalistic. All four canines gleamed as the men considered their strategy.

The Mage swiped his arm and Logan ducked. I heard a blade slice through the air with chilling intent.

I pulled myself up to fight when Logan shoved me to the ground and forced himself over me.

"Don't you dare!" I shouted.

That's when I saw them. His eyes were as black as midnight ashes. Logan was no longer present—replaced by the primal creature that lived within him. Not a single fleck of gold remained.

"Logan, let me up!"

I reached out to the man with the knife, trying to pull the blade, but the metal would not yield. It was made of something I couldn't manipulate the energy from, or it was tempered with magic.

The Mage on our right tossed a flashlight to the ground, blinding us. He made a quick move and Logan lunged at him, shouting out when the other Mage plunged the knife into his side.

I screamed.

"Keep it up. We can get him this way!" one of them said.

They cut him again.

As fresh blood trickled down his arm, and dampened his shirt, it became evident that Logan Cross was willing to lay down his life to protect me.

Me—his enemy.

That fact sank in each time the blade sliced through his flesh.

The Mage continued to bait him and I fought against Logan to get up, but he muscled against me with the weight of his body. They were using his instincts against him.

"Let me up!" I yelled, punching at his arm. "You can't take them both if you're protecting me. Fight them! Get off of me and let me help you."

Logan rose to his feet, tall and brave, as a man who knew no fear. The Mage sliced the cold blade across his chest. When Logan cried out, it shook me to the core. It was not the feral roar of a warrior—one I had heard him use. This time, it was filled with pain. It struck a chord so deep within me that instinct kicked in like an adrenaline rush.

I flew at the unarmed Mage and popped him in the jaw. In a heartbeat, he wrapped his long fingers around my neck. I choked, and that singular sound provoked an explosive reaction.

But not from *me*.

Caged fury spread across Logan's face like a pandemic, hardening the lines around his jaw as he peeled back his teeth. Raw malice glinted behind dark Chitah eyes. I readied myself to fight by his side, but instead of attacking, he knocked the Mage away and smothered me with his body. His chest was wet and warm, and his breath ragged as he struggled for air. The blood loss was taking its toll, and it was everywhere—on his chest, arms, and a gash across his forehead. The intensity in his gaze was so overwhelming, I was afraid to look at him.

"Give her up, Chitah. We have the upper hand. You can walk out of this alive, or die—*your choice*—but the woman belongs to Nero and we're not leaving without her."

Logan's fangs shone in the moonlight like daggers. He dragged my body even tighter beneath him. I couldn't move, not one inch. He spread across me like a shield.

Logan flicked his head from one Mage to the other. He could kill them and I knew it because I had been a witness to his unmerciful violence. I cursed Logan once for never having told me what a Chitah's weakness was. In that moment, I discovered what could bring him down.

His weakness… was *me*.

Everything clicked in that moment. I never asked how his woman died, or the guilt he must have carried from her death. Did he try to protect her? Did he even get the chance? Logan could have abandoned me to fight, but that never happened.

Someone burst through a thicket of bushes.

"Brother!" Levi roared, colliding with the Mage wielding the knife.

Simon stumbled across a fallen limb and skidded to a stop. "*Bloody hell.*"

"Simon, get the other one!" I yelled, and he vanished.

A man screamed, and Levi drove his sharp teeth into his victim— releasing a punishing death sentence.

Logan flicked his attention behind the tree where the sounds of struggle ended. I rolled to my side, but he held me down, pressing his forearm over my clavicle. He was firm, but gentle. Rich, black eyes focused on me for a moment, and his hair tickled my face. He wasn't in there anymore, and the savage growl that sounded from his chest sent shivers across my spine.

Justus charged through the shadows, stalking forward as he looked between Levi and Logan. Levi crouched with a twitching body in his arms. Logan was covered in blood and covering me.

"Silver!" Justus yelled. The look on his face was familiar, one I never wanted to see again. "Come at *me*, Chitah!" Justus challenged. "Fight me like a man." The fingers on his large hands flexed.

Logan's body tensed, ready to spring.

"Get back," Levi warned. "His switch is flipped; he'll kill *anyone* who gets near her. If you die, she'll have no Ghuardian." Levi's voice was calm, as if he were merely discussing the weather report.

But that's exactly what Justus was trying to do—get Logan away from me.

I had to do something.

"Logan, you're bleeding." I reached up, caressing his cheek with my knuckles. "Please look at me. This can't be normal. Let me help you," I pleaded.

His hollow gaze fell on me and my heart quickened. There was something so primal in his body language, expression, and eyes that I had little hope of getting through. He leaned forward and breathed in my scent. The short bristles of stubble pressed into my cheek as he nuzzled—such an unexpected gesture given the circumstance. He had a power over me I couldn't explain, and my body yielded to his touch. I relaxed, slowing my breathing, feeling his body over mine, and a strange calm sank into my bones. Logan's head snapped up to the men circling around us.

Simon emerged from between two trees, brushing dirt from his shoulders with a casual flick of the wrist.

"Sodding bastard. Did you know he actually tried to pull a gun on me? Well that takes care of—"

Logan whirled around and reached for Simon.

Another step closer and it would have been over, but Simon spun out of his grasp and threw energy into him. Logan shook like a bolt of lightning struck him, and I felt the residual power of Simon's light in every part of his body that touched mine. His eyes flicked between all of us with no recognition.

I knew in my heart he was suffering.

"Levi, do something!" I begged. "There's too much blood."

"It's beyond me. You're the only one he is protecting, and only you can bring him back. He's running on pure instinct now. He'll kill us if we don't kill him first. Control your emotions because that's what he's feeding off of. Don't be afraid, and uh… try not to *provoke* him."

"As compelling as that thought is, I'm not in the mood for Chitah jokes," I said through clenched teeth.

"He's in there. Just talk to him."

I spread my fingers across his bloody cheek, and spoke in a soothing voice. "You need to let me go. There's no one left to fight, Logan. They're all dead." I slid my leg up and he shifted his body, growling at the empty space beside Justus.

Adam appeared, and the tension snapped.

"What the *fuck* is he doing?" Adam shouted.

Simon and Justus caught his arms, pulling him back before he got any closer. "Get him off of her! What the hell are you just standing around for?"

His words and scent were inciting Logan to violence. They placed hunger on his pallet and thirst in his eyes.

"Relax," Simon said. "Think of your mouth as gasoline and that Chitah as a raging fire. Silver is the only water who can put him out."

Well said, I had to hand it to him.

I grabbed Logan's jaw and turned his head. "Hey *you!* Don't look at them; look at me you big ol' pussycat."

The cut on his head still leaked blood, and I wiped it from his eyes as I tried to think of a story. "Remember, we have a date to finish. Only this time, I want to do something outdoors. Do you want to know one thing I've never done? When I was a teenager, the kids used to watch meteors out in the field." Telling the story was calming, and removed me from the situation. "They would park their pickup trucks and lay blankets out in the grass. Most of the boys snuck beer out of their house, but other kids used to bring chicken and potato chips. It was a big deal whenever one came around, but I never went. It was mostly something that couples did, and I guess I was never lucky enough to have a boyfriend whenever the stars were falling, and the ones I did never asked. I'm sad those days are gone. I had expectations and hopes about my future, and none of the men

I dated in my twenties lived up to that." Logan's body relaxed and he looked at Adam. It reminded me that we had a captive audience.

"Back off and give us some privacy," I said. "He's not going to calm down with all of you crowding him."

They dismantled from their huddle, nearly dragging Adam with them until we were alone.

I stared up once more at his long, white teeth. "Logan, I need to tell you something important. Maybe all you can understand is the tone of my voice, but I need to be honest with you."

His eyes drifted over my expression and he sniffed, as if that were the only sense he had of what I was saying. I tested the sharpness of his tooth with my thumb. Logan lifted his chin away and snapped his jaw shut.

"I once told you I didn't want you, remember?"

He licked his lips and I averted my eyes.

"I lied. This is something I've struggled with, because I haven't had much luck in this department. I want you, Logan, and I haven't felt like this in a long time about another man. That's a big deal, in case you didn't notice. I don't know how much of myself I can offer you because I'm not ready to be pushed into something serious." I took a deep, shaky breath, not realizing how hard it was to confess my feelings. Logan was not the type of man I would have imagined myself falling for. "You need to give me time if you're serious. I just want you to know that your efforts aren't in vain."

I couldn't explain why I felt such a connection to Logan. I made so many mistakes in my life that I was afraid to make a choice that could end up in me getting hurt. It was easier to admit the truth when I knew he wasn't listening—like a confessional—and a burden lifted from my shoulders.

Except when I looked back up, two golden eyes were staring into mine. The coloring of his skin was normal, his fangs pulled back, and a strong, wounded arm pulled me against him.

"It's about time you admitted it."

That cocky bastard. As much as I wanted to slap him, all I could do was stroke his jaw.

Levi ran in first and slid to his knees. "Lo, how you feeling?"

Logan smiled weakly. "Good to see you, Levi. What took you so long?"

⚊⚊⚊◈◈◈⚊⚊⚊

In the back of an empty van, Logan's head rested in my lap. My fingers combed through bloody strands of matted hair, and his fading eyes met mine with adoration. I tried desperately not to look at the blood pumping out of the most serious wound.

"Where did you get the van?"

"It's an old standby of mine," Simon replied. "We needed something with enough room for the lot of us. The engine was rebuilt for speed, although you have to hang on during the turns," he added with a smile. "That's how we roll, as they say."

"Somehow, that just doesn't sound the same coming from *your* mouth."

Levi attempted to heal the superficial cuts on Logan's face and arms, but he could do nothing for the deep wounds on his side and stomach. My skin went ice cold as I looked at the quantity of blood loss.

Simon pressed a towel against the wound, and Logan's radiant skin was now chalky. *Why wasn't he healing?*

"We're almost home, Logan. We'll get you some help," I said in a determined voice. "The next time you sit on me and keep me from fighting, I'm going to kick your ass."

Logan tried to smile.

"Can he die from this?" Justus asked Levi from the front of the van.

Logan's brother pushed his palms against the dash. "Something's wrong," he whispered to Justus. "A stab wound won't kill us; he should have started healing by now. If he continues losing blood…. What the hell was he stabbed with?"

"Magic," I blurted out. "They kept me in chains that blocked my abilities. Finn implied it worked on everyone, not just Mage." It was possible that when this type of metal mingled with our blood, it would delay healing, or prevent it. Logan was bleeding out. That was a fact.

"Hey," I said, brushing my thumbs over his high cheekbones.

When he saw the worry in my eyes, he kissed my palm. That single gesture opened up the dam, and I turned my head away from everyone. I held my breath and shut my eyes as hot, stinging tears slammed against my lids. My cheeks burned and my chest swelled with a flood of emotion. The reaction was so unexpected that I couldn't control it.

Something tugged at the ends of my hair. I looked down to see Logan twirling some of it between his fingers—the way he did when we first met. Except now, I felt different about the way he looked at me, the way he touched me.

Adam's posture was like a willow tree—knees bent with his arms slung over them. His face was expressionless, until he saw tears spill over my lashes. I threw myself down and covered Logan's face with mine. My hair showered us like a curtain.

"Don't cry, my black-haired raven."

I kissed the soft corners of his lips and whispered into his ear, "You're the most worthy man I have ever known."

He was. He truly was. Of all the men in that van who defended me when the time was appropriate, Logan defended me *always*. Even in a state of mind where he had no control, he was ready to throw away his life for me. I so poorly judged his character, and underestimated that a man could redeem himself. He didn't kill that evening because what I said to him mattered. It did not justify his past, but should I judge the man that he was, or the man that he was becoming?

He fought to stay conscious.

The engine roared as I felt quiet eyes watching us. I kissed him and whispered, *"Kiss me back."*

I jerked my head up. "What are you doing?" I hissed.

Adam's hand was on top of the open wound, and something animalistic raged inside of me when I saw the blood oozing between his fingers. Something possessive.

"Get your hands off of him!"

Caught in a maelstrom of emotions, I tried to shove him away, but he didn't budge.

"Adam, you're hurting him!"

"Silver, *let him*," Simon said, snatching my hand and throwing a serious glare. "Adam can help." Logan lifted a weak arm and pulled Simon's hand away from my wrist. Simon obligingly let go and nodded once at him.

Adam pressed his brows together and I thought I saw a pop of light—like a flashbulb. He groaned weakly and fell back, slumping against the wall on the other side.

My eyes widened when Logan's wound began to close. The skin stitched together by a current of magic, and he strained to pull himself up.

"Adam, what did you *do*? What is it that no one is telling me?"

Justus stared through the visor mirror before turning around to look at us. The van pulled off to the side, and someone reached up to flip on the interior light.

"Logan, lie down," I ordered.

Ignoring me, he leaned forward and rubbed his hand over his stomach, where blood no longer flowed.

"How did you do that? I thought we could only heal our own kind?" I asked in disbelief.

"It's his gift," Simon replied. "Adam is a Healer, and that is a *rare* gift. It allows him to heal all Breed."

"How do you know?"

Justus and Levi climbed into the back, squatting next to Simon.

"Does your maker know?" Justus asked.

"Yes," Adam replied, obscuring his face from mine as he memorized the floor. "We've tested it, and there are limitations."

"A rare gift, indeed," Justus said with admiration. "He must be proud of his Learner."

My Ghuardian gave him a firm pat on the shoulder.

Levi looked at Adam with a solemn gaze. "I'm in your debt for saving my brother, Mage."

Adam never lifted his eyes, but scratched the dark stubble on his face. "You are not in my debt, Chitah. Don't hold that to me because I won't honor it."

When we arrived at Justus's garage, everyone hopped out, including Logan who was on the mend.

"Can you give us a minute?" I asked Logan, motioning to Adam who hadn't looked at me the entire ride back. He nodded and shut the door, leaving us alone.

"Adam, please talk to me." I crawled beside him, resting my head on his shoulder. "I may never know why you did it, but I know all the reasons why you didn't have to."

In a long sigh, he spoke. "If all I can ever give you in this world is happiness—even if it means letting you go—then I'll do it. I saw the way you held him, and kissed him. I know you care for me, Silver, but you've never looked at me the way you look at Logan, and you barely know him. I've done a lot of bad shit in my life. Maybe I don't deserve happiness."

"Don't say that. You know it isn't true." My heart broke for him.

"Isn't it? I've tried to turn a new leaf and look how it's worked out."

"You're a Healer, Adam. That gift could have been wasted on some jerk who doesn't care what happens to anyone, but you care. You have a lot of hurt in there, but I can't fix it. No one can fill the hole your twin sister left behind, but someday you'll find someone to take care of. If you loved me that much, you would have thrown Logan out on his ass when he told everyone he was courting me. I know that much about the kind of man you are. You came into my life for a *reason*. Maybe this is it." It felt like the right thing to say, although I wasn't a believer in fate.

"To save the love of your life, and not to be it."

I chuckled softly. It was all I could do. Adam never professed his undying love for me; that was an unspoken fact we both knew. I never declared my undying love for Logan, either. Somewhere in his words was sarcasm.

"I know," he said, waving a dismissive hand.

"Why did you help him?"

"Because," he sighed, "I'd never be able to look you square in the eye again if I didn't. You would have discovered my secret eventually, and then you would have despised me—resented me—for choosing not to step in."

I tilted his chin to look at me. "I'll always love you. It may not be what you want to hear, or the kind of love you want, but that's where I am right now. You mean too much to me to screw it up with a failed relationship. I'm sorry that I've been harsh about it; I just don't know how else to be. I need you as my friend, and maybe someday you'll tell me the truth about fighting Samil."

His face paled. The primary reason may have been me, and his sense of good and right, but beneath the layer of heroics, there was another secret he kept hidden. I'd felt it for a long time. Adam was worse than a bank vault; I learned early on that I could yell, ask, and annoy all I wanted—but he would never tell me something he intended to keep to himself. Not wanting to risk placing a fracture in our relationship, I didn't press.

"What you said to Levi was true. It's not his debt to pay. It's mine. I owe you for this, and someday I'll repay it."

"I'm sorry," he said.

"For what?"

"I'm done chasing you. Someday you might see you missed a good thing, or not." He lifted a shoulder and looked down at my hand. "I can't see the point of going on like this."

"Me neither, and you are a good thing." I poked my finger at his chin. "Just look at that face; you could get any woman you wanted, you know. Who knows, maybe a thousand years from now—"

Adam playfully grabbed my nose and I laughed. I leaned in and kissed his mouth softly. It was the kind of kiss that let him know I would always be there for him. Through all the missteps in our relationship, I knew more than anything how much I needed him in my life.

"Your sister was lucky, Adam. She couldn't have asked for a better brother, and I hope you know that. I envy the relationship you had with her, and would have wanted someone just like you in my life to look after me. She'd be so proud of you now."

Adam teared up and stared at the ceiling. "I hate to admit it, but I miss you calling me Razor."

"Then let it be between us," I said, slapping his arm. "C'mon, Razor, let's go get some grub."

CHAPTER 32

A S MUCH AS LOGAN INSISTED on licking my wounds, I relied on my Ghuardian to heal me. I sat at the dining table, stuffing a meatball sandwich into my mouth as I recounted my story to Logan.

"He washed your feet?"

I nodded and licked my thumb. "Right after Nero gave him the lashing of his life, there he was, tending to my injuries. He's a tough kid. I just... I can't leave him there with Nero."

Logan exchanged a nod with Levi and left the room.

Justus and Adam went back for the other two who escaped with me; they wouldn't have gotten far in their condition.

"Levi, do you think you can track my scent back to the compound? I left a trail."

"I noticed," he chuckled. "Unless you were setting a new fashion trend."

"Funny," I said, lacking humor in my tone.

Levi stared up at the painting on the wall behind Justus's chair. "For sure. I got a nose for trouble." The bottle of beer tilted, and he enjoyed a long swallow.

Simon was unusually quiet, stirring a spoon in the coffee from the other side of the table. He dropped a third cube of sugar into the steaming liquid, and the metal spoon clinked against the cup. He kicked back the chair and disappeared, returning with his laptop. The next thing I knew, he was staring at satellite imagery.

A man like Nero required a lot of land. I described the size of the house and surrounding structures, hoping Simon found something on the Internet versus Logan snooping around Nero's property. The more I thought about it, the less I liked that idea.

It felt as if my eyes were stitching together. I rubbed at them, tired from the flashing and tree climbing, but I forced myself to stay awake and talk out some of the details. It was amusing to think how my days of eating chips on the sofa as a human were replaced by life-and-death situations. What a remarkable life it turned out to be, after all.

Then there was Logan, who insisted on removing my jeans to run his tongue over a scratch on my leg. Oh, he made it *sound* clinical, but I had no desire to see everyone's reaction as he licked me from head to toe. I could have waited until morning, but Justus saw to the blisters on my feet and the scratch on my leg from the bullet.

Logan strutted in, dropped to his knee, and buried his head beneath my shirt. He rubbed his face against my bare stomach as I awkwardly watched him. He wasn't kissing, nor was he inspecting the size of my jeans. He was inhaling a long, deep breath. I squirmed in my chair when a flutter in his throat tickled my skin. What kind of a world it would be if people freely expressed themselves this way, without inhibitions? I ran my fingers through his clean hair and let go of the embarrassment.

He rose to his feet with hooded eyes, and abruptly left the room.

Simon was busy scribbling something on a sheet of white paper while Levi was sipping his beer.

"Why does he keep doing that?" I asked, running my finger through a candle flame.

"You mean smelling you?" Levi laughed. "I thought you knew."

I gave him a questioning look. Levi stretched his tattooed arm across the table, rolling a bottle cap between two fingers.

"He's tracking the scent on you."

My heart skipped a beat.

"That's right, *Mage*. I never thought my big bro would cross over to the dark side, but I'm not one to lay judgment, as I've taken a vacation there myself a few times. You don't have to tell us the little details of how you got that key from the guard, but it's *all* over you, honey."

Simon glared from his monitor. "What's he on about?"

"I didn't do anything wrong," I said in defense.

"Doesn't matter," Levi mumbled. He can smell the lust all over you. It's thick, and if that man were a Chitah, he may as well have marked you. Logan will help HALO, but he's going to kick some serious ass when he hunts down that man. Eventually, he'll ferret him out. He owns the scent."

"Owns?"

Levi scratched at his chin. "It's what we call it when we've marked a scent to memory. Logan claimed you, honey. His scent is on you, whether you know it or not. Have you two ever gone out in public? I bet the males avoided you like the plague." He chuckled knowingly. "You don't know what that means, do you?"

No, maybe I didn't.

"We don't go around throwing our spice rack on just anyone who catches our fancy, or else there would be a whole lot of boys walking around smelling like me," he smirked.

That rich, heady smell Logan possessed leaked out on occasion, but I assumed it was from getting himself worked up since he didn't seem to have any control over it.

"Logan's only marked one other," Levi said with a rueful expression, "and that was after a long courtship when she finally agreed to accept him. To tell you the truth, I never thought I'd see him do it again. A lot of female Chitah want him; he's what you call a catch. But Logan has always had his head somewhere else." Levi was lost in his thoughts for a moment. "That scent has a lot of messages wrapped up in it, and you don't have to be a Chitah to pick up on the subtle threat." He edged his finger around the rim of his glass. "Simply put, it says '*This one is claimed. Fuck with them, and you fuck with me*.'"

I let that sink in for a moment, and swallowed hard.

"A voice is telling him to hunt down the man, and it's a voice that can't be ignored. Lo may never tell you about it, but he'll do it because it's the only way that he's going to sleep at night—be it one day from now, or in twenty years."

I thought about how he went after Brandon and the look on his face afterwards, like he had scratched an itch. "You Chitah can't go around claiming something that isn't yours," I muttered.

"We don't. You must give him reason to think he can. Hell, you practically have to give him permission. When did he first mark you?"

"The hour we met, when he kidnapped me," I said with an attitude.

"*Fuck*," he mouthed, running his hands through his short hair. Frown lines etched in his brow while he stared at the table.

"Unless you also want to count the fact he marked the *Jesus* out of my bed. It appears your claiming thing isn't as romantic as you would lead people to believe. Back to the first topic—I didn't do anything with the guard, so don't bring it up again."

"Logan will still find him."

"Don't look at me, Simon. I can *feel* your look."

"I'm not judging you. It was a well played move. A girl has charms she can use to her advantage. We have to be cunning where we can. If that's what got you out of there, then it was the *best* move."

"I just don't get it," Levi said, shaking his head. "When our switch is flipped, there's no control."

"So?"

Levi looked up. "We're ruthless when we run on instinct—lethal," he said with a closed fist. "What happened tonight… I just don't get it. Logan should have fought them; it's not in our nature to lay there and take a beating. Hell, I'm surprised he didn't turn on *you*. He hates your kind, you know."

"I heard."

Levi flashed his eyes up to mine. "I mean this sincerely when I say that I like you, but dollars to donuts, Logan is in the hamper with his nose in your jeans. If I were you, I'd throw them in the wash before he gets himself so worked up that he hunts him tonight. *Your blood* mixed with that male's scent is not an agreeable combination. Just sayin'."

I knocked the chair over when I shot up and flew out of the room. Levi's soft chuckles faded behind me.

My energy restored after a long, restful sleep. Logan was sprawled across the bed on his stomach—face down in the covers—with his feet hanging over the edge. There was something comforting about his presence in the room. The same way I'm sure people felt hundreds of years ago, having a warrior in their home. If he lived in those times, he would have been the kind of man to stroll into the house, kick off his muddy boots, and place his sword by the fire.

My growling stomach finally got the better of me and I rose from my lounge chair.

In the hall, I overheard the men planning a raid on orders from the Council. Unlike humans who are innocent until proven guilty, the Mageri proved guilt prior to arrest. All of Nero's possessions would be confiscated and reviewed. If he stupidly chose not to comply, he would be in violation of the law. His rogue status would be bumped up to outlaw. Most endured whatever punishment the Mageri deemed appropriate to avoid becoming an outlaw. They place a bounty on your head, and anyone can legally hunt you—dead or alive. It's all legit.

I breezed past the men in the main room. Candles flickered angrily from the rush of air as I entered the dining room. I lifted two pieces of crispy bacon and a small muffin from a plate.

"What's the plan?" I claimed the vacant spot on the couch.

Justus had pulled an all-nighter in the living room, and it showed. Dark circles wrapped around his blue eyes, while Simon's head looked more like a hairball.

"When are *we* going?"

Justus threw back his head and shut his eyes. "We leave at five o'clock. The Enforcers will go in, and we'll stay connected through radio devices." Enforcers were the equivalent of Mageri police.

"Who's going?"

"Two Enforcers will enter the main gate to present the warrant; the third will be stationed at the rear of the compound. We're bringing in the big guns."

"What does that mean?" Maybe he was talking about those pythons on Knox, but Justus didn't use phrases like that very often.

"It means we have backup. Novis…"

"Novis? I thought he couldn't be involved as a member of the Council?"

"When a search warrant is obtained, a Council member may choose to attend. Your two Chitah friends will also be coming with Leo."

"How did Leo get involved?" He was Logan's eldest brother.

"Will you allow me to finish, Learner?"

I stuffed the muffin in my mouth and shrugged.

"I know of Leo; he's good people. I didn't make the connection that Logan was a relation. I never put much thought into the Cross name," he grumbled.

"I'll remind you that Mr. Cross saved my life."

Justus kept his eyes closed, but I knew he could feel my frosty glare. Despite how our paths collided, Logan deserved his respect.

"Knox will drive the Enforcers, but he stays in the car; humans just get in the way. He has radio communication equipment—very useful. Remi volunteered," Justus said in his baritone voice. "He is a loyal friend, but he never involves himself in these matters, and that does not sit well with me."

"Nero doesn't live there. Finn said he just visited."

"This is to confiscate evidence, serve a warrant, and bring in his men. If Nero is there, then that would just be icing on the cake."

"Simon, why don't you take a shower so you don't blow our cover? They'll smell us coming," I said playfully.

"Wouldn't dream of it, love. Don't you know I'm a dirty boy?"

There went his dimple and I stifled a laugh.

"I'm going with Knox," I said.

Simon's leg slid off his knee and hit the floor. Justus clenched his jaw so tight that even through his eyelids, I felt his burning gaze.

"I'll be *safer* with the Enforcers," I assured him. "The guards will cooperate. They're not idiots. Plus, I doubt you want to leave me here alone." I knew I had him. There was no one left to watch me. "Why are we waiting? We're giving him too much lead time."

"It doesn't matter," Justus interrupted. "They'll have enough evidence after the testimonies and photographs of the facility to serve him an arrest warrant."

"Sure, but what about Finn?" I dusted the crumbs from my fingers, waiting for his answer. Then I looked up, and melted where I sat.

Logan's swagger was unmerciful. He had a way about him when he entered a room that commanded all eyes on him. Leisurely sliding his bare feet across the stone cold floor, he paused in the center of the room. When he lifted his chin and arched his back—stretching himself taut—I stole a moment to admire him. His skin was warm and radiant. Every muscle was toned, and defined by shadows and hard lines. Logan had a prominent Adam's apple, and the way his hair fell over the back of his broad shoulders sent a flurry of tingles up my spine. His shirt was ruined so he went without, and I wasn't about to suggest he borrow one.

The view was too nice.

When I caught him looking at me, I shyly turned my head. He noticed the way I heated up in his presence. A fiendish smile stretched across his face and he sank into the sofa to my right, kissing my neck. I dangled the bacon in front of his mouth to distract him. I didn't consider what that gesture might mean to a Chitah—feeding him.

Logan seduced me with provocative eyes that were the most prominent feature he possessed—aside from his height. His face had strong, masculine contours that were so distinct from other men I'd known. A broad nose and heavy brows set off his gaze. He leaned forward, opened his mouth, and took a seductive bite. Hell, my thighs almost quivered just watching his lips close around my fingers to suck off the juice.

If it's possible to feel someone's aura rub up against you, that's exactly what I felt with Logan.

"It's good to feel like a Mage again," I said offhandedly.

Logan sensed I was uncomfortable and sat back, working his jaw with a half grin on his face. Justus was still out of it, but Simon had a front row seat. He looked like he didn't enjoy the show and wanted a refund.

"When I was in those shackles, I felt human. I never thought I'd say this—but I didn't like it."

Justus stood up, rubbing a hand lazily over his tattoo as he crossed the room. "Shackles," he murmured.

We shared three seconds with Simon before he flew up out of the chair and followed behind Justus.

I took that as my cue and curled up against Logan.

"I heard what you said about looking at the stars, Little Raven. I intend to keep good on that." He propped his feet up on the table with a smug tone.

When I looked up, I noticed the direction of his gaze.

"What are you looking at?"

His features softened as his tongue swept over his bottom lip. "Did anyone ever tell you that you have a lovely bosom?"

My cheeks heated, noticing the top three buttons of my cotton shirt were undone.

"Nobody talks that way, Mr. Cross."

He lifted my chin with his finger and lowered his voice. "I talk that way." He curved a hand around the back of my neck, and his thumb stroked the soft skin behind my ear. "So we're back to formalities? What could I have done to offend you so much? Surely it wasn't paying you a compliment." He smiled.

What I couldn't tell him was that I liked his compliment, as inappropriate as it was. Then again, it was Logan. I didn't *need* to tell him.

He scented it.

CHAPTER 33

During the drive to Nero's property, we left one of the Enforcers at the turnoff. I rode with Knox, while the rest of the men took a separate vehicle. The other two Enforcers sat in the back seat and didn't talk to us much at all.

"You've got a real tricked out ride here, Knox," I said, watching the disco ball swing from the rearview mirror. *Definitely Sunny's touch.*

"Laugh it up dollface, but that ball is fucking beautiful."

"Are you two serious? No offense, you're just not the type of guy she usually goes for."

"I've never met a woman like her," he said in a hushed voice.

I didn't mean to imply she got the short end of the stick, only that I wasn't sure what to make of their coupling, nor his intentions. Knox could be abrasive, and Sunny might be in a vulnerable state after Marco.

I touched his arm lightly. "Don't use her just because she gives you permission."

His steel eyes cut me apart, and I knew in that second that whatever they had was real. I apologetically looked away.

I had never met an Enforcer before, but they weren't very tough looking. One of them leaned between the seats. "This should run smoothly, but if we have a situation, stay in the car. Don't wander off," he ordered, shuffling some papers. "We don't need a woman mixed up in this."

Yeah, whatever.

When we rolled up to the main entrance, they hopped out and shut the door. I looked at the mass of muscle to my left.

"Knox, did I ever tell you I have a problem with authority?"

"My kind of girl." His eyes lowered. "Nice shirt."

The shirt he referred to was a white T-shirt that said "Slacker".

Justus hated that shirt because when I was feeling particularly sassy, I would wear it during our training sessions just to annoy him. Few people ever got my sense of humor in life, and Justus merely endured it.

"That's where we were kept," I said, tapping on the glass at the white building on our right.

The Enforcers held up papers at the door and I leaned against the dash watching them. One entered the house while the other stood on the porch.

Knox lit up a smoke and cracked the window. The sound of burning paper filled the silence of the Jeep.

"What is *that*?" I laughed.

"Menthol."

"Reason being?"

"I'm trying to quit. If I smoke this shit, I'm going to want to quit real fast."

"Or throw up," I added. "You smell like a grandma."

Simon's voice blasted over the radio airwaves. "Godzilla, keep her in the car."

I picked up the radio, irritated by Simon's request.

"How the hell do you work this thing?" I found the button and peeled my lips back. "Bite me, Simon."

"You owe me a game of Risk for that."

Justus chimed in, "Shut up—both of you. I want radio silence unless the sky is falling."

I clicked the button. "*Child.*" I didn't have a good feeling, and I was venting at Simon.

"Whose idea was this?" I asked.

"Someone who enjoys a good clusterfuck."

I grabbed the handle and pushed my shoulder against the door. Knox caught my elbow.

With the cigarette dangling from his lip, he said in a raspy voice, "We're doing this my way. Follow me and stick like glue."

He flicked his smoke out the window and jumped out, pulling the edge of his hat over his brows. I shadowed behind him until we reached the building. He hesitated a moment before pushing the door in and scoping out the room.

"He keeps them down there," I said, pointing to the door on the left. Knox disappeared down the hall.

My focus was on Finn. I went to the right, searching every stall I passed. When I reached the last room, my knees went weak and I gripped the bars to keep from falling.

Finn was lying face down in the center of the room. I didn't notice the bed, books, or personal items that made it his. I only noticed the shackle around his neck... and the blood. Raw wounds covered his back, his fists were bruised and swollen, but what really made my stomach turn was the mark on his arm. Someone drove a hot branding iron into his flesh that would permanently mark him with the letter N.

"Finn!"

I unlocked the door and knelt at his side, trying to find a place I could touch him that wasn't injured. I brushed his hair back to look at his innocent face. Blood crusted around his lip and his left eye was swollen shut. Guilt racked me.

"I'm so sorry, Finn. I should have made you come. Wake up kid." I searched for a pulse and blew out a breath when a flutter touched my fingertips.

The guards were the only ones who carried the key that would free him. I ran into the hallway, frantically searching for an extra. A thick door swung open at the end of the hall, where tools were stored. I lifted a heavy mallet from the nails and went back to the room.

I was the key.

Raising the mallet over my head, I slammed it down on the chain, rattling my bones. "Come on, break!"

Something wasn't right. I looked at the door and took a slow, deliberate breath. For a minute, I thought Knox was stupid enough to be smoking in a building full of wood and straw, but something else occurred to me and I raced down the hall.

My fingers touched a scorching handle that didn't turn—locked from the outside. A fire raged in the entrance room, and my nose burned with smoke and gasoline.

"Knox!" I yelled.

No reply.

I ran back to Finn and looked at the locking mechanism attached to the bars, instead of the chain. I struck twice, and on the third swing, I threw my power into the mallet. It was leaking and I couldn't help it. The metal broke apart, and the chain dropped to the floor.

"I've come to get you out of here, kid."

Somehow, Finn got on the roof every night.

I ran back to the supply room, eyeing the ceiling when I noticed a rectangle outline with a white cord hanging down. I dragged a stool beneath it and pulled the cord. A folded set of stairs lowered and I climbed up—peering into a large attic. On the left, flames were eating through the wood floor, filling the room with smoke. Up ahead was a light, and I jogged forward until I reached it. When the door swung open, sunshine poured in. Several gunshots fired in the building; Knox was in trouble.

I scrambled back down to get Finn.

Being a Mage doesn't give you super human strength. I'd never done anything like this before, but I lifted him over my back, dragging his feet across the floor. I was going to bake Justus a ham for all the strength training he had me do. Flames engulfed the door in the hall, crackling and popping as smoke billowed in.

It was time to communicate. I lifted the radio from my hip, pressed the button, and said in a clear voice, "The sky is falling."

I pulled Finn over my shoulder. My legs trembled, blood rushed to my head, and I stared up the ladder.

"I'm not cut out for this macho shit!" I yelled at the empty room. Thank God Finn was no bodybuilder. *Small favors.*

"Chicken Little, where are you?" It was Logan.

"Where there's smoke there's fi—" The radio tumbled from my hand to the floor. *No time.* I tightened my grip and began the slow ascent.

My muscles shook like crazy, and the coughing was so bad that I almost dropped him. We reached the top and I set him down, pulling up the slack of the chain. His body flopped lifelessly as I took him by the wrists and dragged him to the opening. All I could think about was how much I wanted to chain Nero to a railroad track.

The building was ablaze, and the heat intensified. Outside of the open hatch was a world of clean air and...

My blood froze. I peered over the edge of my shoes; dropping Finn from this height was out of the question. I stuck my head out the opening and screamed for help.

The cavalry never looked so sexy.

Logan and Adam rounded the corner in fatigues and skintight green shirts with every muscle locked, cocked, and ready for action. Logan's hair was tied back, and he wore black lace-up boots. I wasn't sure if I liked him better in those or the leathers, but he was definitely going to have to expand on his wardrobe.

I waved my arm. "I'm going to lower him!"

My eyes and throat burned from the noxious fumes. Finn's legs sailed over the edge while I held his wrists, preparing for his weight. The chain was thrown over the edge so it didn't catch on anything, and it scraped against the siding. I anchored a foot against the wall, leaned back, and eased him down.

"Let him go!" Adam shouted.

Trusting him, I did.

Finn dropped right into Logan's arms. I backed up as a plume of smoke whirled around me.

"Get the hell out of there! Jump!" Adam shouted.

Our eyes met briefly and I shook my head. "Knox. I can't leave him."

"Silver, goddammit don't you dare!" Adam raged.

Knox didn't stand a chance surviving; there was only one way out, and those doors were on fire. He might already be dead—but I couldn't leave without trying. I ran to the other end of the attic until I reached the spot above the other hall. The floorboards looked new; thin panels were nailed over the wood beams.

"Knox!" I shouted. "Knox! Answer me!"

"Down here!"

I paced to the area his voice came from and dropped to my knees. My fingers gripped the edges of the panel. Knox was punching through the ceiling from his end. I stomped my foot, but was overcome with a gust of smoke and covered my face as the heat licked at my side. I frantically pulled at the wood when another set of hands appeared, and ripped it off effortlessly.

To my astonishment, Remi pried away the nailed flooring like sheets of paper. He was a Gemini—dangerous, detached, intuitive, and yet I had no idea they were so strong. Silky brown hair fell over his face as the last board ripped away.

"How the hell did you get up here?"

Ignoring me, Remi lifted a small human girl out by one arm, but even more amazing was when he did the same with Knox. Remi lifted him from the hole like one of those claw machines that plucks stuffed animals from a heaping pile of cheap toys.

Knox was no small human.

"Thank you, brother," Knox said, with a look of surprise when he set eyes on the lean man with the dragon tattoo.

It suddenly occurred to me that this was the reason he intimidated me—the tattoo. It was prominent on his neck, and an ugly bastard of a thing with jagged teeth and fiery eyes. I associated dragons with my ex, and that one stupid fact led me to judge him unfairly.

The human ran towards the opening and a set of massive arms pulled me off my feet. Knox had me in tow as he stormed across the attic—floorboards trembling.

"I told you to stick by my side."

"Quit your bitching," I coughed. "I saved your ass."

With little finesse, Knox flung me out the window like a rag doll. As I sailed through the air, I looked down and saw it wasn't Logan ready to catch me, but Adam. There was nothing graceful about my landing as I crashed down on top of him. It was almost comical to see his outstretched arms and the look of panic in his eyes a half second before impact. Adam crumpled to the ground like a crushed soda can, with me on top.

Splat. Just like the cartoons.

"Nice catch, Adam," I said. "Real suave." I dusted the dirt from my cheek and tested my shoulder.

He groaned, shoving me off. "Maybe you need to lay off the ice cream."

"Guess you can't say that I never fell for you." I patted his unshaven cheek.

Remi leapt from the open hatch, landing on his feet with grace. Adam stood up, and hooked his arm beneath mine, lifting me to my feet.

"Why did you come for me?" I asked Remi, coughing into Adam's shirt.

Gemini are only loyal to friends, and don't have many. It's not in their character to put their lives in danger for a casual acquaintance.

"Remember what I said to you at the Red Door not long ago? Never let go of your humanity; most who were human eventually do." Remi's eyes—shades of green and orange—caught brilliant shards of sunlight. "Justus told me of the lives you saved from Nero. Even now, you were once again willing to risk your life for a Shifter and a human. How many of us would sacrifice their immortal life for a human? This was foreshadowed, and I made a decision to steer fate."

"I don't believe in fate," I said dismissively. I knew Justus respected his words of wisdom, but I found it hard to believe that our lives were predestined, because if that were true, it meant that destiny hated my ass.

Remi dusted his hands over his pants, ignoring my remark. "I do not turn a blind eye to a warrior in need."

"Hear that, Adam?" I said, coughing hard. "I'm a warrior."

I may have been coughing up black poison in the form of sarcasm or soot, but his compliment warmed me like the sun. I glanced up to see the real sun was sinking below the horizon.

On the way to the car, Adam revealed that an Enforcer lost his life. After that, all hell broke loose. They captured five guards, and Logan brought in three more with Leo's help. In a last-ditch effort to destroy evidence, everything was set ablaze. We would never know the full extent of what was lost, and I realized capturing Nero was not as attainable as I thought.

"Where's Finn?" I asked.

Adam popped the door open and my eyes feasted on a vision I could have gone my entire life without seeing.

Finn was face down in the back of the Jeep with Logan straddling him. They pushed the seats down to make room, and the chain was removed and lying in a pile by the door. Logan pressed his palms flat on the floor as he licked Finn's wounds. Breed did not catch or carry disease, and I shouldn't have been so uptight about something that was natural among his kind, but I was. My nose wrinkled until I saw the wounds healing. If Finn was too weak to shift and heal himself, Logan was nursing him to a point where he could. He was a stranger to Logan, and my heart squeezed with unexpected admiration.

"Is she okay?" Logan looked over his shoulder at Adam.

I climbed between the seats before fainting like a sissy girl.

Finn's eyes drifted open, and I lay beside him, pressing my cheek to the floor.

"Help Finn," I said to Adam. I could tell he wanted to help me first, but that would have been energy wasted.

The hard edges of Adam's face tightened, and he placed his hands over Finn's back. Finn's cheeks splashed with color. Still, he did not move from whatever hell he endured at the hands of Nero. Adam gave him as much healing magic as his body would allow before collapsing on his elbows. His dark eyes were sunken in, and his skin paled beneath his unshaven jaw. Whatever magic he gave, he gave a lot.

"What about his arm?" I asked.

Adam rubbed his temples. "It doesn't work on wounds that have scarred."

The jeep hit a bump and we all groaned at Knox.

I touched the glass, searching for the last slice of sunlight. It was painful to cough, so I struggled to hold it in.

"I'm going to have to touch her, Cross. If you so much as hiss at me I'm tossing your ass out on the pavement, feel me?"

"I trust you."

We both offered Logan the same skeptical look. My injuries were not severe, but it didn't matter. Logan didn't like seeing me hurt.

Neither did Adam, who slid his hand up my shirt. I instinctively reached up to slap him when Logan caught my wrist and chuckled. "You can do that later, my sweet… or allow me?" His fangs punched out, and I knew despite everything, he was offended.

Logan smoothed his hand across my forehead. I loved the way he was unabashedly affectionate with me.

Adam closed his weary eyes—concentrating. I took a moment to look upon the wave of dark, thick hair he loved to run his fingers through, the strong jaw, and masculine lines. He was the serious sort, but whenever he laughed his eyes just radiated. I always loved the little lines at the edges in particular. His light moved within me—stimulating my own—and delicious oxygen moved throughout my lungs.

Logan's voice was a hush in my ear. "I'm not entirely happy that another man's hand is up your shirt. I promise I'll do my best to refrain from knocking his lights out later on."

He smiled at me with his eyes, but something told me it was a promise he would only *try* to keep.

"Where's Leo? I didn't get to meet him."

"You will… someday."

"They'll be placing an arrest warrant on Nero," Remi interrupted from the front seat. "He's an outlaw."

Logan's fangs extended. "Then let the hunt begin."

CHAPTER 34

"WHAT DO YOU MAKE OF it?" Simon asked, running the chain through his fingers.

Justus knocked back a shot of tequila and the glass tapped against the coffee table. It was clear he had no answer.

An Enforcer collected our statements, and after an hour of signing paperwork, we had enough. Justus was right—Novis was too involved. It wasn't required that he go, and instead of accompanying the Enforcers, he followed the other men, ready to fight. Maybe he wouldn't admit it, but that's what it came down to. His death could have led to severe consequences for everyone. Now he was taking in Ray and Cheri, and not just for questioning, either. They were displaced and in need of a safe house until the Council decided their fate.

"It doesn't just neutralize our power," Simon suggested. "It's strong enough to prevent a Shifter from turning. Looks like it has to be circled around the skin," he said, wrapping it around his wrist. "Holding it has little effect Feel like testing it out, Silver? Bind with me, for the sake of science." He wiggled a brow.

I rolled my eyes and Justus cleared his throat. You couldn't have paired two more opposite men. Simon was a chatterbox who talked a mile a minute, while Justus was a man of few words.

Simon freed his arm from the chain. "I bet those men were armed with a similar metal; that explains why Logan didn't heal quickly. I've seen a lot of rubbish selling on the black market, but this takes the cake. HALO has no record of such metals?"

Justus shook his head.

"Why chain him?" I asked. "He didn't have any power to fight back."

Simon studied it with concentrated eyes. "They wanted to punish him without promise of healing. If Finny healed, he wouldn't learn—he would *endure*. Nero wanted him to scar, to hurt, and to remember what he did. This," he said, jingling the chain, "would break him of his disobedience. The elders see Shifters as nothing more than pets. This dates back to the era when men rode horses with steel at their side. Shifters served as guards for the villages—utilized for their abilities, but treated as animals. They're weak in human form, except the alpha males. We've evolved since then, but Nero is playing by his own rules." Simon threw up his hands and abandoned the subject. "Clearly!"

"No one else was in the building?"

Justus stroked his jaw. "Only the human you found."

"Will they kill her?"

"No," he sighed. "The Vampires will erase her memories."

I strategically slid my feet further down the sofa. Justus was leaking body heat, and it was the next best thing to fuzzy slippers.

Midnight was approaching and the air held a frosty chill. Justus rarely used the fireplace anymore, and it wasn't fair that he had his own internal thermostat. Some of us had cold feet.

"Why did Novis want Adam to keep his gift a secret? That's a remarkable gift that could help a lot of people."

Simon dropped the chain on the floor. "True, but you must think with a devious mind. His gift—like yours—is one many would find... useful."

"I think it's ridiculous that we have to live in fear of others finding out what we're capable of. We should embrace our differences."

Simon raised his hands like a conductor, as if I were an orchestra playing a sad song. I tossed a pillow at his head, but missed.

"I'm serious, Simon. The laws don't offer enough protection."

I slid my feet farther down.

Justus circled his fingers around his temple. Something vexed him. "Why did you risk yourself for a human? You could have burned alive."

"How can you ask a question like that? I did it because it was the right thing to do."

"It was foolish."

"Sometimes smart and right aren't always in the same zip code.

How many times are we given a choice that matters? I couldn't live with myself if I didn't try."

"You barely know him."

I puffed out a breath, "I don't have to love someone to value their life; he would have done it for me."

"Are you so sure of that?"

"Why don't you ask him?"

Simon chortled, "Do it, Justus. *Please?* I'd love to see the look on Gigantor's face when you challenge his integrity."

"I want tickets to that show, too." I laughed as Simon made a face.

A hand caught my ankle when I started to curl up my legs.

"Give them here," Justus said.

He lifted my feet, covering them with his large, warm hands for a brief moment. My soul released a heavy sigh. Justus drove me crazy, challenged me, kept his distance physically, and yet one touch meant the world. I hid my smile because his affections came around as often as Santa Claus.

"You should have bought me slippers for my birthday."

He lowered his brows, sharpening those blue eyes. "What?"

"My birthday was last month."

"No it wasn't," Simon interjected. "Your human life is over. We don't recognize *those* birthdays. Just a few more months before your first year as a Mage," he said with a sly smile.

"What's the tradition? Sparklers?"

Justus couldn't mask his smile. "No fireworks for you. The house is liable to burn to the ground."

I dropped my head on the sofa and groaned. "Why does everything have to happen to me?"

Simon arched a brow. "Are you *seriously* pulling the 'woe is me' card? For pity's sake. Well, I'll see your *barn* and raise you the gallows," he sniffed. "Don't even get me started on the firing squad."

Simon acquired a sour expression as his thumbs were beating up his phone.

"Who are you texting?"

"He had a date tonight," Justus revealed.

Dating would be a step up from the one-night stands he usually had. "With a real live girl, or do you mean the fruit?"

"Jealous, love?" Simon inquired, cocking an eyebrow without looking up.

"Not really. I just didn't think you were dating anyone."

"I *am* of the male persuasion. It's what we do by nature: hunt, eat, kill things, and shag."

"*Simon has a girlfriend,*" I sang.

"She's not a girlfriend. Just a lovely lady with a lovely bum."

"What's this about a girlfriend?"

Levi didn't just enter a room—he owned it. I guessed it was in the genes, because the Cross men knew how to make an entrance. The steady way his eyes soaked in everyone gave it a personal touch. His legs swept forward as if he were carrying something large between them. Stopping short of the sofa, he tucked his fingers in the slit of his jean pockets. Levi possessed a distinct look that was different from Logan. His face was fuller, frame wider, and his body hair thicker. Not much, but I noticed the details.

Levi's gaze slid over to Simon, who crossed one leg over the other, feigning indifference. Didn't matter. I could tell the Chitah made him nervous.

"Now *I'm* jealous," Levi remarked with a secretive wink. I curled my hand over my smile.

Simon's eyes narrowed, never missing a beat. "Mind cluing me in on the inside joke?"

"Wouldn't dream of it, honey," Levi said, falling over the arm of the leather chair. He stroked his lower lip with a wide thumb.

"I'm going to go check on Finn," I announced. "Is he doing any better?"

Levi laced his fingers behind his neck. "Messed up. He still thinks Nero owns him. No clue that owning a Shifter has been illegal for a century. You can't find that on the Internet. That mark on his arm is better, but he's always going to have a scar. It was too deep. He must have shifted at least once and started the healing before they chained him."

I had heard enough and left the room.

It was so still inside of my bedroom that you would have thought the candles made a clamor. The air smelled of fresh citrus from a reed diffuser on a small table by the bed. My eyes adjusted to the low light and there, on top of Goliath, was a blanket of men. Logan draped himself over Finn's legs. He helped a person he had no reason to trust—because of a promise. The circumstances of how I met Logan became irrelevant in those moments that I watched the way he offered a Shifter warmth and compassion. I found him to be a remarkable man.

Finn was awake. Logan, on the other hand, was passed out cold.

"Do you want some company?" I closed the door behind me.

"I think your friend likes me," he said with embarrassment in his cheeks.

"Take it as a compliment; it's just his way. How are you feeling?"

I brushed a strand of hair from his forehead. They cleaned him up nice and dressed him in a cotton shirt. It was about five sizes too big, but he looked great.

"Better."

The silence stretched between us.

"Why did you come back?"

"I keep my word, Finn. We had a search warrant, but it looks like they were prepared to tear it all down. Maybe Nero got spooked; he knew we were looking for him. Lucky I found you when I did."

"Yeah." He nestled his face into the pillow. "Did you really carry me up those stairs? He told me," Finn said, nodding his head towards Logan.

I squeezed his hand and smiled. "I'm just glad that you watch your figure. I don't know what I would have done if you had one too many Happy Meals."

A line of confusion etched in his forehead. "What's a Happy Meal?"

I was angry that Finn had never had a taste of a normal life. Why wouldn't his leaders have protected him? Was this type of violation of so little importance? Breed law focused on the big fish and didn't seem to look out for the little guy.

"I made you something." His eyes lit up, watching my reaction. "Look in the pocket on the lower left leg."

I lifted the flap from his baggy cargo pants, reached inside, and pulled out a small piece of wood.

"It's a little wolf!"

Finn had a natural born gift, and it showed in his art. The object fit in the palm of my hand—an intricate carving, down to the last details.

"Carving is my hobby, and I like to give them away. You left before I finished it. I had never carved a wolf before; it was hard getting the snout just right."

I treasured it in my hand before showing him my gratitude with a kiss on the cheek. He turned red and shrank from my touch as a child might. By his reaction, affection was not something he was used to.

"Anyone ever tell you how special you are?"

Logan lifted his head, attempting to throw off a jealous gaze through a storm of blond hair. He peeled away from Finn, rubbing the sleep from his eyes and yawning wide.

Finn combed his hair over his ears. "They found the guard chained up, but he was—you know—naked. I'm sorry I left you, I should have found a way to get you the key—"

Logan flipped over and my heart skidded to a stop. Finn stared wide-eyed at his fangs, but avoided his gold rimmed eyes. The throaty growl was how I imagined a saber tooth tiger might sound.

"Finn, I haven't really talked about all that," I warned, flicking my eyes back to Logan. "It wasn't as bad as you think."

"But Diego is strong and—"

"*Diego.*"

Logan spoke as if summoning an enemy. The word rolled off his tongue, tasting each delicious syllable like blood from a fresh kill.

I shot Logan a nasty glare that filed him down like an emery board. Finn needed to feel safe, and I was not about to start this shit.

"Finn, you're free now. You don't belong to him. Do you understand?" I sat on the edge of the bed, signaling Logan with my hand to calm down.

"I'll never go back to my father. What am I supposed to do?"

"Stay with me," Logan replied as a fact, not a suggestion. "My home is yours and you are welcome to live there for as long as you want. We take you as a brother."

Finn stretched his wide eyes to Logan.

"That's right, Little Wolf. We're not the same, but you're family to us now. You cared for someone I…" He looked at me sideways, "…respect. You eased her pain and I thank you for that. You're a free man. Paper is paper," he said, leaning forward and placing his hand on Finn's chest. "But they cannot chain you here… or here." Logan touched his forehead. "As long as your mind and heart are free—no man owns you, no chains can hold you. The key to your freedom has always been in your own pocket."

I squeezed Finn's hand and left the room, allowing him the dignity to spill tears without an audience.

"Follow me," Justus said, and led me to his bedroom from the hall. He shut the door behind him and I crossed my arms nervously as his room was always off limits.

"I want to speak with you. Sit."

I took a few tentative steps towards the sofa and seated myself.

His voice was stern, and I wrung my hands together. "What do you want to talk about?"

"Certain things need to be said."

He sat on his heels before me and found my eyes. "It's my responsibility to see that you are taught to fight, educated in our history, and given the laws. I took a vow when I offered my services for this role. It's not a position I can easily walk away from without it becoming a mark on my honor. Time and time again, you have disobeyed my orders."

My heart sank. A lecture was one thing, but I wasn't sure where this conversation was heading.

"Is this the part where you disown me?" I asked in a fragile voice. "I'm not making excuses, but this life was not my choosing. I've accepted it, but it's hard to let go of my human life, and it doesn't help when you start imposing unreasonable rules. I'm struggling with this and doing the best I can to acclimate. You may not approve of Logan, but it's not your choice. I don't know where that's going—if anywhere—but I still have a life to live, and some decisions are mine to make. I screw up. A lot. I know this… but it's been a difficult adjustment for—"

"Will you shut up?" he said, laughing with a shake of his head. "Or should I hand you a spade for deeper digging?"

I chewed on my thumbnail. I couldn't pretend that what Justus said to me didn't matter.

It did.

"Novis was right when he said we can learn from your example. You saved lives of lesser value than your own; you are a reminder that immortality is more than self-preservation. We all want to bring in Nero, but some men we chase for years." His voice softened. "You may *never* have closure. Are you willing to accept that?"

It was a poignant question that led me to believe he was speaking from personal experience. My heart wanted to say no, but my mind knew he was right. Not everything wraps up neatly the way we'd like. If I didn't look beyond Nero, then he would consume me and remove any chance of leading a normal life. Well, as normal a life as a Mage can lead.

"But I *want* him. What was the purpose of all of this," I said, waving my arms in frustration, "if I couldn't catch him?"

He caught my wrist, and lowered my hand. "You granted freedom to those who did not have it. Is that not purpose enough? Perhaps it's not in the fates for you to find Nero."

"I don't believe in fate."

The muscles in his face relaxed, and the tips of his short hair seemed to absorb the light in the room.

"Some things do not *need* us to believe in them. Don't pursue something with a vengeful heart, or it will destroy you. Hate wraps a cold hand around your heart and hollows you out. You're young; live your life. I don't want to see you get hurt," he said with an uncomfortable pause. "You cannot continue to put yourself in harm's way. Time will give you the wisdom you need to make better decisions."

"What decisions have I made that were so bad?"

He popped a knuckle. "Your trip to Hell? You shouldn't have bartered flesh for knowledge. That is something Simon would do.

He tries to guide you, but don't be like him. He's more broken than you realize."

"I understand."

And I did. Sacrifice only means something when you're willing to give up everything for a greater purpose. Finding Nero was nothing more than a thirst for revenge, and I knew it.

"This is not a free pass to disobey me," he said firmly, "but know that I am honored by your actions."

Justus placed his hand on mine and pulled away. That simple gesture was the most profound thing he could have done. He didn't like to be touched, and I could tell that it was hard for him as he averted his eyes. "You're just lost. No one should come into their creation the way you did. But remember that you are more than Samil's progeny."

My heart swelled because deep down, he wanted to do right by me. He fumbled just as much in his attempts as I did.

"Do you like the Chitah?"

I half smiled. "Yeah. Actually, I kind of do. Logan was a twist in the road that I didn't see coming, but I like being around him. He understands me when I don't understand myself. He gives me the space I need, and respects my opinions. Maybe I'm not supposed to pair up with someone outside of my Breed, but I need to figure that out for myself. I didn't much like you when we first met," I added, watching a smirk rise on his cheek, "but I trusted you. I don't know where that comes from, but I think maybe I need to follow my instincts for a change."

I glanced down as he slid a ring on one of my fingers. I wasn't a big fan of jewelry, and searched his eyes for understanding.

"What's this?" The ring was smooth and black with a silver lining.

"You mutter and moan that I spend money foolishly. I purchased that for a dollar," he said proudly, rubbing his chin. "The lady said it was a mood ring."

I twirled it between my fingers, watching the darkness change. It was a tender moment and I didn't want to spoil it with jokes. Justus was a proud man, but quiet about his feelings. In his own way, he cared for me. He treated our relationship like a car: constantly tuning it up and improving the parts, but every so often, he gave it a good polish. What developed between us was natural, and something I never knew in my life. Justus was like a father I never had. We were both stubborn and would always have our arguments, but at the end of the day, he was my compass.

I stroked his brow with my thumb and he flinched, moving out of reach.

"Why don't you accept kindness?"

His jaw clenched. "I'm a hard man, and that's just the way it is."

The only touch he allowed came from strangers—women at the bar—that he wanted for nothing more than sex. But when a touch meant something, Justus would push away.

"I don't have a nose like your Chitah friend, and my telepathy is a little rusty these days," he said, changing the topic. "Maybe this will tell me what's going on in that head of yours."

"It's perfect."

Damn if I didn't see that man blush.

The bristles of his short hair made a scratching sound as he rubbed a hand across it. "Teach me what the colors mean. What is your mood?"

A deep shade of violet bled through the darkness, and I peered into the reflective band and saw that time stretched before me like an infinite road of possibility.

I lifted my chin and smiled.

"Optimistic."

"Kiss me, Little Raven."